BITTERSWEET BROOKLYN

ALSO BY THELMA ADAMS

Playdate
The Last Woman Standing

THELMA ADAMS

PUBLISHING

Text copyright © 2018 by Thelma Adams
All rights reserved.

Published by Lake Union Publishing, Seattle

www.apub.com

Amazon, the Amazon logo, and Lake Union Publishing are trademarks of Amazon.com, Inc., or its affiliates.

ISBN-13: 9781503904606
ISBN-10: 1503904601

Cover design by Shasti O'Leary Soudant

Printed in the United States of America

To my grandmother

AUTHOR'S NOTE

True events inspired *Bittersweet Brooklyn*, which is based on meticulous research. However, in narrating the story, certain factual elements, characters, and timing of events have been altered to dramatize lives that passed largely under the historical radar. Fiction often requires good guys and bad guys—real life is rarely so clear-cut. Every individual is the protagonist of their own life story. To quote a favorite African proverb, "Until the lion learns how to write, every story will glorify the hunter."

Chapter 1

Brooklyn, October 1935

It's tough torching a fresh corpse, so the Williamsburg Boys Club killers stuffed their shredded victim into the back of a Buick. They'd douse the stolen car with gasoline and ignite it. Then, at least, the cops would suffer distinguishing the upholstery from the body. It wasn't pretty, but it *was* Louis "Pretty" Amberg in the back of that green sedan on October 23, 1935.

Amberg was no near-and-dear to Thelma Schwartz. The thirty-three-year-old hadn't met the mobster while he was still alive, swilling vodkas at her older brother Abie's Brooklyn hangout beneath the ramp to the Williamsburg Bridge. But she'd heard stories about the mean drunk with the lazy left eye. Abie's gang said the Russian immigrant had good table manners, meaning the opposite: he'd stuck a fork in Milton Berle's face when the performer had insulted Pretty's bulldog mug from the Vanity Fair Club stage.

Word to the wise: never sit in the front row at a comedy show.

Unlike Pretty's eyes, Thelma's were her second-best feature: glowing green below arched eyebrows and thick auburn hair. A skinny widow with a kid, she knew she got looks when she wore lipstick and stiletto heels and bent over, showing a neckline more daring than the next. And those looks improved as the night wore on. Her best feature: her legs. Like everybody else's, they began at her ankles and connected to her hips—but they took their sweet time. Her long limbs had magic in them, at least according to Abie.

That Wednesday, Thelma had dropped by Abie's Marcy Avenue dive unannounced and desperate, fresh from being mauled by a bruiser in the alley behind the Arcadia Ballroom. Feeling raw and ashamed, she'd sought brotherly comfort—and cash. Late nights like this had left her with a female problem that Abie's money might solve, if not soothe. When she was hurting, she turned to Little Yiddle, although she never used that nickname herself. It used to be that she was always welcome, but lately that had changed as her brother's underworld "business interests" had appeared to expand.

She'd hurried down the two steps to the basement entry of the three-story redbrick building, strangling her lapels as the wind rose. Rocking from one foot to the other in thin-soled shoes, she regretted being on her brother's doorstep. Turning, she glanced up and down the street to assess her exit, but she observed a stranger lurking in the shadow of the bridge. He hovered just beyond the circle of streetlamp light, a fedora sheltering his eyes.

As she watched, the man also shifted from one leg to the other in the frigid night. She was afraid of being alone in the dark without a man's protection, but not as terrified as she was of being stuck at home with a kid every evening for the rest of her life. When Abie failed to answer, she let herself in with the spare key she kept for emergencies. She hung her coat on a hook before pouring a drink. After kicking off her heels under the octagonal card table, she settled down to play solitaire and nurse her grievances with a vodka neat (the poor person's martini), when she heard grunts from the kitchen. She stayed seated, doing nothing to investigate the source, feeling nothing but trouble rising and her nape hair prickling under the clasp of her cheap heart-shaped locket.

After a while, Abie swung through the kitchen door, unrolling his sleeves.

"You gotta get out of here," he said, his eyes dead, the whites red streaked. When she didn't move, he became agitated. "Now! Grab your coat. Go!"

Thelma choked, stung by his betrayal and frozen by the gut punch of disgrace—the familiar emotion of being unloved and unlovable. "That's some welcome, brother."

"You don't get it. Get outta here. I'm not kidding, kiddo." His creased face gray and sweaty, Abie removed his handkerchief from his pants pocket and swabbed his brow. At forty-one, he was a very short, fit, bigheaded man with a strong chin, handsome between flappy ears that would have dwarfed a man twice his size. "This is for your own safety. Grab your stuff now, baby, and scram."

She didn't recognize this desperation, his frenetic urgency. "You're calling me *baby* like I'm one of your cookies? Where am I supposed to go, Abie? I can't find a cab this late and I'm broke."

"Shh," Abie hissed, looking over his shoulder. "Maybe you should have thought about that before."

"Since when am I unwelcome?" she hissed back. She felt three years old, wet and weak. He'd always understood her. He'd always championed her. Who was she without her reflection as the favorite in his eyes?

One after the other, she'd made the choices that landed her here on Marcy Avenue in the bridge's shadow on a dark block after midnight. She'd taken the risks, a widow trying to squeeze a spritz of joy from a cold night, packing up her cares and woes, feeling low and hoping she'd meet another man to rekindle her heart's flame before it was too late. "You sound like Annie," she said.

"Our sister wouldn't be so dim to come here this late."

"Kick a girl when she's down."

"Get in line. Take a number." Abie fumbled for a cigarette. "You gotta learn to pick yourself up, Temmy. This is my last warning: get out."

"I've always been here for you."

"So now you've gotta shovel on the guilt? I'm your brother, for God's sake." He smacked his forehead, resigned, and then sank down beside the card table. Thelma slid an ashtray closer. He sighed, adding a smoker's cough to its tail. "If you're staying, Temmy, then pass me the deck. We'll play a hand while we wait. It's probably too late anyway."

It was 2:00 a.m. Abie riffled the deck on the felt. The cards scattered, escaping his jittery fingers.

"You're shuffling like an old lady."

He stopped and glared at her, the whites of his eyes wide. She'd never seen him so unhinged. She extended her hand. He flinched.

She began, "What can I—"

"Play cards."

"Deal," she said. He did.

Once the game started, Abie quietly unloaded, as if he were filling Thelma in on a radio serial she'd missed while she was out dancing. She reached over and removed the cigarette from his dry lips and placed it between hers. She puffed, then discarded as he began to explain that Pretty had angled for control of the Brooklyn rackets, crossing the ambitious Louis "Lepke" Buchalter, who'd slain the Russian's brother Joseph the previous month. Enraged, Pretty entered the rival gang's headquarters, roaring that he'd be avenged. But Lepke struck first, telling Abie to set the trap by inviting the bereaved sibling over to the Marcy Avenue apartment that doubled as the Williamsburg Boys Club for drinks and girls.

The kitchen door swung open, revealing a husky, pockmarked man in his undershirt, his eyes feral. "You didn't get rid of her?" he asked, incredulous. "What, Little Yiddle, is this amateur hour? Bring me the girl."

"She's my sister. Leave her out."

"Quit stallin'," said the stack of bricks.

"I begged you, Temmy. I'm not the boss."

"But we're in your place."

"Right, like I planned on opening a kosher butcher shop," he snorted. "Just shut up and follow orders. You'll be okay."

"What're my odds?"

He didn't answer, so she crammed her blistered feet back into her heels and stood up. Whatever she was facing beyond the door, she was certain she wasn't dressed for it. She yanked up her neckline, but it wasn't getting any higher. Her heart pounded. With these party shoes and the corner guy, she wasn't running anywhere this late in the game.

After squeezing Abie's shoulder, steely beneath his shirt, she shoved the door with false bravado, sending it banging against the wall. She was trying to play it as cool as Jean Harlow in that Jimmy Cagney gangster movie Abie loved, *The Public Enemy*—but that didn't last. The first thing she saw was an empty vodka bottle standing on the kitchen table beside three glasses, two empty, one full—the dead man's glass.

And then she saw a corpse stretched on the floor. Even in her wildest imagination, this was not what she'd expected. She ran to the sink and puked.

"Don't block the drain," said the goon with a half smile, as if her terror amused him. "Take a last look, sister, but make it snappy. You got work to do."

She swiveled, propping the small of her back against the sink. Beside the stove, the body lay on the checkerboard linoleum. She swallowed hard. Her palms sweat. She couldn't see Pretty's face. The assassins had rolled him into Abie's bedspread, his wing tips visible, feet splayed. Although she knew he was no angel, she felt pity viewing his Florsheims. She'd been aware her brother broke the law, but this was murder: she'd stumbled into a crime scene with a victim whose name she knew. She was an accessory after the fact, abetting a felony, a loose end. She turned and spewed in the sink again.

Pretty was Jewish, like she was, an immigrant like her European parents. Now he'd been reduced to a flesh puddle on the ass end of Williamsburg. This was where they'd ended up: Jews killing Jews before the Gentiles had a chance. Thelma refused to believe that they'd become the embodiment of the crude caricatures anti-Semites published in the city's broadsheets. But she couldn't explain this: the man in the chenille wrapper. One bloodstained shoelace had come undone. Red gore like a cow's afterbirth splashed the floor.

The pockmarked stranger handed Thelma a bucket and mop. She raised her hand to refuse, but the man shook his head no. Apparently, if she was there, they were going to use her—the story of her life. Maybe the killers had to tie her to the crime or flay her, too. She glanced from the gore to the goon, unable to figure out how she was going to clean her way out of this mess, but when he said, "Quit stalling," she realized she'd rather scrub than be rubbed out and join Pretty.

Looking away from the stranger, Thelma removed her good dress and stripped to her slip, as if she were about to clean her mother's kitchen floor. She threaded her hem through her bra so the fabric wouldn't absorb the blood. Her protruding ribs humiliated her—but this wasn't the situation for vanity. Nobody would be ogling her flesh that night.

With Pretty's cheap cologne still clinging to the air, she mopped up the dead man's body fluid, which turned the rinse water pink. After a while, she hoisted the heavy bucket and sloshed the filth into the sink and, retching, her eyes stinging with sweat and tears, refilled it again and again. Just when she sighed in relief that she was almost done, she spied splashes on the underside of the baseboard, on the insides of the table legs.

A second stranger with a sandpapery voice entered while she knelt, searching out stains with an old rag. She observed the guys' ankles as they muscled the body from the room. They should have called him Lumpy, not Pretty, the thugs *kvetched*. When the back door slammed, she rose, grabbed the third glass, and gulped the dead man's vodka before leaving the kitchen in bra and soiled slip. The shock began to diminish as the liquor did its work. But the horror increased.

From his armchair, Abie spat smoke and said, "Get dressed."

"I hadn't thought of that." She carried her crumpled clothes before her, heels in her left hand. Red had been her favorite color. Not anymore. Entering Abie's bedroom, she noticed the way the bedspread had been stripped away, revealing the shabby, torn sheets beneath. She'd bet his linen was clean over at his apartment on Rodney Avenue, but he still didn't want anything to do with Tillie and their son.

Zipping her dress, she kicked herself for dropping by after midnight, for assuming Abie needed her as much as she did him. How could she ever look up to her brother again after scrubbing a corpse from his kitchen floor?

Chapter 2

Thelma felt her older sister enter the room before she saw the tips of Annie's brown shoes, her good ones, and then the heels, rotating in circles, stamping a dance of impatience. The fourteen-year-old was rushing toward womanhood, which included keeping her three-year-old sister quiet and off their widowed mother's nerves. Thelma, hidden under the kitchen table by the oilskin cloth the color of *shmaltz*, chicken fat, cradled a lighter in her lap.

Even with her back flush against the metal leg farthest from Annie, she felt the furnace blast of her sister's anger as she called, "Thelma," and then "Thelma" again, as if it were a curse.

Thelma felt a sudden, urgent need to pee as Annie raised the oilcloth and knelt. Her sister's close-set blue eyes flashed, enraged, as she spotted Thelma. Mama had warned the little girl not to touch the lighter. She had said *Don't play with matches, don't touch the stove.* As the littlest cowered under the table in a hostile apartment where her family were visitors but not guests, she braced but did not resist. She was terrified and helpless and horribly guilty. Annie didn't bother to ask her to come out. She reached in with her long nails, as if her sister were a stray cat, grabbing her by her arm above the elbow, where there was so little meat. The little girl squealed as Annie, digging her talons deeper, dragged her out on her rear end over the sticky linoleum.

"Leave me alone," Thelma said, emerging sideways into the kitchen's dusty light. Mrs. Junger had warned the lodgers to stay out except at mealtimes, and this was *verboten*, forbidden. Annie, spiky brush curlers framing her shiny, round Polish doll face, collapsed on a wooden dining chair. It was August hot, and there had been a long argument among the tenants over whether to open the kitchen windows during the day to create cross-ventilation or shut them. Nothing worked.

That humid, oppressive New York summer of 1905, the widow Lorber and her four children were living on Manhattan's East 106th Street. The United Hebrew Charities paid their rent directly to the Jungers, who leased a large second-floor railroad flat above a pediatrician's office where babies cried from morning until night. Even with the windows closed, Thelma could smell the corpselike ripeness of garbage in the courtyard and then Annie's sweat, undisguised by her penny cologne.

Annie felt her curlers and sucked her teeth in disappointment before reeling the child in between her thighs, which were strong despite their outer softness. Already well into puberty, Annie boasted breasts larger than were good for a girl her age.

Exhaling peppermint and garlic, Annie demanded to know what Thelma clasped in her fist. The younger sister wondered where the older had gotten the mint and if she had another and if, after the fuss to come, she could request one. Even at three, she knew that simple negotiation. Wait for it. Pain first then, perhaps, pleasure.

Annie clamped Thelma between her thighs, gripped her right wrist in her left hand while holding the gadget aloft in her right. "Schmulie's?"

Thelma nodded yes. She called him an uncle, but he was really a boarder, too. Tall and rickety, Schmulie was a happy bachelor who had two tricks to entertain children. Settled in the kitchen in his undershirt, as much fluffy white hair on his back as his chest, he thumbed the lighter's trigger and dared Thelma in his raspy voice to blow it out. She never could. He dared. She blew. This inevitably inspired delight and frustration and maybe a penny for her labors if he was flush at the races. His other trick? Removing his dentures and flying the bared teeth at Thelma, clicking like maracas, until she crumpled with laughter, breathless, ruined for any further attempts snuffing the dancing flame.

As uncles went, Schmulie was a good one, meaning benign, just coaxing a burst of laughter. He never caressed Thelma's knees beneath her yellow flour-sack dress with its red birds on the pockets, or searched to ensure she was wearing panties like some other uncles did. Although, Uncle Schmulie did pinch her face—she bore a lot of cheek for a skinny girl.

Annie peered at the lighter as if it were a weapon, rolling it around in her fingers, perhaps considering the crime and punishment before saying, "Fire isn't a toy."

Thelma nodded in agreement, although she wanted to respond *So give me toys*. But she sensed how dangerous this moment was, riskier than fire. She felt an emotion that she would come to recognize as betrayal, when it was one's family administering the pain and not a stranger, a kid on the street, a schoolteacher shaming you in front of the whole class for filthy fingernails.

"Do you want to touch the flame, silly girl?" Annie flicked the trigger with her thumb. She did what Thelma had been unable to do— summon fire from the lighter's mouth, letting the oily butane smell waft into the room of a thousand leftover kitchen odors, the cabbage and the liver, the stew of unknown parts. "We warned you, but you knew better. You wouldn't listen. You wouldn't mind."

"I'll mind. I'm a good girl." Even that simple truth felt like a bad, livery taste in Thelma's mouth as she tried to avoid Annie's eyes. It smacked of a lie. Lying was bad. She was bad.

Annie now shook her head. "With this foolish game, you'll burn to death. The flame will catch your skirt, your sleeve, your curls, your eyelashes. It will swallow your arms and legs and toes. You'll crisp like chicken skin. And all that will remain is a pile of ashes and a handful of teeth that I will have to sweep up. So I am going to teach you a lesson about fire today so that I never have to teach you again."

"Please, Annie, please, no." Thelma wiggled her hips and pulled at her hand to get it back. The sound of a handball bouncing against the courtyard wall could be heard, and the screams of ordinary children playing.

Annie gripped Thelma's right hand tighter as the little girl strained, folding the fingers down in a fist and covering them, leaving only the pink thumb unable to run for cover, held aloft as Annie clicked the lighter. Then she depressed the trigger, leaving the flame on. "This is what happens to little girls who play with fire," she said, holding the fire beneath her sister's thumb but still only threatening, leaving an inch so that Thelma could feel the heat but not the burn.

The butane smell filled Thelma's nostrils. She was angry at Uncle Schmulie for introducing the game, for showing her the lighter, for befriending her and then abandoning her to this witch. She felt the increasing warmth on her thumb but couldn't detach herself. She felt absolutely alone. It was loneliness like hunger that couldn't be solved in the belly with bread and jam. Annie clearly didn't want her, not there in the kitchen, not anywhere. Annie, her enemy, had taken play, a harmless game, and turned it into this. Thelma had to pee, to escape from the butane and the smell of Annie's floral perfume that masked her sweat and woman's smells.

"This is what fire does," Annie said, letting the flame lick the surface of her sister's thumb. There was a moment of shock where the child felt nothing. Then pain arrived, her own skin crying out in agony to her stunned mind. The girl's eyes teared as much as she struggled against crying before Annie.

Thelma's knees buckled. *"Please. No."*

It smelled like cooked meat. Thelma feared she would combust, becoming ashes to ashes, dust to dust. Her scorched thumb throbbed. She flinched, but Annie pinched her between her thighs, continuing her work, teaching her horrible lesson.

Alarmed that she was melting, Thelma worried she would lose the thumb and then the hand. Meanwhile, the warmth and shame of the liquid soaking her underwear and flowing down her bare leg became one more crime. But Annie was apparently not yet aware of that (or the possibility that the pee flowed dangerously close to her good shoes). She said, "Fire is dangerous. Lighters are not toys, Thelma"—the name again, the hated name—"this is what it's like to be burned. This is the pain. I need to teach you so you don't hurt yourself."

Let me hurt myself, because I would never hold a match to my finger. Where was her mother that she couldn't hear her daughter's screams? Where was her father looking down from heaven's fluffy clouds, refusing to send down lightning to strike this villain? Where was Schmulie to grab the lighter and spank her as was the proper punishment?

The harsh physical pain only increased with time, but the sense of being scrawny small in the world, unloved and unlovable, was a deeper and longer-lasting wound for which there was no salve.

A new smell wafted into the room: burning paper. Briefly, the little girl wondered if that was what she was—a paper doll that would soon catch fire and disappear.

Her brother Abraham emerged from the room she shared with her sister and mother. The eleven-year-old stood, legs spread, as if he were Harry Houdini with a trick up one sleeve and down the other. Abie refused to cower in the shadows with his head down and his shoulders rounded, like so many other Jewish men and boys. The world was his ghetto. He never shuffled except when he played cards. He had a spring in his step and a chin that jutted forward. No one decided for *him*. He lived in Papa's vacuum. His response to those who disliked or disrespected him was *schmuck*. It was his favorite Yiddish word in a language that contained more bendy terms for shaming and cursing than the Eskimos had for *snow*.

Schmuck was the first word Abie had taught Thelma. It took half a day. What a beautiful, defiant word that filled every curve and cranny of her mouth. He roared with laughter when he deployed his sister on Mama, his hands launching her forward. Afterward he comforted her through the slap and inevitable mouth soaping. Later, he led Thelma to the corner candy store, where he had a line of credit for unnamed services rendered, and bought her a paper sack of lemon drops. When she offered him a candy, he refused, saying, "Don't share. You earned that whole bag."

Now, when Thelma saw her brother through her tears beyond Annie, the air returned to her lungs. He raised a flaming dollar bill in his right hand.

Annie swiveled her neck, turning from her torture, indignant at the interruption. "What are you doing, *meshugener kop*, burning your money? Are you crazy?"

"I'm not *that* crazy!" Abie replied. "I'm burning *your* money. Why are you burning the baby?"

There was love in his voice, a treble that had yet to change despite the recent appearance of a wispy mustache.

Annie dropped her grip on the girl's arm while still keeping her sister captive between her thighs. "Where did you get that?" she shrieked.

"You think you can hide anything from me, sistah?" Abie asked, employing the term a newsboy might use on a street-corner mark. This *sister* was no term of endearment. It was not *baby*. He dropped the flaming bill on the floor when the fire singed his fingertips. He stamped it out on the linoleum, leaving a smudge. Then he removed a second crumpled bill from his pocket and lit it. "I'm burning *your* cash."

In the shock that followed, Annie relaxed her legs. Thelma kicked her shin. The larger girl pushed the child backward and rose, slipping in piss. She didn't pause. A head taller than her little brother, she still outclassed him in weight and reach, but she stopped when she saw smoke escaping the bedroom she shared with her mother and sister.

Annie rushed past Abraham, hissing, "You delinquent."

Abraham had set fire to Annie's underwear drawer, where she stashed all her secret things, including the silk-satin brassiere for which she'd slaved and had hidden from Mama beneath the cottons. She screamed; the *geschrei* summoned the neighbors. Thelma flew to Abie, wrapping herself around his leg, as close as red paint on a barber's pole. He examined her thumb and kissed it, but they lacked time for a reunion. Disentangling his little sister, he leaped to the kitchen window and slammed it up. He turned, blew a kiss, and then shot out onto the fire escape. Thelma vowed that when she had kids of her own, she would love the child like she loved Abie, unconditionally.

Chapter 3

Three hours after Abie dashed out the Jungers' window onto the fire escape, his mother returned to 106th Street from her twelve-hour shift at the Ansonia Hotel laundry. They say that in hard times some women lose their appetites, others their capacity to nurture: the latter was Rebecca Lorber née Minzer.

Gazing down, she saw a stranger's hands, gnarled and old, her red fingers stiffened by starch. Crossing the alley to the service entrance, she kicked aside a stray cat nosing in a garbage pile. Her arms dragged like two overstuffed suitcases. Her advice to landsmen fleeing Eastern Europe: "Pack light." The fellow emigrant would end up carrying the world's weight on top of the featherbed and silver. Better to cast off those possessions early and keep the old world alive in your heart.

Born into an extended clan in the trading hub of Galicia's Drohobych, where the Tysmenytsia River met the Seret, the widow Lorber plodded the Manhattan streets as if invisible. Nobody here recognized that, of all her sisters, she most resembled her mother. Her close-set blue eyes appraised the world from a round face above flaring nostrils in a thick root of a nose.

Standing five feet and a pinch, Rebecca had swollen ankles that ached from an entire shift standing. After a day scrubbing white linen stained with shit, blood, and wine, and then working the industrial steam iron with a foot pedal, she didn't want to touch or be touched.

A hug was as good as a blow. Rebecca didn't recognize this crotchety old donkey she'd become. She'd nothing but trouble to anticipate going forward, and looking back was no picnic.

At thirty-one, Rebecca felt herself an old woman, even though it seemed so recently that she had curls in her hair, fire in her cheeks, and the gall to yell at her children herself. She'd borne five children, four still living, and been pregnant eight times. She'd lost an infant late in a pregnancy as her husband, Jonas, began to succumb to the slow death of tuberculosis, the plague of Norfolk Street on Manhattan's Lower East Side. The girl was almost fully formed. Rebecca had let herself get fully attached, and she couldn't escape the mourning, particularly to welcome Thelma within a year, as if a baby for a baby could wrap up sorrow. How could a dying man manage that? But somehow he had the energy for sex that he couldn't summon for work. After Thelma arrived, Rebecca felt betrayed by both husband and child. The weak-chinned Jonas had hardly stuck around to see the girl's first hairs. He'd hidden in final prayers, salvaging his eternal soul while leaving his wife carrying around that saggy torn sack of a uterus and no prospects, no safety net.

In that hopeless state of mind—with Jonas buried in a distant pauper's grave in Mount Zion Cemetery, alone with two sons and two daughters—she cracked for the first time. She couldn't make herself get out of bed. Rebecca's worst nightmare had occurred: she'd become a *betteljuden*, a begging Jew, those impoverished souls she'd condemned in Galicia, always assuming laziness, not a series of misfortunes, had left them penniless.

She didn't know how to be an individual in the new world. Annie's strength and toughness, despite being only eleven, pulled her through the darkest days. Rebecca had passed Thelma to her oldest daughter. She never tickled or touched the baby. She couldn't bear the child's crying when she herself buckled in pain. Rebecca called it grief for Jonas, but that was just a black felt bag to shove her woes in: she missed having a husband to take care of what the external world demanded of a citizen.

In her eyes, he became a martyr who'd never done anybody a wrong, but did she really miss *him*? That was less clear. His absence from her bed was a relief. No more of the monthly terror: will the blood come or not. She believed that if she became pregnant again, she'd die, ripped from the inside out. No child was worth that. And yet there was Annie: through her daughter's strength, Rebecca survived that period, creating a bond between them that spared no room for the baby or her brothers.

Now Rebecca relied on the United Hebrew Charities to pay the rent. She was deeply ashamed. She lacked control, sharing a room with her daughters, another woman patrolling the kitchen, a padlock on the icebox. She'd often spent her day off fighting long lines at the aid office. She lived in fear of home visits and losing the very little independence that she had, or her children.

Once she'd been proud, surrounded by family that seemed only to exist in memory like an embroidered folktale. She'd never had to face abuse alone, even if it came from her father, who treated all his girls as if they were farm animals to be bred and sold. All he loved was that weakling son. Let them both have each other and swallow the spit in the soup from the many daughters.

As the widow lifted one heavy foot over the other on the stairs, the apartment's back door banged open. She almost fell backward, reaching out to clutch the banister with a chapped hand that cried in pain at the touch. Above, the landlady appeared like Moses with his stone tablets. She stomped onto the landing, a yellow thread of a woman with brown bug eyes. She seethed down at the boarder, sniffing at the smell of work sweat that rose with that of the garbage below.

Rebecca felt humiliated even before she heard the latest outrage, an old donkey steadying herself for another whipping. She hoped this would be the last, her legs almost folding beneath her. She recognized that sharp tone, the entitled way that her mother had addressed servants, poor relations who'd overstayed their welcome in the barn, beggars who'd arrived at the back door on a black mood day. What a ridiculous notion that all Jews would stick together, German and Hungarian, Russian and Rumanian, assimilated Americans who worked on Saturdays and wore pinstripes. The landlady didn't know Rebecca's father or her mother, her grandfathers, the great Torah scholar who had been her father-in-law. How could she know Rebecca without knowing her family? Instead, Rebecca was some kind of savage, a necessary evil to pay the rent, a charity case to demonstrate a generosity Mrs. Junger lacked.

Mixing German and English in a harsh tongue Rebecca hardly understood, Mrs. Junger raised her right hand and yelled, "Take those demons and go, you good-for-nothing *Galizianer*. This is how you repay my hospitality? I open my home to your *Wildfang*, your *Wolfsjunge*, and your boys burn it down. Dogs, I'd rather rent to mongrels."

"What now?" Rebecca asked, huffing up the final steps, shoulders dropping lower in anticipation of a beating despite the awareness that it would be verbal, not physical. She couldn't imagine how this foul day could worsen. Pushing past the landlady into the kitchen, Rebecca was immediately surrounded by the other boarders rushing to the kitchen to witness the fireworks. Her gorge rose in reaction to the public dressing-down, and yet she knew enough to bite her tongue and take her punishment.

She longed to stretch out on her bed without even washing away the *shvits* pooling like syrup beneath heavy breasts. She shut her eyes, wanting to be a cow in a field of her homeland lying in the high grass, the smell of mown hay, a boy's hand up her skirt when all of that was still a mystery and not a leaky pipe, all plumbing, no pleasure.

Mrs. Junger pointed at the door. "The street!"

Although they were not friends, the women weren't complete strangers, living as they did together in the thin-walled apartment. They both knew Rebecca's biggest fear: homelessness. In Galicia, the government exiled the penniless to remote precincts. The Jewish elders, on instructions from the Christian magistrates, sent the *betteljuden* to labor in distant fields, because the poor lacked the coin to pay the candle tax on Jews, a sum for every wick lit in the ritual prayers or on holidays.

Her youngest, Thelma, waited in the kitchen, demanding attention. The red-faced girl grabbed her mother's skirt, thrusting her thumb up for inspection. The child cried anew, unable to explain through the tears and snot what had happened and why she was waving her hand so urgently at her mother.

Rebecca saw the child in her peripheral vision, hopping from foot to foot, but only wished for her to stifle herself and stop the tsuris. Embattled, impoverished, Rebecca had nothing left for her. Thelma's cloying closeness, the heat, Mrs. Junger's insistence that the Lorbers pack and leave immediately, shut Rebecca down. Her head began to throb; her swollen legs bent beneath her. She reached for a chair. It collapsed, splintering under her deadweight. A smoky black cloud swirled inside her mind. She could neither see nor hear.

In that darkness, Rebecca felt suddenly weightless, as if she'd returned to the bed shared with her sisters in their thick-walled home with many rooms. There, she'd fit like the scent of fresh, eggy buns in the oven. When she awoke from her faint, stretched out on the featherbed that she had stitched as part of her dowry, she thought she saw her older sister Fanny leaning close. But, no, it was her eldest, her survivor.

A burned smell made the air in the windowless room almost unbreathable. When Rebecca coughed, Annie offered her mother a tumbler. Forced by Annie, Rebecca sputtered the warm water down her chest as if she were a baby. She didn't want to drink. She didn't want food. She didn't want anything but quiet, the peace of the grave. She whispered, "Enough."

"Drink some more, *Mamaleh*."

"*Enough!* I'm done."

"You just had a shock, your blood pressure . . ."

"I can't wash another sheet. I can't raise children on my own. This is my last breath."

Annie removed the rag from her mother's forehead and dipped it in a bowl. She wrung out the excess, then replaced it. Rebecca shut her eyes. Her head throbbed. She could hear a thrumming in her ears and a banging on the door, low to the ground, and Thelma's cry of "Mama, Mama, let me in."

Rebecca opened her eyes. "I can't."

Annie shrugged. "So don't."

From outside, again, "Mama, Mama, let me in." Ignoring the cry, Rebecca noticed the bureau drawers were ajar. Scorched linen piled high atop the chest. Hanging from a wooden knob, part of a strange blush satin undergarment stippled with burns. She looked back at Annie, whose face neared her own as the girl shifted the wet cloth and held her mother's hand.

"Will she never leave me alone?" Rebecca asked.

"Ignore her." Annie stroked her mother's eyebrows with her thumbs, as Rebecca had done to her when she was younger and sleepless.

As Rebecca began to calm down, Annie started to cry and snuffle. First quietly and then building until her mother asked, "What's the matter, *maideleh*, why tears?"

"Don't leave me, Mama," Annie said, hiding her face in her mother's shoulder. She remained there for a long time, Rebecca's hand toying with the curls at the nape of her neck. When Annie pulled away, she wiped her eyes and then began crying anew. Her mood had changed. These were now angry and righteous tears, as if they arose equally from seeing her mother incapacitated and from yet another looming crisis. "I have to tell you something that I don't want to tell you."

"Tell me."

"You need to rest," Annie said. "Later."

"Better now than when it's too late."

In that scorching, airless room, Annie narrated her side of the story: Abie had opened her dresser and, unprovoked, set her clothes ablaze while Annie played with Thelma in the kitchen. Her crazy brother hadn't stopped there. He had burned the money she'd been saving for her mother. Annie leaned closer, confiding quietly in Yiddish. Occasionally, Thelma rapped on the door with a piteous "Mama."

"How did I raise such wolves?"

"Papa died," Annie said. "Don't blame yourself."

"Where can we go? We can't move. I just can't."

"We won't have to," Annie said. "Listen to me. I have a plan."

"You're a good daughter, Annie, but this is too much to bear."

"For you, maybe, but it's not for me."

"What can you do? You're only a girl."

"I'm young. I'm strong. I'll take care of it."

"How?" Rebecca's head began to throb again. This wasn't the rest she needed. She could hardly decide between a pear and a pickle, much less make serious decisions. "I'm too weak."

"Something has to be done, Mama, and fast. I'll protect you. Trust in me."

"Always and forever, if I live so long," Rebecca said, her voice wet with emotion.

"I can't control Abie any more than you can. He's running wild on the streets. Mrs. Junger called him an arsonist. I begged her on my hands and knees not to contact the police. Instead, she sent word to the United Hebrew Charities that Abie tried to burn the apartment building down. By breakfast, when the social worker arrives, either we'll all be tossed out—or he goes and we stay."

"I can't split up my family," Rebecca said, pushing herself up from the pillow onto her elbows. The damp cloth slipped down her nose and she fell back, grabbing her head, as if she were having a stroke.

"You don't have a choice. I've talked to Mrs. Junger. We can put the boys in the Jewish orphanage."

"I can't. I can't give up my Abie."

"It will have to be the two of them, Abie and Louis both. And, think, that way they won't be alone. They can watch over each other until we can afford our own apartment."

"They're my sons," Rebecca protested. "They bear my grandfathers' names."

"They're my brothers," Annie said, cupping her mother's hands within her own. "This pains me as much as it hurts you, Mama, but what choice do we have?"

"Tell me what my Louis did to deserve this? Abie, yes, but did Louis light a fire, too?" Rebecca asked, considering her little gray-eyed boy, only nine years old, who'd never caused her a day of trouble. He wasn't affectionate, but he was a sturdy son of whom a mother could be proud, who never made a promise he didn't keep, who preferred the outdoors to the kitchen table.

"Whatever Abie does, Mama, Louis does. They're inseparable."

"Should the sins of one weigh on the other? It doesn't feel kosher," Rebecca said, sucking her tongue. She tried to measure her choices but felt so bone-tired that her mind could barely follow a thought to its conclusion. "What would my sisters in Drohobych say? That, after losing so many babies, the Lord blessed me with two sons and I threw them away? They would judge me harshly. They would never look at me the same way again."

"Your sisters are far away, Mama. And the boys will return. They're strong. They'll be fine. For now, we have to save ourselves."

Rebecca had no more fight left in her, as wrung out as the sheets she had scrubbed and pressed and steamed at the Ansonia laundry all day. She surrendered to her eldest. "If you think there's no other solution, Annie, then it must be true."

"What choice do we have?"

That evening, mother and daughter soldered their bond. Rebecca sighed as Annie relieved her of the burden of responsibility. She rolled on her side and curled into a ball, abdicating to Annie without even noting the exchange. She never even opened the door to Abie, or the baby, to hear their accounts of that afternoon.

The next morning after breakfast, when the female social worker arrived in white gloves and hat, Rebecca remained bedridden. As she awkwardly beckoned the stern stranger into the bedroom, she heard Abie and Annie yelling, throwing voices like knives. All Rebecca felt once she took the pen in her hand was anticipation of the silence to follow. She couldn't control those boys. She heard something solid hit the wall. Thelma wailed. It made it easier for her to sign the papers, claiming (as she coughed dramatically) that she was too sickly to keep her sons, which wasn't the same as she was just sick to death of them.

What mother wouldn't feel guilt at this moment? Village mothers on the outskirts of Drohobych, Galicians from good families, never gave away their children. There were so many hands to hold on to a child— sisters, brothers, aunts, uncles, cousins, neighbors. Food appeared on the table, fresh in summer, preserved in winter. Money came in from farming and trade that daughters never had to touch. She missed that garden of Galicia, the breadbasket, the wheat growing in black soil, sunflowers exploding in midsummer. She recalled the dust rising on the roads, the closeness of animals and the dairy's stench.

This wave of homesickness was at the root of Rebecca's malaise. She recalled Fanny, with the dry wit that always kept them laughing, who ran interference when Papa raged. Her sister could have held the hand of a gorilla. She would have made a success in America. She wouldn't have had to discard her sons like trash. If her husband had died, she would have walked to the matchmaker the following week in her torn black dress and found a new one. Rebecca had failed, done the unthinkable. She'd made a devil's deal and then turned over in the bed, blinding her eyes to it.

Chapter 4

No matter how much Thelma wept and pleaded and promised goodness she could never deliver, Annie wouldn't take her to see Abie and Louis. The little girl lacked control and felt it keenly. Her burned thumb blistered then burst then healed—and, still, no brothers to kiss it better. They'd taken the fun and play and tickles with them in a single cardboard valise. When Thelma hid in the closet, no one looked for her. She felt a wild anger, because Abie had protected her from Annie and been exiled. She bit her own arm to keep herself from screaming that it wasn't fair. She missed hiding behind her big brother with her head beneath his coat, her arms hugging his knees and her nose pressed against his bony back. When she wasn't in the closet, she sat on the floor beside the kitchen window, waiting for him to return for her, hearing every cat paw on the fire escape, every dirty pigeon's scratchy curse. No Abie. No safety.

Once Mama finally rose from her bed for good, three months later, she took Annie and Thelma to visit the New York Hebrew Orphan Asylum. Slapped by sleet and rain, they caught the Fifth Avenue horse-car uptown. Loneliness banged in the little girl's chest despite being sandwiched between her mother and sister in a seat made for two. She'd forgotten Abie's penknife that he'd left behind. Surely he needed it if he was going to escape.

Annie and Mama talked over Thelma's head in hushed tones, but she didn't listen. Instead, she studied a golden-braided girl. The slightly older child wore a red wool coat, holding a black terrier in a basket. She kissed the puppy on the mouth. Its pink gumdrop tongue licked her lips. The girl laughed like bubbles. Thelma coveted the dog and the basket, the coat and her shiny black rain boots. She wanted her joy and laughter and to be free of Mama and Annie, who she was convinced didn't love her. It was a tough-nut truth she knew like the numbers from one to ten or the color blue. She just did not know why, or what mistake she'd made.

As much as the child longed to see Abie and Louis, she feared the institution. Annie often threatened, "If you misbehave, we'll send you to the orphanage." But at least there the girl would be with her brothers. Sitting in the circle of Annie's flowery perfume that masked an unrecognizable bodily odor, Thelma envied the braided blonde across the aisle. She sat beside a white-capped nursemaid exhibiting a gentle patience. She wanted to trade seats. Even so young, she suspected this red-coated Gretel with her raised chin was one of them, a Gentile.

Thelma knew she was Jewish, different, and should look down and away. Annie had warned her about these people. The goyim chased them from the old country to new ghettos. They were not their friends. But she couldn't see that evil in this girl. Surely if they shared a playground, she would skip rope like Thelma and let her pet the Scottie dog with its red collar to match her coat.

Mama pinched her elbow, but still, she stared.

"We don't have to go today," Annie said, even though the fare had been paid. She'd left school to work six days a week, including the Sabbath. "If I wasn't such a good sister, I would stay home. This is my only day off and I have plans tonight."

"I have to go," Mama said. "They're not animals."

"I like animals," Thelma said, thinking of puppies. She twisted Mama's dull gold wedding band, trying to make it turn on her swollen finger. When Mama had enough, she swatted her daughter's hand away.

The previous night, in preparation for the visit, Annie had sheared her sister's hair, claiming it was so that she wouldn't get lice. Now, with her cold neck exposed, Thelma felt ugly and ashamed, a boy in a skirt. Abie would tease, but that would be okay. Her anticipation to reunite with him became breaths too big for her chest—and to see Louis, too, the silent soldier, and be one among three again.

The women rode the streetcar forever among folks in their Sunday clothes whose skin was increasingly dark. As the horsecar approached Harlem's 136th Street, Mama rang the bell. The vehicle slid to a stop. They shuffled to the exit. Thelma had to leap from the high platform and nearly slipped. A stranger steadied her by her collar, calling her "boy." She blushed, glaring at him with burning girl eyes.

Slush slicked the streets. Thelma viewed knees and boots and black puddles. Annie had stuffed newspaper into Thelma's boots. The dampened daily held the chill between her toes. She struggled to follow her mother's hippopotamus rear. Clenched by the wrist, the little girl occasionally slid behind her mother. They covered long foreign blocks among brown-skinned residents often hostile in reaction to Annie's fearful glances.

The sleet began, then freezing rain.

The soggy trio arrived at the red stone building that stretched between 136th and 138th Streets on Amsterdam Avenue. Thelma bent her neck back but couldn't see the sky above, only the Hebrew Orphan Asylum. Four stories high in the middle and three at each wing, it had a confusion of towers and spikes and gloomy windows. It resembled a witch's fortress, not a children's sanctuary. A high, spoked iron fence encircled it.

Mama threaded between stone pillars. "Not so bad."

"Not bad at all, Mama," Annie said.

Thelma shook her shaved head. If it hadn't been for the promise of Abie and Louis, she'd have spun around, sped into the cobbled street, and begged any stranger to snatch her up.

Scurrying under eaves that protected them from sleet that had bunched into hail, Mama knocked on the front door. No response.

Annie pushed the door open. The astringent smell of ammonia assailed them. Even ferocious Annie wiped her stinging eyes.

Giant black-and-white tiles covered the foyer. Thelma tried to stick to the light blocks, but Mama yanked her onto the black as they penetrated the gloom. A half-open dutch door yawned to the left beside a brass bell that Mama slapped with her palm.

From deep beyond, there were scrabbling noises, then a woman yelled, "What, are you crazy? Are you in such a hurry to leave that child?"

The crone, who had one milky-blue eye, poked her sour face over the double door. She fixed Thelma with her one sighted yellow eye. "Isn't the boy a little small?"

Thelma froze. She'd believed they were there to visit Abie and Louis. She panicked, wondering if Mama was now abandoning her, too, the monkey child that couldn't stand still. But she had no bag. She had nothing, not even underwear. "This isn't fair, you *dybbuks!*"

"Stop fussing," Mama said, pushing Thelma at Annie, who caught her in her claws. Mrs. Lorber addressed the matron: "We're here to visit Abraham and Louis."

"They've been waiting since breakfast and have missed lunch." She pushed open the half door, advancing with a knot of keys dangling from her waist. "I am Mrs. Feingold," she said as if that explained everything.

"Mrs. Lorber." Mama followed Mrs. Feingold up wide stone steps past a splash of vomit.

"Moishe, the mop," Mrs. Feingold said. Then she proceeded.

After Thelma paused to stare at the sour-smelling pink-and-yellow puddle, she hurried to catch up. They climbed the stairs as if ascending to heaven. The girl, feeling even tinier than usual, almost expected an angry bearded man with a raised right hand to greet her at the top. Instead, a ball rolled by, plopped down the steps (awkwardly, because it was not fully round) and splashed in the barf.

"Mop, Moishe, mop," said Mrs. Feingold, who led them past a tall door where dark, lemurlike eyes peeped out. Curious, Thelma stared back but turned away when a girl her age stuck out a pasty tongue and an older boy shook a fist. She hurried to catch up as the group entered a long, open hall on the second floor. Tall windows received a wintry light. The chill that had claimed Thelma's toes now crawled up into her ankles as the group passed through double doors. They entered a long lounge that felt as frigid inside as out. Abie perched at the far end in a big chair capable of holding a rabbi, swinging one leg over the armrest impatiently. Beside him, Louis inhabited a child's chair, still and wary. Two years younger than Abie, he was a gentle boy, the catcher of Abie's pitches, his lieutenant and coconspirator. He had crisp gray eyes that, when he chose to look up, seemed to monitor the horizon but resisted domestic tides.

Dropping Mama's skirt, Thelma ran to Abie, carrying a hurricane of love. She leaped into his arms and took his tickles and gave him kisses on cheeks that had oddly begun to sprout soft whiskers. She pecked his earlobes, and he bit her cheek and gave it a hard suck until she slapped him and pulled away, happily wiping the slobber on her coat sleeve.

By the time Mama and Annie arrived, scraping up child-size chairs, Thelma had climbed into Abie's lap. She faced her mother and sister from his throne, as happy as a birthday girl. They couldn't touch her. She had her Abie, his bloody-knuckled hand tucked around her tummy. This was family. This was safe. Without Abie, Thelma wasn't herself.

Louis inched closer to Thelma, smelling of harsh soap, the same foul scent from when she'd had her mouth washed out at shul. She kissed his elbow, like she always did, and his cheek. Blood pooled in the white of one eye; his split lip hurt Thelma as if it were her own. He rested his hand on her shoulder as she sat on Abie's knee, looking down at Mama and Annie. *See,* she wanted to say, *the boys love me. Abie loves me.*

"Stop bothering Abie, Thelma," said Annie.

Squeezing the girl in his lap, Abie said, "Temeleh never bothers me. She's my sister."

"I'm your mother. Don't you have a kiss for me since I've come all this way?" Mama held out her hand as if expecting Abie to shove Thelma off his lap and come forward. He stayed put and so did Thelma, her gaze bold with her brother at her back. Louis shuffled toward Mama, but one withering glance from Abie stopped the boy.

Abie stroked what hair she had left and said, "I don't want you to catch anything here at the Hebrew Home for the Criminally Unloved."

"The Hebrew Benevolent Orphan Asylum," said Annie.

"It is what it is," said Abie, "and it's no playground."

"You've had it too good," said Annie.

"That's funny coming from you, princess," Abie said. Even though Thelma was safely on his lap, she hoped he wouldn't pick a fight. She feared their anger spoiling her good feeling. From her roost, Thelma watched Annie and Mama. They shared the same small eyes without brows, round faces, and high foreheads. Mama's gray hair twisted in a tight bun, with a wild frizz. The rain had flattened Annie's careful curls. Side by side they were two hard mountains, their shoulders bent. If it weren't for Abie, the child would have felt weak against them.

Mama pursed her lips. "You're looking thin, Abraham."

"You're not," Abie said.

"I've been sick in bed since you left. I can hardly touch my food."

"It doesn't show," Abie said. "And, by the way, we didn't leave. You dumped us here."

"You've worried her sick," said Annie. Mama had stopped working at the laundry and retreated to her bed, leaving Annie to mother Thelma with slaps and shoves. "I left school to become a bookkeeper's apprentice."

"Sorry if I don't get out my hankie to dry your tears while I'm stuck in this hell house for Hebrews. The grub here would make a rat puke, or maybe it *is* rat puke. Look at my fists, you squinty-eyed *yenta*. Look at Louis's lip. We're not at the Ritz."

"You brought it on yourself, you *no-goodnik*."

Thelma wanted to defend him, to cry that Annie was no good. But even facing her sister from the security of Abie's lap, the older girl's rage still terrified her.

Abie said, "I pity the boys you spread your legs for when you finally open that mouth and they see who you really are."

Yellow and sweaty, Mama belched. *"Enough."*

Annie encircled Mama's shoulders. Once the older woman caught her breath, she said, "Why should I visit? Like I need more tsuris? Since I'm here, tell me, Abraham, they have school here. What do they teach?"

"I can pick a lock in under a minute. If I had better tools, I'd be faster. See, Ma, I've learned a trade."

"You are a rascal," said Mama. "At least are you learning your numbers and letters?"

"I could read your letters if you sent any. Can you write?"

"Well enough if I have something good to say, but, Abraham, tell me why I should write to you when you have no shame?"

"You could send your love," Abie said. Silence descended on the great big room. Thelma knew love: Abie showered affection on her. Abie gripped Thelma tighter. Louis moved nearer.

Mama didn't soften. "When you're worth it."

"If you're worth it," Annie sniffed.

"I can't control you, Abraham, so I won't comfort you. You behave like an animal and you land in a zoo, dragging your brother behind. Are you tending Louis now that your bad deeds landed him here?"

"Are you minding Temmy?" Abie asked. Thelma shivered. She feared being in the middle. It was the lighter all over again. She rubbed her scarred thumb. "Look at her: turn her sideways, she'd disappear. And what's with this hair? What horrible thing can a baby do that deserves such punishment?"

"Temmy is fine . . . ," said Mama.

". . . not a scratch on her, but what are these bruises on her arms? She looks sad, just like I'd be if I was left alone with you two."

His caring unleashed the tears stuck inside her.

"You've grown since I saw you last, Abraham, with that dirty fluff under your nose. But Louis has shrunk."

"Unhappiness can do that. I protect him the best I can, but it's no picnic for a skinny kid without the belly for a fight. Hey, Ma, here's another lesson we've learned on the inside: how to walk back-to-back. It's like having eyes behind your head when some big bum tries to rush you. So I've learned how to take better care of Louis, but looking at his lip, well, nobody's perfect."

Turning to her younger son, Mama asked, "Louis, what happened to your face?" Louis hung his head. Thelma took his hand.

"He fell down the stairs," Abie answered.

"Which stairs?" Annie asked.

"The joint has tons of stairs. We've had to clean 'em all."

"You always make a big tsuris from nothing," Mama said, "even when you were a baby."

"I was never a baby."

"My firstborn son, you are. If only Papa had survived to see you here."

"Was that the only way Papa could escape you?"

"Why would he want to escape me?" Mama's fury rose, shrinking her eyes, twisting her mouth. She leaned forward like a witch casting a spell. Annie mirrored the action, the anger sparking from mother to daughter. But while Mama focused on Abie, Annie narrowed her eyes at Thelma. Thelma feared Mama would rise and strike her, even in her weakened state. Young as she was, she knew that hurting her hurt Abie.

"Always the funny boy, Abraham, always with the joke," said Annie, her fists balled up and ready to strike. "Has that mouth of yours helped you make friends here?"

"Better than friends, I have a gang."

"He has a girlfriend, too," said Louis.

Abie plumped up his chest and stroked the few dark hairs above his lip. "I don't put up with *drek*, and I take my lumps."

"Why should you get lumps unless you asked for them?" asked Annie.

"Like I asked to be here, Annie? Welcome to the institution, Ma."

"I brought you here . . ."

". . . dumped us here . . ."

". . . they promised to take care of you."

"You should be thankful that we came here on my day off," said Annie.

"And all you give me is heartburn," said Mama. "Can't you see my stomach can hardly support this visit and yet here we are, to show that you have a family? How many of those orphans dream of having a family like yours?"

"They call those nightmares," Abie said. "The other kids, most of their parents died. My mother's alive. My big sister's no beauty, but she's healthy. I got sent because I set fire to Annie's drawers. She stays home because she only burned the baby. Where's God's justice in that?"

Mama rose, her face pale and her neck red. "Who are you, you little *pisher*, questioning God?"

"What's there to question? The high holidays came and went with no word from our mother. The others look at Louis and me and wonder what we did to deserve this stone shithouse. Those children cry because they have no families. But at least their parents didn't abandon them here. They mock us as unlovable." Abie had worked himself up. He wasn't quick to anger, but once he was angry, it couldn't be stopped. "Those jerks don't envy us, Mama, because we are lower than low. We're orphans with a mother beyond the iron fence."

"Don't make Mama feel worse than she already does," said Annie.

"The fix is simple," said Abie. "Spring us today. Call Mrs. Feingold right now and take us home. Tell her we won't be eating chipped beef on toast tonight."

"I can't do that," Mama said.

"Can't—or won't?"

"Please, Mama," Thelma said. "I'll never be bad again. I promise. Bring them home."

"We don't have the money for the horsecar," said Mama.

"Annie does. She tucks coins in her handkerchief," Thelma said.

"Have you seen my money that I worked so hard for?" Annie said. "Have you stolen it?"

"The kid doesn't steal," said Abie. "She's a kid."

"We can work," said Louis. "We'll deliver newspapers. Just take us home."

"Please, Mama, let them come home with me." Thelma buried her face in Abie's neck, feeling his thighs stiffen beneath her. He must have known her tears didn't move these boulders.

"Come, Thelma," said Mama. "Enough of this."

Annie approached. She ripped the child from Abie, holding her collar and waistband as if the girl were a dirty diaper. Annie set Thelma down roughly, and they hurried away behind Mama's hippopotamus bottom.

It crushed Thelma that she hadn't said goodbye before leaving with the enemy. She twisted around and saw Abie, sitting still like a king in his big rabbi's chair, fingering his baby mustache. Louis wilted beside him, his head bowed.

"I love you," she called, voice squeezed tight. "When I'm grown, I'll marry you both."

As Annie dragged her behind Mama, the child promised herself that she would never treat her own children so harshly. They would know love and affection. She would protect them, whatever happened.

When Annie tugged at her bruised arm, Thelma winced, wishing she had left her there in the Asylum for the Criminally Unloved with the boys.

Chapter 5

Annie knew she'd done good. Who could argue? Problem solved. She washed her hands of that bad business with the boys. She wasn't yet fifteen, and already she had a woman's tits and a man's *kishkes*, guts. She owned the family, and no one would stand in her way. It was her rightful price for protecting Mama.

Feeling powerful, Annie strode away from the orphanage, an imposing building under the capable care of the solid Mrs. Feingold (no beauty for sure—would it be so terrible to use tweezers occasionally?). The matron ran a haven for Hebrew youth. It wasn't perfect, but what was? It was a palace compared to where those boys, those *goniffs*, could have been. They should have been in jail. It could always be worse.

In Europe, it *was* worse. The boys should count themselves lucky they weren't among those panicked Jews trying to flee Russian persecution into Finland that Annie had read about that morning in the papers. This wasn't Saint Petersburg. There was no czar. No one had chased those rascals into the orphanage.

Burning money! What kind of animal did that? They were American-born citizens. And, if you misbehaved, you got what you deserved—not because you were a Jew, but because you were a thug. That was justice. That was fairness. That, she was certain, was never going to happen to her. She wouldn't let it.

Annie wasn't dumb enough to get into trouble. She was going to enjoy the freedom America had to offer: work hard and rise, marry and have children, send them to school and let them be doctors and lawyers and pillars of industry. Maybe even buy a house, a mezuzah on the front door and a yard at the back to hang laundry where no one could see your intimates. A place she didn't have to share with people like Mrs. Junger, the landlady, who sniffed the air around Annie as if she stank, who shrieked at Mama as if she were a bum. Sacrifice, yes, be patient, survive setbacks, but keep moving forward, like she was today, on the wet sidewalk of Upper Manhattan. She'd won.

It had begun to snow. The air seemed charged with potential and her power to control her future with Abie shut away. She was going to work hard, get herself and her mother off charity, and improve their situation. Annie believed in a better life, and that included dresses and shoes and occasional trips to the hairdresser. She would find a husband and marry for love—none of this old country arranged-match *mishegas*. She wasn't a breeding cow waiting to be milked, not here in America. Of course, she would marry an observant bachelor, but what was the rush? She wasn't above having a little fun now that she was out of school and learning how to keep books.

Annie had taken to accounting quickly with her head for numbers. The same in Yiddish or English, they weren't open to interpretation. They stayed in their columns. They didn't lie. Add them up and they equaled the same number every time; multiply them and they grew. Annie enjoyed working outside the 106th Street apartment, the daily routine, the smell of the green canvas ledger and the way her boss, old Mr. Nutkis, slowly nodded his head as he reviewed her work, pausing occasionally to put his eyes near the figures, closing the right and focusing with the left. The owner of a wholesale women's undergarment business, the widower would run his stubby, ink-stained fingers down the debits and then appraise Annie over his wire-framed glasses, tutting contentedly and saying, "Not bad."

Not bad. She knew in the language of old Mr. Nutkis that that was good, praise even. She appreciated compliments, given their rarity. Even without completing eighth grade, Annie was already better than her employer's two red-haired sons, who sat and read the racing forms the moment their father went out to do his business, as if the bell over the front door were the starter gun that had them running for the petty cash.

Annie wasn't working at Nutkis & Sons for the entertainment of lazy *nudniks*, neither of whom were marriage material. She'd figured that out on the first day of work. She didn't want ginger-bearded sons. She deserved better, even if they would likely inherit their father's company. And, when she bent over the files, when a son's frisky hand landed on her behind, accompanied by a high giggle, one hard smack clarified that she was there for her business, not their pleasure. "Do it again," she'd said the first time, "and I'll slam your *schlong* in the file drawer."

In general, when the father was out meeting clients, Annie dealt with the boys firmly and swiftly, secure in the knowledge that she had more on them than they had on her—and she was willing to use it. The old man was the one who mattered. He earned her best white-toothed smiles in the morning while her lipstick was in full force. She served him strong tea made the way he liked it, in a short glass with three sugar cubes on the saucer. At the end of every week, she received her paycheck gratefully, not too proud to mention how much it meant to her sick mother and how she appreciated his charity in hiring a young woman without experience. She made the old man feel good about himself, and that encouraged him to feel good about her. At the end of the day, she pinned on her hat, walked onto the sidewalk in shoes she bought herself, and purchased beef at the kosher butcher that went a long way toward smoothing relations with their landlady. This was autonomy, a new kind of freedom Annie relished with small gifts to herself: lipstick and hairpins.

Annie prided herself on her daughterly devotion, but she was no altruist. A debt was owed, a life saved. She'd first shown her mettle when

Papa died, and now she'd done it again, unbidden. She was the mother now, the family boss. But control came at a cost. Without her brothers, Annie had more responsibility for Thelma. The curly-haired *kvetch* constantly harassed her older sister, always wanting this or rejecting that. Annie hated dragging her kid sister wherever she went. With wet puppy eyes and a perpetually runny nose, the skinny *meeskait* embarrassed Annie. Her sister wasn't the kind of kid that strangers admired, saying, "What a pretty girl!" Instead, people on the street stared at Thelma's emaciated legs and knobby knees and seemed to judge the *zaftig* Annie, as if she'd intentionally starved the kid. Was it her fault the monkey only ate bananas?

If Annie stopped to talk to a boy, say, in front of the candy store or by the shoemaker's, Thelma would hop from foot to foot as if the sidewalk were burning, crying to pee. Or she'd sock the kid right below his belt to steal his attention from Annie, or pick her nose and wipe the booger on her sister's arm. Exasperated, Annie would lift the girl's skirt from behind and potch her right there on her droopy underwear. Thelma deserved the punishment, but it only ignited the child. She'd wail and scream and pull away so that by the time Annie turned back to the boy, red-faced and annoyed, he'd be skulking away.

Who needed all the *mishegas*? That feral child, forever underfoot, dragged on Annie's freedom, needy and pleading, "Play with me." If the usual discipline—pinching and pushing and slapping—didn't work, Annie needed to show Thelma the harsh alternative. The trip to the orphanage should have made the point that there were worse places to be than by Annie's side, but it hadn't gone as she'd hoped. Abie had had to ruin it, sitting there, dry-eyed and unapologetic, blood on his knuckles beside a battered Louis. He even had the chutzpah to demand an apology *from them*! The schmuck just had to crawl under Mama's skin and kick her in the heart when she was down.

Now, as the snow fell softly, Annie felt tempted to peer over her shoulder up the block at the Hebrew Asylum one last time, victorious.

But she wouldn't let herself look back, even to check that Mama and Thelma were close behind her. They could keep up, as far as she was concerned.

Snow or no snow, she intended to rescue her day off. She had to get home, touch up her hair and makeup, and change shoes. She'd already laid her dress out on the bed. She had a date to meet Frank, the shoemaker's eldest son, the one with the brush mustache. He was a little older, a little dangerous, muscular, but if she could handle Abie, what couldn't she handle?

Energized, Annie paused impatiently at the corner, allowing her mother and sister to catch up. She rearranged her mother's woolen scarf to cover her rounded head. "I'm so ashamed," said Mama.

In answer, Annie hugged her tight, breast to breast, rubbing the older woman's back with gloved hands and feeling the fat rolls beneath the old woolen coat.

Crossing the street, Annie took Thelma's hand. She glanced down at the head she'd shaved last night in anticipation of the visit, fearing the spread of lice. Shorn of her copper curls, the child looked even more pitiful, not that Annie felt the pity herself.

Thelma glared up at her sister, her wet eyes full of fire.

"What?" Annie asked.

"I want Abie."

"He's never getting out," she said. "That orphanage is too good for him. And if Louis isn't careful, Abie will drag him down, too, and you with them, little girl. Just you see."

Thelma tried to yank her hand away, but Annie clutched the child's twiggy wrist harder and hurried until she was dragging the girl behind her. Thelma tried to bite her sister's arm but couldn't reach it as the older girl jerked her up on the curb. Despite Thelma's yelp and a piteous "Mama," their mother didn't turn around.

Chapter 6

Manhattan, 1908

Two lonely years later, the Hebrew Association dispatched a match-maker, a *shadkhn*, to 106th Street. The widow Pressman wore a black straw hat with a goldfinch perched on top. The bird bobbed as she balanced across the dining room table from Mama, drinking hot tea through a sugar cube and whispering. Thelma sat nearby on the windowsill, her hands squished between her thighs and feet pressed together. She thought the *yenta* said something about a carrot and a stick: that either Mama could move, or she could marry.

Within a week, Mrs. Pressman had introduced Mama to Moritz Mandel. The virile younger man had an unkempt nest of curly hair and dense black brows that could have been considered romantic in a situation where that mattered; he and a sister, Clara, had arrived on the Lower East Side from Austria in 1902, the year of Thelma's birth. Declaring the match, the *shittach*, perfect, Mrs. Pressman stitched the pair together: a foreign-born goldsmith with steady employment and an experienced American citizen who could keep a home in the old style and make sons. Perhaps Mandel should have struck a better bargain, but he was homesick, overworked, and accustomed to obeying maternal figures in domestic issues.

After a lunch-hour wedding, Thelma, Annie, and Mama moved to Brooklyn's Hooper Street. A week later, Abie and Louis returned from the orphanage wearing ragged clothes three sizes too small. They were tougher now, lean and rangy with calloused knuckles and practiced sneers. Abie hardly slept. The pair spent most of their time outdoors, never explaining where they went or who they met. If pushed, they claimed they were at shul, *davening*, praying. When Mama attempted to direct them, they ignored her. They'd been beaten by professionals. For Annie, Abie only had scorn. He held her responsible for his institutional stretch.

Louis, never chatty, hardly spoke as he approached his twelfth birthday in May. For a young man, he had sad eyes. The boys no longer romped with Thelma like before—no more hide-and-seek, but they did play cards together. Abie told Ma it was educational because it taught his sister addition, and if she learned to count cards, she could earn money gambling. And Abie, who'd spent the last three years protecting Louis, now took Thelma under his wing, too.

The Lorber kids assumed Mandel's surname, calling him Uncle Moe, not Papa. He stayed off the boys' backs, so they liked him okay. Thelma was fonder. With her, he was easygoing and affectionate. Her stepfather held her hand. He stroked her cheeks. He brought her lemon drops in paper sacks from the corner candy store. It didn't take much attention to win the girl over.

Mama worked hard for Uncle Moe, cooking his old-country dishes at 5:30 p.m. every night. During the day, she cleaned the new apartment in Brooklyn's Williamsburg, a lively immigrant neighborhood that mixed Jews and Italians. Mama no longer washed strangers' laundry. She claimed that removed ten years from her age (aided by the boxed hair dye Annie bought her).

Now the family had their own boarders: Mama's nephew from Austria moved in, and Uncle Moe got him a job. Since his name was Morris, to avoid confusion he went by his last name, Minzer. The boys called him the Mint, the big spender, because Minzer never pulled a coin from his pockets. The bachelor wore thick glasses, his neck like the pipe under the sink. In his early twenties, he seemed content to sit like a sofa cushion when he wasn't working beside Uncle Moe on Manhattan's Maiden Lane. It was the diamond district, which sounded sparkly and glamorous to Thelma, although when Uncle Moe and the Mint came home, they acted as if they were returning from the salt mines, with aching shoulders and heavy sighs.

The other boarder was also in his twenties. Jesse Lazarus clerked in a nearby warehouse while saving money to lease a Manhattan newsstand. He promised to hire Abie and Louis. They would work together, becoming their own bosses, which seemed to be what everyone wanted in America. The immigrant men wanted to be their own chiefs (and yell at someone else for a change, at least when they were out of the house).

A handsome-ugly man, Jesse had beady eyes and a shiny smile, broad muscular shoulders and comparatively skinny legs. None of his shortcomings affected Annie, now an office bookkeeper. She had Jesse in her sights from the moment he entered the apartment and loosened his belt.

The pair pretended to loathe each other. They were a regular comedy act, but Thelma had caught them wrestling awkwardly in the stairwell two flights up. And Annie no longer stalked the apartment in curlers or her ratty robe. As long as Thelma remained far from Jesse, she was safe from her sister. If they were in the same room with him, she wouldn't hit her little sister or pick on her skinny calves.

The family expanded with a man at the head of the table and the boarder uncles. They all ate meals together. Thelma was a picky eater, which peeved Mama. To her, rejecting food was a *shonda*, a shame. The youngest was such a little stick that neighbors asked why Mama was starving the child; Thelma embarrassed her. But when it came to food, she ate three things: rye bread, mustard, and cornflakes. Organ meat disgusted her. She refused mushy green beans that tasted like dirty laundry. Only Uncle Moe could halt the arguments between mother and daughter. Demanding peace for his digestion, he insisted Mama let Thelma eat what she wanted. He would finish her food, and if she starved to death, he would say kaddish, the prayer for the dead, over her skinny corpse.

If Thelma could have consumed strawberries every day, she would have been content. But in February, when her seventh birthday arrived on Groundhog Day, berries were pricey. Another *shonda*: buying out of season. Fruit in itself was a luxury and often arrived in the pockets of Abie and Louis, squished but no questions asked.

Mama held the birthday party on a Sunday, two days early. Now that she had her own Brooklyn apartment and a working husband, she played the *balabosta*, the big hostess, marking every birthday with a spread of food. She invited a few neighbors and friends but not that many children. She didn't want to clean up their mess. Still, because it was the bleak of winter, and they were falling over each other in a claustrophobic apartment, she knew they required some festivities. She even let Jesse (the only Russian immigrant among them) set a vodka bottle frozen in a block of ice on the table.

On the morning of the party, Thelma joined Mama in the kitchen. The mother strapped an adult apron on her daughter, rolling the cloth at her waist so she wouldn't trip over the hem. Mama was a short-tempered if capable cook, working hurriedly as if on the cliff of a disaster. The broth threatened to boil over; the sponge cake to fall. Once she started she never stopped, not to drink water or *kibitz* with an uncle. She had one chore for Thelma: chopping cooked chicken livers. The organ meat smelled weird and sour as Thelma steadied a shallow wooden bowl with one hand and cranked the metal meat-grinder handle with the other.

Mama wasn't a patient teacher. Thelma knew that within those walls, she must follow instructions and not question. She never mastered the more intricate lessons of making potato pudding or stuffed cabbage. Mama never had time, or money, for the girl's beginner mistakes. Still, in the kitchen they usually called a truce. Thelma felt as close to Mama there as she ever did. Until Thelma minced the last liver and surrendered the bowl, they were united in their labor, wordless, simply mother and daughter. But when Annie waltzed in and donned her apron, the balance shifted.

When the time came to eat, Thelma would have a mustard sandwich on rye, maybe taking a single slice of sticky salami just to appease Mama. The rest had pickles and delicatessen and things that were wrapped in beef guts, the *kishkes*, and tongue. Just the thought gagged Thelma: Who would eat the speckled flesh pulled from an animal's mouth?

As the room filled, the guests descended on the table and praised Mama, who continued to shuttle back and forth bringing new dishes and clearing empties. Jesse poured vodka into small glasses and passed them to the men. Annie took one, too. The liquid seemed to release smiles before unseen. For a time, no one picked on anyone else.

"Where's Abie?" Mama wiped sweat from her broad brow, the table still full but the tongue decimated. Between the oven and the radiator, the apartment steamed.

"Who knows?" said Annie.

"He'll be here," said Louis. "He just had a little business."

"Monkey business," said Mama. Only then did the birthday girl begin to worry that Abie, who still lived at home, might miss her party, because Mama seemed so sure he would disappoint. But he promised he'd come. He'd be there in his own time. For now the celebration fizzed. Thelma sat on the sofa on Uncle Moe's lap, beside Minzer and a jeweler in a skullcap she didn't know. They passed around more vodka. When she begged, Uncle Moe gave her a tiny, stinging sip and said, "Hey, Minzer, grab your accordion."

After some reluctance, Minzer pushed off the sofa. He entered the room he shared with Jesse and the boys, returning with his music box.

Jesse retrieved his clarinet. A neighbor produced his violin. Two men shifted the table against the wall while Mama scolded, "Watch the food!" They pushed the chairs against the living room walls beside the hissing radiators ("Watch the curtains!") while Minzer, Jesse, and the neighbor tuned up, no longer workers but players.

The musicians began with boisterous old-country tunes. The melodies arched up to the ceiling corners and crawled down into the mouse holes. Once the music started, Thelma couldn't sit still, hopping off Uncle Moe's knees and wiggling with the band. She started with a grapevine left and another right, a kick left and one right, walking forward with hands raised and bowing backward. She wasn't just a jangly bag of knobby knees and sharp elbows but something else, something that might even be beautiful. She felt at the center of the living room, the apartment, Williamsburg, Brooklyn, the world, happy and flying and even graceful. And while she began dancing with her head bowed, she now raised it, inhaling happiness and exhaling joy. Uncle Moe and the Mint clapped with the music; Louis grinned with his small yellow teeth. This was bliss, freedom. The girl couldn't, wouldn't stop.

As the music got wilder, Thelma abandoned the steps and leaped and twirled and spiraled, until she became light-headed and landed with a dramatic fall to the floor as the song ended. The guests applauded.

Mama flung her dish towel over her shoulder. "Don't encourage her."

"Why not, Becky?" asked Uncle Moe.

"Once she starts dancing, she never stops until there's a fight."

"It's a party *for* Temeleh, *nu?*" Uncle Moe asked. Mama sucked her teeth, disappearing into the kitchen with Annie. To Thelma, he said, "Such a dancer! My Temmy has talent."

She ran back to Uncle Moe's knees, dizzy and gleeful, unleashed. He smiled down, raising first his right eyebrow and then his left. She giggled. He raised his right eyebrow and lowered his left. She bubbled with laughter. He was her first papa, since she'd never known any other.

Uncle Moe touched Thelma's cheek. "Hey, fancy-schmancy dancer, do you know the box step?"

"What's that?"

"I'll teach you, Temeleh." He lifted his stepdaughter off his lap and carried her to the center of the room. She liked being held. She liked his soap's sweet, sharp smell. "Minzer, play something American."

Uncle Moe set the girl down, shimmied his shoulders, and planted his feet on the wooden floor. He stretched his right hand, palm up, keeping his left hand behind his back. He bowed so that he was close enough to wink. Uncle Moe opened a door for her that had been shut. She was crossing into the real world where things happened, the world of adults who danced and laughed and drank. You didn't need money to move your feet. She looked straight into his eyes and read their mischief. They shared a common killjoy: the madwoman in the kitchen.

Mama returned, clearing dishes with a clatter to rival Minzer's accordion. Thelma took Uncle Moe's right hand and then he gave her his left. She felt the eyes of the room on them but didn't look away or down in shame. She looked up and raised her eyebrows. He waggled his. She shook her shoulders, planting her feet in their shabby oxfords. For a moment, their ugliness didn't embarrass her. Suddenly, this actually *was* her birthday. Attention flowed toward her. For a moment, she felt whole, like being Thelma wasn't a *shonda*.

The musicians swung into "I Want to Be a Popular Millionaire." Thelma entered an enchanted circle as Uncle Moe showed her the steps, saying, "Forward-side-together; backward-side-together."

She tried to follow, mixing her right with her left, going ahead when she was supposed to retreat so that her knees bumped into Uncle Moe's shins. She felt breathless and awkward with every wrong step. But then the steps became more fluid, and Uncle Moe led her through the box, through the square, again and again, until they were one rhythm with the music. She became giddy from the flight around the room as they began to take up more floor space. He spun her out and under his arm and then caught her, returning to the steps that were becoming simpler: forward, side, together; back, side, together. She felt trust in his arms, that he would lead her and her feet would follow instinctively without her bidding.

As the song ended and there was laughter and clapping and Uncle Moe gave her a last twirl and rested his arm on her shoulder, the door opened. Abie arrived, carrying an enormous bouquet. "Thank you! Thank you! No applause, just throw money!"

Thelma ran to her brother and flung her arms around his waist. Mama had been wrong; Annie, too.

Abie handed Thelma a bouquet of yellow daffodils tied with gold ribbon. "Mazel, *shayna punim.*"

Pretty face. Only Abie called her that. She floated with happiness.

Annie muscled forward. "Where have you been, Abie?"

"That's a stupid question. I've been buying flowers for the birth-day girl."

Mama came over, asking, "Who died?"

"Not me, Mrs. Gloom," said Abie.

"What kind of person buys flowers?" Mama said, twisting her dish towel. "They'll be dead by morning. They're a waste of money."

"Yes, Mama, but they are a waste of *my* money. And so are these." Abie bent down. He handed Thelma a bag, which she juggled with her arms full of sun-bright yellow daffodils.

Thelma peeked into the brown paper sack. "Strawberries! You bought strawberries in winter, Abie!"

Mama snatched the bag. "I'll cut those up for the guests."

Thelma scanned the room. Her jaw fell: so many people, so few strawberries. She was disappointed, then enraged. She couldn't, wouldn't, share them. It was unfair. Here were shiny red strawberries for her, and Mama was snatching them before she'd had a chance to taste one. There would be hardly any for her if they passed them around.

"No, Mama, these are for Temmy. She can share them if she wants—or gobble them down."

"Then *she* can wash them." Mama slapped her dish towel on her shoulder. Thelma worried, unable to reach the sink by herself. Also, as much as she wanted the fruit all to herself, she feared Mama's anger: selfish little girl.

"*I'll* wash them. Here, Moe," Abie said, handing Uncle Moe a vodka bottle, "for the boys."

Heading for the kitchen, Abie stopped, swiveled, and said, "Here, Ma, catch!" He threw a green sausage of cash at Mama. She didn't react fast enough. It bounced off her fingers and dropped to the floor. Silence fell as Mama knelt and grabbed the roll.

"*Goniff,*" Mama said—*thief.* But she tucked the money in her apron pocket, knees cracking as she rose. Still gazing downward, Mama disappeared into the bedroom she shared with Uncle Moe. She was always complaining about money, so why wasn't she happy? Confused, Thelma hid in the daffodils, feeling their soft petals as the Mint began playing the accordion again; the neighbor scratched his fiddle.

Jesse set his clarinet aside and stood, rolling up his sleeves. "Stand back," he said as he strutted to the middle of the floor. The music intensified. Crossing his hands over his chest, he squatted and began to dance the *kazatsky.* He shot out one leg and then the other, stiffly at first, while the men shouted, "Hey! Hey!" and the women clapped. Kicking and crouching, trying to get lower each time without tumbling backward, Jesse sped up. Sweat spread under his arms. He breathed heavily, shifting from one leg to the other, heels pounding. Then he leaped up and grabbed Annie's waist, dancing her around the room until even she was panting and laughing and red cheeked.

Later, after Mama and Annie cleared the table and the neighbors disappeared down the hall and up the street, the birthday girl sat with her elbows on the tablecloth and her chin in her hands, admiring the daffodils in a milk-bottle vase. The Mint sat beside her with a flower that she'd placed behind his ear. He took a butter knife and raised it above the table by its tip. With his jeweler's hands, he gently swung the silver and, below, the handle swung widely. A bigger shift at the top created an earthquake below. "Even the tiniest movement from above shakes the bottom, where we are," said the Mint. Uncle Moe called him a socialist, and the conversation went in a man direction the girl couldn't follow.

The Mint taught Thelma something that day. He wasn't as dumb as Mama said he was. She learned that if she waited for the world to stop swinging so she could get her feet under her, she would never find her place. She couldn't wait for life to start after things settled down, because they never would. The ground was always shifting, cracking, falling away beneath her feet. At least when she was dancing, she floated above the mess.

Suddenly, Thelma was in a rush. She was a big girl now. She was seven. She needed to settle at the adult table, because she couldn't care less for children her age. The family was never around long enough at any one place, dolls were deadweight, left behind in apartments abandoned in the dark of night, and other kids were never Abie or Louis. They didn't know Thelma's secrets, and when she shared them, the other kids pulled away. She thought she saw horror and disgust in their eyes. Who knew if it was her or them?

Part of Thelma wanted to be invisible. The other part wanted to be seen, brightly, like Abie viewed her, like Uncle Moe. She knew she was different, but maybe she was also better, at least better than Annie and Mama. She wanted to be still at the center of the universe and see it spinning, tossing, and turning. She didn't want to stand on a stoop watching the fun from a distance as if it were a Ferris wheel the Williamsburg Italians erected for feast days five blocks away.

Thelma loved that old neighborhood of constant celebrations. She adored the grease-pole races where boys competed to climb to the tip to knock fat salamis off the top into the cheering crowd below. She never caught a sausage. The fun was watching the boys and men slide down again and again, oil slicked and angry, laughing or beating their chests and leaping up to try again.

The year's biggest, craziest celebration was July's Giglio, the feast of Saint Paulinus of Nola and Our Lady of Mount Carmel. But every day, just outside, just down the street, Thelma spied Italian men on the corner. They were loud and didn't bow their dark heads in shame; whenever there was the least bit of sun, they'd strip down to their undershirts, revealing gold crosses, tanned and hairy chests. They swaggered and joked; they whistled at girls. Their teenage sons wore cologne, and even at seven she would have followed a boy down a back alley for that smell.

Chapter 7

Brooklyn, 1913

Four birthdays followed on Hooper Street, with Moritz teaching Thelma the fox-trot and the polka, and Annie marrying Jesse, and a sense that the broken family, if not healed, at least had begun to put down roots in Williamsburg. In the news, Woodrow Wilson entered the White House. The American people—meaning men—might as well have elected a six-legged giraffe, for all Thelma understood of this thin-lipped Gentile, the twenty-eighth president, from Virginia, who said, "I would rather fail in a cause that will ultimately succeed than succeed in a cause that will ultimately fail." Even then, at the ripe old age of eleven, Thelma would have rather succeeded one way or the other, but she seemed destined to snatch at a life where she had few choices of success or failure, little independence, just her bloody fingertips grasping for survival.

By then, Abraham and Louis had been gainfully employed as newsboys, shouting the daily headlines until their voices rasped, yelling at the Manhattan crowds where Fourteenth Street crossed Fifth Avenue. Jesse had leased the newsstand, a narrow green shack with room for one on prime real estate. His bride did the books for the family business.

At night, the brothers returned to Hooper Street, sharing stories from the world beyond the neighborhood. They both read the paper from front page to sports, starting at dawn when piles of papers landed heavily, tossed down from a horse-drawn wagon beside the green kiosk—and stolen by rivals if they hadn't arrived to stack and sort them. In 1915, the Germans bombed the British. The Allies—take that!—landed on the Gallipoli Peninsula pressing for Constantinople. Up in Inwood, female inmates at the Magdalen Home for Wayward Girls on 191st Street rioted. They tossed plates and broke windows, Abraham cheering them on. Despite ten arrests, the cost of their struggle may or may not have embodied President Wilson's idea when he stated that he valued a setback on the road to a just cause over a victory. Abraham preferred local crime stories, like the Magdalens, while Louis scrutinized world politics. The younger brother felt the call to war, waiting only for armed conflict to get close enough to sweep him up and out of the house.

During that time, Thelma's best friends were Italian girls from the neighborhood clustered around Our Lady of Mount Carmel Church: Nina, Paola, and Maria or, as Abraham called them, the Nina, the Pinta, and the Santa Maria. They became the soul sisters lacking at home. Their news was not the kind that made the papers. Maria's father fell off a ladder and broke his neck. What was he doing on that ladder on a Saturday night anyway? wondered her aggravated and now-widowed mother. Nina's little brother drowned in a rain barrel. Paola had her first tongue kiss, with an altar-boy cousin in the sacristy. She described it to the rest of the girls, down to the salty taste of spit like anchovies, and the smell of sex that seemed to her like frankincense and myrrh—an odor completely alien to Thelma.

At home, the thirteen-year-old idolized Uncle Moe, although he was no big *macher*, simply a craftsman carrying his salami sandwich in a metal pail to the jewelers' each morning. To her, even so young, he was a steadying influence. He rarely raised his voice and, then, only in the most extreme circumstances. He had simple tastes, relishing the sweet foods of his Austro-Hungarian childhood, the sugary *lokshen kugel* dotted with raisins, which she liked, too, and the gefilte fish, which she spat out and refused to chase with that vile magenta horseradish.

When Moritz returned home at dusk, Thelma ran to him. It was as if he had returned from the Alaskan wilderness, a pickax on his back rather than a lunch box in his hand. She'd fling her arms around his waist and bury her forehead above his belt buckle. The world seemed lighter when he was around. His pale goldsmith's hand on hers kept Thelma from disappearing into that invisibility that seemed to envelop her. She imagined that this was what it was like to have a father, someone who liked you best in the world, even better than your siblings, even more than your mother. Her needs were so large they were bigger than her field of vision. She was the only child who hadn't known their real father, had no memory of his voice or touch, the scratch of his beard, of his authority over them, of what he expected from his children.

She'd learned not to mention her father's name, Jonas, which meant "gift from God," a present she'd never shared. Annie filled that gaping hole in the family where their father had been with blame, linking Thelma's arrival with Papa's departure, as if the two things were connected in a puzzle that the youngest couldn't solve.

And so Thelma attached herself to Uncle Moe. Making him comfortable became her pleasure. The rewards had been a simple intimacy: he twirled her curls, stroked her cheek that others had been so quick to pinch. She'd plump sofa cushions, urging him to take his comfy corner of the couch while she retrieved his worn blue-leather slippers from their hiding place below. She knew he liked baseball and klezmer music, particularly the clarinet. On a Saturday night after Shabbos, he liked a bottle of beer and a cuddle, narrating folktales about a mischievous child who happened to share his name while Mama cleared the dishes and retreated to her room, easing her swollen ankles.

With Mama gone, a shoeless Thelma knelt beside Moritz on the couch, brushing his rhapsodic black curls that crested over his forehead.

He submitted to her attentions with a doll's patience, sighing with apparent pleasure. Then he would pull a small comb from his pocket and let her groom the lavish mustache that ran from beneath his wide nose and joined up with muttonchops on the side. Afterward, he would gaze at Thelma with topaz eyes, which had already begun to squint from the close work of twisting fine platinum into diamond rings. She basked in the gentle kindness, only turning away to nestle deeper into the crook of his arm and snuggle into his neck.

They'd been dancing together since her seventh birthday. She'd held his hand walking to the synagogue when Annie had wed Jesse and hidden in his arms when Annie gave birth first to Julius (named after Jonas) and then baby Adele, the blonde bubble.

Thelma had never understood how Annie could envelop these new arrivals with such maternal affection after the horrors she'd experienced as a child under her sister's brutal care. The unfairness had rankled her as this new generation filled the apartment with their screams and hungers, shoving Thelma farther down the food chain. When Annie demanded more room so her kids could sleep in peace, Mama had relegated Thelma to a bed made of two kitchen chairs pushed together and covered in a sheet. She kept her clothes nearby in a kitchen drawer beside a rotary eggbeater.

At night, the saving grace was that both Mama and Annie slept soundly, immobile until the morning once their heads, set with curling rags, compressed their pillows. In the kitchen, Thelma, having tossed and turned, her legs dangling through the back of one chair, her arms outstretched and wrapped around the back of the other, would rise, drawn to male voices in the living room. She wanted to join their circle. She'd wander as far as the doorway, dragging a moth-eaten blanket, announcing, "I can't sleep," to the assembled men, insomniacs all.

"Go to bed," Jesse would say, playing the responsible father who brooked no dissent.

"Go to chair," Abraham said, lowering his voice, mimicking Jesse.

"Go to hell," Thelma would say, as Abie had taught her, and they muffled their laughter so as not to awaken the gorgons and babes. Uncle Moe would pat the couch beside him where he sat scanning the Yiddish paper with the ripped cover that the boys had retrieved from the newsstand.

Thelma became part of the insomniac conspiracy . . . and then something more. As the night wore on, one by one, the males would disappear. Jesse crept away to join Annie, clicking their door behind him, succeeded by the squeal and release of the box springs under the expanding husband's weight. One settled, Thelma thought as she tucked herself deeper into the crook of Uncle Moe's arm. The thirteen-year-old nestled within his body's musty cave so that she smelled the workday's sharp sweat and smoky pipe tobacco, her head resting on his shoulder. Increasingly impatient, she would watch the Mint rise, cracking his back and neck with sounds like bones snapping in a noose.

Shortly thereafter, as the streets beyond the curtains calmed, the hollow hoofbeats of a workhorse retreating, she swallowed her impatience as she waited for Abraham to smoke, then squash his last cigarette. The young men left last, Abraham often poking the sleeping Louis to urge him toward their bed for the few hours before 3:00 a.m., when the brothers, now twenty-one and nearly nineteen, had to rise to return to Union Square.

Uncle Moe remained with his left elbow on the armrest, but she could feel his right arm's power as he'd squeeze her tighter. He removed his glasses and rubbed his eyes with his left hand, setting the gold-rimmed specs on the side table as if preparing for sleep. That was when their game began. Thelma inquired whether she could remain on the couch beside Moritz, where it was soft and comfortable and she could sleep. Was that too much to ask? He agreed it was an insult, banishing a daughter to the meanness of two kitchen chairs shoved together as if they were a bed and not a penalty.

Moritz and Thelma began each night in concord: she'd done nothing wrong to deserve such mistreatment, and, he sympathized, it was unfair. What followed in the midnight quiet, punctuated by a cough from beyond the bedroom doors, or the flip and flop of unsound sleep, was an unspoken union against Mama, an old crone who fed their bellies but remained blind to their inner lights.

After a few minutes, Moritz would sigh with what sounded to Thelma like satisfaction, as if shedding the day's adult responsibilities. His voice would soften to a whisper and deepen as Moritz narrated the folktales he'd heard as a boy, mixing English with Yiddish. To Thelma, he seemed a gentle man who loved children but was forced to marry a barren witch. He described remote villages where geese and cows wandered packed-earth roads beside fields of sunflowers. In the old country, he explained, men married girls of thirteen—twelve, even. She interpreted this as a preference for her over her mother.

An intense tenderness filled her as she listened to his soft, accented speech. His eyes unfocused, he would praise Thelma's graceful body, her spirit, her dancing. His reassurance eased her anxiety that she was inferior: skinny, good-for-nothing, and foul tempered.

Some nights, Moritz asked Thelma to scratch his back, hiking up his shirt and exhaling deeply at her touch. And, afterward, it was only fair he would scratch *her* back beneath *her* nightshirt. And this was where it began.

Thelma cast aside the thought that what they were doing, whatever it was, betrayed Mama's trust. She was too far down the road, too close to the man, and she couldn't keep her hand from rising to his cheek, gently, tentatively, tugging the woolly mustache. Down swooped his lips, covering her mouth until she could hardly breathe, the spit tasting of smoke and herring. His tongue pushed past her teeth, the snail seeking its shell. It frightened her. And it excited her, too, because it seemed to be the only real thing that happened to her, an unexpected portal to the adult world toward which she was rushing.

When Moritz's fingers migrated from Thelma's back to her bottom and snaked in between her thin thighs, an alarm sounded. But she was torn: so grateful was she for his attention that she was willing to give him anything he asked. She convinced herself that by each pat of his, each stroke, he was reciprocating her affection.

Despite the possibility that, at any time, someone might enter, seeking matches for a final cigarette, sneaking a sandwich, Thelma couldn't resist the man's gentleness as he pulled her onto his lap. Terrified or intrigued—she couldn't tell the difference as her heart raced. And then she was lost. It was not one night but many. She would fall asleep, turning toward Uncle Moe as if they were a couple, and awaken as he took her hand. She hoped for affection, wordless tenderness, only to have him guide her fingers to the rod between his legs, teaching her to stroke until he gasped and fell immediately asleep, leaving her with a disturbing gooey handful. She would wipe her messy fingers on her nightshirt, but long hours passed before she fell asleep again.

❧

Many months later, Thelma awoke to Annie screaming, standing at her bedroom door. In her arms, the infant amplified her mother's cry. Thelma had been dreaming that she held on to a stick to defend herself from the disapproving glares of her mother and sister, who were like ghosts surrounded by other women who resembled them but whom she didn't recognize. She knew from their faces that she'd disappointed. She was late, or in the wrong place. She had broken something, or was broken herself. She became aware that she was in the curve of Moritz's arm, like a pussycat, or a stuffed toy, or a woman.

As Annie shrieked for Jesse and the children joined in a chorus that roused everybody else, Thelma realized that Uncle Moe was seminaked. Her hand rested on his pickle, which was doing what it did in the morning—popping up with the sun. Her first thought was that he loved her more than anybody else, more than Mama, or Annie, or those brats.

Thelma's second thought shriveled as Moritz picked her off him like lint. Rising, he rushed to the bathroom with an uneven gait, abandoning the adolescent to Annie's rage.

Annie's face flushed red at the edges of her white cold cream, already streaked with tears. "Get up, you floozy!"

Thelma, crusty eyed, recoiled at Annie's curled-lip look of disgust. Had her nightmare continued? Awake or asleep, she cringed, still careful not to rub her sticky hands on the upholstery.

Handing Jesse the baby, Annie pounced on Thelma. She slapped her, hard, with follow-through, a pause, and then a backhanded, knuckled fist. As her head snapped back, Thelma realized she wasn't dreaming. She cried out, "Moritz!"

"Shut your mouth," said Annie. "Don't speak his name."

Annie grabbed Thelma by the collar, lifting her off the couch and into the air, bare feet dangling and juice dribbling down her thigh. Annie shook the girl with two hands, violently. Between flashes of light and dark, Thelma wondered, why hadn't Uncle Moe come out of the bathroom? Why had he abandoned her?

Meanwhile, Annie jerked the child's stinging face close, flush with her own. The closeness terrified Thelma, the hate-filled eyes, the anger that radiated heat. But it was Annie's words that seared: "You sick, twisted, filthy little husband thief. We should throw you out with the garbage. What do you think you're doing with Mama's man?"

Thelma tried to raise her chin in defiance. "He loves me."

Annie snorted. She looked to Jesse, who laughed outright.

"How'd you trick Uncle Moe, you shameful hussy?"

She shrugged. "He likes me?"

Hoping for an ally, Thelma eyed the bathroom door that hid Uncle Moe. She felt his betrayal deep in her belly, a familiar hollow love hunger more painful than Annie's violence. Out of the corner of her swollen eye, she saw Mama enter. She knew immediately that her mother had already heard the commotion, because Mama, appearing at the bedroom door in her ratty bathrobe and curling-rag crown, was already weeping and howling in operatic torment.

Mama strangled out the question: "What now?"

"Ask Moe." Jesse gestured to the bathroom door with his chin.

"Ask your daughter," said Annie. "She had her hand down Moe's pants."

Mama ignored Thelma, falling to her knees outside the bathroom. She began to bang on the door, her arms raised above her head, her handkerchief waving like a flag of surrender. "Moe," she pleaded. "Moe, Moritz, Moe!"

Baby Adele wailed and wiggled in her father's arms, while four-year-old Julius slipped into the room behind Jesse. The curly-headed boy, who had yet to have his first haircut, ran to his kneeling grandmother. He threw his arms around her, crying, *"Bubbe, Bubbe."* He tried to pull her up, but she continued her banging.

"Always tsuris," said Jesse. "I have to get to the newsstand."

Annie shook her head. "Look what you've done, Temmy, lying with Moe. Look what you've done to Mama."

"She's killing me," Mama cried as she ripped at her nightgown's neckline. Met with Moritz's silence, she creaked up on her knees, leaning on her grandson. She shuffled to Annie and collapsed on her in a tearful embrace. Her grandson, excluded from the circle, began to cry.

"Julie," Thelma called to her nephew, opening her arms. She squatted and he came running. She held him tightly, kissing the light-brown curls, his eyelids, tasting the salty tears. Were they his? Were they hers? What did it matter? A beautiful boy blessed with Jesse's balanced disposition, his affection temporarily filled her stomach's hollow.

"Julie," Annie said over her mother's head, "come away from Aunt Temmy. She's no good. She's nothing."

The words smarted, and Thelma hurled back, "He's older than me when you burned my thumb. Have you tried that lighter trick on *your* own kid yet?"

"What's she talking about?" asked Jesse.

"Bubba maisa," Annie said. *Bullshit.* "She makes things up, the tsuris queen. Always she turns a chicken into a turkey."

"You should burn in hell, Thelma," Mama said, the curse landing on the startled girl like a slap so that she automatically covered her face with her hands. "What wild animal *shtups* her own father?"

"It was him first. It was his idea."

"Liar," Annie said, assessing her sister's chest. "You don't even have *broisten.*"

Thelma wondered how Abie would have handled this situation, how he'd have defended her. He'd have known the perfect response. But he was already at the newsstand, miles away. So Thelma sharpened her tongue and spat the words he'd often spoken behind their mother's back since her remarriage: "Who'd want to touch an old hag like Mama?"

Annie had to hold their mother back from rushing Thelma, who regretted the cruel remark as soon as she'd said it. But, cornered and alone, she only had her sharp tongue to defend herself.

"You're nothing to me," said Mama.

The rejection cracked Thelma, releasing all her feelings of self-hate so that if she were capable of crawling out of her worthless body, she would have, gladly, and wormed down the drain. Instead, she collapsed, crying, inconsolable, with no one to comfort her. Her family was no family. Without her brothers, she felt alone and abandoned.

The toilet flushed. The bathroom door remained shut.

Chapter 8

Later that same morning, after Moritz had slipped out the bathroom, donned his suit, and crept off to work, the time came for Thelma to walk to school. Mama and Annie ignored Thelma, huddling in the kitchen, whispering. Their teaspoons jangled in short glasses. She exploited the opportunity and tiptoed into Annie's room and palmed her sister's loose change (stuffed beneath the baby's bassinet, where the angelic Adele slept beneath her crown of curls).

Skipping school (where she was quick and good at math, which pleased the teachers and alienated the boys), Thelma slunk in the shadows of doorways on South Fourth Street. She paused under stoops in sticky spots smelling of man and dog pee, avoiding the truant officer. She sprinted across the street to the Marcy Avenue BMT Station, bought a nickel ticket with her stolen change, and hopped the train across the Williamsburg Bridge to Manhattan. The span was only a year younger than she was, but its birth had been greeted with magnificent fireworks displays, not mourning as hers was.

She headed for Fourteenth Street, where Abie was hawking papers with Louis, having left for Manhattan long before Annie had shrieked Thelma and Moritz awake. She had to find Abie. He'd be angry at those bitches—and offer a soft shoulder where she could weep until she hiccuped. At twenty-one, he resembled a full-grown man with whiskers on his chin and a swagger in his stride, but he'd never risen above five foot two.

Abie would have made Napoleon look tall—and he blamed this shortcoming on the orphanage cook who'd conked the kid's cranium with a cast-iron pan. He'd never confessed the misdeed that agitated the cook but insisted the blow had stunted his growth. He'd gotten *his* back: dumping laxatives in the soup. But the damage had been done.

On the other hand, Abie's thirteen-year-old sister now towered over him, giraffe legs and jutting ribs. But, despite her height, she looked up to Abie. He was quick with a fix. She sought his counsel in everything but algebra. They were both suspicious by nature (or nurture), but he trusted her, deputizing Thelma as his eyes and ears in the house when he was on the streets. She spilled her guts religiously.

For Thelma, the early morning Hooper Street blowup seemed like a news flash, which she had to relay to Abie before he got someone else's version. She must be the first edition. She needed his advice about what to do next and after that. She knew Annie and Mama were wrong, but she didn't understand what kind of father Moritz was. Why had Uncle Moe hidden in the bathroom, abandoning her? He had said he loved her best, but had that been a lie?

Thelma was angry at Uncle Moe, but she still, in her mind, imagined him leaving the bathroom and exclaiming that he wanted her for his wife, not Mama. She had young skin. She had dancing feet. She held his secrets. She scratched the itchy skin between her legs but couldn't find a way to quiet her heart's hungry hollow.

She'd tossed these feelings over and over again while on the el to Manhattan, coating them like fish fillets in flour. She had no one to blame but herself. She should have remained where she belonged in the kitchen, propped up between two chairs, either her butt sinking in the crack between them or her legs dangling. She scolded herself: she was stupid, stupid, stupid. She was unlovable—worse, despised. Did she become who she was because they didn't love her—or did they not love her because of who she was? She was weak—weak when Annie was strong, Annie who owned their mother as if she were gloves. Annie, who'd reversed the order of things, climbing to the top of the family and pissing downhill. All Thelma had was Abie, and he was around less and less these days. Who could blame him?

For a brief moment, during the comforting clack-click-clack of the train on the rails, Thelma snatched at a sense of well-being. No Mama. No Annie. No Uncle Moe. She could breathe again, leaning her cheek against the warm glass. The world hummed as long as her back was to Hooper Street, far from her sister's shrill judgments. Beneath her on the East River, sailboats skipped under taut white canvas. On the opposite shore, Manhattan's skyscrapers rose as she approached. She recognized the Metropolitan Life Insurance Company Tower from her Corn Flakes box, now visible like a tiny toy beside a model train that she could reach out and touch and reposition. But she wasn't deluded: it was big—you could hide there, you could get lost there, you could become everything or nothing.

Thelma exited with the crowd at Delancey-Essex near her Norfolk Street birthplace. A mid-April heat wave made it feel like July. The bad-temper weather inspired pushing, shoving, and accusations between strangers, as she navigated uptown as she'd done in the past with her brothers. Occasionally, they'd roam the city—tough-guy Abie intimidating strangers out in front, Louis guiding them with his strong sense of direction and memory of landmarks, and she, rushing to keep up with their gang. The trio had run together for a few years. A march—a political rally or a union protest—was an opportunity to separate a wallet from its owner and have some fun. Abie loved crowds. They jacked him up. Louis had his back. And Thelma was their audience. She was their keeper of stolen property, because who would question that monkey face—and who would suspect brothers soft enough to bring their kid sister along? The Lorber kids measured all the angles.

The boys had taught her how to ride the trolley for free, shifting from seat to seat, sidling up to maternal-looking women to avoid buying a ticket. The worst that could happen was she'd have to slip her fingers in that lady's hand and guilt the adult into paying her fare with eyes that pled poverty backed by a body suggesting starvation.

At Fourteenth Street, the broad thoroughfare that sliced the island below Union Square, Thelma stumbled onto the sidewalk and into the mass of purposeful humanity, alone in Manhattan for the first time. It was different from carousing in her brothers' wake, always an arm's grab away from the familiar. Thelma tried to repress her rising sense of panic. She gasped the ashen air, spinning to figure out which direction held the family newsstand on the corner of Fifth Avenue. Without Louis, she couldn't tell uptown from downtown, east side from west. She moved momentarily with the crowd and attempted to get her bearings without asking for help in a voice that would betray her vulnerability. Girls who didn't know where they were going were snatched up and sold into slavery, or so her friends Nina, Paola, and Maria had told her. She felt like a candy wrapper caught in a gutter dust devil.

Thelma needed Abie. She needed him to explain the error of her ways and determine whether it could be fixed. She needed him to explain how Mama hadn't even come to see if she was all right and hear her brother's sympathetic outrage. This was always the cruelest blow: that their mother never took their side. She couldn't erase the pathetic image of Mama, prostrate, begging at the bathroom door, calling for Moritz with her back to her own child.

Meanwhile, a crowd had gathered on the corner of Fourteenth Street and Third Avenue east of Union Square. Thelma tried to thread through but became tangled in the knot, pulled toward whatever had united the mob. She heard snatches of information: "blood," "stabbing," "murder," and the strange name "Little Yiddle." As she neared the center, the crowd's excitement grew along with her apprehension. Nearby a jostling scrum of newsboys in knickers and caps postured, yelling at each other, raw and loud, their stock in trade. For a change, the boys were at the action's center, not just peddling the news: czarist troop movements across the Atlantic or the ravages of Typhoid Mary closer to home.

She sought her brothers among the youths, rising on tiptoe, looking for a familiar cap, Abie's square jaw, the scar crossing Louis's right brow. Instead, she spied a circle of policemen, their eyes concealed by billed caps. They wore navy wool uniforms with two parallel rows of shiny buttons on the front, gold shields pinned over their hearts. The lawmen had formed a barrier around something half-visible. "Back up," they shouted at the crowd. "Step along." They claimed that nothing was happening, nothing to see.

But something *had* happened. Beyond the coppers, Thelma detected a lake of blood with irregular shores. The air bristled with electricity. Something had happened. Right here, but what? A trail of red footprints moved west, first backing away and then turning, but then there was also a helter-skelter of shoe prints and handprints and knee prints and what appeared to be a drag mark, first left and then right. A few feet away, a pigeon pecked at a brown tweed flat cap abandoned on the sidewalk. She gasped in recognition, trying to convince herself that it could have been anybody's hat, even though it was identical to Abie's.

The crowd surged forward. Beside Thelma, an angular, middle-aged man with pointy elbows suddenly appeared. A vivid, jagged scar sliced his left nostril, deep lines scored his face, and above, his press card sprouted from his greasy hatband. He freed his arms to lift a notebook balanced on his left hand. In his right, he clutched a thick pencil. Neglecting her, he began to grill two bickering newsboys, asking, "Who's the victim?"

"What's it to you?" asked one brown-eyed boy, who couldn't have been more than thirteen but had the shattered nose of a welterweight.

His companion, a red-haired cupid with a devil's sneer, squinted at the stranger. "Who's askin'?"

"John Atherton, *Tribune*."

"We got your story, mister," said Broken Nose. "I was right there."

"No, you weren't," said his sneering companion. "*I* was there. It was Rothman, the *putz*. Nate to his friends, only he don't got no friends."

"I was there because Rothman asks *me*, 'Who's the toughest kid on Fourteenth Street?'"

Atherton nodded. "Who *is* the toughest kid?"

"You're the reporter," said Cupid. "You tell us."

"I'm a newspaperman, boys, not a spiritualist," said Atherton.

"Okay, okay, it's who I told the *putz*: Little Yiddle."

"That's not news," said Broken Nose while Thelma eavesdropped. "Everybody knows that."

"Is that Yiddle's blood on the ground?" Atherton asked.

Thelma leaned in. The sneering cupid laughed derisively. Broken Nose sucked his teeth. "Hell, no, mister, that beet juice is all Nathan."

"Got what he deserved," said Cupid. "When Yiddle passed by, pacing like he does, back and forth on Fourteenth Street, Rothman laughed."

"You don't laugh at Little Yiddle."

"Not if you like your nose, mister, no offense," said Broken Nose.

"None taken," said Atherton, scribbling without watching his hands. He anchored his gaze on his sources, switching back and forth between the two boys with the glow of a journalist who'd found his lead.

"Nathan starts braying like a donkey. He says, so that everybody can hear, 'What? That kid tough? Ah, stop!'"

Thelma's chest tightened. Her anxiety rose, amplified by the crowd continuing to push forward. She struggled against the current, trying to stay beside the reporter so that she could hear the boys. Little Yiddle was an odd nickname. It made her uneasy. Abie wasn't tall, but there was no kid tougher—still, she couldn't imagine he'd let anybody call him an insulting name like that more than once.

The reporter tapped his hat brim with his pencil. "Why was this Nate laughing?"

"Little Yiddle got his moniker 'cause he's short, and he's bony . . ."

". . . but he's no pushover."

"He's quick with a knife."

Thelma's hands felt clammy. Short. Like Abie. Bony. Like Abie. But, no, there was no shortage of angry little men on Fourteenth Street. Abie was too smart to make waves in Manhattan. *He'd never stab a guy,* she thought, *not in broad daylight.* Not that Thelma doubted he'd pull a blade if somebody looked at him sideways.

"You don't mess with Little Yiddle unless you want to drink your dinner through a straw."

"It's orphanage rules," said Cupid.

It had to be Abie. What could he have been thinking? They'd take him away from her. Again. She couldn't let that happen.

The kid continued, "This was Little Yiddle's territory, not Rothman's. They don't call you the toughest because you're a weakling. He hears the *putz,* approaches Rothman, and says, 'I'll show you!'"

"And he did. He gutted Rothman like the chicken he was."

"He *was?*" asked the reporter.

"Dead," said Cupid. Thelma felt dread, her face flushing. She looked down at the blotchy skin on her shaking fingers. He'd killed a boy. Dead.

"Last legs," Broken Nose corrected.

"He's as good as dead. The ambulance carted him off."

"A knife to the stomach is more than a bellyache."

"That's a lot of blood," said the newsman as the law started to disperse the crowd, supported by a flank of mounted policemen who'd just arrived on the scene. The reporter buttonholed the redhead and asked, "Where do I find this Little Yiddle?"

"You don't. Not if you know what's good for you."

"We ain't squealing."

"What's his Christian name?"

"He don't have one, stupid."

"His Jewish name is Abie."

Gutted like Rothman, Thelma wanted to fly up and out of that crowd and find her brother. She'd punch her way out. She turned away from the reporter so he couldn't see her flushed face. Wouldn't he be surprised if the girl standing right next to him knew everything he wanted to know about the perpetrator, even where he lived? But she wouldn't be talking.

The cupid chimed in, "Abraham Lorber."

"How do you spell that?" the reporter asked. She knew it like her own name, knew that he was born Abrem, but this little sister was already struggling against the crowd, panicked, kicking shins and punching, running toward Fifth Avenue and the newsstand. Now her brother might need her protection. Sure, she was weak, and she was sad, a fatherless child, but what she was didn't matter right then. She had to be strong for Little Yiddle—even the toughest kid on Fourteenth Street needed family.

❦

Thelma fled the gawkers circling Rothman's blood. The mounted police converged from the front while a wall of cops squeezed from the rear. She hunched down, scrunching her stomach, making herself as small as possible, her eyes innocently pleading to let her through while her pointy elbows ripped holes in the mob. A rising panic snuffed her breath. She felt claustrophobic, wanting to kick out. Her shakiness, almost nausea, made it harder to get her bearings. She hated being lost. How did Louis, the human compass, find his way? If Union Square was north of Fourteenth Street, then uptown was to her right, which meant the newsstand should have been straight ahead. But it could easily have been behind her.

Having escaped the crowd, she dashed for the newsstand, arms outstretched, desperate to discover if Abie was okay and what had really happened. She registered alarm in the strangers' faces she passed, as if they perceived her secret knowledge of the assailant. A terror that naked could be contagious, and no one wanted to catch what she carried. To avoid pedestrians, she sidestepped off the curb, only to be nearly squashed by a crosstown streetcar. As her heart raced, a nearby matron jerked her back to the sidewalk, but then the woman's grasp tightened around her wrist. With difficulty, Thelma shoved the lady away with her free hand while twisting her entrapped arm from the stranger's viselike grip. As she sprinted away without looking back, she sucked in her tears and swiped her nose with the back of her hand. Distress was dangerous in public, where young girls could be traded like secondhand clothes.

When she arrived at Fifth Avenue, sweaty and disheveled, Thelma leaned against a cast-iron street marker. Canvas-sided horse carts lined the way. She jumped when a white-speckled nag stamped its right hoof and blew out its nose, raising its head to expose black gums. Across the street stood a tall limestone building with broad shop windows that exhibited the wares of S. N. Wood & Co. Cloaks & Suits.

A white banner stretched above the display: CLEAN-SWEEP SALE NOW GOODS AT YOUR OWN PRICES. And, in front of that, was the fir-green newsstand beneath a hand-lettered sign: LAZARUS & SONS. To Thelma's dismay, the shack was shuttered. Gone were the stacks of newspapers, the issues of *Photoplay* magazine with images of Charlie Chaplin or Lillian Gish, the glass case crammed with chewing gum and cigarettes. She crossed the street and circled the seemingly abandoned wooden hut barely high enough to contain one man. She banged on the side door, with one fist and then two, despite the padlock that cinched the metal loop beneath its hasp. They never closed the newsstand.

"Girlie," said a ragged peddler as he extracted a stone from his horse's hoof with his pocketknife. "Yeah, you," he said. "They're shut for the day."

"Why?"

"Maybe I know. Maybe I don't. But I'm not the only workingman who can handle a knife. If you want some advice, *maideleh*, disappear," he said, "and don't speak to coppers."

"But," she began, "I gotta find my brother Abie."

The peddler raised the blade to his cracked lips, signaling silence.

While Thelma shut her mouth, her mind raced—but her feet couldn't follow. Without Louis, she didn't know the city well enough to pursue Abie now that she'd discovered the newsstand closed. Her heart pounded; sweat streamed down her temples. She feared for Abie's life, however quick he was with a knife. Where could he be? Was he hiding from the police? And if that reporter got her brother's name in print, did it mean that he was lost to her?

That reporter didn't know Abie like she did—how much love he had for her and how, time and again, he'd been forced to defend himself, a scrawny kid, from bigger foes as he had in the orphanage. To hesitate was to become a victim. She understood that. There had to be justification for his attack on that Rothman kid. Abie would explain. She felt fear, yes, but something else, too, as she paced the sidewalk bracing herself to return home. It was pride. Her brother was the toughest kid on Fourteenth Street, and he would always protect her. No one on the street would dare harm her with such a daring brother in her corner.

Chapter 9

Enraged, Annie refused to talk to Thelma or Moe when they returned home that night. They were dead to her. They deserved the burning flames of hell and roasting on a pitchfork for how they'd crushed Mama, who had spent the day beating her breast and breaking plates on the kitchen floor, or looking up at the ceiling, raising her fist and cursing God. She'd held her mother as she had her own children, Julius and Adele, rocking the older woman until her sleeve was tear soaked and Mama had quieted down to an occasional snuffle.

Annie didn't need the aggravation: she was early in a pregnancy and feared the tsuris, the anxiety, would cause her to lose the baby, the child changing its mind about entering this world, this family. That night, even Jesse couldn't comfort his wife, and when he touched her, she slapped away his fingers, handed him a pillow and exiled him to the couch. At least there he would ensure that nothing further happened between the perverts: her stepfather and the husband thief.

The following morning, she didn't emerge from her room until she heard the door close behind those going to work and school. In the silence that followed, she remained in her nightgown and curlers, lacking the energy to get dressed and begin the day. She felt a heavy weariness that began in her uterus and tugged her down so that almost without thinking she cupped her hands beneath her expanding belly that created a table on top where her enormous breasts rested. She sat for a long time in front of the mirror, looking at her angry eyes in their cold-cream mask, and only when she heard Mama crying her name did she wipe off the gelatinous goo and shuffle out in worn slippers that had once been robin's-egg blue but were now mouse gray. She knew she was the only one in the household who had the chutzpah to do what had to be done—but her gut said that one of the participants had to go. With his steady paycheck, Moe was still valuable to the family, but what could she do with Thelma?

By the time she reached Mama, Annie felt hot liquid dribbling between her legs. She ran for the water closet with Mama beside her, entering the bathroom where Moe had hidden his weak self the previous day. She pulled down her underpants and witnessed her worst fear: bright-red blood spots. When she sat down on the toilet and pushed, the flow became heavier. Panic flooded her and she considered her dear baby, already beloved and tight inside her. Now her anger returned with a level of fear: this was her third child and it had been stolen by Thelma's selfishness, as if the girl had reached her hand up and ripped the infant from her.

By early that afternoon, after Annie fought her living children down for an early nap and admonished them not to move until she awakened them, she planted herself on the ratty armchair abandoned by previous tenants. A wet washcloth covered her brow, swollen feet soaking in a tub of Epsom salts. Her brain throbbed as if it were too big for her skull and would burst through her eye sockets. In her veins, the blood rushed up and down like uncontrollable children pounding the walls in an empty hallway. A roaring anger erupted from the ache and emptiness of her womb, where the baby had been sloshing and content until yesterday. Now, a bucket in the bathroom held rags clumped with blood and that bit of baby on to which she'd clung when the cramping began.

Wait until she got her hands on Thelma. It was all her fault. Annie's fists clenched at the thought of wrapping them around her sister's skinny neck until it cracked and she was silenced. Always wanting, needing, and demanding. Her siblings were rotten, all of them, corrupt, dissolute, reckless. They endangered her family's future, the security of Julie and Adele. Only she could halt them before they were all ragged and begging on the Brooklyn streets.

That *goniff* Abie had ruined Thelma and Louis. And now Thelma had stolen her unborn child, wrapped her legs around Mama's Moritz, and would suck them all down into her lazy, lustful hell if Annie didn't step up and squash her immediately while she was still weak, young, and ignorant of her power over men. The safety of Julius, Adele, and Annie's future children depended on her complete control.

Anger coiled up Annie's spine. She'd never wanted to be a mother to Thelma. Even when their father had been alive, she'd wanted nothing to do with that colicky infant. She'd have been content to abandon her to the wolves. She didn't even want to be her sister, not then, not now. She hated the curly-haired child who resembled their father, long legs and arms, green eyed and excitable, selfish and weak. Annie had been a girl herself when Papa died, only eleven years old, still sleeping with a rag doll, still dreaming, obedient and devoted to her mother.

Annie had watched her father's last breath curl from his lips in the stifling Norfolk Street tenement. She'd cleaned the bloody bubbles from his wiry beard after Mama had collapsed by his side. Her mother had cried, "Take me now," wailing for a Galicia she would never see again, for the sisters she resembled, the mother with the house keys dangling from her waist who knew right from wrong as she knew salt from pepper, absolutely. And so Annie took the bowl from her mother's shaking fingers before the water splashed on the floor and washed her father's emaciated body with a rag, learning his scars and bumps, the rosy nipples, the way a wife would, the way no daughter should. She had felt disgusted and enraged but had also felt the birth of something new, of her own ability to take control in a crisis. She sensed a path to power and, without reflecting, grabbed it.

It was not an easy road. With Papa gone, Mama disappeared in her own mind, playing hide-and-seek with her oldest living child, physically visible, still sweating and shitting, but mentally absent, incapable of making even the smallest decision. Annie had become responsible for children she didn't want surrounded by strangers loath to help but quick to comment, always judging, coughing, the men *davening*, the women cleaning. Mama couldn't scrub anymore, couldn't feed her family. She wouldn't rise from bed. She screamed like her feet were aflame whenever they touched the rough wood floor and cowered back on the featherbed, fetal.

No one had ever asked Annie if this was what she wanted, if she could handle the responsibility. She just did. There was a fire. She extinguished it. She'd summoned the strength. It had been her or no one, her or the street. If they'd eaten gruel, so be it. At least they'd eaten.

Now cursing Thelma for the miscarriage, Annie groaned. She would kick her, pull her hair, shove her out of the apartment and onto the streets like the mongrel she was. Let her take care of herself from now on. Her sister threatened the balance that Annie had achieved with the goldsmith's arrival, lifting their mother's weight off the daughter's shoulders and onto the second husband's. Steady paychecks paid for food and rent. Mama, in turn, had kept the Sabbath, had cooked in her own kitchen, had cared for Annie and her grandchildren, repaying a debt to her eldest child that could never be retired. They all owed her. She was the family's backbone in America. She had rescued the past for the future—and she was the only one with the sense and spine to make decisions for their survival.

She blamed the girl for seducing Moritz, a good provider, a talented craftsman who loved her mother's cooking. So it wasn't an ideal match, but what was? It was still a bond in God's eyes. She cursed Thelma for upsetting Mama and unleashing the chain of *mishegas* Annie worked so hard to quell. All the yelling and the screaming after the men had left for work yesterday, Mama crying, picking up the sharpened scissors and claiming first she would kill Moritz, and then Thelma, and then herself.

Annie shook her head in disgust and immediately regretted it as the pain swelled. She'd prayed inside herself: let the baby live. But she'd feared from the first blood leaking down her leg that it was a lost cause.

Her own belly had betrayed her. She still had bits and pieces of the child inside her, cells that clung to her, a boy, she believed, whom she would have named Friedel, after her father's father, a peacemaker, a leader. Now there would be no calm, no child. She felt like she had expelled her uterus along with the baby bits, anxious that she would never be able to make children again and would lose Jesse's love and devotion. Like Moritz, he would turn elsewhere—to her sister.

As Annie flipped the damp cloth on her forehead so that its coolness touched her skin, she heard a rap on the door. "It's me, Mrs. Dickman. Let me in."

The neighbor was the first, but not the last. Annie, still heavy and sore, couldn't force herself to rise in answer, but that didn't deter her neighbor, who opened the door unbidden, crying, "Have you heard?" With excitement in her wheezy voice, she asked, "Mrs. Mandel, where are you hiding?"

Mama entered from the kitchen, her meat-hook hands splotchy with fat and flesh. "Heard what?"

"Abie," Mrs. Dickman said. "They found him."

"Was he lost?" asked Annie. "*Mamaleh*, please, do me a favor: go back and wash the *kishkes* from your hands before you touch something."

Mrs. Dickman pursed her fish lips. "Look at you, queen of the May, sitting on your *tuchus* while your mother works."

"As if it's your business in my house who sits and who stands," said Annie, slitting her eyes and glaring, yet Mrs. Dickman remained. Mrs. Famant rushed in next. The third floor's childless beauty, with lavender eyes and strawberry curls, played the cello, a melancholy instrument, and feasted on others' sadness. "Have you heard?"

"Your Abie killed a boy," said Mrs. Dickman.

"A Jewish boy," added Mrs. Famant. "Such a *shonda*."

A lament escaped Annie's lips. It sounded foreign to her, as if she doubted herself capable of that horrible sound. This news of a killer under her own roof beggared belief. Was Abie capable of murder? Yes. He was an animal. She herself had been tempted to kill him and, although she'd never resort to that level of violence, she recognized his rage because it mirrored her own.

Mrs. Spiegelberg shouldered her way into the apartment, dragging her twins behind her. "Have you heard?"

"In Manhattan," said Mrs. Dickman.

Mrs. Famant added, "With a knife, no less."

"A knife?" asked Mama, her cheeks reddening.

Annie couldn't handle her mother's ululation. She had no more comfort to give, drained as she was herself. She feared what would happen if she fell prey to Mama's hysterics and cracked. Jesse, in all his good nature, lacked the strength to navigate conflict and protect their children. "Get out, all of you."

"You should know," said Mrs. Dickman. "We didn't want you to find out from the police. Abie butchered the boy."

"In broad daylight," said Mrs. Famant, pointing at the ceiling. "Before God."

"A Jewish boy."

"*Shonda.*"

"The shame."

"The newspaper called him Little Yiddle."

"That can't be Abie with that ridiculous name," Annie said, bristling, her voice thready and unfamiliar. "It must be another ape. My brother's too tough to take that insult."

"It's in the newspaper," said Mrs. Dickman.

"It has to be true," agreed Mrs. Famant.

"So show me," said Annie. But the women hadn't bought the paper. They carried rumors overheard on the street and at the grocer's but no proof. Annie's rage rose, attended by heartburn, even if she remained too weak to stand and spew her anger at these *yentas*.

Her family, which she'd struggled to glue together, continued unraveling. How much tsuris could she stomach? Surely she'd been tested enough. Her jaw ground and her chin jutted. She had to push through—and yet she couldn't. Not today. Not having lost so much blood. Then it gradually dawned on her, through her anger and resentment, that maybe, just maybe, she could exploit bad news for the advantage of her and her children.

What if Abie *had* slaughtered a boy before witnesses? Wouldn't he go to jail? Let them lock him up and drop the key down the sewer. He was the only remaining threat to her power within the home and, as she had told anyone who'd listen, he was his own worst enemy. She was only a sister, a daughter, a mother—he was lawless.

Glee: that was what she felt, like a shot of morphine for the pain. Prison was too good for him. Even as she growled, "Get out, you *yentas*," and the neighbors looked daggers at her before dispersing, part of her hoped their gossip was true. If the police wanted Abie, she'd turn him in herself. What was bad for Abie might be good for her growing family, despite the disgrace.

After the hens left to cook for their husbands, Rebecca locking the door behind them, Annie passed out in her chair despite the sad, needy looks aimed at her by her mother. She dreamed of giving birth in their old tenement apartment with her father lying shrouded beside her, the baby arriving too soon. In her dream, she tried to hold the child in with all her muscles, to no avail, and she wept tears of anger at Abie and Thelma for their curses that caused this theft of life. She didn't awaken until she felt a wet kiss at her temple and the weight of her husband's muscled arm on her shoulder. "Anechka," he whispered, removing the washcloth from her forehead and feeling the skin gently with the back of his hand to check for fever. "How's my little girl?"

Annie put her hands to her hair, raising her lips to accept his kiss, ready to cry about the loss of their third child and be comforted. And then she spied the *New-York Tribune* tucked under Jesse's elbow. Scanning her husband's gray eyes, she recognized that the news was as bad as the gossips had reported. When she said, "Give it to me, Jesse," he winced and complied.

"Show me." Annie grabbed the *Tribune* while Mama crept next to her, collapsing onto the couch with a groan of relief, still wearing her bloody apron, her slipper-shod feet barely touching the ground. Making a big display of opening the paper, Annie flapped the pages as she prepared to read the item to Mama and Jesse.

Just then the front door cracked as Moritz returned from work, hat in one hand and metal lunch pail in the other, round-shouldered and apparently repentant. Annie said, "Look who's here." Mama made a loud spitting noise, *ptui*. She tightened her grip on Annie's arm.

Moritz said nothing, just slowly followed his usual routine, removing his hat and coat and carefully hanging them on hooks by the door, shuffling into the kitchen to put his pail by the side of the sink for Mama to wash as she did every day. Meanwhile, the Mint followed, head bowed, a nothing to Annie but at least he contributed to the family pot, despite consuming more than his fair share. He was neither ally nor foe, which she couldn't say for her mother's husband, a coward who deserved the curled-lip look of disgust she dispatched as if he were the poor relation rather than the savior whose salary had rescued the family in troubled times. Yesterday, Moritz had squandered all his capital. Now, she sucked her teeth and shook her head but believed she restrained herself by not cursing him aloud on sight for the pervert he was, plowing his wife's daughter while Mama slept a room away. He was an animal, even if that wasn't apparent now in his mud-brown suit and scuffed shoes, his shirt she had ironed, using her own spit to smooth the creases.

Annie returned her attention to the broadsheet, squinting to find the article. "It's not here," she said, suspecting the neighbors had lied.

Jesse pointed, saying, "Look there, down on the left, below 'Husband Beaten; Wife Pays Fine.'" Jesse scraped a wooden side chair, placing it beside Annie. "See that headline, 'Toughest Kid Proves It'?"

"Oy vey ist mere," cried Mama. Annie moaned, holding her side as if wincing from the aftershock of a delayed contraction.

Jesse stroked Annie's shoulder. "I had to hide this copy under the counter. We sold out. It's not every day the family makes news."

"Here it is," said Annie, "'Newsboy Stabs Boy Who Doubted Title Given Him'? It's not exactly the Nobel Peace Prize."

Jesse shrugged. "He's no Teddy Roosevelt."

The door opened. Annie gazed up from the newsprint. "Speaking of no Teddy Roosevelt," she said as she coldly eyed Thelma, dragging her schoolbooks tied with twine, her scabby knees dirty and infected. "If it isn't the hooker of Hooper Street," she said.

"Annie, please" was all the mournful child answered, her hair frizzing out of her pigtail braids from the humidity. She reached up to hang her books on a hook by the door, revealing a sliver of underpants, and pivoted.

"Stool," Annie said, pointing to the corner.

"I have to *pish*," said Thelma.

"Sit," said Mama.

Thelma sat.

"In the corner," said Annie.

Mama said, "Face the wall."

"Why punish me? What about Uncle Moe?"

Moritz said nothing. Keeping his eyes down, he leaned on his elbows at the head of the dinner table beside the bowl of walnuts, which he began to crack like bones with his bare hands and, occasionally, his molars.

"Hey, schoolgirl," said Annie, "pull up your socks, because you'll want to hear this. Your favorite brother made the news. Such a big man, a *macher*! Look, the paper says 'toughest kid on Fourteenth Street.'" She snorted. "He's not even the toughest kid on the block."

Thelma, glued to the stool, swiveled her head toward Annie, her eyes wide. "He is too."

"Don't defend that monster," said Annie.

"Don't underestimate him," said Moritz. He dug for nut meat in a half-broken shell and studiously avoided looking at Thelma.

"Who asked you, Moritz?" said Annie while Mama examined her hands, digging meat scraps out of her fingernails, wiping them on the soiled apron.

"I can talk in my own home," said Moritz, his attention focused on cracking a shell.

"Like your opinion matters," said Mama.

"My name's on the lease, Rebecca, not yours," said Moritz, pausing to split the recalcitrant walnut with his back teeth. "You're welcome to leave at any time."

Mama's lips began to twist uncontrollably, her chin jutting left then right, a dam trying to contain the waterworks. She shrieked, "You have shamed and dishonored us."

"Aren't you in the kitchen yet, woman? Is it too much to expect dinner on the table when I return from work?"

"Yes," said Annie, defending her mother while extending her arm to prevent Mama from standing.

Moritz ignored Annie. "Five thirty has passed. Where's my food?"

"You don't deserve Mama's cooking," said Annie.

"Don't push me, Annie," he said.

"Let Thelma cook for you. Maybe she can boil an egg."

Moritz paused, glanced for what might have been the first time that afternoon at Thelma, humiliated on the stool, her shoulders hunched and her chin gouging her knees. In the daylight, she was a child. "That's not all your sister can do, Annie," said Moritz.

The Mint, seated across from Moritz at the foot of the table, shook his head, silently, like an old burro. In her corner, Thelma hid her head in her lap beneath her crossed arms.

"Shut your dirty mouth, you *putz*," said Annie, gazing over to where Thelma slumped on the stool, her skimpy skirt revealing her slender thigh. "She's weak, a *meeskait*, homely. Look at her: a nothing. A strong wind would blow her away. Hell, a breeze would knock her down."

"I'd like to knock *you* down," said Thelma, twisting on her stool and raising her fist. "What'd I ever do to you, you cow?"

"Cow? Me? Get me a pencil, you little monkey, you tramp, and I'll write you a list. You couldn't stay in the kitchen like you were told—don't expect any mercy from me. I have enough worries without your tsuris. From now on you sleep in Mama's bed far away from Moritz, who can sleep in the gutter for all I care," said Annie, her knife-sharp voice feasting on the girl's flinch as if from a blow. "And you, a grown man, took advantage. Tell us now, here, to Mama's face, Moritz. No hiding in the bathroom. Explain why your own daughter's fingers were in your crotch?"

"Stepdaughter," said Moritz, cracking a walnut in his fist.

"In God's eyes she's your daughter." Annie pointed at her stepfather as if backed by the Torah itself. Jesse stood behind her, her army of one.

"And what god would have me marry my grandmother and lie beside her on her pallet of aches and pains, breathing her stomach gases? Is it my place to rub liniment on her back like a nursemaid?"

"You'll be the death of me," cried Mama, clenching her fists. She leaped from the sofa with unexpected vigor, but Jesse caught his mother-in-law by the wrist and restrained her.

"How would you know, you old *kvetch*? Every day you wail will be your last. You *geschrei* as if you already have one foot in the grave—so why not let the other join it?" Moritz wiped his hands and then nodded in thanks as the Mint set a beer tumbler before him. The bachelor sat across the table with the crossword puzzle and a pen. His voice low, Moritz continued, "The matchmaker offered me a bride, Annie, but gave me this used-up crone. I am a man. I am vital still. I have an appetite—and not just for roast chicken. Your mother sees me and shuts her legs. Fine! I don't want to fill her with my seed. The thought disgusts me."

Thelma looked from Moritz to her mother with marsupial eyes as Mama recoiled. Her mouth dropped, exposing many missing bottom teeth. "You devil! To speak of these things in front of my children . . ."

"I'm no devil. I'm a husband whose woman doesn't want him like a wife should. The walls are thin enough that this should come as no surprise to anyone. You want a moneymaker to release you from taking in laundry, from walking the streets. I am trying to make my peace with that, and with having Annie's angry puss bossing me around as if she owned me. Remember this: I own you. When you didn't have a pot to piss in, I rescued you from charity. You can't tell me what to do. Anything you say, I *let* you say. I have fulfilled my side of a bad bargain, you ill-tempered sow. I do my part. I am the husband. I provide—but I have needs, too."

"So is that what you call your nursery games with my sister?"

"*Your* sister—don't pretend to care about the girl," Moritz said. Thelma looked longingly at him. He ignored her. She pulled her hands in her sleeves and hugged herself. He continued, "Do you think I'd coming knocking at your door, Annie? Is that why you're so angry? One look at Thelma and it's easy to see she's better looking."

"You animal," Annie screamed.

"You bitch," said Moritz with a chilly calm, as he flicked a bread crumb off the tablecloth.

Incensed and insulted, Annie grabbed the chair arm, but she lacked the strength to rise. Silence fell momentarily, and then Moritz cracked another nut. When he spoke he didn't return Annie's gaze. "So, Jesse," he said, spitting out the bitter shell, "what's this newspaper story that seemed so urgent . . . ?"

"Don't change the subject. We're not done with you and that little flea there," said Annie.

"Yes, you are."

Jesse rustled the paper, saying, "Here it is: 'Nathan Rothman, of 101 Henry Street . . .'"

"That's near where we lived with Papa," said Mama. "We knew Rothmans on Suffolk Street."

"Rothman is a common name, Mama," said Annie.

"Let me read," Jesse said. "This Nathan 'was told by a friend on April 13 that the "toughest kid on Fourteenth Street" was "Little Yiddle" Lorber.' That's our Abie in black and white."

Annie slapped her free hand to her damp forehead. Her blood pounded in her skull, and nausea constricted her throat. Except for her wedding announcement, a moment of intense pride—she the bride of someone she loved from the heart and who adored her—she'd never seen their family name in the newspaper. A burning shame rose in her cheeks as she imagined that *yenta* Mrs. Dickman going from door to door, spreading this story of their humiliation. Imagine if the woman discovered what she'd seen with her own eyes yesterday morning: Moritz slumped on the sofa, his legs sprawled, bare feet flexed, head thrown back, mouth open—and her sister's pale hand in his lap. Now, her brother had stabbed a boy, a Jewish boy, and this was what the Gentiles would read. This was what they'd think Jews were: animals who sliced each other on street corners, bloodthirsty criminals who would creep into their homes at night and slit their throats and those of their innocent children. Her people would be persecuted again, like they had been in Galicia, tossed off their land and forced to start over with what they could carry on their backs, families split and separated, mothers from children, husbands from wives. She felt a rising panic that fused into a certainty: Abie had done this just to humiliate her and Mama.

"It's him," Mama cried. "It's him!"

"Sure it's him," said Jesse. "That's why I brought the paper home."

"Schmuck," said Annie. Thelma remained silent.

"They even know his address: '372 Hooper Street, Brooklyn.'"

"They know where we live? It's in the paper?" asked Mama. She stood up. She sat down. She looked at Annie. "We have to move."

"I'm not moving," said Moritz. "If you have to go, pack your bags, and take your tsuris with you. Leave me in blessed peace and quiet."

Mama grabbed the hem of Annie's housedress. "The *shonda*! Everyone will know, Annie."

"You saw the neighbors swooping down like vultures, Mama. The news is out. What can we do about it?"

"Lock the door! Kill me now! These Rothmans will slay us in our sleep. They're not good people."

"No one will slay you in your sleep, *Mamaleh*," said Jesse.

"Unless it's Abie," said Annie. "Who knows what will happen with the wolves Abie has brought down around us?"

Mama gripped her apron hem, shaking her head. "We'll never live this down. We'll have to move away to someplace without Jews."

"Omaha," said Thelma, raising her head from her hands.

"Shut your mouth before I scrub it with lye," said Annie, and the girl did.

"What comes next?" asked Mama. "Frogs? Boils?"

"Let Jesse finish," Annie said as her husband bowed his head to the paper.

"So Rothman says, 'What? That kid tough! Ah, stop!' Knowing Abie, that kid was no genius."

"Keep reading," said Annie. A walnut cracked loudly.

"'Well, I'll show you,' said Little Yiddle, as he plunged a knife into Nathan's stomach."

"Is he dead?" asked Thelma, her voice strained.

"Who?" Mama shrieked. "Abie?"

"Not Abie, Mama Becky. He had the blade. The kid, Nathan, he's as good as dead, it says right here: 'Nathan went to a hospital, and last night asked the doctors to take him home so he could die in peace.'"

A sobbing sound rose from Thelma's corner. Annie cut her sister off. "Stifle it, Thelma. That good-for-nothing doesn't deserve your tears, and the sound is shredding my head." She grabbed the paper and read the conclusion: "Lorber, whose parents call him Abraham"—she snorted—"was arrested last night in Brownsville and locked up in police headquarters, charged with felonious assault."

"Felonious assault," Moritz said, rubbing his ribbed forehead.

The Mint whistled, glancing up from his crossword. "That's a mouthful."

Outside, a raw-voiced Italian knife grinder offered his sharpening services, which chilled Annie, considering the bloodstained blade that must have been in her brother's hand. It might have been honed by this same neighborhood vendor who pushed his cart down the street accompanied by a tinkling bell. When Moritz opened another nut, Annie jumped at the loud crack.

"How many walnuts are you going to eat, big spender?" she said, but in her head she calculated. *Felonious assault*: the crime would demand prison time. It said so in the paper: *locked up.*

Realizing that her headache had lifted, Annie placed a hand on her shoulder where Jesse's fingers rested. She touched his gold wedding band, reassuring herself of what mattered: her family, her husband, her children (present and future), and Mama. She refused to be dragged back into the gutter.

The front door opened suddenly, so wide it sent Thelma flying off the stool. Abie swaggered in, all smiles, with Louis behind him. Annie blinked and opened her eyes. She'd imagined her brother subdued in handcuffs, shuffling his chained feet, humbled and filthy, with police spittle on his back. The degree to which his being brought low had pleased her became clear with her shock and disappointment at seeing him at large standing before her, grinning, energetic, self-satisfied—and dressed like a peacock. He wore an outrageous double-breasted gray-flannel jacket unbuttoned to reveal a yellow waistcoat straight out of a fancy catalog. Removing his dove-gray fedora, he bent low and announced with a sweep of his hat, "Don't believe everything you read in the papers, suckers!"

Thelma fled to her brother, wrapping her arms around his waist and squeezing him monkey-child tight. "I was so worried," she said, rubbing her cheek against his chest and then peering into his eyes as if to make sure it was really him. "I looked all over for you."

"I heard," he said, smiling at her with a ray of love and tucking a corkscrew curl behind her ear. "And here I am to save the day, bearing gifts!" Louis stood stiffly behind his brother, carrying a bottle and a box of chocolates, a bag of lemon drops and baked goods, lox and cream cheese from Coney Island Bialys and Bagels. "They were out of salt, Jesse—onion okay?"

"I'll suffer," said Jesse, seemingly unsurprised at his brother-in-law's swift return from lockup.

"Stop crawling all over Abie, Thelma," Annie said. "You'll strangle him."

"I'm guessing you want to have that pleasure to yourself," said Abie.

Annie's hands indeed itched to circle his neck. She felt her anger beating above her left eye. "I didn't expect to see you so soon. What, now they have bagels in prison?"

"And chocolates," Abie said. "Louis, hand her the box."

Louis gave Annie the red box of chocolates from the top shelf of the candy store, the fancy kind that nobody ever really bought—at least nobody like them.

"You're welcome," Abie said as Annie held the big box with two hands, trying to squelch her curiosity. She liked nice things, but she didn't like them from bad men. It wasn't a gift but a bribe.

"Thanks for nothing" was all she managed to say.

"You can't believe everything you read, sister dear."

"You look great," Thelma said.

"Like a pimp." Annie grunted as she rose from her chair, still holding the lavish red box. "What are you doing here, Abie?"

"It's where I live. It says so in the paper. Can't you read, or has that hair dye bleached your brain?"

"I can read, all right. The paper says you stabbed a kid."

"So you've seen my press clippings." Abie pretended to shine his fingernails on his lapel.

"We sure have, Little Yiddle," said Annie.

"No one calls me that," Abie bristled. He squinted at her. It was just the two of them again, while those remaining in the room apparently had the sense to avoid coming between brother and sister. "It's a gimmick. The writer made it up to sell papers."

"The paper says you're in jail. Did they make that up, too?" Annie stepped forward, shaking off Jesse's hands. Placing her right leg in front of her left and clenching her hands, she assumed her fighting stance. "Little Yiddle."

"Call me that again," said Abie, raising his right fist, "and I'll disappear that big mouth of yours."

"What, you'll cut me with your little knife?" Annie raised her right pinkie, waggling it at her brother as she approached.

"Leave it, Annie, I don't want to sweat in my new suit," Abie said, pulling out an overly friendly grin while hugging Thelma to his side. "Do I look like a jailbird?" Abie inflated his chest, nearing Annie so that they were almost nose to identical nose. She smelled his aftershave. Only an inch taller, Annie had nearly fifty pounds on him. He stared her in the eyes. "Who are you going to believe—me or the ink?"

"So, Big *Macher*, now the whole block knows what a stinker you really are," Annie spat, raising her voice. "I had that *yenta* up my nose already. You think we can keep this quiet?"

"Quiet?" Abie sucked his teeth. "Who needs quiet? For someone who considers herself so smart, you sure are a dope. I'm sending a message in black and white: don't mess with me. I'm the toughest kid on Fourteenth Street—nobody else. The Brownsville coppers hauled me in for a *schmooze* and then released me. I'm untouchable. I'm not blabbing, and Rothman ain't pressing charges."

"Will the boy live?" asked Mama.

"Sure he'll live," said Abie, waving his hand dismissively.

"Praise God," Mama said, looking up at the ceiling.

"What's a little poke between pals?" Abie smiled and winked at Annie. "He might piss blood, but he's already back in his mother's arms. So, Mama, where's *my* hug? Aren't you happy to see me?"

Mama stayed put beside Annie, shaking her head. "What will the goyim think, a Jewish boy stabbing a Jewish boy? They'll come down around our heads and send us away. Where will we go? I'm too old to run again. Why, Abie, why'd you do it?"

"Rothman crossed me. I couldn't let him get away with it. I've got a reputation to maintain."

Annie stared at Abie, disgusted. He was filth—and yet he boasted. He never changed. How could he remain so arrogant despite such shame? If it were her, she wouldn't have been able to leave the house. But it would never have been her. "What kind of a reputation does a *pisher* like you need? You sell papers for pennies, Mr. Big Shot. Jesse employs you out of the kindness of his heart and this is how you repay us?"

"You got the order wrong, sister mine." Abie laughed. "You think I work for Jesse, you silly cow, and not vice versa?"

"You're just a know-nothing kid. He's the boss," Annie scoffed.

"He's not even the boss of you. You lead him around by that ring you put in his nose. We know who wears the pants in the family."

"Like you know so much about marriage, Chief Can't Keep His *Putz* in His Pants?"

"I know enough about living with you to pity the poor schmuck. I've never seen a guy so happy to get out of the house and go to work."

"He's a happy guy," she said.

"Does that look like a happy puss to you?" asked Abie.

"You just stabbed a guy, you expect smiles?" Annie glanced at Jesse. She registered his discontent. He looked glum, squirming in his silence. "You're an idiot, Abie."

"I'm a lot of things, but an idiot I'm not, right, Louis?"

"Right, boss."

"Tell me, Jesse," said Annie. "Tell me who runs the business."

"You want him to lie to you?" said Abie. "This is why we didn't tell you the score. You'd try to muscle in and meddle even if you knew nothing about what we do or how we do it or who we have to grease to stay in business."

"Bribery, too?"

"That's the cost of doing business. Every cop on the beat has his price; every *goniff* who pisses on our corner gets his piece. If you don't know that, you don't know nothing. You don't even know your own husband. You should see Jesse when he's a free man—that's happy," said Abie. "He arrives in Manhattan skipping, a regular elf, and whistles all day selling papers—and that's what he does. Man the kiosk. Shift merchandise. Take betting slips. He's the *kibitzer* in chief with the customers, but is he the brains of the operation? Think about it, Annie. Did he propose out of the blue, or did you have to lead him to water and make him drink?"

"You're an idiot!" Annie spat, but that didn't keep the wheels from turning. She had to admit to herself that Jesse was no genius and hadn't been in a rush to face the rabbi and stomp on the glass. "You're not worthy to shine his shoes."

"True—there's not a nicer guy in Brooklyn, but is your husband the top dog? Whose idea do you think the newsstand was?"

"It was his. We've discussed it for years."

"Right—and who do you think filled his head with the idea? Who knew what would make you happy and keep you off my back? He'd still be stacking boxes at the warehouse if it weren't for me and my connections. You wanted him to be his own boss, but I'm as close as he'll get. You're looking at the top dog right here. Ask that kid Rothman. Ask anybody on Fourteenth Street. Jesse can't control me any more than you can. Think about it, know-it-all—does he strike you as a leader?"

Annie looked over at Jesse. He didn't contest the point. Tension mounted in the room. Annie disliked silence, and in her husband's refusal to contradict Abie, she realized her brother might be telling the truth for a change.

The full weight of Abie's words registered like a gut punch. Stepping backward, Annie shoved the candy box under her armpit in order to clutch her belly, which twisted like a contraction. She gasped from the pain and broke into a sweat. It made no sense that Abie told her hardworking husband what to do. And yet, what terrified her was the way it made sense. Abie had never struck her as the lowly newsboy type, kneeling to cut the twine on the paper bundles at dawn and tipping his cap to strangers, subservient. Jesse, on the other hand, seemed more clerk than kingpin.

Abie raised his eyebrows. "I'll bet you a silver dollar I'm right."

Annie shifted her gaze for reinforcement to Jesse, but he looked away. So it was true. She sensed it in the air, and it strangled her, but she squeaked, "Please, Jesse, tell me he's lying."

"It's not just me that lied, sister mine," Abie said, a glimmer of triumph in his eyes and a sneer on his lips. He'd outsmarted her again, the schmuck.

"Don't speak to me that way, you killer."

Abie just laughed and stroked Thelma's hair as she clung affectionately to his waist. Annie wanted to wash out his mouth with soap, to
slap the smile off his face and feel the righteous sting on her palm.

Abie sneered. "Like I would answer to your husband, Annie? Look
at him: he's a mensch, too nice for a *farbissiner* like you, but does he
look to you like a boss? I don't think so. Does he resemble someone who
can hold down prime Manhattan real estate?"

"Abie," Jesse said, his voiced strained with emotion. "Don't rock
the boat."

"It's already rocking, thanks to that mouth there. I'm tired of your
wife's boot on my neck. She should know where she stands—and it's not
on top of me. You think you can get that lease on Fifth Avenue without
a thumb on the scale? You got this racket confused, big sister. Jesse and
Louis work for *me*."

"Jesse, tell me he's lying." Annie's husband just shook his head.
What had he gotten them into, the weakling? She felt attacked on all
sides. "It's your business—Lazarus and Sons—we signed the papers."

"Don't make a whole *megillah* out of this, Anechka. Money's
money—it's all in the family. Roast your chickens and be happy."

"Now you're telling me what to do, too?" Annie felt rage roar up
from her guts, a betrayal that included both husband and brother. Her
eyes stung as if she'd been slapped. "I won't be played the fool."

"Too late, sugar puss," said Abie, as he stroked Thelma and stuffed
his free hand in his pocket, rocking back on his heels. "Tell her, Jesse."

"What now?"

Jesse swiveled from wife to brother-in-law, alarmed, raising his
hands, palms out, before his chest. "Abie, you had to go and open your
mouth?"

"If you could control your wife's tongue, I wouldn't have to."

"She's your sister."

"What are you keeping from me, Abie?"

"Read this and weep, Annie: we run numbers. That's our business, the Italian lottery. Sure, Lazarus and Sons sells papers and shifts girlie rags under the counter, but the big dough comes from the bookie racket. Where there's cash, there's always someone trying to steal it from you. So you gotta have muscle, and that's me. Jesse's the front. Louis takes orders. We're a three-man team. If you're going to survive, you gotta outsmart the competition, and you gotta have a good relationship with the coppers and *essere amici* with the Italians. It's a family business—just the family is a lot bigger than you and me and Mama."

"That isn't family."

"Like you're the expert," Abie said.

"Better than you," Annie said, quivering with anger, uncertain whether to pounce or cry. "Did you know, Moe?"

"I thought you knew," Moritz said.

"I didn't." Annie turned toward Minzer. "How about you?"

He shrugged, scratched back his chair, and padded to the kitchen as if walking on eggshells. After a pause, water rushed from the tap.

No one would make a patsy out of her. Her eyes welled with angry tears as she spat, "You knew about this stabbing before it was in the paper, Jesse? You lied to me to protect that schmuck?"

"I didn't want to get you excited, Anechka."

"Don't *Anechka* me, you. Either you were in or out. Which was it?"

"You were pregnant. I was protecting you."

"Did you hear that, Little Yiddle, yesterday I *was* pregnant?"

"Mazel tov!" said Abie. "I didn't know you were hatching a kid. I just thought you were eating for two like always."

"Shut your mouth," Annie said.

"Shut yours, you sharp-tongued shrew. Never, ever tell me what to do. Don't let these pretty looks fool you—I can be way uglier than you ever imagined. Ask Nathan Rothman's mother."

"Are you threatening me in my own house, you coward?"

"Is it *your* house? Who pays the rent, sweetheart? You make the rules because I let you—and I'm feeling particularly generous today, having slipped the noose. But don't cross me. I know who you are. You sent your own brothers to the orphanage, but you burned the baby."

"What's he saying, Annie?" said Mama. "What baby got burned?"

"I don't know what he's talking about, Mama; he's *meshuge*," said Annie, waving her hand as if swatting a fly.

"I do, Mama," said Thelma, proffering her scarred thumb. "When we lived—"

"The only baby I know about," said Annie, cutting off her sister, "is the one I lost today thanks to you two."

"It's not my fault," said Thelma, defiant.

"What, Annie, we lost the baby?" Jesse said with a strangled cry, falling to his knees before his wife. "I'm so sorry. Why didn't you tell me?"

"Isn't it obvious? How could I tell you with all this craziness? Why do you think I'm still sitting here in my housecoat?"

"I'm so, so sorry, Anechka."

"What did I do to deserve such trouble?" Annie turned to Abie and Thelma. "You're animals and I'm the one who suffers."

"You're not the only one who suffers, you miserable bitch. If I were the child in your belly, I'd get out, too, while I had the chance."

"Take your stinking chocolates and get out!" Annie shrieked, throwing the heavy box at her brother's head. He dodged and it clocked Louis, who cried out in surprise. Jesse straitjacketed Annie from behind, dragging her backward on her heels as she struggled forward to claw Abie.

"Ungrateful bitch," Abie said. "I'm going around the corner to get a corned beef on rye while you cool off. C'mon, Temeleh, it's my treat. Louis, grab the candy. They shouldn't go to waste."

Chapter 10

After gorging at the deli, Thelma and her brothers sprawled on the Hooper Street stoop, sucking up the soft April warmth. She'd spread her handkerchief beside her, smoothing out the cotton on the stone step so Abie wouldn't get *schmutz* on his new pants. Between sips from his beer bottle, he dug between his teeth with a wooden toothpick. When Abie passed his bottle to Thelma, she took a sip. It tasted sour and disgusting and adult. Abie broke out laughing at the squished-up face she made, so she took a long pull and felt swimmy as she returned the bottle. Behind them, Louis leaned in the doorway, always on watch, his face in shadow. He raised a brown bottle to his lips. They were as full as a wolf pack after decimating a sheep, and Louis burped aloud as if to underscore the point. Thelma, surrounded by her brothers, was feeling triumphant, seizing that rare moment of having a leg over Annie. This was her tribe, her band of brothers. Abie was violent, but he'd never raise his hand against her; he'd always be her defender.

From their spot beside a row of trash cans marked with the address "372," Thelma examined the identical limestone apartments across the street that mirrored her own. The building had four stories with a five-step stoop that stuck out like a tongue from its front door. On the top step, a head-scarfed mother rocked gently, her shoulders slumped, singing the Yiddish lullaby "Lyalkele," little doll, in a quivery voice to her fussy baby. A small child who could easily have been mistaken for a burlap sack curled at her feet, asleep.

Above the mother's head, each level had four arched windows with ornamental bricks fanning out above the frames. Built by an Italian in 1910, the buildings were young, like she was. Thelma liked that, the newness. Gone were the tenements, the rooming houses, the dreariness of charity and the self-loathing it inspired, the warring scents of ammonia and shit and thin chicken broth. Despite all the strife upstairs in 2B, she felt relatively secure on Hooper Street for the first time in her life.

Looking up, Thelma spied a young boy carefully raising the window sash and exiting backward, sticking one leg in knee britches outside, his foot reaching hesitantly for the first fire escape step, and then the next. He turned around with a cat burglar's grace, only to have Abie yell, "Hey, Mikey, does your mother know you're sneaking out?"

Thelma laughed as a light immediately brightened the adjacent window and a woman in curlers stuck her head out, screeching, "Mikey, get back in the house now!" Before the boy complied, he raised his right fist at the trio across the street and slapped his left hand on the opposite biceps.

"You made another friend," Louis said to Abie, laughing.

"Friends are overrated," Abie said, leaning forward, his elbows on his knees.

But not brothers, Thelma thought.

For a while after that, the trio was agreeably silent, digesting, observing the parade of pushcart vendors returning to their warehouses, couples arguing, cops on the beat. Abie slit the ribbon around the chocolate box, handing it to Thelma, who'd never seen such riches. Two dozen chocolates, squares and rectangles, stars and hearts, nestled in ruffled paper cups. She said, "I don't know where to start."

Abie, without hesitation, grabbed the biggest nut cluster in the very center and placed it in his mouth, sucking the sweetness. "Annie doesn't know what she's missing."

Louis reached over Thelma's shoulder and plucked a spherical sweet. "Make mine a cherry."

"Caramel," said Thelma, her teeth sticking together and mangling the word. "Thank you."

"Thank Annie for slinging them at my head."

"She'd have made a great shortstop," said Louis. "She still has a good arm."

"Then that's the only thing good about her," said Abie. "I'd rather be interrogated by the Huns than try to be nice to that hag. There's no payoff."

"Nope," said Thelma, shutting her eyes and circling her palm above the candies before picking one. She took a nibble and then a bite, and recoiled. "Weird cream—ick! It tastes like medicine."

"Spit it out," Abie said. With his permission, she launched it all the way to the sidewalk. This was what it must feel like to be rich: not only did she have more candy than she could eat in one sitting, but she had the luxury to reject the ones she didn't like.

Abie swigged his beer. "Good form," he said. "If I'd known Annie was going to aim for my head, I would have bought her a smaller box. No good deed goes unpunished."

"Annie," said Louis, shivering as if he were crossing his own grave.

"Getting on her bad side is more dangerous than fire," Abie said.

"Does she have a good side?" Louis asked, and they laughed.

When it was quiet again and it appeared her brothers were dropping the topic, Thelma said, "Can you imagine: The first thing I remember is my own sister torching me?" Betrayal had been her first emotion, the shock that family could hurt her.

"What's left to the imagination? I was there," said Abie. "Annie was on the warpath that week."

Thelma looked over and asked, "Why?"

He passed her the bottle. "We got the Annie treatment a few days before. She locked Louis and me in the closet," Abie said. "Mama was at the laundry. Annie wanted to paw the landlord's boy at the front of the apartment. So instead of watching us, she locked us in the bedroom closet. We banged on the door with our fists, yelling."

"'Let us out!'" Louis said, remembering.

"Louis hated small spaces."

"Still do."

"So we sat there in the dark, telling stories until I ran out. Time passed. Louis got more scared."

"I swear the closet shrank."

"And he started to pass gas."

"I tried to hold it in."

"He couldn't. We tried beating the door, but zip. And then it happened: his *tuchus* exploded, and he crapped his pants."

Thelma grabbed her guts in sympathy. Their sister had terrorized all three of them at one point or another, and if not for Abie's rage, Annie would have crushed them all.

"God," said Louis, "it stank."

"He was nine years old already."

"I was so ashamed I started crying, and that made it more shaming," said Louis. "I was a big boy. That shouldn't have happened—shit or tears."

"We're only telling you, Temmy, so you know you're not alone. Hours passed and Annie opens the door. She *geschreis*."

"She yanks me out by my hair, crying, 'You stink, you little stinkers!' Sure I did: crap was running down my legs."

"A shit fountain! When Louis stood, crap streamed down his legs and covered his boots. She had to remove his shoes to clean him. When Annie got on her hands and knees, the laces were double knotted and covered in shit."

"She ordered Abie to untie them."

"I refused, and I wouldn't let Louis do it. She coughed and gagged and worked the knots, cursing us as if we'd *chosen* to hide in the closet.

And that's when the landlord's boy strolled in, took a whiff, and called us *betteljuden*. She was rabid."

"She pinched my balls, she was so angry."

"Yeah, and you doubled over, and shit sprayed her hair."

"She got what she deserved."

Thelma puckered her face. "Disgusting!"

"But effective," said Abie. He passed her the bottle. She took a bigger bitter sip. "Enough with the happy memories. So, Temeleh, I hear you came by to visit me in Manhattan."

She felt like she'd been caught out of school (which she had). Attempting to sound tough like her brothers, she asked, "Says who?"

"That horse guy doubles as a lookout."

"I saw the blood and I panicked. Abie, I'm sorry." She remembered the red splash on the sidewalk, the excited crowd, the strange reporter grilling the boys. They hadn't mentioned Rothman since they'd left the apartment, and she needed to hear Abie's side of the story. "What did that kid do to you to deserve that?"

"Deserve? None of my business," said Abie, sucking his teeth. "The whole thing was rigged. He was a schmuck, but I know a lot of schmucks and I don't stab them all. Some, but not all, and that Rothman kid was a patsy. He'd been showing up on the street, trying to throw his weight around, spitting on Monk Eastman's sidewalk. Rothman had been bragging he told the cops, and now he shows up in new shoes and a new coat. The bosses hatched a play. I got my pal Gersh to egg this Rothman on, to build him up as a big man, tell him how I talked tough but I was lily-livered. Then it was just a matter of walking by and he was all full of himself. He took one look at me and burst out laughing, and he called me Little Yiddle—it made it easy to shove the blade."

"How could it be easy?" Thelma asked, leaning in, repulsed and curious.

"Orphanage rules," Louis said.

"Someone smacks you, you hit back harder. You gotta gain respect right away, because later it hurts more if you don't make it clear who's on top and who's on the bottom. I wasn't mad at the kid. I had my orders. It's the cost of doing business on Fourteenth Street."

"At least he lived," said Thelma.

"Yeah, but he's never going to shit straight again. He's out of the game."

"Don't you feel bad about hurting him so bad?" asked Thelma.

Abie scanned the street, then sniggered. "It was him or me."

"Yeah," Louis agreed, "it was Abie or that dirty rat."

"You don't see me crying any tears."

Thelma waved a fly off her scabby knee. "I cry all the time."

"Yeah, but you're a girl. You're supposed to be soft. Not us," said Abie.

"Abie and me, we're hard as nails," said Louis.

"Harder," said Abie. "As if we had any choice."

"So, Abie," Thelma asked, "since when do they call you Little Yiddle?"

"Since yesterday when Rothman said it—and it landed in the papers."

"Isn't that insulting?"

"It's not Handsome, but my gut says it's gonna stick. And it's a name—I'm not a nobody anymore."

"Are you really the toughest?"

"Until the next guy . . ."

"Were you scared?"

"Shit, yeah—the trick is not to show it."

"How do you do that?" Everything Thelma felt splashed across her face, making her vulnerable—especially to Annie. But she didn't want to harden and crack. She wanted to unfold and figure out just who she was. It seemed to her that Abie had always known exactly who he was—and she envied that.

"It's acting. Like the theater."

"But how did it feel? Can you teach me?"

"You're kidding, right?"

"No," Thelma said. She wasn't joking. Anxious about his safety, she wanted to know what made him tick so when the time came and the tables were turned, she could protect her brother.

"Oh, you want the inside scoop, kiddo?"

"C'mon, Abie, stop stalling." She pinched his elbow. "Louis knows."

"I got blood on my shoes to prove it," he mumbled.

"I'll pay for a shine," Abie said, rubbing his stubble.

"Big spender," said Louis.

"All right, already, this is how it played. I was antsy and itchy. I'd been sweating it since sunrise. When someone strikes me, I hit back. It's like—what's it called?"

"A reflex," said Louis. "If you show weakness, you might as well hand your enemy a hammer to hit you with."

"Take your fear and bend it into anger," Abie said.

"Anger I got," said Thelma, trying to sound older than she was. She gazed up and back toward home, where the lights still shined in the second-floor apartment. Framed in the window, in curlers and cold cream, Annie scowled, touching the rollers to check if her hair was dry. Thelma didn't ever want to go upstairs again. She dreaded seeing Moe at the table, turning his head away from her as if she were the shame, not him. She didn't want to join Mama in bed in the place where her stepfather belonged. No one cared what she wanted, but it was this: sitting with her brothers, her family, on the stoop until the sky grew light and the pushcart men returned. She wanted to grow up fast so that nobody would ever tell her what to do again. Shifting her back to the window again, she said, "You don't like anybody bossing you around, right, Abie?"

"Not me. I like singing my own tune." Abie scanned Hooper Street. In the apartment building next door, a clarinetist was slaughtering "It's a Long, Long Way to Tipperary," repeating the opening bars until they surrendered and swung into "By the Beautiful Sea."

Across the way, the mother stood and dusted off her shift, cuddling the now-sleeping infant and jiggling the sack of a child with her toe. They disappeared inside with the kid letting the heavy wooden door drop behind him. It banged and the baby started wailing.

"Enough with the bedtime stories—maybe it's time for you to go inside, Baby Snooks," said Abie.

"I'm in no rush. Let me stay a little longer, please?"

"I got to see a guy about a thing."

"Just a few more minutes, please, please, please?"

"Just don't be a *nudzh.*"

"Never," Thelma said, stretching her legs out in front of her and sucking on a chocolate. A pipe-smoking stranger strolling past slowed and ogled Thelma's calves. Her brothers laughed. "What did I do wrong now? Why'd he look at me funny?"

"Not funny," said Abie. "It's just . . ."

"Is there something wrong with my leg? Too skinny, right, like Annie says?"

"As if that pug-ugly knows," said Abie. "There's nothing wrong with those gams, little sister. You got the magic leg. You step off a curb and shake it, and the Prince of Wales is going to stop his carriage."

"I've never heard of that," Thelma said, but she liked the way it sounded. She had something special besides brothers who comforted her when she was low.

"We each have a magic thing. Louis can find his way anywhere with his eyes closed. I got a magic tongue: I can talk a cop into letting me go. Hell, I can talk a nun out of her panties. But you, you got the magic leg."

They looked the same to Thelma—schoolgirl legs, scabby and pale and long, but she believed her brother. He would lie—but not to her.

Just then, a wine-colored Packard with yellow spokes trolled down the street.

Abie rose nonchalantly, as if new cars routinely picked him up curbside. He stretched his legs, smoothing the front of his new pants, and then strutted down two stairs. At the bottom he turned, light on his feet. "So why'd you really come to find me yesterday, Tem?"

In answer, she crossed her legs and stuck out her tongue. Hugging her knees under her chin, Thelma surveyed the car, but her thoughts returned to their apartment—and Uncle Moe sitting at the table playing cards with the Mint like they did every night.

"Uncle Moe and me . . . ," she began, and then she stopped, and began again. "I . . ." She'd thought her story would spill out with her brothers. And yesterday, when she was running toward Abie, it might have, if nothing else had happened. But now, with all the *mishegas*, with all she'd seen, she couldn't form the words. She worried that Abie might not love her the same way once he knew—or even worse, he might not believe her.

What a knot. How could she untangle it? How to explain the cat-like comfort of curling into Moe's sea-salty neck at the end of a long day, the way he began to gather her up when the light under the crack of Annie's door extinguished and the bedsprings squawked? She cringed at the memories, how he touched her chest where the buds were forming with his jeweler's hands, her shame at not being entirely a woman yet, her apologies at her inability to please, her eagerness and her inexperience, the way their noses bumped and her arms became bent at awkward angles.

It felt wrong, she knew that. She should have, could have shoved him away. She didn't—so wasn't she as much to blame as her stepfather? She certainly felt guilty. Uncle Moe and her: she loved him. Maybe from that first time she'd followed his lead as they box-stepped on her seventh birthday. The world had whirled around them and she couldn't stop laughing for fear she'd misplace her feet, breathless. Maybe before that even. Moe saw her, not just the shabby shoes, the frizzy hair, and the spit-upon posture. He nurtured the softness underneath the crust. When he was in a room, she gravitated toward his side. He read to her from the paper, cut her an apple slice, clipped her nails. Moe was the attentive parent, waiting with open arms to cuddle, pinching her shoulder muscle until she squirmed and fell to the floor, slipping her hand in his. She kicked herself inside, aggravating an old bruise: she was so needy that she couldn't turn away when it became too much.

She saw Abie glance down the block and then return to the stoop beside her. Louis descended and parked himself on her other side, forming a brother sandwich. Their hatred of Annie united the trio.

"That stuff on the couch?" Abie asked. "Jesse told us."

"Annie exploded," said Louis, "and the poor schmuck vented to us like he always does."

"Who is he to tell you about my private stuff?"

"Nothing that happens in that apartment stays private," said Abie. "That's a luxury for rich people."

"So why didn't you say anything?"

"I'm saying something now, aren't I?"

"Maybe," she said, suspicious. "I thought I came first."

"I try to protect you, but I'm no prince. You know that. I wish I had, and so does Louis. Nobody loves you more than we do. But you gotta see I've been a little busy, what with the police and all." Abie patted Thelma's knee, simultaneously peering out of the corner of his eye. The circling Packard was heading their way again. He must have nodded, because they passed, crawled to the corner, and hung right.

"I didn't know, Abie. I didn't know what we were doing was wrong. Or maybe I did." Thelma shrugged. "He's Uncle Moe. I trusted him."

"Sure you did," said Louis.

"You didn't ask for this, baby. You're a kid, just not anymore. You got the magic leg. That's what I've been trying to explain to you," Abie said, apparently distracted by the rising pressure to enter the approaching car.

"It wasn't your fault. Not at all. But maybe you didn't realize that you're not a little girl anymore, at least on the outside. Men are animals."

"Dogs," said Louis.

"And I know that personally."

"But you're not like that, Abie."

"Right," he said. "I just stabbed a kid; otherwise I'm a peach. I know you want answers, but I'm no expert on creepy old guys. I like my dolls taller than me, fully grown. Want my advice? Try not sitting on men's laps. Maybe pick on somebody your own size—and stay away from Moe."

"Easier said than done, right, Tem?" said Louis, who extended his hand to escort her inside. "Ready to go up?"

"I'd rather go to hell," she said.

"What's the difference?" Abie asked, laughing.

"You're my family, not those *putzes*," Thelma said. "Do I make you happy?"

"Of course you do. You're aces!" Abie leaned over to kiss her cheek with his mouth open so that when he pulled away, the suction popped. She wiped her wet face with the back of her hand while Abie stood and jazz stepped backward downstairs with all the vigor of a man used to starting his day job late at night. Thelma plucked her handkerchief from where he'd been seated, waved it in the air like a magician to shake off the grit, and then stuffed it in her pocket, sighing. Abie had a point. He was her big brother. She believed him, and she believed in him. Abie pivoted, crossed the sidewalk, and ascended the Packard. The shotgun door shut like applause.

Chapter 11

While her boys and the husband thief conspired on the stoop, Mama lay alone in her room like a widow. She'd never allow Moritz near her bed again, and she'd keep Thelma in her room to ensure he didn't try. Enraged, she counted grudges instead of sheep and so was sleepless.

She'd positioned a line of hairbrushes, bristles up, along the mattress's center, marking the boundary Thelma couldn't cross. Every once in a while, as she waited, she pushed it farther so that now she had two-thirds of the bed and that skinny little thing would have a sliver by the wall under the window. She was fortunate to share a bed with her mother and not an orphanage cot.

The girl hadn't yet come upstairs. Every few minutes Mama would extend her right leg to touch the floor and feel for her slipper with her toes, as if she would go and grab the child herself. Just the thought of the girl made the sting of Moritz's rejection rise in her throat like bile. How dared he take her homely daughter in her place, that nothing without breasts? It was a *shonda*, an embarrassment that would ruin her if it reached the temple sisterhood. And now she had a killer son, too, a *dybbuk* who gave her money and took her soul. Who was she to tell Moritz how to behave when her own son ran wild in the newspapers for everyone to see? This would never have happened in the old country.

Three short knocks struck the bedroom door. Silence, then three more raps, louder, quicker, followed by Moritz demanding, "Wife, let me in."

She said nothing. Having wept outside the bathroom on her hands and knees only to have him ignore her, she now rejected him.

"I'm your husband," he said. "Obey me."

She would have snorted, but instead she sucked her breath and hid beneath the comforter. A small satisfaction curled up inside her: now, he approached her. He'd feel how it was to break a marriage.

"Let me in for my clean linen," he said. "You can't deny me that."

She could. Having always been duty bound, she perceived the freedom of slipping her chains. She had a briquette of power and let it smolder. She bit her tongue. Eventually he retreated. He wasn't one to beg. She remembered how Moritz had entered into their marriage: politely, dutifully, carrying a paper sack of cherries and new linens tied with cloth ribbon. He was younger than she, sure, but only eight years, not a lifetime, with a head full of hair and still humming the melodies of her childhood. Energetic, he took the steps two at a time, but after having all those children, dead and alive, she felt like an old gray-haired crone beside a juicy youth.

To her, Moritz meant a roof, a kitchen of her own, a full larder. Jonas had been her husband and she remained as mad at him for abandoning her as if it were yesterday, as if she hadn't remarried a goldsmith with a steady job born in a village sixty miles distant from her own. In heaven, she would reunite with Jonas and give him a piece of her mind. She wondered if he would listen to her above the clouds as he'd refused to do on earth, or if he'd found someone else there among the spirits who didn't get impatient being lectured about the Torah.

Heartburn flared at the top of her belly, and pain crawled up her throat, releasing itself in painful wet burps that soured her mouth and made her gag. She pressed her hand against her breastbone and thought it wouldn't be so long now before she joined Jonas. She was ready. Would she give *him* a piece of her mind! She collapsed back on her pillow, gasping while her foot retreated under the featherbed she'd stitched with her sisters before her wedding, now stained with man spots and menstrual blood.

From behind, Mama could hear Annie and Jesse talking, since their headboard shared a wall with hers. This, too, was another source of annoyance, *shpilkes*.

"They're animals, Jesse," Annie said in a loud whisper. "They're outside laughing, eating *my* chocolates right in front of me."

"Anechka, you threw the box at Abie's head."

"Don't start," she said. "Don't *you* defend them!"

"I'm not defending them. Give it a rest. I have to get up in a few hours."

"You can sleep after a day like this? I don't know how, after you lied to me about the business. Do you think I'm too stupid to understand?"

"Never, Anechka, not stupid—I didn't want to upset you."

"Or were you too weak to hear the truth?"

It was news to Mama, who wondered what else was happening under her nose of which she was ignorant. Her own mother would have had more control over her children's lives. She, who had been such a dutiful daughter, would have been a disappointment. On the other side of the wall, Annie started in again: "Those chocolates are mine, and now they're downstairs laughing like the criminals they are. They're eating my candy and pissing in my soup and you don't have the guts to stop them."

"We only had the one box of chocolates. Did you want me to throw something else? A chair, maybe, a table? A lamp? Go to sleep, Annie, enough already."

"You think I don't know that they hate me. They wouldn't *be* here if it weren't for me. What did I ever to do them?"

"You hate them, Anechka, so what do you expect?"

"So now you're blaming me? I'm not the one who knifed a kid."

"No, and you never will be. Knives aren't your weapon. A box of chocolates, maybe."

"Stop!" she said, but her voice was huskier.

"Now come to Papa for a cuddle."

Usually Mama was asleep by now, but tonight she was listening for the front door to open and Thelma to enter and find the hairbrushes. As the minutes clicked by, surrounded by darkness, the dead were more real to her than the living. She was acutely aware of the little ones who waited to hold her hands as she walked in her dreams, the souls of the children she'd miscarried, the first daughter she'd held to term who died at the lip of life. She'd felt her move, dance, leap inside her until that last night. What happened as the moon rose? Who'd sinned? She'd felt ill will, perhaps from Jonas's first wife. Mama knew—no, she loved—that child. She'd felt the infant's hand outside her body. Saw enough to know she'd looked like her little sister when she'd been born. If she'd survived, maybe they would have remained near her mother and sisters, but, no, they'd buried the child and then left.

In New York, she'd had Annie, Moishe, her favorite, Abie. Feverish Moishe died quarantined, on the opposite side of the apartment, far from the comforts of his mother, because she'd had to protect Louis, who'd arrived as easy as breath but at such a high cost. Moishe—with the girlish curls, the chubby cheeks, the smiling sweetheart lips—had died in agony. After that, she'd miscarried, miscarried, and then came Thelma, and she buried Jonas. The children kept her awake: the ones who survived and the ones who cried out in the night from beyond. Jonas had found her belief in spirits ridiculous. She'd once told him about their children who surrounded her in her sleep. Disgusted, the rabbi's son shooed her away, curling his lip at her superstitions. But these absent sons and daughters were real to Mama. She walked sadly in a graveyard of her own womb.

Conspiring with the matchmaker and Annie, she'd tricked the guileless immigrant Moritz into thinking she could still have children. But Mama didn't feel life there anymore. It had been so long since her body had experienced pleasure. She'd felt mortified when she viewed the revulsion in the young man's eyes, the expression that this was the ultimate duty he had to perform in the match and that he might not be able to rise to the occasion. On their wedding night, she'd lain on her back like a martyr with her legs splayed, in a new nightgown buttoned to her throat, ashamed to display her flesh, the belly mountain, the veined breasts with nipples sucked dry. He had been a good boy, small, shy, and he'd tried, and failed, to mount her. She was confident that she'd done her duty. Lay still and submissive, hardly crying.

She overheard her children laughing outside, conspiratorially, and she felt no joy although merriment brightened their voices. What could possibly make that trio happy? Pleasure-seekers, they were corrupt, *drek*, garbage—strangers. They would get what was coming to them; she'd ensure that. She only hoped she'd live long enough to see their come-uppance and, on that day, she would show no mercy. Thelma was still young but, following her brothers, she'd already chosen the wrong path. She could skate into hell beside the boys.

Convinced they mocked her with their sniggers and snorts, she felt the weight of their betrayal like a winter coat in summer. She was their mother. That should matter. That should command loyalty and respect, as she had honored her mother unquestioningly, as Annie did. Who were they to judge her? If Jonas had survived, maybe things would have been different, but he'd been weak and homesick, not a husband to cling to in adversity. She'd drowned in a sea of troubles and he'd denied her a life vest, that selfish man who loved God and hated her. It remained a bitter pill, her feelings torn between love and hate. She was shipwrecked in America.

Meanwhile, her children heed and hawed as, somewhere, Nathan Rothman twisted in pain from Abie's wound and Mrs. Rothman sobbed. Mama grabbed her belly in sympathy; there wasn't a pain in the world that didn't manifest itself in her stomach lining and crawl up her gullet. Both mothers wept that they could not control their children's actions when they roamed the streets of an endless city with dangers on every corner, where there was no stern neighbor to grab the children by their ears and drag them home to the punishment they deserved. Where was their shame?

Jealousy gnawed at Mama. Once, she'd had that connection with her sisters, a magic circle that cost nothing, that cloaked the night in ease until sleep came. Mama longed to be a happy cow hidden among the herd of her sisters. But now it seemed like she would never reunite with her *mishpokhe*, her family. She'd left the village a young woman and was now a grandmother, unrecognizable, even if at night she dreamed herself young again. Her crepey skin repulsed her, the rolls of fat snuggled beneath other rolls.

She seized the smothering nightdress at her throat and made to rip the neckline, still after all these years mourning her loss of a home where she knew her place between betters and inferiors. In America, there was only low and lower, despite Annie's insistence that they must rise and confidence that education was the way. She had no time for learning anymore.

In Drohobych, Mama had made sense. Here not so much, and her children even less without their cousins to shape them, grandparents to separate right from wrong, rituals to shelter them. In her village, Mama had been secure, knowing her value as part of the whole. If her father married her off to the rabbi's middle son, then the family would ascend to better seats within the synagogue. Profitable contracts would pass their way. She'd understood the give-and-take. She'd given. Taking was her father's right. She would live across the village, but what sacrifice was that? She would still be near her family, her sisters, her herd. Her children would have grown old surrounded by cousins, and cousins' cousins, and they would have remained strong and righteous. Now, lost, they straggled away from the herd, vulnerable, ungovernable.

Family meant everything to Mama. Yet hers was shattered—betrayed on the stoop tonight and in the fields of the past. What pained her deeply was how easily she'd been forgotten and abandoned. She was expendable. Did they even remember her? She doubted it. Where were the sisters and cousins to follow in America? Why, if they prospered in the old country, had they not sent her money to rejoin them once Jonas passed? These were night questions without answers.

Finally, the bedroom door rasped. Through slitted eyes, Mama observed the girl carrying her shoes, which she slipped under the bed. Thelma stripped down to her undershirt and underpants. In the wan light from the single window, Mama watched with heartburn and anticipation as Thelma gathered her thick hair atop her head and crept into bed, smelling of sour beer. She was a slut. She was nothing to Mama. The girl, so stealthy, depressed the bedsprings. They screaked. Then Thelma cried out in pain and surprise as her knee landed on the first upturned brush. She cursed as her palm landed on the sharp bristles of another. Mama turned her head away, giving the girl her back. She smiled in the darkness.

Behind her, the girl whispered, "Good night, Mama."

With her back to Thelma, Mama said, "You want my husband? Take him and go. You're no daughter of mine." Then she shut her eyes and began to feel sleep approach.

Chapter 12

After that night, Thelma avoided Hooper Street as much as a penniless thirteen-year-old student could. Mama made even sleeping unbearable with the scratchy blanket of distrust between them. And then there was Moe: the apartment was too small for both of them, their every movement scrutinized by Annie, who lived in a postmiscarriage rage that she exorcised by criticizing others. He tried to play the stern stepfather now, telling Thelma to shine his shoes or iron his handkerchiefs or finish the food on her plate. At dinner, he hid behind the newspaper, eating his meal slowly so that the table was already cleared and the family dispersed while he ground his way through the meat and ate each overcooked carrot with care, saying nothing to anybody, scraping his knife against the plate in a way that made Thelma shiver.

Occasionally, she would be doing homework cross-legged on the floor and she would feel heat on her cheek and glance over, catching him looking at her as a husband might look at a wife. She immediately looked down, hiding within a round-shouldered posture. She disappeared into algebra and grammar, ashamed of her loneliness and the loss of an ally, feeling the guilt of pissing in the family soup despite Abie's absolution and reassurance that it wasn't her fault but Moe's. Everything she studied was about rules and order—the right and wrong of every answer—but she lacked the road map to navigate a hostile home where

Annie and Mama made her feel that her behavior, and hers alone, had brought shame on the family.

After dinner, Moe would go through elaborate motions to prepare his pipe, puffing the sweet-sour tobacco and then cleaning the bowl and the chamber before pushing back from the table, walking to the hook, and retrieving his coat and hat. The Mint would join him at the door, and they would leave together without a word of goodbye or a hint of when they'd return, until the day that Minzer left altogether, having found another place to live nearer to work, where he and Moe could return to playing cards in peace. Her brothers began to skip dinner, coming and going as they pleased, more often than not sleeping behind closed doors and standing at the icebox to drink milk from the bottle or grab a hard-boiled egg to eat during the day.

For safety, Thelma gravitated toward the nearby homes of her Italian girlfriends, where adding another bowl was no problem if a clean spoon could be found or pulled from the maw of a teething baby. Chairs could easily be shared. There was so much activity in those fertile households that she could just be one mouth among many and not the lightning rod she was at home.

Her favorite kitchen was in Nina Gigantiello's apartment overlooking Our Lady of Mount Carmel on North Eighth Street, a full floor of a four-story building above the Knights of Columbus. Shy and olive skinned, Nina had short legs and short arms and a basset hound's mournful brown eyes, blinking her stubby lashes frequently in a constant battle against ash and pollen. She was a superior student but would often finish only two-thirds of a math test so as not to stand out and inspire the wrath of neighborhood curs ashamed by their own limitations. When Nina became the first girl in the class to get breasts—a large shelf on her slight frame that got in her way when she leaned over and tried to tie her tattered laces—she unbalanced the equation of girls and boys in the class.

The Gigantiellos, like most of their immediate neighbors, were deeply Catholic and, like so many of their countrymen, they sinned and repented, sinned and repented, with much drama followed by heavy meals. Crosses hung everywhere—above the beds, nestled in a sideboard altar, even between Mrs. Gigantiello's breasts. Was the cross a warning for men to stay away, or an invitation to look closer? Thelma didn't know. Over time, she became accustomed to the crucifixes and even the way that Nina's mother was constantly crossing herself and raising her eyes toward the water-stained ceiling, as if their Lord would answer conversationally on cue like a nosy neighbor.

With a smile that could melt mozzarella and a single gold front tooth adorning the white, Mrs. Allegra Gigantiello was a woman of big laughs and loud sighs. She flowed through the house carrying a large wooden spoon, which she would cover with a cloth to sweep out a spider at the corner of the ceiling or thump on the close-shaved head of a child who stole the baby's animal cracker. She took an immediate liking to Thelma, whom she called *stuzzicadenti*, which meant toothpick. At Mrs. G's table, the skinny girl found her appetite, eating anything put in front of her: pasta bolognese, eggplant parmigiana, and *pasta e fagioli*. She did the unthinkable: fell in love with sautéed spinach with garlic and baby peas, when before she had never met a vegetable she liked. She discovered she was Jewish by birth but had an Italian palate.

As Nina's blond, bullet-headed little brother—they called him Giorgio Porgio—buzzed around her, teasing the guest while avoiding his mother's wooden spoon of justice, Thelma always finished the meal by clasping Mama Allegra in gratitude. Mrs. Gigantiello would pull her tight into the smell of musky sweat and spice and rose water—nose to nose with the cross—and compliment the child for giving meaty hugs despite such slender arms.

"She's a good hugger, this *stuzzicadenti*," Mama Allegra had said, scratching the girl's scalp. Melting into Nina's mother, Thelma hoped that, someday, she could become this kind of mother, nurturing and wise. Praise seemed to come as easily as sweat to Mama Allegra, and the Italian woman's embraces would inspire more affection from Thelma as Nina looked on, increasingly withdrawn.

Giving her friend the evil eye, Nina would ask Thelma, "What's the big deal about Mama?"

"Everything," Thelma replied. Just as she'd never tasted *rapini* before, so she'd never felt the warmth of uncritical maternal love. It was heavenly, more filling than pasta and more nourishing than vegetables.

After dinner, Nina would drag Thelma away to join her sisters on the fire escape to try to catch a breeze, gorging on stone fruit and spitting the pits on unsuspecting passersby entering the Knights of Columbus. The older daughters claimed this artillery practice strengthened the kisser—they could tie knots in cherry stems with their tongues—but that exercise was less important to Thelma and Nina than eliciting a big upraised fist and curses in Italian from the gold-chained men, their crosses nested in chest fur.

Once darkness fell, Thelma would linger, waiting for an invitation to spend the night, and then join the long line to the bathroom, having the backs of her ears scrubbed hard by one older sister or another, Trulia or Gabriela. She was accepted like a puppy among piglets, without asking permission. And she found that on North Eighth Street, the gears of her mind stopped grinding. For those hours she didn't wait for the next shoe to drop. She floated in the world of children.

In the dining room, the girls would set up the kitchen chairs in two rows, with the youngest in front, including Thelma and Nina. Then Mama would take the boar-bristle brush to Thelma's knots, praising her curls and their reddish-brown glow, smoothing them with olive oil, the movement of her sure fingers a tonic and salve so that the chore that Thelma hated the most at home became a luxurious pleasure. As Mama Allegra spun her wild locks into well-behaved braids, one on each side of her head, Thelma's shoulders dropped, her hands folded into her lap, and she lost the thread of the parish gossip, which Trulia called Our Lady of Perpetual Hullabaloo.

Then they would turn to Mama, unfurling the intricate braid created the night before. She would sigh with pleasure as Nina and Thelma combed through the thick straight hair with silver strands mixing with the blackish-brown. For a moment, the mother appeared girlish, her hair full and floating over her shoulders and down her back, framing a gently smiling face happy to see a night's rest after a day of labor. Then the younger girls stepped aside, making way for Gabriela to weave her spider magic on her mother's hair, slowly and deliberately knitting the strands back up into their captive, civilized state.

It was on one of these July nights a week before the Giglio feast that Mama Allegra sat behind Thelma, untangling the knots in her hair, twirling curls around her fingers, and proclaiming her jealousy. Then, after shooing Giorgio away like a pesky fly from beneath Thelma's knees, which he was trying to tickle with a chicken feather, she asked the question that cut deepest: "You are a treasure, *stuzzicadenti*, so why doesn't your family treasure you?"

The question sucked Thelma's breath away. It was so direct and simple, and yet she couldn't answer. Why didn't they? A tougher girl would have said *ask them*. But she was not that callous girl. She picked at the scabs of herself, wondering how she had erred from the beginning. Why was she worth less than her sister, and now her niece and nephew? Why were Mama and Annie so close, knitted together by a fierce love, while she remained on the outside looking in? Their rejection ripped through her. She was not affectionate; she was needy. Her legs weren't magic; they were skinny. She didn't dance for joy but demanded attention.

She didn't fit, didn't do as she was told, didn't submit, didn't keep the right secrets and tell the right lies. If only she spurned Abie and Louis. If only she did these things, she would be loved—but there was always something else that was not good enough, never good enough.

It wasn't fair and she angrily searched inside herself for more flaws to justify their criticisms. And, searching, she found them: a dirty mouth, a lazy ass, a husband thief.

How could she begin to discuss her stepfather when she didn't even know how to explain it to herself? Silence spread through the room as the Gigantiellos awaited Thelma's answer. Trulia and Gabriela leaned in. In the expectant quiet, they heard a tenor practicing his solo for the feast. Then came the frazzled response of the brass, followed by the singer excoriating the musicians for entering too late and at the wrong tempo. The song began again and Thelma looked at Nina, who knew her secrets and nodded, saying, "Tell Mama."

"Tell me, *bambina*," said Mama Allegra. "What could you possibly do that would be so terrible?"

Shaking her head, Thelma said, "But it was."

"I look at you and I don't believe it. Not my sweet *stuzzicadenti*. Did you drown a baby? Set fire to a cat? Rob a bank?"

"No." But there were other crimes. "Uncle Moe."

"Who is this Uncle Moe, Nina?"

Nina looked to Thelma, who nodded permission. "The stepfather."

"Ah, stepfathers, *patrigni*," said her mother. "There's a special place in hell for them."

"He's a good man," Thelma protested, squeezing her hands between her thighs. "He was kind to me. And then this . . ."

"This what?" asked Mama Allegra. "Gabriela, get me a hankie. What did this man do to you?"

"He did nothing to me, Mama Allegra. This thing at night we did, me and him, on the sofa when everybody else was asleep. That thing was my fault." She crumpled in her chair, feeling the pressure to confess but not the words to explain: she lay with her stepfather, the *shonda*. She'd opened her legs to him and shut all rights to be part of the family. She was guilty of this crime—the husband thief.

Her remorse mixed with loneliness. She missed the nights, the attention, and the secrecy. It angered her that she'd risked everything for his embrace and, then, like Mama, like Annie, he'd deserted her. His promises dissolved like sugar in water.

She looked at Nina's mother and recognized kindness with such clarity that she blushed. She feared that if she revealed what had happened, it would be the end to pasta, hair braiding, hugs. Nina's mother would reject her. The Gigantiellos would no longer welcome her if she confessed, but, with their encouragement, she couldn't hold back. It was too much to carry alone. She said, "Uncle Moe, my stepfather, at night, we did stuff."

"*Stuff, bambina*, what is *stuff*?"

Thelma paused, her mouth open, trying to form the words plucked from the confusing images in her head.

Nina said, "What a husband does with his wife."

"Oh, that never happens in Jewish households!" the matriarch said ironically, laughing in a way that made Thelma cry in relief. She pulled the girl in close with a hug and a kiss, saying, "As if you were the only little girl subject to a lecher under her own roof."

"It was my fault," Thelma said.

"How could it be? You are a child."

"Children don't behave that way with men. I am a woman."

"No," Mama Allegra said in a stern voice. "You're not. He's the adult, *bambina*. He wore the wedding ring and took the vows. He ate your mother's cooking and shared her bed. He should have known better, but men are men, unscrupulous, stealing fruit from others' trees and convincing themselves it's theirs."

"He didn't force me. I was willing."

"You were vulnerable. He pounced. Have you seen your long legs, your green eyes? No wonder he couldn't keep his hands off you. In the old country, a girl your age would already be married to keep you safe from the uncles under your roof. Your mother and sister should have protected you from him. Don't blame yourself, *stuzzicadenti*. We'll guard you."

Giorgio leaped to Thelma's side and saluted, grabbing a broom like a bayonet. The youngest son was always in motion, kicking a can, making a slingshot, bouncing like a rabbit on the sisters' beds and crying, "I'm going to the moon." The crack that had formed on the ceiling showed how far he'd gotten.

The blue-eyed beauty of a boy, far prettier than Nina, Gabriela, or Trulia, appeared to take his duty even more seriously than expected, as if he were in the army and Thelma was his captive. A year younger and a head shorter than her, he remained beside her for the rest of the summer like a warrior cherub, despite Nina trying to shoo the pest away from her friend. Thelma, having never experienced this level of attention, found his devotion both cloying and pleasing. She was no longer the one who tagged along. He was. And so he pushed her farther into the group, tormenting and tickling and bringing her strange presents: a bottle opener, a purple ribbon, a linen handkerchief with a blue windmill and the initials *K. J.* on it.

During that summer, Thelma became a shadow daughter of the Gigantiellos'. Occasionally she'd slip in and out of the house on Hooper Street, trying to avoid conflict, dodging Annie's gibes that she was spending too much time with the Italians. She'd hoped that if she lay low, relations would stabilize between Mama and Moe, and the husband would return to Mama's bed where he belonged. But she had no such luck, and spending the night still meant sharing Mama's bed, a waking nightmare of belches and sniffles and a pervasive sense of unwelcome and unease that followed Thelma into her dreams, where her shoulders ached from the weight of bending low.

In the week leading up to the feast, Allegra, her mother, and her sisters cooked and competed, letting the girls and their cousins taste the sauces, the *panna cotta*. Thelma praised Mama Allegra's cooking, which pleased the older woman, teasing a smile that revealed her gold tooth, which the woman normally tried to conceal. Her own children agreed that Grandma's was superior, followed by Auntie Bettina's. Thelma remained loyal. She did little things to please—bringing Allegra glasses of water as she cooked, finding a misplaced spice or stepping on a stool to pull a stray hair from the woman's mouth.

"Stop it," Nina would say. "You look at her like she's the Madonna. Don't be confused. She's not. She's only my mama."

"That's plenty for me," said Thelma, not recognizing the difference and disregarding the warning. She was now part of a pack, joining the girls as they leaned out of the third-floor windows, their stomachs bolstered on bed pillows. They watched the men prepare for the Giglio feast, hammering temporary platforms and hanging streamers that arced over the narrow street, transforming the neighborhood into a party that lasted twelve days. Giorgio danced behind them, asking, "When will it start? When will it start?"

Trulia and Gabriela ranked the barrel-chested workers down below, choosing between them like ice cream flavors, trading them like baseball cards—but ducking down whenever the males looked up to discover the source of the giggling. In contrast, Thelma had given up on males, content to watch others play the game in hopes she would eventually learn the rules. She preferred being at the center of the girl storm, finding safety in the pack where she no longer stuck out.

Freed from worry only blocks from Annie and Mama, she gazed up and out with new eyes, saw white clouds floating in crisp blue sky above; below, the food stands took shape and gained paint, garish yellow and red stripes, banners proclaiming "clams," "pizza," and "*braciole*." Just to say that word felt good in her mouth—*braciole*—the way it rolled off her tongue as if she knew the whole language. She began to talk more with her hands, to shout and pinch, bargain and brag. Now she shimmied her hips when she walked, imitating Gabriela, the prettiest of the sisters, and yet no match for the beauty of Giorgio, the only son.

When Mama Allegra wearied of them underfoot, she'd reach to the top shelf for a glass jar containing rubber bands and thumbtacks and her household money. She'd entrust change to Trulia so they'd disappear to the pizzeria. Located around the corner, the brick oven made the restaurant Hades hot. The owner's broad-shouldered son with the girlish waist tied a red bandanna around his head like a pirate to catch his sweat and had the nervous habit of licking the twist of his wispy mustache with the tip of his tongue.

Thelma, emboldened by the pack, would strike up a conversation with anybody, asking the youth at the oven if he was married. When he said no, she asked him why not—and offered him Trulia, cheap, just for a pizza.

"I'll take her for a pizza," said an old man resting in the back, ice cubes tied with a rag around his forehead and water dripping down his long nose. "I'll even give you two!"

"You're too generous," Thelma said.

"I'm not that hungry," laughed Trulia.

"What about you, *bella bella*?" Thelma asked an old widow in black who stood waiting for ices with three grandchildren tugging at her hem.

"What about me, what?" asked the widow, pausing to request two rainbow and a lime.

"Do you like this handsome man here with the runny nose?" Thelma raised her eyebrows. "He has some years on those tires yet."

"I'm off the market," said the woman. And then she eyed the young man behind the counter and raised her eyebrows. "Or maybe not."

Thelma had begun to feel freer again, like a young girl, having found not only refuge but joy in Nina's family. "Love is in the air."

Gabriela snorted. "No wonder it stinks in here."

Chapter 13

Brooklyn, 1915

That July, and the two that followed, the feast days in Nina's neighborhood offered Thelma an escape from Hooper Street, which was only a ten-minute walk away. The annual Our Lady of Mount Carmel celebration transformed the neighborhood of narrow streets into an outdoor party, the air thick with the smell of sausage and peppers grilling, and the vinegary sweat of men standing shoulder to shoulder supporting the Giglio. This, Thelma discovered, was a monumental papier-mâché-and-wood tower, the centerpiece of a celebration with roots in Naples, Italy.

The imposing seven-story structure included a platform a full twelve feet above street level that supported a twelve-piece band, a singer, and the parish priest. Underneath, a network of poles radiated out in four directions. The 112 *paranza*, or lifters, young and old and older, wearing white shirts with red sashes, shouldered the beams. And then, together, legs planted, they hefted the gigantic float with a universal grunt to encouraging shouts from their peers and admonishments by the year's *capo*, a burly, tri-chinned man with a baton, clearly accustomed to yelling and being obeyed. That the task was challenging was visible in the furrowed brows and pulsing veins of the men as they raised the monument and briefly danced down the street before the audible squawks as they replaced it.

Thelma vibrated with the tension of the crowd, caught between terror that the tower would topple, squashing the neighbors standing in such close proximity, and awe at the strength of the united community of men protecting them from possible disaster. She joined with the throng on North Eighth Street calling out "lift, lift" to the *paranza*, the muscled neighborhood men, who raised the tower on their shoulders while, above, the band began to play.

The beat thrummed in Thelma's stomach and she, too, began to dance, her feet shuffling in the small square of space below her, her fingers entwined on one side with Nina's, while holding Giorgio's wrist with the other. Trulia and Gabriela had disappeared with their boy-friends and left the younger children unattended, with many warnings about what would befall them if they misbehaved; all the while it was the older girls shirking their responsibility. Sweat pouring down their brows in the July heat, the trio shouted "lift, lift" in unison with those around them. Thelma envied a curly-headed little girl bouncing hap-pily to the music atop her father's shoulders while she ate a *gelato* that dribbled on the man's straw hat.

Right then, Thelma wanted to be Italian, speak Italian, and marry Italian. But she'd never admit that to Nina. She feared her friend would withdraw her affection. It was too much closeness for the thirteen-year-olds. This was that girl's neighborhood, not Thelma's. She didn't want to poach—but she did desire to know the names of the men who bore the tower, to climb onstage with the singer in the white suit with the lily boutonniere. While he was the man they'd heard earlier chastising the band during rehearsal, now he was the proud focus of all attention, his black hair slicked back above a large forehead, confident as he crooned out over the audience. He planted his feet like a sailor on a ship at high seas and waved at the crowd before turning the backs of his hands out as if conjuring their excitement. He was a man she wouldn't notice twice in the pizza parlor. But there, on the stage held aloft by over a hundred men, Thelma wanted to join the sweet-voiced stranger made suave by his sway over the crowd—and dance for him.

Thelma hadn't even noticed that Giorgio had threaded his arm around her waist until he recoiled when Nina pinched his hand, hard, and he cried out. "He's fine," Thelma said.

"He's a pest," said Nina.

Afterward, they took their pooled pennies and nickels, even a quarter that Thelma had mooched off Abie, and felt like royalty, buying more food than they could eat, Thelma sampling a clam and spitting it out on the ground as if she'd tasted mud, without regret over the penny it cost her. They played games of chance, throwing balls into water-filled jars to try to capture a goldfish that neither mother would let them keep and shooting air rifles at deer leaping in the air and hearing the ricochet of their misses.

Thelma never wanted the day to stop—and then the greased-pole competition began. Jews didn't do this: Tests of strength out in the open for everyone to see? What would they think of next, these Italians? They tied sausages to the top of a tall pole slathered with oil, and tan guys flexed their muscles climbing toward the meat. One by one they ascended, slipping and slithering and hugging on for dear life, their lips pouted sideways to avoid a mouthful of goo. Sometimes they tried as a team, with one man standing at the base, the next mounting his shoulders, and a third with his feet on the previous man's head until yet another scrambled up his friends' strong backs—inevitably tumbling back into the crowd. Neighbors screamed encouragement as time and again the seekers crept up, only to slide back down covered in filth, mocked by friends and enemies alike.

Suddenly Giorgio broke away and rushed through the crowd. Nina elbowed Thelma and said, "Watch this! Tonight we eat the best sausage in Brooklyn!"

Grabbing Thelma's hand, Nina followed. When they got to the clearing, they found her little brother eyeing the pole. He pointed to the sausages and cried, "Who wants dinner?"

The spectators roared. "Me! Me!"

Leaping like a trapeze artist, Giorgio cupped the pole below him with the soles of his feet, his arms hugging the wood. Thelma smiled, feeling pride in the boy who inchwormed up as the crowd began to chant, "Giorgio! Giorgio!"

When he lost his grip and slid down a man's length, Thelma gasped with the crowd. Her stomach twisted as Giorgio climbed, hoping he would be spared the humiliation of tumbling, fearing grave injuries.

Refusing to surrender to gravity, Giorgio rose again, bit by bit, toes grabbing. An arm's length from his goal, he paused. The crowd roared, chanting his name. He reached one arm over the other and hoisted himself to the top.

"Gigantiello," he cried, slinging down sausages to the cheering, scrambling crowd. Afterward, he swooshed down in one motion to pose at the bottom, as triumphant as a prizefighter. "I am the winner," he said, laughing, slathered with grease, grabbing the ten-pound sausage that was his reward. "I am the wiener."

Nina and Thelma jumped up and down, laughing and poking each other and crying, "Gigantiello!"

Returning home, they let Giorgio swagger ahead of them. Despite his greasiness, Mama Allegra hugged him tight, saying, "You are the best boy in the neighborhood." Then she turned and found the twine, cutting a length with a large and deadly pair of shears. She tied it to the sausage, hanging the trophy out the window overlooking North Eighth.

By the next year, when Giorgio ascended the greased pole, his sisters were nowhere in sight. They had left the apartment as a pack—the dark-haired Gigantiello girls and their blond baby brother. But when they reached the sidewalk, Trulia and Gabriela scurried to meet their boyfriends, who were gambling in the church hall basement, while Nina met her Antonio. The son of a postman didn't look like much. At least he was tall. Tonio walked beside Nina with pride as if her ample bosom were his, which in a way it was. Nobody would bother to look at his sallow features when he stood beside such a magnificent chest.

Thelma begged Nina to stay beside them, but the couple had other arrangements. What a difference a year made, particularly with Giorgio. He now towered over Thelma, awkward in his unfamiliar body. Thelma hardly noticed that he'd become quiet around her, no longer teasing or tickling. She looped her arm through his so the horde couldn't separate them. Together they watched the Giglio dance through the crush, the hoarse shriek as a man fainted beneath the platform and was trampled by his neighbor before being carried away on a stretcher.

Afterward, they ate grilled corn, blackened on the outside, until the butter dripped down their chins and they wiped the slop off with the back of their hands. It was so sweet and fresh it could have been dessert. He paid with hoarded change from who knew where. The pair pitched pennies into jars without luck. They strolled to the air rifles, where the barker had a curled mustache that stretched from his nose hair to the tufts at his ears. When their turn came, Thelma flubbed it pathetically while Giorgio hit the moving target every time and won the girl beside him a kewpie doll with a hideous grin. That was when she first became aware that these weren't younger-brother affections. The attention felt so good that she couldn't reject it, pretending she was protecting his feelings. It was the Giglio, after all. Nothing that happened during those twelve days was real.

The afternoon steamed. The sun hung high in the sky. Everywhere tired children cried, tugging away from their parents, falling in fits on the filthy ground. Heading for the greased pole, Thelma and Giorgio cut through the human snarl. Giorgio led, his hand extended back for Thelma's. Her sweaty palm embarrassed her, but she surrendered it. After all, he was only Nina's little brother, only Giorgio.

As the pair entered the circle surrounding the beam, they heard a young man in free fall, yelling, "The sausage is mine," as he tumbled. There was an unnerving crunch when the bricklayer's son hit the street only a few feet away from them. His right arm bent up and back unnaturally. A white bone shard poked through his dark skin. Thelma turned her face away, holding tighter to Giorgio's hand.

The crowd surged forward, seemingly split between concern for the laborer's son, who now might be unable to help his father, and the desire for some local hero to appear before anybody else got hurt. Seeing Giorgio, the crowd's mood shifted. He dropped Thelma's hand, nodded to the judge sweating in his summer suit, spit on each palm, rubbed them together, and confronted the pole.

Filled with pride, Thelma retreated to the front row of spectators, where a shabby widow tugged her waistband for restricting her view and cursed her in Italian. The humidity suffocated. Ominous clouds bunched up above.

Last year, Giorgio the boy had beaten the men, but now he, too, carried a man's body. She wondered if he would be able to shinny up so quickly without falling like the bricklayer's son. He began by climbing up the backs of the trio who had launched the previous climber. Ascending without haste, he made it seem easy. Crouching on the shoulders of the top man in the totem pole, he extended with all his body height, pushing off with his feet and advancing arm over arm, leg over leg. Just when he was about to hoist himself up to the top, his left foot slipped and then his right, splashing pitch gobs into the crowd. Disappointed, Thelma swallowed her breath. He'd come so close. And, then, exhaling, she shouted, "Giorgio! Giorgio!" and the old lady next to her picked up the cry in a shrill voice, and it rippled through the crowd so that even strangers from distant neighborhoods who had no idea who the boy was, or that he was last year's champion, joined in.

Frogging his knees up, Giorgio grabbed the pole with his thighs. He swayed backward to wipe away the sweat and then reached up with sinewy arms, revealing his hairy armpits, then scooching his legs behind him. He slid then recovered and lunged, taking the top, his face covered in pitch. He began to rain sausages down on the crowd, which now throbbed, "Giorgio! Giorgio!"

As he slid down like a fireman racing to extinguish a blaze, Thelma skipped forward, hurdling the kids grappling for spoils. They were winners! When she reached Giorgio, pitch and blood streaked his right cheek. She went to dab the spot with her hankie as he leaned down. He kissed her pop on the mouth. She started, handkerchief still raised. This was Giorgio! But it wasn't. She briefly tasted oil and salt before the judge separated the pair unceremoniously with a ten-pound sausage.

As they returned to the Gigantiellos', Giorgio's arm encircled Thelma's waist, but when they turned the corner and became visible from the upstairs windows, she shook him loose, afraid of what Mama Allegra, who missed nothing, might think.

Chapter 14

The feast created a temporary topsy-turvy world in the neighborhood but, afterward, the Madonna returned to her niche inside the church, the men warehoused the Giglio for repairs, and life returned to normal. The summer passed, and without Thelma's encouragement, Giorgio kept to himself. When his sisters went out in a group, he often stayed away, joining neighbors in elaborate games of hide-and-seek among the narrow streets that lasted until their mothers called them in to dinner and continued immediately afterward until bedtime.

That fall, Thelma attended her final school year. She was smart enough but had a mouth, she'd been told, that begged to be scoured with soap. She despised the fussy Mrs. Hammerstein, who saturated herself in sweet gardenia perfume and wore her hair with a ruler-straight middle part. The geography teacher made them spend class silently etching detailed maps with colored pencils and rewarding with gold stickers those who drew added doodads, ships, monuments, or dolphins. Thelma didn't need to know Venezuela's shape or its major exports—and she didn't care who knew about it. That didn't make her teacher's pet.

Instead, Thelma wanted to earn money, buy stockings, and cut loose. Most weeknights she ascended to Trulia's insurance office over the pizza parlor for mechanical typewriter lessons. Typing was the only sport in which she excelled, reaching seventy-five words per minute over time. In contrast, Trulia didn't like to rush or ruin her nails, so she'd save her daily correspondence and let Thelma complete it with fewer errors. That way Thelma could contribute while learning a practical skill. She appreciated the concentration: when her fingers were moving, she stopped thinking about anything else, embracing the challenge of being swift without mistakes. While Trulia bribed her with bread and cheese and then plopped nearby reading a *Photoplay*, Thelma pounded the keys, feeling competent and modern.

As Thanksgiving approached, Trulia casually dropped the fact that Nina was pregnant, as if it were a *Photoplay* spread, expecting Thelma to know already. She didn't. Angry, she went the next day after school to confront Nina but stopped short when she noticed that the girl was pale and green and seemed to be swallowing back either tears or bile. Nina sat with a hot-water bottle tucked behind her lower back, solemn with double bags beneath her pleading brown eyes and a single braid down her back. Thelma teased her that she would go to any length to escape Mrs. Hammerstein. How could she survive without knowing the capital of Uruguay?

"Montevideo," the fourteen-year-old Nina sobbed, fleeing toward the back bedrooms, the rear of her dress damp, looking so much like the little girl Thelma had often chased and tagged on the playground. Nina didn't have time to explain how she could let this happen before they'd finished school or the question that plagued Thelma: How come Nina didn't tell her first? She could understand falling asleep beside Tonio, because no boy was duller—but how did this baby thing happen?

Thelma encouraged Nina, who was hardly showing, to escape with her, but the girl rarely strayed from the apartment above the Knights of Columbus, which meant that Mama Allegra hovered nearby with aunts and grandmothers and widowed sages in the childbearing arts. This infant was to be the first grandchild, and the women circled around to protect the eldest of that new generation of cousins, praying for a boy. Nina sat in the middle of the flurry of knitting and crocheting, listening to one childbirth story after the next with what appeared to be a rising dread, disappearing into dullness as the baby slowly began to take shape. As a warning, the elders had told her the story of a young Italian woman crushed during a demonstration on the streets of Brooklyn, so Nina became deathly afraid of crowds. She hardly ventured outside.

One afternoon Nina yanked Thelma into the bathroom and shut the door. "I'm choking, Temmy. I don't know who I am anymore."

"You're Nina! Who else would you be?"

"They've taken over my body and I don't have any choice."

"What can I do to help?"

"I don't know. Have this baby for me?"

"Not going to happen."

"Is it possible to be smothered by love?"

Thelma shook her head, not that she'd ever experienced it. Nina's plea was a message in a bottle—and, after that, the old Nina all but vanished. Feeling abandoned, Thelma resented the situation, but there was no longer any room for her on the couch playing with her friend. She couldn't fight the black-dressed widows who side-eyed the outsider as they closed the circle around the pregnant child. She didn't knit. She didn't sew. And her attempts to cheer her friend up with wicked tales from school brought scowls from their elders and a longing look in Nina's eyes. "I never thought I'd miss math," Nina confided before racing to the bathroom with one hand over her mouth.

The week before Christmas, Nina married Tonio in the modest chapel at Our Lady of Mount Carmel. Her small, round head stuck out of a big, fluffy white dress that suited her like frosting on a plum. With sugary, angelic smiles on their faces, her jealous older sisters surrounded Nina as she approached the groom, who puffed out his sunken chest at the altar, standing beside his brothers as if it were an undertakers' convention. Thelma felt awkward in her loud polka-dotted party dress borrowed from Trulia, her bra stuffed with socks to make it fit, uneasy about being under Jesus's roof. Strangers sat beside her beneath his martyred gaze, nailed as he was to the cross above the altar, and confusion set in when those around her knelt during the long Mass. She didn't know what to do, so she gazed up at the marble Madonna in her niche coddling her infant son and hoped that benevolent lady would be kind to Nina, however skeptical Thelma felt about a life with Tonio. To her surprise, she felt like the woman responded, assuring her that Nina would be fine. Thelma wouldn't admit to anyone that the Virgin Mary had seemed to address her, and yet it had a calming effect.

Afterward, the family catered the lasagna dinner, while Tonio's uncle provided the cake for the church hall reception. One man after the next stood up to toast the couple, praising the sanctity of marriage and the bride's virtue, while Thelma sat at the children's table attempting to keep Trulia's polka-dotted dress clean from the flying food. After the cake, she tried to thread her way to the bride, but she only managed to stick the cash-filled envelope Abie had given her into Nina's *borsa*, her satin pouch, before Nina was snatched in another direction by Tonio's strict father.

Immediately after the ceremony, the groom moved into the Gigantiellos' so that the women could usher Nina through pregnancy, leaving little space for Thelma. She couldn't stifle her anger at Nina for leaving girlhood—and her—behind so suddenly. Without regular visits, Thelma's bitterness soured their friendship as much as Nina's exhaustion and the gap in their situations.

She slunk back to Hooper Street, half a mile and a world away, crawling into bed beside Mama. The springs croaked. She recoiled, afraid of waking the sleeping giant thrashing beside her. It was cruel to notice the whisker that sprouted on a mole above her lip but there it was, waving in the wheeze. On the bedside table, a glass of baking soda and water awaited late-night indigestion.

Loneliness stuck in Thelma's throat, and she tried to spit it out. She'd felt secure with the Italians, but now? With her brothers launched in the world, no one understood her here. Moe had seemed to care, but that had been a trick. She'd been a chump. She smacked her forehead. She was a freak, a problem, not a person.

She missed Mama Allegra's care. At Nina's she'd felt wanted. Even if she resented that it had to end, she didn't entirely blame her friend: their changing bodies betrayed them before they were fully aware of what was happening. Sure, Nina's sisters had warned the younger girls, but how many times could you tell a child not to scratch an itch? Sooner or later they always did and there would be blood and blisters and scabs, bandages and scars, possibly a kiss to make it feel better, possibly not.

She needed to unload to Nina, but she cared enough to know that bigger problems plagued her friend. Thelma suspected Nina worried not only about the unborn infant poking her innards with unseen elbows but also about yoking herself to the first boy who walked out with her during the Giglio. She'd gone too far too soon and was too good a girl to deny the consequences. Perhaps there was a shy boy who'd been watching, and waiting, who would have been a partner for Nina a few years down the road. Now he'd never get the chance. Thelma wondered if that might have prompted the fear in Nina's eyes: that Tonio was a good match for her family but not for her.

Thelma tried to imagine Nina and her together in the future, with or without babies. Bolstered by Mama Allegra, Nina would be a good mother. Thelma hoped she would be as well, but she lacked Nina's patience, her obedience—and she had Mama beside her, a constant reminder that she wasn't good enough. Stuck and frustrated, she feared becoming an adult too soon like Nina but resisted reverting to this stifling childhood. She was a curiosity, not a kid but not yet a woman.

Over time, awake in the dull, dark hours as Mama slept, Thelma waited for her body to change beneath her cotton undershirt. A few hairs sprouted in one armpit, then the other. The left breast softened and grew, shaming its stunted sibling, still hardly more than a bud above protruding ribs. She would have arisen to pee, drink water, watch the moonrise over Hooper Street—but she feared bumping into Moe, who now came and went at odd, unpredictable hours.

Mama Allegra had warned Thelma to avoid her stepfather, calling him that harsh word, degenerate, *degenerato*, which clashed with the mild-mannered daytime Moe. But the apartment was too small to dodge him, and the continued hostility of Annie and Mama that had begun long before the stepfather's arrival worsened the situation. Mama Allegra had told her to make peace, but how?

One night, after squashing a relentless mosquito drawn to her sweet blood, she curved into a fetal position and drowsed. She dreamed of running through the Giglio pursued by boys flinging firecrackers. Jerking awake, she stared directly into her mother's eyes, which conveyed a searing hatred. Mama's raw hostility slapped her, and she hadn't had the time to raise her defenses. She considered what Mrs. Gigantiello would do—and sought peace by treating her mother with tenderness. "What's wrong, Mama?"

"Nothing," Mama said, flopping away.

"Please, tell me, did I do something wrong?"

"What didn't you do wrong?"

Silence snapped between them. Panic spread through Thelma's chest: she wasn't good enough. Now Mama would remind her why, gouging her weak spots. She would snap, attack, and prove her mother's point. The snake ate its tail or, as Mama Allegra explained, *il serpente si mangiò la coda*. Anger begets anger.

Upstairs in the neighbors' apartment, hinges squawked and a couple began sawing against each other. A gasp followed as if someone squashed a cat. Then the door above opened and shut again. She would have giggled if she were with Nina, but not now. "Is this still about Moe? I'm no Mata Hari, Mama. Why didn't you protect me?"

"I should have protected him from you!" Mama flipped back toward Thelma, eyes enraged. "I should have thrown you out a long time ago. I was glad you left. You stole him from my bed."

"Did you want him here?"

"He was mine, not yours."

She wanted to say *who would want you?* It was ready to fling off the tip of her tongue, yet she held back. "Then why isn't he here instead of me?"

"You ruined him, you slut."

The words stung and bees buzzed inside her head so that she could hardly hear what her mother was saying. Breathing deep, Thelma looked up at the ceiling. She struggled to restrain her voice when she wanted to scream and scratch. "Please, Mama, don't pick on me. Can't you see I'm trying to help? I made a mistake. I'm sorry. I can't change what happened."

"You're still a dirty husband thief."

Thelma rose up on her knees and pointed. "You brought Moe into our family, not me. Shouldn't he have protected me like a father in my own house? If he's a devil, is that my fault?"

"How dare you accuse him?" Mama snorted, and then she belched, raising her hand to her sternum. She'd begun to sweat. "Who do you think you are?"

"I'm your daughter, Mama."

"No," she spat, wriggling back to raise her head on her pillow. "You're not. Annie's my daughter." The young girl yelped, but the mother continued, "She's loyal. You and the boys do what you want, say what you want, behave like animals, so you get what you deserve. Go live with the Italians, if they're so fond of you. Get out!"

"They're not my family, Mama."

"So they don't want you, either?"

"Why do you hate me? All I want, Mama, is a little bit of the love you have for Annie. Is that too much to ask?"

"Yes." Mama stiffened. "You think you've got it rough?"

She didn't know how to answer. Yes. She thought she had it rough. Night after night sharing a bed where there was no rest, no affection.

Before she'd hungered for something she didn't know—a mother's love for her daughter—but now that she knew how it could be, she didn't know how to get there with her own mother. Part of her insisted it was the mother's responsibility to create and maintain that connection, but that wasn't how it was between them. She tried to retreat when she said, "I'm not complaining," but somehow it came out as defiant.

Mama sucked her teeth. "You're always *kvetching*. Look at you: born in America, clothes on your back, food on the table, a roof over your head, a mother and father, a sister and brothers, and still you piss in the soup."

"*Mamaleh*, I'll try harder." She was young, but she could be the bigger person. A little crawling wasn't impossible if afterward she could stand taller. She was capable of the greater love. "Please, I beg you, what can I say? What can I do to make you love me?"

"You *putz*, there's nothing you can do. You aren't my daughter."

"That's a lie," Thelma said, but a blade couldn't have cut as deep as that rejection. Her mother's confession shattered Thelma like cheap glass right when she'd tried to compose herself. Mama treated Papa's death like a personal tragedy, but his loss had devastated them all, and their mother had ignored her children when they needed her most.

Fatherlessness had defined Thelma. That shadow never disappeared, no matter how high the sun. She hungered for the man she'd never known, the one capable of explaining why she was the way she was. Affection starved, she craved all men, seeking hugs whether appropriate or not. And that was why in those jagged bits of her heart she believed she deserved Moe, the only father she'd known, the man who'd loved her with his hands, not his heart.

She inhaled shallowly to ease her nausea and then felt suffocated. There was no safe place. She knew neither mother nor father. She was an orphan, unlovable, the sight of her unbearable. She realized that was what she'd always seen reflected in her mother's eyes: disgust and rejection. They hadn't bonded because she was nothing to her mother. She would have been better off with Abie and Louis at the Hebrew Home for the Unloved.

Mama now cried loudest, as if what she'd said hurt her more than it did the broken girl beside her. The girl wept, too, sharing the sagging bed but remaining separate. Thelma could have consoled Mama, offering kindness in adversity. But she desperately needed comforting herself. She was the motherless child. She heard Mama's voice catching, the muffled trumpet when she blew her nose. From next door, Annie banged on the wall. "Shut up. We're trying to sleep."

"I must have done something horribly bad to deserve such cruelty, but what can a baby do so wrong? It's not fair."

"You want fair, see a judge. Let Abie introduce you," Mama said. "You always make an elephant out of a fly."

"But this *is* an elephant."

Thelma cursed Papa for leaving her with these shrews. She climbed out of bed, left the room, saw Moe sit up on the couch and splay his legs. Speeding past him to the bathroom, she sat on the pot, stood up, splashed water on her face, and returned to bed. She saw Mama's pale profile, tears reflected in the moonlight.

Much later, as dawn rose, Mama began gasping for air. She kicked her feet. She clutched her breastbone, coughing wetly.

Let her die. But Thelma couldn't.

"Sit back," Thelma said, creeping off the mattress and tiptoeing to the bedside table. She stirred the baking soda mixture. Settling beside Mama, Thelma cradled the woman's head while she drank the chalky liquid, as if Mama were the little sister and she the mother.

Kindness and caring were her only escape. She would show them how capable she was. Maybe then they'd appreciate her. She had to be better than they were, because if she became like Mama and Annie, what was the point? She refused to let them twist and taint who she was. Reaching over, Thelma grabbed her pillow and propped up her mother. Her head raised, the older woman fell asleep within minutes.

As the room got lighter, Thelma curled up, resting her cheek on her praying hands.

The next morning, she awoke by herself. The sun hung high in the sky; laundry sagged from the clothesline. Her first thought: *I'm unlovable.* Whatever hope she'd had nursing Mama had faded. She was alone. No one would come and inquire how she was, braid her hair, rub her temples. When she got up, threw on her clothes, and entered the living room, Moe was already gone and she could hear Mama clattering in the kitchen. Seated on the sofa, Annie wrestled Julius's arm into his sleeve. She glanced at her sister with amusement in her eyes and snorted. "Well, if it isn't the Grand Duchess Anastasia! Can I pour you your tea, Your Majesty?"

Chapter 15

By the time Thelma was fifteen, Abie and Louis used the Hooper Street address only to register for the draft. They were adults navigating New York, and although Thelma begged to accompany them, their impatient expressions told her she would be a burden in their chaotic outside lives. They claimed they couldn't protect her and that her moment would come, but the rejection still stung.

She was anxious for the time when she, too, could leave but, for now, after years of wandering, the family had taken root in Brooklyn. "I'm not going anywhere," Annie had said with apparent pride, admiring Julius and Adele. Her sister's declaration seemed more a threat than a promise to Thelma, too young to become financially independent and too sharp (given Nina's enslavement to an annual pregnancy and the constant demands of small children when she was hardly more than a child herself) to view marriage as an escape.

She could depend on Annie to be a *farbissiner*, a grump with a whiplike tongue, but also to keep house and tend Mama. Even when Thelma fled to the Italians, which she did less frequently now that Nina had become a mother with a wife's responsibilities, she didn't worry that her folks would disappear in the night—although she frequently wished they would. As for her brothers, they'd typically return for Shabbos supper. On Friday nights, they'd arrive together, hike up their pants, and relax. They'd bow their heads as Mama lit the tapers on the silver candlesticks (a gift from Abie), mumbling the weekly prayers beside Moe, arguing politics and battling Thelma over the wishbone.

Sometimes Mama reserved dinner, scorching the chicken, but neither son surfaced. A furious Annie would curse those *no-goodniks*, galling Thelma: Abie was a criminal, corrupting Louis, who, the eldest insisted, wasn't quiet but slow and impressionable. One was quick with a knife, the other overly fond of guns. Thelma knew that on the street Abie occasionally broke the law, but at home, where it mattered most, he protected her when Annie and Mama didn't. She felt disloyal if she didn't defend her brothers. But without allies at the table, she didn't risk raising Annie's hackles and becoming her next victim—"Is that a pimple on your *schnoz*, or is that a room divider?"

When Abie and Louis did come home, they bore presents, proving they weren't poor relations: cakes in string-wrapped pink boxes and Joyva chocolate-covered halvah or, responding to relentless nagging, an electric iron for Annie, who craved everything new.

Recently Louis had quit the newsstand to guard the Grand Theatre's stage door near Chrystie Street in Lower Manhattan, surrounding himself with chorus girls. He never discussed his personal life, no matter how much Annie grilled him: "Got a girlfriend? She must be blind! When are you bringing her to meet the family?"

Louis would shrug his shoulders. He stonewalled Annie, preoccupied by the Great War. The German troops advanced while the British failed to take Gaza. He joined public demonstrations, striding to City Hall Park, where, in March, former ambassador James Gerard proclaimed, "We are on the brink of war with Germany."

When he turned twenty-one in May, Louis announced his commitment to defend America. In contrast, twenty-three-year-old Abie was in no rush. He claimed he'd had his fill of institutions, whether orphanage or army. Never again would he let anyone tell him when to piss or how to shine his shoes. If his teeth fell out from not brushing after meals, he'd put 'em in a bag and buy new ones.

While Abie officially referred to himself as a newsboy, he'd diversified. He still protected Lazarus & Sons, where his six-year-old nephew, Julius, had now joined his father hawking papers. Housing the bookie racket opened up a spectrum of criminal activity to Abie, joining the shysters and *goniffs* operating south of Union Square. And he'd proved with that Rothman kid that he was no pushover.

Crime suited Abie. And he wasn't an aberration among the *yidlach*, who tended toward crimes of property rather than passion. He appreciated variety, a little bit of this and a little bit of that. He liked every day different—some days burglary, others *shlamming* for the garment union when the bosses introduced scabs or clubbing strikers if the bosses paid more. Sometimes he'd say he had to meet a guy about a thing, a friend of Lepke or Gurrah, which could mean a shakedown or a robbery, nothing complicated. *In and out,* he'd say, *one, two, three.* He acted as a courier for skulls like Monk Eastman and performed some conflict resolution that could involve words or fists. People talked to him; he was that kind of guy, a *kibitzer*. And he'd sell what he knew, maybe stopping by the cop shop that took a piece of the newsstand and prepaying for some future infraction. He had friends everywhere but, he told Thelma, he wasn't confused. He could only trust her and Louis—and that made her feel important.

The newsstand and the permanent address were good investments, making him appear to have ties to the community, which never hurt with the law. So, in that respect, he and Annie had common interests. And since his cash helped underwrite her household, he didn't appreciate it when she nagged him about his new suits or pinkie ring. She'd criticize him for making the Jewish people look bad, but that didn't keep her from lobbying for a bigger house for her growing family.

If Annie pushed too hard, he'd grab his crotch and tell her to go bake a cake. If he was going to come home on Friday nights, he preferred to discuss taking dates to see a Douglas Fairbanks or Charlie Chaplin picture at Broadway's Rialto Theatre with a full pit orchestra. Even when prodded, he wouldn't name his girlfriends.

This refusal enraged Annie, who lashed out, "No good girl would date you more than once, Abraham."

"Who said anything about good girls?"

While Abie was enjoying himself, Louis was antsy awaiting America's entry into the fray. In April, President Woodrow Wilson obliged, declaring war on Germany. On June 5, the brothers went together, compelled to register for the draft, joining ten million other American men. They filled in the blanks—white, medium build, no dependents: the only visible difference between them was that Louis was two inches taller than Abie's five foot two. And his eyes were gray, not brown.

Having registered at the local draft board, the brothers lingered on the stoop with Thelma, bringing two beers and a sack of lemon drops, reluctant to go inside. Louis seemed energized, as if his world were cracking open. Meanwhile, Abie was unusually quiet, saying, "I'm not really a khaki kind of guy."

"We have to do our duty."

The thought of their going overseas shredded Thelma. She needed them all together. She sucked on a lemon drop, hard, to keep from crying. They were all tired of her tears, no one more than she was, but the goopy suckers formed at the inside corners of her eyes and threatened to tip out over her lower lashes. She was embarrassed, sitting outside, that strangers would see her and judge. She felt panicked, like the boys, her boys, were already gone, the way one day they'd been at home to protect her from that beast Annie and the next day disappeared into the orphanage. She breathed, feeling what it was to still sit beside Abie with Louis at her back. How this was something good in her life. She reached out to take Abie's hand. Instead, he passed her his beer. And even that had an intimacy she appreciated. What was his was hers. She didn't have to ask. And yet, she sensed a growing distance that she tried to dispel with a swig of his bitter adult brew.

Louis, who typically stood, the sentinel, sat down on the other side of Thelma and took her hand in his. He had nice hands, with square fingertips and a strong grip. It was as if he sent her love through his touch. She'd been so self-involved that she hadn't noticed something new about Louis, how much he'd grown into a handsome man she would have smiled at on the street if they were strangers. He'd become a person separate from his brother, the quiet man who watched and listened, who didn't care about opinions. Actions were everything to him and all of hers were loyal; the pressure of his fingers told her that.

As much as she didn't want to be a damper on Louis's rare high spirits, the idea of their leaving her behind permanently terrified her. What if they died under enemy fire? What if they came home in a box? She wouldn't have a family without them. And she knew that only then would Annie praise them, hypocrite that she was.

She reached her free hand out and when Abie handed her the beer, saying, "Go easy," she shook her head no.

"Don't leave me," she said.

"I'm too short for the army," Abie said. "They'll throw me back."

"There's something fishy to that story," Louis said.

"Did you just make a joke?" Abie asked. "We should register every day!" Thelma could tell her brothers were trying to be funny for her sake. It wasn't working.

"You won't like it, Louis," Thelma said. "They'll force you to salute and make your bed, Private."

"At least I'll have my own bed, unlike some of us," he said.

"You never know," said Thelma. "Mama may come along with you."

"Nope: Annie's the killer," Abie said.

"We've been trained by the best, Abie. We've been battling that bitch all our lives. What's boot camp after the Hebrew Orphan Asylum?"

Abie made a noise, a cross between a swallow and a harrumph. "I've never hated anybody like I hated her that first night, not even the Huns," Abie said. "If curses could kill, she'd have been dead five times over. When she finally showed up to gloat, I was surprised to see her alive."

"By then, we didn't give a shit."

"We'd met scarier people than Annie."

"What happened?" Thelma asked, digging her elbows into her thighs and cradling her chin in her hands.

"Some kid crapped in our cots."

"That stinks," said Thelma, wrinkling her nose. "But it's better than sharing Mama's bed."

"I'd take her hairbrushes any day," Abie said. "This was no prank."

"The big boys were gunning for Abie and me."

"There was a guy with one eye and an empty socket—Blinky."

"Another, Floppy, had the bottom half of his ear bitten off."

"The thugs asked us who wanted to go first. Louis asked them what they were talking about."

"I was just a kid. They snickered. Then they dropped their pants and wiggled their *schlongs* at us."

"So I said, 'It's kosher weenie night,' mouthing off, acting like the big *macher* I wasn't. But I blamed Annie, not those boys. They weren't doing this to us. She was."

"So we sat on the floor . . ."

". . . back-to-back on the cold concrete all night. Didn't sleep a wink," said Abie.

"I could barely keep my eyes open, but I felt Abie awake through my back, and when he felt my head drop, he'd shove me with his shoulder."

"And, then, on the third night . . ."

"I just couldn't keep my eyes open," said Louis. "I started to slide and all of a sudden . . ."

". . . wham!" Abie clapped his hands. Thelma jumped.

"Someone was hovering. I'd fallen asleep."

"Not me."

"Abie struck—bang—like a cobra."

"Blinky was never gonna see again."

"Abie saved me."

"I bought us some time, that's all."

"So, Temmy, if you wanna know how we got so tough . . ."

". . . or why we hate kosher hot dogs . . ."

"That's the story."

From above and behind, a window slammed open. Annie stuck her head out and shrilled, "What, are you going to keep me waiting all day? Come up already."

Abie spat. "Like we said . . ."

". . . the army's going to be a cakewalk," Louis concluded.

Chapter 16

That summer of '17, the army plastered posters all over Williamsburg. One showed a gruesome gorilla wielding a club in his right hand, while a swooning damsel, her breasts exposed, languished in his left. The message: "Destroy This Mad Brute: Enlist." Wartime anxiety and excitement swept Thelma's third Giglio. Uniformed men—some local, some not— cruised the festival, buttoned up early in the evenings but increasingly disheveled toward midnight. Thelma saw the soldiers' flushed faces, so full of life, and imagined those of her own brothers, gray and lifeless, with blown-off bits. It was unsettling, to say the least. But she wasn't alone. Mothers cried in public. They shot lovelorn looks at grown sons preparing to cross the Atlantic to fight after the family had struggled to root themselves in America. These women spoiled their younger boys who lingered behind while watching their daughters with a jailer's eye.

Despite Giorgio's kiss last summer, Thelma sensed he now avoided her when she went to gossip at Nina's across the head of her little girl still in diapers as she nursed the boy. The girls were in different situations now, with her friend subject to the will of her husband and his parents as well as her own. Having always been the more serious of the two, Nina now treated Thelma with patience, as if she were still a child unburdened by the obligations of being a wife and mother. When her brother came up in the conversation, Nina downplayed Giorgio's attentions and Thelma was quick to agree: she considered the smooch sweet but not serious, a practice kiss. He was Nina's kid brother, after all, the pest.

Maybe that's why her guard was down that July when he invited her to the fair. She couldn't miss it; she might as well accompany him, since Nina was tending her newborn baby boy, Enrico, the blessed first grandson, and would remain safely upstairs with her mother. Thelma buckled her good shoes and embraced that first night; after a long year, she was hungry for warm evenings when a breeze would rise and she felt like she could stay out all night and become someone new by dawn. The lights arching over North Eighth Street in brilliant curlicues gilded familiar blocks, while the brassy Giglio band inspired her to skip, not walk, hurrying toward the action. On those vibrant streets, she felt like she was in a foreign country, and yet it was also familiar—like Giorgio.

Thelma resisted linking her arm through his as the pair passed the clam bar. They followed the men carrying the plaster statue of Our Lady of Mount Carmel, which they placed in the outdoor niche where she'd remain for ten days. Thelma wasn't yet ready to celebrate Christmas, but she felt more at home here than on Hooper Street. She wouldn't confess, but she'd even come to revere the Virgin Mary: compassionate, generous, patient. What was not to love?

In sight of the Madonna, a somber Giorgio claimed Thelma's hand and laced it through his elbow, covering it with his left palm. He'd grown even more over the last year, shoulders spreading and neck thickening. By the jealous glances of the neighborhood girls, she registered that he'd become truly good-looking. She laughed, and it sounded strange and high to her, girlish in a way that embarrassed her. But she knew the baby boy lurking inside the man: she'd seen him running around in his underwear, slopping in the bathtub and weeping over a lost horse carved from soap.

They did the usual things that night: munched corn, tossed pennies, aimed air rifles. He wasn't chatty and so she filled the void discussing movies—Charlie Chaplin in *The Immigrant* and Douglas Fairbanks's

Wild and Woolly. They turned a street corner, where a band played "Goodbye Broadway, Hello France" surrounded by singing soldiers. When she asked him his favorite song, he shrugged, so she dropped it, letting the silence wash over them with the warm night.

He stopped at a relatively quiet spot down Havemeyer Street, removing a packet of sparklers. He lit two and gave her one, like a suave leading man sharing cigarettes. For a while, they faced each other making arcs of light, watching them glow and sizzle gold and bright. Oblivious, she hardly noticed anyone or anything else, although neighbors passed by, shouting greetings and asking Giorgio whether he'd win the greased pole this year. *Bring me a sausage,* they'd say. He shrugged, distracted, smiling into her eyes, forming a charmed circle between them, an isolated island of two. She removed her shoes and danced barefoot with her sparkler, creating fiery figure eights and spirals. He wrote her name in the air. She wrote his. They lit another and another, the pure luxury of it, making big circles and stars. And then he said, "Look," and she watched as he made a big heart. She smiled. He spelled the word *L-O-V-E* and, this time, she dropped her sizzled sparkler and rose on her toes to kiss the familiar cheek.

He pulled away and dragged her farther from the noise as she laughed and protested half-heartedly, his hand gripping hers so that all her blood rushed to the fingers touching his. He ducked down an alley, descending the four back stairs of a shuttered bakery. There was no pause to acknowledge the change as he twirled her around, flattening her back against the bricks with his hips. She grabbed a breath before he swooped and there was absolutely nowhere else on earth but his lips on hers. She felt the truth of his confession. His kiss communicated love, soft then urgent, as if all the words he hadn't said earlier came rushing out.

Surrendering to the thrill, she repressed her doubts. Wasn't it satisfactory to be loved for who she was, even if the feeling wasn't quite mutual? Given all she'd experienced, would she recognize love when she felt it?

In the days that followed, the Giorgio nights, she lied to herself. On North Eighth Street, the lifters danced the Giglio, the singer sang to make his mama proud, the priest prayed, old women fainted, gamblers pinned dollar bills to the Madonna's shrine. The pair returned to their spot behind the bakery earlier each night and would emerge inflamed, love bites on their necks. Sometimes they bumped into Trulia and Gabriela, who smirked at the sight and wagged their fingers.

Thelma loved the old Giorgio like a sister, which was a relationship she understood. Propelled by that kinship, she fell for the full lips, wide shoulders, and strong hands of this golden man who adored her. She was in love with love, which wasn't the same as Giorgio.

That year, the boy didn't climb the pole, didn't bring home the sausage to Mama Allegra. He made promises the world wouldn't let him keep. On the fair's final night, as the street cleaners swept the stinking garbage into piles and carpenters began to dismantle the food stalls, Thelma ascended the stairs to the Gigantiellos' apartment, having promised to return the borrowed shorthand manual to Trulia. It was strangely quiet there, as if no one was home—no one except Mama Allegra, who sat on the sofa, squinting slightly as she mended Giorgio's pajamas. She raised her eyes when Thelma entered, a little weary, and she smiled but kept her lips together as she patted the adjacent cushion. Thelma sat down. A bowl filled with green beans rested on the side table. Placing it on her lap, Thelma pinched the tips, discarding them into a rag.

The odor of rancid oil and nearly two weeks of sidewalk sausages clung to the room. Then Mama Allegra set aside her needle and thread and put her veined hands on top of Thelma's. "Stop, *carina*, we need to talk."

"Why?" Thelma tasted a metallic tang: disappointment. Mama Allegra's measured, slightly chilled tone dismayed her. "Where are Nina and the baby?"

"They're at Tonino's." Mama Allegra traced her fingertips on the girl's face, as if marking the familiar features before a journey. Resigned, she said, "I love you like a daughter."

"That can be good or bad," Thelma said with an awkward laugh. "Look at my mother."

"Not bad, good, *carina*. But hard," she said. "I need you to be loyal—like Nina, like Trulia and Gabriela."

"I *am* loyal."

"Maybe yes," she said, clasping the girl's chin and reading her eyes, "and maybe no."

"Maybe nothing: I love you more than my own mama."

"Yes, that's true, but we both know about your mama." The mother studied the girl's eyes. She shook her head. "Turn around and I'll braid your hair." She smoothed Thelma's collar, collecting the curls made antic and sticky by the humidity. Her tender fingers gentled the girl's scalp, parting the hair into two and each half into three. She combed each strand until the knots melted. Thelma's shoulders relaxed as Mama Allegra worked, brushing then braiding. "This thing with Giorgio . . ."

"It's just the summer, the feast," Thelma said, trying to sound light despite feeling caught, a fish on a hook, flapping.

"No, it's not. Not even the summer. Not even tomorrow."

Thelma opened her mouth, but no more words formed. Of course Mama Allegra knew—hadn't Gabriela and Trulia seen them? The neighborhood was a sieve. They might as well have printed an announcement in the *Brooklyn Daily Eagle*.

"He's serious about you, my boy. I know his heart even though he tries to keep this secret. He never hides things from me, and that's how I knew this is serious. He loves you and that's a dangerous thing for a boy in a man's body. Do you love my Giorgio?"

Thelma paused. That was the question. Did she love Giorgio?

Yes.

No.

She hadn't figured it out herself. She was only fifteen. Confusion was everywhere. During the feast she'd enjoyed his company with no promise of a future, and that high was the yummiest. She'd sped toward

Giorgio without brakes, as if, like the movies, his regiment left at dawn. They only had tonight. They'd last as long as the fireworks glowed. Today she had brothers. Next summer, who knew? Life's transitory nature was in the air like popular music—"Goodbye Broadway, Hello France."

She adored him. He made her heart race. He was more than the delicious darkness at the bottom of the stairs. She wanted to be there for him, too: to be that beautiful spark reflected in his eyes. If he believed, then she almost did. He was the most beautiful boy, Tarzan to her Jane.

But love? She scrambled. Against what yardstick could she measure romantic feeling? Did you know it when you felt it? Fearing she was broken, she doubted her ability to experience serious Mama Allegra–worthy emotion. She wondered if it had been burned out of her, whether Moe had twisted it. She'd loved and trusted Moe, and that exploded.

"You don't love him, Thelma, do you?"

"Please, let me think!"

"If you have to think about it, it's not true love. You'll break his heart."

"No, I won't."

"Not on purpose, no, not you. But even so it will get broken. And I'll have to glue together the pieces. Do you want to marry him?"

"I dunno."

"He knows. With all his heart, he knows."

"We're so young, Mama."

"Not too young to get into trouble." Mama Allegra pulled the first braid tightly so that it pinched.

"Where's Giorgio? Why can't he tell me himself?"

"I sent him upstate to cool off."

"Why punish him?"

"It's not punishment. He's harvesting corn at his uncle's farm."

"When's he coming back?"

"When he's back, you don't need to know."

"We haven't done anything."

"Not yet, then, but you're not the type to turn away from free *gelato*. Look at Nina, as young as you and a mother now. A good girl, an obedient wife, but you aren't her."

"I make him happy. And, Mama, he makes me happy."

"Happiness," Mama Allegra laughed softly. "Happiness comes, it goes. You can't sole a shoe with happiness. If you loved him as much as he loves you, we might talk differently. But now we know that's false. And, even then, if you did love him, I would challenge you. He's my only son, my golden baby."

"I would never hurt him."

"A marriage isn't only between a man and a woman; it joins two families. You fled your home to live with us. A stepfather touches you, a mother shuns you, and a sister shoves you out the door, slamming it behind you. I've read your brother's name in the papers—and not for rescuing a child from a burning building. That's no recommendation."

The truth crushed Thelma. She'd run to them, revealed her secrets. "I trusted you!" she said, her voice rising. "And now you're using everything I told you against me. I'm better than my family. You know me. Can't you see that?"

"Calm down, *cara mia*," said Mama Allegra. "You've told me their worst—and I believe you. Isn't that what you wanted, someone to have faith in you? We do. You're a good girl, but where's the joy in uniting our families? I love you, *carina*, but I have to protect my own. I don't want to have anything to do with that flock of yours, and I won't have them mistreating my baby boy."

"Doesn't Giorgio have a say?"

"What say? He loves you. He doesn't see beyond that but, me, I see in decades. It doesn't take a fortune-teller to foretell the future. I'm a mother, a grandmother, a daughter, a sister. I'm a Catholic. What would our Christmas be? Where would your children play? What if your brother Abraham who's so quick with a knife offers Giorgio a job and he does it because he's family, a brother like Louis? What happens then? Love doesn't question—but a mother must."

Mama Allegra smoothed Thelma's stray hairs away from the back part and then tugged each braid as if to say, *There, that's done.* Thelma twisted into the older woman, pushing her forehead into the crook of her neck and embracing her. She wanted to sob, to beg for asylum and never leave, but the tears resisted. After kissing the girl on the crown of her head, Mama Allegra pushed her aside, gathering Giorgio's pajamas and retrieving the needle from the tomato-shaped pincushion.

Thelma waited, watching the even stitches appear side by side, neither tight nor loose, the older woman squinting slightly. She would need glasses soon. "Now I'll braid *your* hair."

Mama shook her bowed head no. Thelma thought she heard a sniff but couldn't tell whether the woman was crying. She turned and rushed out the door, rumbling downstairs and breaking into the street, slapped by the summer heat. And yet, she couldn't cry. The rejection hurt too much. She couldn't swallow. Her skin burned. Was she hot because of the temperature or the shame? Her money was on the latter. She was alone again: not good enough, unwanted, shabby, repulsive. She was poison.

She walked down the sticky street smeared in *gelato* drips, beer, and vomit. She stepped across a broken red-white-and-blue pinwheel; when she looked up, a withered yellow balloon flapped from a fire escape. She sped southeast on North Eighth, turned left on Meeker, ashamed that everybody knew about her and Giorgio and considered her unworthy. She'd been so stupid, as if they could hide anything down four steps during the Giglio.

How could she explain her feelings to Giorgio? This love/not love she didn't understand. She hadn't even asked Mama Allegra for his address to write him a letter. He would think she didn't want him, but that was false. She needed to talk to him. But that was a lie, too. She wanted to kiss him, to touch him, to bury herself in him so deep that she came out the other side, clean.

What was this if it wasn't love? She didn't know. She was too young to see her mistake. She set her back to the beautiful boy who had been a pest and then became so much more, leaving behind the Italian neighborhood, that foreign country she loved better than her own, her hair wrapped tightly in two braids that tugged at her scalp. Without thinking, she removed the ties and loosened the hair, pulling apart what Mama Allegra had made, no longer a sister to Nina, Trulia, and Gabriela.

Thelma's feet entered Union Avenue of their own accord, nipping over on Grand Street and then veering onto Hooper, flagging only when she could see their building. Down the way, the knife grinder in his faded-green felt hat, rang his bell. She hesitated on the sidewalk, not wanting to enter. But she couldn't retreat. She didn't know where to run. She didn't fit anywhere, not with the Gigantiellos, not with her own people.

Mama Allegra had been right. Their families could never unite. Annie would have chewed Giorgio up and spit him out with the seeds. She'd have called that sweet boy names: blondie, Adonis, Talaina, *sheygets*, Gentile. They would have told him about her and Moe in the crudest way and asked Giorgio if he was ready to be fitted with horns because Thelma couldn't commit, was a slut. How could she ever bring someone she had feelings for home to a family like that?

And suddenly even her memory of Giorgio, of two friends melting together under the cover of night as the trumpet blared in the distance and the drums kept a beat, became tainted. If she could have scraped off her skin and become someone else, anyone else, she would have right then and there. The scrawny knife grinder in the felt hat stopped his cart to whistle at the magic leg. She turned. When he smiled, revealing black gums and a few straggly teeth, she spat at him.

Chapter 17

The summer passed, leaves crisped and fell, and the record-setting, frigid winter of 1917–18 surrendered to a timid March. While the war effort ramped up, men in uniform weren't much on Annie's mind as she spread on the padded bench before her vanity, absorbed in her reflection. The twenty-six-year-old removed with gentle strokes of her middle fingers the cold cream that tingled her pores, leaving her fair skin soft to the touch. She didn't have a single blemish because she cared for her face morning and night, which required a heavier-duty lotion that worked wonders, even if she had to cover her pillow with a towel when she went to sleep. She had a thirteen-minute routine and she stuck to it however much the kids cried. She needed her beauty time and woe betide anybody, including Jesse, who interrupted her when she was seated at the mirrored set he'd bought her for their seventh anniversary. She'd trained her husband to behave the way she liked him to, and that included how to wrap the back sections of her hair that were hard for her to reach in curlers. (And how to clip her toenails, because he was better on his knees.)

That's who Annie was: diligent, reliable, and well maintained. She loved order the way a drill sergeant might, both for its results and its own sake. She could say that she primped for Jesse, but she was self-aware enough to know that her standards were higher than his—he always said he'd love her as much in shabby slippers and a housedress with her roots showing, but that was not who she was. She pinched her cheeks hard three times for rouge, leaned in to pluck three dark hairs from between her brows until her eyes stung.

With her pinkie, Annie prodded the beginning of a tiny wrinkle below her right eye and then realized it was nothing, an eyelash. She put the hair on the tip of her forefinger and blew, wishing for what she wanted most: her child's safe arrival. She wiped her hands on a rag and felt herself up. Her breasts were sore. She was sure of it: pregnant. She had that feeling of well-being from the inside out that she wasn't alone—and she wouldn't let this baby go if she had to strap her legs together with a belt. This child would go far, she was sure of it. Maybe not president—that was for the grandchildren—but doctor or lawyer, maybe even a judge or a rabbi.

Smiling into the mirror, she removed a poppy seed from between the straight white teeth and unclipped her blonde curls. She was the good-looking one, the successful one, with her husband the news dealer earning regular money from the family business and handing it over without resistance. He didn't know how to manage finances. She did.

As soon as Annie had discovered the newsstand bookmaking racket, even before her anger had subsided, she'd demanded the ledgers. (She now knew too much for Abie to rebuff her request.) With her book-keeping skills, she'd taken over, ensuring the flow of cash that could be siphoned off safely into the household budget after making the proper payoffs to police and not-so-silent partners. She understood how to bury assets and inflate expenses on the ledger. In the name of Lazarus & Sons, she'd purchased life insurance on Jesse and Abie and Louis—after what happened to the Rothman kid on Fourteenth Street, she wasn't taking any chances. In filling out the forms, she named herself as the sole beneficiary. Who else could be trusted to secure the family's interests?

What she wanted now—more than anything except the infant's safe arrival—was her own house with no strangers walking on her head or ramming a broomstick up her *tuchus* from the apartment below. She'd had enough of neighbors and landlords. She wanted to raise this child under her own roof and lift the family into respectability. Then she'd be content.

She smiled into the mirror, her bottom lip full and the upper curved. Looking among the lipsticks aligned like toy soldiers, she selected one, shook her head, exchanged it, and carefully applied a bright orangey red. She looked happily at her reflection: beautiful. Two short raps interrupted her pucker. She rose, calling, "Hey, Thelma, get the door already!"

Glancing outside where young trees bent in March winds, she plucked her cardigan from the chair back. Upon entering the living room, she saw a soldier in uniform and Thelma wrapped around him like the stripe on a barber's pole. Louis looked different in his uniform, the fitted tunic, military jodhpurs: taller, more handsome, like a movie star. He had shoulders and a waist she envied.

"Why'd you knock, Louis? Like we should get up and answer the door for family? Look at you: a soldier already! Should I salute? What are those, short pants? Thelma, let him breathe, for God's sake."

"Hello, Annie," he said in a voice deeper and more measured than she remembered but no warmer. With his arm circling Thelma's shoulders, he turned to his older sister. If he were a stranger, he was the kind of young man you'd see on the street and think he treated his mother well. Following basic training, his face was thinner than it had been before he enlisted in December, his cheekbones more prominent, but his wide nose would always have the broken bend to the right with which he'd returned from the orphanage. His gray eyes held hers with an unfamiliar boldness, as an equal. She would see how long that lasted. He handed her a pink string-wrapped box that looked small in his hand. "Where's Mama?"

"What, where's my kiss, soldier boy?" she asked, extending her freshly cleansed and moisturized cheek toward the twenty-one-year-old and awaiting his approach.

He touched dry lips dutifully on the surface, asking, "What's that smell?"

"Noxzema," Annie said. "Soft, huh?" She detached his hand from her sixteen-year-old sister's, leading him away from the door. "Wait until you see your niece and nephew. They're so big! They've never met a soldier. Did you bring them something from the army? Mama," she screamed over her shoulder, "your son the soldier's home."

As if on cue, Mama entered from the kitchen in her apron, her cheeks flushed from bending over the oven, wiping her fingers on a flour-sack towel. She hesitated, eyes widening, twisting the cloth in her hands, as she stared at the man in uniform. It was a look of horror, as if he'd come to take her away, not visit. "For this we left Drohobych, that you should fight another man's war?"

"Ma, he's an American," Thelma said.

"Who asked you?" said Annie.

"Pardon me for living," Thelma said.

"It's my war, Ma. It's our duty to join our allies and defeat the Huns."

"What did they ever do for us?"

"Plenty," said Louis. "Britain and France are all that's between us and the Germans bombing Brooklyn."

While Thelma started singing "You're a Grand Old Flag" and doing a little kick–ball change, Mama began crying. She advanced toward Louis, planting her face into his chest. He awkwardly patted her head. She began to wail, "Don't go!"

"Annie?" he asked, as if dealing with an unwanted family pet.

Annie approached, pulling his mother off him like lint, one piece at a time. A big wet spot remained on the chest pocket of his woolen uniform. She handed Mama the cake box, saying, "Can you put this on a plate?"

"Babka," he said.

"Mama's favorite," said Annie. "Look at how short they cut your hair! When did your ears get so big?"

"You should talk about ears," said Thelma.

"Who asked you?" Annie assumed her usual spot on the sofa, crossed her legs, and patted the cushion beside her. Instead, Louis pulled up a chair. Thelma dropped a pillow and sat on the floor beside him, one elbow on his thigh.

"You're a dead ringer for a movie star," Thelma said, looking up adoringly at her brother.

He struck a noble pose, propping up his chin with his fist and dropping his voice an octave. "Yeah, my regiment leaves at dawn."

Thelma squeezed his leg. "Wow, muscles!"

He nodded. "Boot camp."

"Those Mississippi girls near Camp Shelby must be throwing themselves at you."

"I hurt myself picking them up," he said, placing his hand on his lower back, "so I've had to go easy."

"Meet any Jewish girls?" Annie asked.

"It's Mississippi. Not a bagel in sight," Louis answered. "Where's Abie?"

"He'll be here," said Thelma.

"What did he tell you?" Annie asked.

"Like I said, he'll be here. If he said he'll come, he'll come. What am I, his parole officer?"

But Abie didn't arrive. Jesse returned from Manhattan with six-year-old Julius, who now worked the newsstand, too, learning his reading from the headlines and his sums from counting change. Moe followed, wearing a skullcap, the fringe of his prayer shawl visible below his woolen vest. Since he'd exited Mama's bed, he'd become increasingly religious, a man of rules and limits. He rose early to join the minyan for prayers before hastening to the jewelry district, often returning to the synagogue after supper. It was either atonement for past sins of the flesh or a desperate urge to escape the company of his wife and her daughters.

Annie, who rarely took anything at face value, never considered Moe's *davening* true faith as a desire to get nearer to G_d. She kept the milk and the meat separate according to kosher dietary laws, rested on the Sabbath, and honored the high holy days but wouldn't expect thunderbolts to fall from the sky if someone ate a ham sandwich on the stoop. When four-year-old Adele awoke from her nap and padded to her mother, Annie opened her arms wide and gave the girl twenty pecks on the forehead below her crown of blonde curls before looking over at Louis. "Here's my Baby Snookums," Annie said. "Isn't she a princess?"

"A princess," he said, reaching his arm out to the grumpy child in the red-checked jumper. She recoiled, diving farther in her mother's arms.

"More like a big fat baby," said Julius, a dead ringer for his father. "Hey, can you teach me how to shoot, Uncle Louis?"

"Not indoors."

"Have you killed anybody yet?" the boy asked.

"Julius," warned his father.

"Not while I've been in uniform," Louis replied.

"What do you got for me? Ma said you were going to bring me shoes from boot camp. Where are they?"

"I left them in my other pants," said the uncle. "Want a shiny nickel?"

"I'd rather have a shiny dime," said the boy, sticking his thumbs in his belt loops.

Louis doled out the change and, not to be left behind, Adele came over and snuggled her head on her uncle's shoulder before slowly extending her palm. He gave her a dime, too, but she shouted, "No! I want a penny. They're prettier. Mama says so." He obliged.

And still they waited for Abie. Added to the shmaltzy, savory scent of Mama's cooking was a new charred smell. Jesse offered Louis schnapps from the decanter in tiny glasses, but he declined. He ribbed him for not being a real fighting man, because a soldier would never refuse booze. And, because Louis wasn't drinking, they couldn't, either, not the good stuff that Annie reserved on the high shelf for special occasions.

"When's dinner?" Jesse asked.

"I'm starving!" said Julius.

Annie sighed loudly. "Mama, get the chicken out of the oven before it's as brown as a brisket. Thelma, give her a hand."

"Why don't you?"

"I'm entertaining."

"That's a laugh."

After that, Mama served a Shabbos dinner on a Tuesday, with Thelma beside her ferrying platter after plate after bowl, carrying enough eats for an army. It included what Annie believed to be Louis's favorite, sweet noodle pudding with raisins. After everyone else began inhaling the food, Louis waited until Mama approached the table after the last dish had found its place. He rose, walked to her side, drew back her chair, and slid it in behind her.

"Fancy," she said.

"You're welcome," he said, returning to his place beside Thelma. Dropping the napkin on his lap, he shut his eyes for a moment, as if praying. He pushed the kugel to the side of his plate, moving the roast chicken thigh to the center. He carefully cut the meat with a fork in his left hand and the knife in his right. He put down his knife, shifted the fork to his right hand and took a bite, chewing it slowly with his mouth shut and then swallowing. The rest of the family stopped to watch, as if he were a giraffe at the zoo. These were not the customary table manners.

When Jesse offered to fill the guest of honor's glass with kosher wine, Louis covered the opening with his hand, saying, "I'm in training."

"How are they treating you?" Jesse asked.

"Never better, sir," Louis said, cutting another morsel of meat. "I'm getting three squares, exercise and fresh air. Now I can load and shoot a rifle. If you follow instructions and keep your head down, you get by easy as pie."

Annie shook her head in disbelief. "That sounds too good to be true."

He shrugged. "They call me Brooklyn."

"Is that an insult?" Annie asked, prepared to be outraged. It sounded like a Jewish slur.

"They think I'm a loud city boy."

"Imagine if they met Abie!" said Thelma.

"Imagine if we met Abie!" Annie said. "I can't believe your beloved brother doesn't care enough to see you. It's a *shonda*. How long is your leave?"

"Twenty-four hours. I have to be on that noon train tomorrow."

"This is how it always is with that little schmuck," Annie said, standing to clear the chicken carcass from the table, "coming and going with no respect for the family. Everything he ruins."

"What's ruined? We're all here and happy," Jesse said.

"Speak for yourself." Annie's anger rose into her throat. As she gritted her teeth, her forehead contracted and she felt her blood pressure ascend. She wouldn't let them do that to her baby. Her earlier sense of well-being evaporated, replaced by hate. Abie was a short, selfish rat who would just as soon smile as slit your throat. He always kept her waiting, even when he knew it wasn't good for Mama's health. He couldn't arrive on time. He couldn't do what she asked. For once in his life, would it kill him to be a decent brother?

If there was one emotion she could always count on when his name was involved, it was rage. If it weren't for him, she'd have peace of mind. "You can't depend on your Little Yiddle, Louis. If he cared for you, he'd be here. You shouldn't be seen with him anyway, a good soldier like you. He's a criminal. He doesn't deserve your loyalty. He's not fit to shine your shoes."

"I can spit-shine my own shoes," Louis said. When Thelma began to speak, her brother reached over and rested his hand on hers. She clammed up.

The slamming of dishes in the sink, the rattling of flatware in their drawer, and the clumping of Annie's heels as she paced filled the rest of the evening. "Where could that devil be? What is he doing now? He could be dead in a gutter. I can only hope."

Annie watched her kids brush their teeth, and then she scrubbed behind their ears with extra vigor until Adele cried out, "Mama, stop, you're hurting me!"

"No *kvetching*," Annie said. After tucking them in, she went and shut off the kitchen light before going to bed.

Louis cleared his throat in the dark. "Annie, we're in here."

Switching the light back on, Annie saw Louis and Thelma talking, their foreheads touching. What could they possibly discuss so intensely in her absence? They must have been knocking her—and at her own kitchen table.

"Shut the lights when you're done, night owls," she said, her tone critical as if staying up late was wicked. Even while Annie judged her brother and sister, she resented that their kinship excluded her, making her the odd woman out in her own house. When they were younger, she'd scrubbed behind their ears like she had with her children just now. She'd fed those *pishers* when nobody else would.

Annie had sacrificed her childhood for them. No one had taken care of her! She deserved their respect and gratitude, and she was unable to grasp why Louis loved Thelma and not her. It was unfair. What did that runaround slut have to offer that Annie lacked?

Peeved, she said, "We're not made of money."

As she swiveled away, Annie overheard Thelma whisper, "What *are* you made of?"

"Shh," said Louis, "don't poke the snake."

Annie pivoted, ready to raise a fist and explain who was really the snake around here, but Jesse called out, "Anechka, come to bed." And she did, crawling under the blankets beside Jesse, who couldn't sleep without her. She rested her head on his shoulder.

"Abie doesn't show and they *still* love him more than me," Annie said. "Some people get away with murder."

"So what else is new?"

She took his hand, put it on her belly, and held it there. As the night got quieter, he made her soft promises: "He's going to go to school, and have his bar mitzvah, and keep on going. He'll go to college, become a lawyer, marry a girl from a good Jewish family . . ."

"Become a judge," Annie said, feeding their shared fantasy.

"Are there Jewish judges?"

"There will be."

"We'll name him after my father."

"Elias."

"He'll make us proud." And those were the last words Annie heard until a pounding at the door awakened her. Annie jumped straight up in bed and felt her curlers and patted her night cream. Panic accelerated her heartbeat. Nothing good ever came knocking past midnight.

"Who died?" Annie asked.

"Go back to sleep," Jesse said, "I've got it."

"It's the police! I can't go to jail!" she said, considering her handwriting in the newsstand ledgers. "I have babies." She rushed into her slippers, struggling to find her robe sleeves as she waddled out of the bedroom while Jesse yanked his pants over his pajama bottoms. Crossing the living room, she reached for the bolt. As she unlocked it, the door burst open. Abie stood there smirking in a black tuxedo, a chorus girl on each arm. The blonde and the redhead, standing six feet tall in silver heels—not counting their feathered headdresses—dwarfed the man. Each dancer carried a champagne bottle.

The cheeky trio burst into the darkened living room, with Abie flipping the lights on abruptly, illuminating Annie in robe and slippers. "Surprise," the two stunning women cried in unison as if they were leaping out of a giant cake, their slim arms raised in victorious Vs above their heads.

The showgirls filled the room with bubbly laughter, fueling Annie's shame and rage beneath the dime-store cream *shmeared* across her face. Annie realized it was as if her own shocked reaction were the punch line of the world's funniest joke. She felt fat and dumpy, unwanted, an immigrant reject destined for the dung heap. The women laughed at her until they bent over and cried. "I told you dames," said Abie, "was I right or was I right?"

"Right," said one.

"Right," said the other.

"Oh, Abie, you are always right!"

"Do you animals know what time it is?" Annie shrilled as Julius and Adele toddled in and Jesse caught them by their hands to keep them away from their mother.

"No," roared Abie, "do you?"

"The night is young," said the blonde, tossing her head back so that her brilliant yellow feathers brushed the doorframe. She was the kind of woman who made old men thirsty and young men hungry. That was also the kind that irritated Annie.

"Young is the night—and so are we!" said the throaty-voiced redhead with the green-plumed cap. She shimmied out of her coat, revealing her costume, a mix of jade-colored sequins that snaked over her private bits and sheer netting everywhere else. She was all legs except where she was breasts. She had a beautiful oval face with arched brows worthy of the Roman Colosseum above wide-set, flirtatious eyes, but it went largely unnoticed considering the live flesh undulating below her beaded choker.

"She's all but naked," said Annie.

"The mystery is all in that *but*," said Abie, wiggling an imaginary cigar.

"How could you?" Annie asked, gripping her robe's collar to her throat and aching to remove the goo from her face, the metal curlers. She felt hideously ugly. Abie would pay for this night. "There are children here."

"There are children everywhere," said Abie. "These girls are children—aren't you, babies?"

"We're children of the night," sparkled the blonde in a squeaky voice. She had blue eyes so pale they verged on freakish.

"Do you want to hear me sing a high C?" asked the redhead. "Everybody says I'm the best singer in the chorus."

"Save it, Charlotte," said the blonde. "First, we have to find Louis."

"Louis, come out, come out, wherever you are." The two women raised their fists in front of their chests like stage mice and wiggled their tails, crouching as if playing hide-and-seek. They knocked on every door, crying, "Louis! Louis!"

When Charlotte cracked Mama's door, she sniffed and said, "I think something died in there."

As the chorus girl pivoted, Thelma slipped out behind, barefoot, wearing a ratty nightgown. Eyeing Abie, she leaped toward him, wrapping her arms around his neck. "I knew you'd come. They didn't believe me."

"Have I ever let you down, my Temeleh?" Abie said and pulled his younger sister close.

"Careful we don't smash your toes, baby girl," said Charlotte. "These heels are lethal, right, Gloria?"

"I've slayed more guys with these shoes than the French have shot Germans."

"Ah," said Charlotte, "your dancing ain't that bad!"

"You're a laugh riot," said Gloria, fluffing her feathers and shuffling her feet before a kick–ball change that got a response from the downstairs neighbors' broom handle.

"Now, Annie, look at Temmy—that's a welcome."

Annie shook her head. "Maybe you're not so welcome in my book."

"He's welcome in mine." Louis left the darkened kitchen, a cigarette hanging from his right hand and a glass of buttermilk in his left. He'd removed his shirt, revealing a muscular chest and arms. "I'd say my brother's a sight for sore eyes—and these eyes are very sore. What's home without Abie?"

"Look what I brung ya," said Abie. "Your pick: blonde or redhead."

"I only diddle brunettes," said Louis, laughing.

"Don't insult the girls," Abie cautioned.

"Insult the girls?" Annie asked. These weren't girls; they were whores. "You bring *shiksas* into my house and you worry about insulting *them*?"

"What's that, a *shiksa*?" asked Charlotte. "Is it like a malted milk?"

"It means angel who doesn't scream at my ass for breakfast," said Abie.

"That's not what it means," said Julius. Jesse clapped his hand over his son's mouth before the kid could explain.

"It means a goy," Annie spat.

"I'm no goy." Charlotte giggled while rubbing her back against Abie like a bear scratching against bark. "I'm all goyle from top to bottom."

"*She* might be ignorant but not me, sister. I know the poison you spew behind my back, but mock my friends to my face, you may as well insult me. I don't roll over." Abie lowered his voice to a growl as he neared Annie.

"It's the truth, Little Yiddle." Annie shrugged. Having crawled under his skin, she paused to consider where to plant the next knife and how to twist it. She found a racket in the middle of the night contemptible. And she realized she had the power to embarrass him as much as he'd shamed her.

"The truth, Mamaleh, is you're a bossy battle-ax who'd rather toss your brothers into an orphanage than admit you torched the baby."

"Ancient history," said Annie, sucking her teeth. "You can't still be angry about that."

"Try me, you fat, ugly bitch."

She boiled. "Jesse, are you just going to stand there and let him abuse me?"

"Abie, please," said Jesse. "Lay off. Don't talk to my beauty that way."

"Who asked you, Newsboy? Move along. This is between me and my sister. Annie, you don't want to be on my bad side."

"Or what, you're going to stab my belly?"

"They never charged me."

"Like you didn't do it," Annie said. "It was in the papers."

"Don't believe everything you read. Like you're so respectable," said Abie as he placed his face uncomfortably close to Annie's so that she could smell his cigar breath. His proximity and his glare threatened her. "Don't act holier-than-thou just because you married the first sap who liked the way you jiggled his circumcised *putz*."

Annie slapped him, hard.

"Annie!" Jesse said, shocked.

Abie laughed. "Is that the best you got? Are you going to burn me next? Lock me in a closet? Rat me out to the police?"

"I'm going to sit *shivah* for you," she said. "You're not welcome here."

"But my money is, you schnorrer. We're not done."

"Yes, we are."

"Not until I say so." He took one step back, popped his cuffs, and, smiling, backhanded her, catching his pinkie ring on her nose. Cartilage crunched.

The painful blow made Annie's eyes water. She covered her nose with her hands, feeling shock, anger, shame—and dripping blood. "Jesse," she said, "punch him."

"No need," said Abie, raising his hands in the air. "We're even."

Her cowardly knight shuffled backward, saying, "I'll get ice."

That weakling, Annie thought, disgusted that he let Abie shame her before the entire family. Raw emotions surged through her. The caged fear that roared inside escaped, exposing the degraded woman in a shabby robe shackled to her mother. She dreaded becoming Mama, stranded on her bed with her aches and pains, despondent and dependent on others. Panicked, she was too ashamed to look at her own children after being beaten.

Julius said, "That was funny, Uncle Abie. Do it again."

"Once is plenty."

"Why'd you slap Mama, Uncle Abie?" asked Adele.

"To make her behave," Abie said. "Like when she slaps you, my little kosher deli. We're done here. Louis, grab your stuff. You're not coming back."

"Aces," said Louis, disappearing into the kitchen to gather his kit.

"Can I come?" Thelma asked.

"You can't go where we're going."

"Where's that?"

"A place I got on Marcy Avenue."

"C'mon, Abie, we can't leave the girl here," said Gloria.

"Throw on some clothes, Temmy. We'll be out on the stoop. After you, my beauties," he said, ushering them out and leaving the door ajar. The popping of a champagne cork echoed in the vestibule. Then came the girls' tinkly laughter and Abie saying, "Sweet, sweet, sweet ass."

Within minutes, Louis and Thelma followed them out, with the younger sister carrying her shoes. Annie slammed the door behind them. She heard her mother call out, "Annie! Annie!"

"Go to sleep, Ma," she called, lacking the stomach to cope with Mama.

"Come to bed, Anechka." Jesse moved to embrace his wife. She sloughed him off without a thought for how he felt, remembering the stink of Thelma's burned flesh, the shit stench when she'd unlocked the closet door at the Jungers' apartment on 106th Street, releasing Abie and Louis. She'd struggled with Mama in pieces—why hadn't they understood that? She'd only been a kid herself. They'd stolen her childhood. What did she know from raising children? Should she have let

Mama go after Papa died and taken to the streets? She alone had united the family. They were here because of her, not Abie. She had to regain control.

Annie switched off the living room light. Darkness flooded over her. She was agitated and sad in a way that she typically repressed. When she felt this way she lashed out—but at whom now? Abie was an animal, but he hadn't stuck around to get the punishment he deserved.

"Anechka, come to bed," Jesse called from their room, but she ignored him. If he hadn't busted Abie's nose for her, he was incapable of improving her mood. Staring out the window, her fingers gripping the sill, she saw a full moon illuminating Hooper Street. She observed the quintet heading toward the Italian neighborhood. Thelma walked in front between Abie and Louis, who was lifting the drink to his lips. Then they began to skip, the three of them, with Thelma leading until they all had the same bouncy rhythm. She could hear their laughter in the wind as they tried to remain in step even as the champagne bubbled over.

Behind them, the showgirls pranced arm in arm, kicking up their impossibly long legs while passing the second bottle between them. What a waste: opening another container before they'd finished the first. Annie had never tasted champagne. Somehow, if this night had unfolded differently, she might have. It probably tasted sour anyway.

Alone looking out, Annie resented the closeness of her brothers and sister as they scooted toward fun, their backs to her. Louis was going to war and she hadn't even wished him luck, given him a photo of the kids to carry. She might never see him again. And what bothered her even more than the possibility that he would die on the fields of France was that she'd hardly known who he really was on the streets of Brooklyn.

She waited for one of them to look over their shoulder at her waiting in the window, to acknowledge her sacrifice for them. But they didn't. They couldn't care less. They hated her—and for a moment she let herself taste that big cup of bitterness.

She'd make them pay.

Chapter 18

1918

After that March night, Abie no longer visited Hooper Street. Simultaneously, when Annie did the business accounts, she noticed that the newsstand's take appeared to diminish, but she couldn't tell whether it was demand slipping, competition rising, or her brother's sticky fingers. Since she was no longer talking to Abie following their fight, Annie couldn't confront him. Instead, she prodded Jesse to grill Abie, but although he agreed, he never accomplished his task. Some days he said he forgot. Or Abie didn't show up. Or someone attempted to muscle in on their turf or the suppliers refused to deliver. The truth was that Jesse was the weakling that Annie needed to control, loving but unthreatening. She'd more or less made peace with the fact that while Jesse would never set the world on fire, he would also remain faithful to her until death parted them. She would have to remain the family's backbone, as she had been since Papa passed. There would be no rest, but she'd sleep when she died, which she hoped was a long and increasingly prosperous way off. On evenings when Jesse returned home flushed and shaken but silent, Annie recognized that he'd witnessed risky activities but protected her pregnancy by keeping mum.

Annie sat with her ledgers, furious but stymied, and yet as months passed her anger lessened. This pregnancy was a good one, infusing an unfamiliar sense of well-being that coated her raw nerves. Between their income from the newsstand, Moe's goldsmith salary, and Thelma's secretarial paycheck from the women's shoe factory, the rent got paid and they didn't have to run a tab at the kosher butcher. In the happy stage of her pregnancy, the newsstand receded in importance and Abie's disrespect chafed her less. She was the only one with children and that apparently wasn't going to change anytime soon.

On March 25, Private Louis Lorber shipped out to France on the *Corsican* with the Thirty-Eighth Infantry, and Annie went from being a sister shamed by Little Yiddle to one who could brag of her soldier brother bolstering the war effort. That he was fighting with the French and English against the Germans and their people, the Austro-Hungarians, bothered Mama more than it did Annie, as the older woman often expressed her fears that Louis was battling their own relatives conscripted into compulsory military service.

Ever striving to be an American in full, Annie put her faith in Woodrow Wilson, the reluctant wartime president, who had said, "*Neutrality* is a negative word. It does not express what America ought to feel. We are not trying to keep out of trouble; we are trying to preserve the foundations on which peace may be rebuilt."

Come April, as the baby expanded within, she felt a domestic peace she'd never known even as the world raged at war. She began to live entirely in the present, two hearts beating within one large and well-moisturized skin. She felt the quickening of this baby earlier than she had with the previous children born and unborn, watching an elbow cross her belly like a submarine, feeling a playful kick. Her attention turned inward, talking to the little life inside her, certain he would understand. She acquiesced to the cravings she ascribed to the infant: pickles, fresh grapefruit, barely seared liver. For once, she'd spent a little money at the beauty parlor and was blonder than ever, a regular movie star. She left the housework to Mama, who watched Adele while newsie Julius labored beside his father. She allowed herself the luxury of relaxing in the middle of the day with her feet up, a pile of movie maga-zines and an egg cream from the corner soda fountain with a double shot of Fox's U-bet Original Chocolate Flavor Syrup.

As April blended into May and then June and Annie became as mellow with child as she would ever be, Jesse and Julius returned daily from Manhattan with a pile of free newspapers. These included the *New York Times*, which covered the Great War like a tablecloth. Julius, now seven, a natural-born American, had become obsessed with the European war, in which the Yankees were expected to enter and save the day despite German dominance against the French and English allies. Correspondents attached to the troops revealed the condition of the millions of soldiers on foreign soil, and Annie's neighbors on Hooper Street—Mrs. Dickman, Mrs. Famant, Mrs. Spiegelberg, and their children—would come downstairs to hear the latest news without having to buy a paper themselves.

In the evening, when Thelma returned from the factory office with fingers stained black from typewriter ribbon, Julius would hand her the *Times* while Adele crawled into her lap. As Mama finished overcooking, Thelma would read the paper aloud. She used a clear voice that Annie found affected, as if her skinny sister were one of those loose suffragettes speechifying on a soapbox. Thelma encouraged Julius to sound out the words as he read along, *Allies* and *Germans* and the tricky *artillery*, which he especially liked because it had to do with big, bad armaments that went "boom-boom-boom." Everything was toy soldiers for him that year: if he had a bar of soap, he'd make a pistol; a stick became a rifle; he begged for a slingshot but Annie refused.

The family followed the frequent dispatches of reporter Edwin L. "Jimmy" James, since he was embedded with the Americans in France. His first-person accounts gave the sense that if the correspondent just looked left or right, he would see Louis and capture him in a paragraph. A private in the Thirty-Eighth Infantry led by Colonel Ulysses Grant McAlexander, their brother was armed and ready to change the balance of the war far from Abie, his constant companion since childhood. On May 17, Thelma read:

> The great task of the Allies is to block the plans of the Germans to make further advances now. This is a task for America, no less than for England and France, especially since the Kaiser hoped to win the war before our growing weight could be thrown in serious strength against him. Therefore, the chance for Americans to help fight the foe on his chosen battlefield at this time is nothing less than an opportunity to make our role the more glorious.

While this notion of their uncle as "glorious" excited her children, Annie wasn't buying. Although he was raised high on his paper pedestal, Annie questioned her little brother's hero status. Having witnessed the new and improved army version of Louis meticulously cutting his meat, dabbing his mouth with a napkin, and behaving like a Gentile stranger in his own home, she was skeptical. His treatment of her and Mama had been polite yet distant—not how you handled family. Yet when he had a chance to take her side, he'd scampered away as fast as he could collect his gear, joining Abie and his two sluts without defending her. Louis always made his choice—and it was the wrong one.

She considered Louis disloyal, doubting his commitment to the military, too. Annie expected him to appear on her doorstep one day, AWOL. For now, so convinced was she that Louis was damaged goods that, initially, she sniffed and said, "He always liked guns," as if this unhealthy fascination paralleled Abie's being "quick with a knife."

When a postcard from Private Lorber appeared in late May addressed to Thelma alone, Annie's resentment increased. She anticipated there would be another sent to her and the family, but it never arrived. She explained to the neighbors that the mail wasn't dependable, but inside she boiled that Louis preferred Thelma to herself. She resented both the snub and the way it emboldened her sister.

The postcard bore a drawing of a soldier poised on a rock writing a note with a pencil upon his knee, the words *Love to all at home* printed on its face. On the reverse side it read:

Grub good, girls friendly, and gun shoots straight. Learned a French word: merde! Love always, Lou.

The next card for Thelma came in late June, with Louis describing enemy artillery: "Shells go screeching overhead like giant skyrockets. Oy vey! Made friends, brave-hearted boys, and will never let them down. We'll keep the Huns from Paris. Our colonel says, 'They may kill us, but they cannot whip us.' Love always, Lou." Annie tossed it in the garbage "by mistake," but Thelma fished it out and placed it beside the earlier one on the mantel.

All through the summer, Thelma continued to read to those gathered on Hooper Street. According to the *New York Times*, the green Americans hardly had time to train before joining their weary French and English allies to draw a line at the River Marne, a tributary of the Seine. The mission was to thwart the German offensive to capture Paris, only fifty miles away to the northwest. Even Annie began to warm to the notion of Louis as a valiant fighting man as the Dickmans, Famants, and Spiegelbergs regularly took over the living room for the nearly daily reports from their pal Jimmy of the *Times*.

Come mid-July, Private Lorber, under McAlexander's command, participated in a critical victory, the Second Battle of the Marne. Defending a long, bendy stretch of water that was all that stood between the enemy and the French capital, the inexperienced Americans—outmanned and outgunned by superior German troops—refused to allow the Huns a foothold on the western riverbank. And any time there was a mention of the Thirty-Eighth

Infantry, the Brooklyn observers imagined one of their own armed with a Colt revolver and a bayonet, defending his country.

Annie found it astonishing that Louis could be so distant that she couldn't nag him about not writing to her, and yet the war was as near as newsprint. Despite her bias, Annie's pride began to grow as Julius haltingly read aloud from James's July 17 dispatch, with Thelma correcting him when he faltered, her finger tracing the words on the page.

> The story of how the American soldier, who had never before played a role in this world war, stood against the most savage rush of the German foeman and held fast at one of the most vital points of the allied lines will make a glorious page in American history.

James could have been writing about Louis himself. The neighbors actually applauded and, from then on, brought victory cakes, vodka bottles, kosher salamis, and covered dishes of stuffed cabbage. The local candy store sent over Hershey bars. And at 1:00 p.m. each day, a shy boy in a white apron knocked on the door with a tall chocolate egg cream in a glass that he'd carried from the corner soda fountain. No one asked why all the postcards were only addressed to Thelma; they cheered on Mama and Annie, whose claims to have raised her younger brother right increased with each new report.

Under the headline "Swift Success of Our Men" on July 18, James breathlessly chronicled the rise of the allied offensive, noting:

> I was present at the fighting this morning in the Château-Thierry region, where our boys had done so much to aid the allied cause already . . . Our troops swept down the hill north of the Bois de Belleau toward Torcy. Shouting as they went, the American

soldiers advanced on Torcy, and at precisely 5:30 the commander reported that they had captured the town.

"I bet Louis was right at the front," said Julius.

"I bet he was," said Thelma, smiling as if on the verge of telling a story and then setting it aside. "They don't come any braver than your uncle."

Annie didn't bother contradicting her. Heading into her ninth month, she was feeling foggy. Everything around her was like distant gunfire, and she was slow to react, whether to slights or praise. Unlike some pregnant women, who grew angrier as the months passed, Annie's rage seemed to recede. The child's final development, the expanding of his lungs, his daily weight gain, his punching out for more space, stole away her thoughts and left her dull and uncommonly serene, the embodiment of motherhood. She, like Louis, was a winner—only on the Domestic rather than the Western Front.

Meanwhile, the Second Battle of the Marne had put the Germans on the defensive. Now, the family cheered each Allied victory, big or small. Come August, Annie's movements slowed further, although she remained in the chair in the middle of the living room—and beware anyone who took her favorite seat. With the afternoon heat, she claimed she was sweating for two. The soda fountain boy arrived with a tray carrying a pair of egg creams while the newspaper reported win after win, despite the continued might of the enemy's artillery. On August 18, under the headline "American Snipers Busy in Fismette," James described the danger of American sharpshooters confronting equally agile German riflemen in a small hamlet. Thelma, sucking on a lemon drop, read, "The American soldiers there have revived the old quip about there being in the place only the quick and the dead."

Annie said, "Quick! Quick!"

"Pow! Pow!" cried Julius, playing rifle with a yardstick, slaying his sister.

Adele fell dutifully on the floor, crying, "Dead! Dead!" as Thelma concluded the article.

"France will never forget what America is doing."

"Quick, you dummies, the baby's here!"

"Mama!" Thelma shrilled, dropping the newspaper. She grabbed Annie under the armpits and hoisted her out of the amniotic fluid–soaked chair. Mama scurried in, buried in an armload of rags, her eyes wild. Ignoring Mama, their bossiest neighbor, Mrs. Spiegelberg, ordered an agitated Mrs. Dickman to escort the children upstairs, although the synagogue *yenta* lingered, apparently not wanting to be excluded from the front.

"Must I get a broom and sweep you out?" asked the widow Spiegelberg, turning to the cellist Mrs. Famant. "Grab Jesse before he faints and I have two patients. Brew him tea upstairs or, better yet, schnapps." Decisively removing and repositioning a hairpin, the widow Spiegelberg marched into the kitchen, announcing, "Boiling water."

Meanwhile, Thelma led Annie to bed. The pregnant woman collapsed and then crawled into a fetal position. She felt like a mule had kicked her lower back, paused to improve its aim, and slammed her again for spite. She'd been here twice before, but the pain was worse than she recalled. Between contractions, she felt oddly elated. "Thelma, bring me some chocolate."

"You ate the last one."

"What, now you're counting? I stashed an emergency Hershey bar in the embroidered *afikomen* cover under the good tablecloth."

"I'll find it," Thelma said.

"Don't take any for yourself."

Thelma winced. "God forbid I steal the chocolate from your mouth!"

"Are you calling me fat?"

Thelma rolled her eyes. Her mouth worked as if trying to bite her tongue, but then she spat, "If the shoe fits, squeeze your foot into it."

"Get out!"

"Door open or shut?"

"Go already!" Annie couldn't bother with her sister's attitude. She was a bug. Squish. Crunch. "You don't belong."

"Who carried you in here?"

"I forget."

"Why don't you stand up, Annie? That's how cows give birth."

"Mama, get her out of here."

"I'm going." Thelma slammed the door behind her. The formal wedding portrait of Annie and Jesse fell off the wall, glass shattering.

"Pain in the neck," Annie said.

"Troublemaker," Mama agreed as she rushed to collect the big shards with calloused fingers and sweep up the smaller.

"Always with the last word," said Annie as the angry mule kicked again, harder, to get her attention. In agony, she flopped around, trying to find a comfortable position. She didn't know whether to stay reclined or rise—but then she weighed Thelma's words and remained in bed.

Stretching her legs, Annie pushed at her heels, curled her toes, and then balled up. She exhaled as the ache eased between spasms and realized she was clutching the sheets. She loosened her grip and actually smiled, poised to meet this beautiful baby who'd been swimming around inside her *kishkes*, a part of her, party to all her secrets. It was happening. No more waiting. No more strangers touching her belly as if she were a cow.

Annie struggled to squelch Thelma's comment. She turned her thoughts, instead, to pondering her hopes for a boy, to be named Elias after Jesse's father. Before long, she'd cradle Eli, if the infant were a boy. She'd kiss his little fish lips, pinch his *tuchus*, and latch him on to her breast. It would be the first meeting of a lifetime of closeness. With each child, she was knitting her family tighter around her. She could tell by how heavy her chest already was that she'd have buckets of milk. Like a cow, she thought, and then said, "Stinker," brooding about Thelma, the husband thief, the fly in the ointment.

But, no, her sister was a speck, a nothing with neither children nor husband nor dollars. *She* was the good daughter. Her third baby would be the child born in wartime in a household of peace and plenty, with a father and a mother, a sister and a brother and a grandmother, drowning in affection. She couldn't wait to meet this child.

Mama shuffled in with more rags, followed by Mrs. Spiegelberg carrying the boiling-water basin. "Out of my way!" the neighbor warned as if no one were more important.

In the rear, Thelma padded in, removing the candy wrapper and dispensing a small corner. Stroking Annie's shoulder by way of apology, she asked, "How can I help?"

"Get the hell out," Annie said, snatching the candy bar. Thelma flinched. That was the way Annie liked to see her: paralyzed with terror, stifled. "And shut the door behind you."

Annie didn't want that bitch anywhere near her baby. It was bad enough observing her show off beside Julius teaching him to read or letting Adele crawl into that nasty lap of hers. This infant was coming out and so were the knives. Her serenity month was over. She'd switched to her delivery mood, no longer pliable. She broke off a larger chocolate chunk, sucking the sweetness. The mule kicked, and she ground her teeth. She placed a pillow between her thighs and hugged a second cushion that smelled like Jesse's coal-tar shampoo. It was disgusting, but it was him.

The pregnant mother began to mouth breathe deeply, wishing only that she'd stashed two chocolate bars in the *afikomen* cover. "Hey, Temmy," she yelled through the door, "send Julie for more chocolate."

"Where's your wallet?"

"Take money from your purse."

"Will you pay me back?"

Annie didn't answer. Fearless, relief flooded over her. It was starting and she was ready, a true Eastern European: plow wheat in morning, have baby at night. At least that's what Jesse said, although she was glad he was upstairs with Mrs. Famant, because his fussing infuriated her. Whatever he could do to help he'd contributed at conception. Hopefully the kid would have his father's typically pliant temperament but not his knobby knees. And she'd ensure the infant knew the meaning of a spanking if he displayed his uncle's sticky fingers. No, this kid would be righteous, lawful, and fair. He would excel in school and she would warrant that he had perfect attendance. Unlike his brother, Julius, he wouldn't have to work. He would be as close to a Torah scholar as she could manage in America. He would toil with his mind and not his hands, a studier, not a laborer.

Mama settled at the top of the mattress, where two pillows normally rested, lifting her daughter's head into her lap with fingers made strong from domestic work. With a damp rag, she traced a circle on Annie's sweat-slicked forehead; the eldest daughter cooed in response to let Mama know to continue, that it soothed her. Her shoulders relaxed against the older woman's knees. They were the image of mother and child, and Annie knew it would irritate her brothers and sister to see how close they were, nearly identical in looks but for the difference in their ages and experience. Her siblings' imagined jealousy made it all the sweeter.

Removing a boar-bristle brush from her apron pocket, Mama gently parsed Annie's curls, smoothing the snags as if fingering fine wool. She had often told Annie that in Galicia young women received knotty balls of yarn to untangle to prove their patience before they could marry. She'd said there weren't enough skeins in Austria to prepare Mama for her marriage!

Mama scratched Annie's scalp, stroking the thin brows plucked like those of a silent film star. Humming a lullaby in a minor key, she held on as Annie's body shuddered when contractions slammed her harder and quicker.

Their mutual exchange of comfort was a tradition rooted in mourning for Papa. She'd cradled Mama's head when the woman had suffered in that tuberculosis-riven tenement, when she had threatened to abandon this new world and all its old disappointments, forgetting her sons, who were only nine and six at the time, and Thelma, the baby. There had been only Annie to rescue her, rubbing her temples, soothing her sobs.

Fifteen years later, Mama nurtured Annie with the attentiveness she'd learned from her daughter. For them both, the world had stopped rushing past and they clung to each other, survivors sharing a life raft. Annie reflected, as the mule kick became stomping and Mrs. Spiegelberg demanded she push, that she was the love of her mother's life. And it was this thought that held her as the contractions crested and receded and the baby's head battered against her insides, simultaneously reluctant to leave and demanding exit. She began to scream and Mrs. Spiegelberg tried to put a rag gag between her teeth, but she swatted the woman's hands away. She raised herself on her elbows and growled and spit and howled, falling back to pant and then rising again.

"Stop kicking me," said Mrs. Spiegelberg.

"Then get out of my way!"

"Hold still!"

"You hold still . . ." The comment ended in a curse as Annie grunted and groaned and heaved as much to push out the baby as to chase the aggravating Mrs. Spiegelberg out of the room. As this third child slid from between her legs, following the path widened by Julius and Adele, and gave one healthy *geschrei*, she felt her heart expand and a fierce desire to protect this life even if she had to die trying. She knew as he curled into her arms, all tiny fingers and toes and a little pecker and pink testicles, that he was going to be the love of her life.

"Get Jesse," she said as an afterthought.

∿

Weeks passed and the baby prospered. She held him constantly, a bulwark between herself and the world. When she needed to change clothes, she handed Mama the infant. Even four-year-old Adele had her turn (with close supervision), but not Thelma. Annie justified the rejection by telling herself her sister was irresponsible, but there was an underlying jealousy twisted up with anger: the fear that the child might bond to the sister and reject the mother (like Abie, like Louis, even Moe). As for Abie, she snubbed him, not inviting him to the circumcision, the *bris*. She wouldn't let him upstage the holy event with showgirls or distract the mohel with schmuck jokes.

After that, most evenings the family followed the Thirty-Eighth Infantry's progress against the Germans. In late September, after a fifty-six-hour assault, the Allies breached the enemy's last defensive position on the Western Front, the Hindenburg Line. Louis had not only fought with the winning side—he'd survived enemy artillery, snipers, and mustard gas. The army promoted the family war hero to private first class. The French awarded him the *Croix de Guerre* for bravery. His division became known as the Rock of the Marne for changing the course of the war.

Louis remained in Europe as autumn folded like batter into winter. On a dank December 23, Annie held a newspaper, watching out the window for Thelma to return from work. Before the sixteen-year-old had shaken the sleet from her shoulders, Annie pounced, handing her the *Brooklyn Daily Eagle*.

"What's the rush?" Thelma asked, removing her damp gloves. "Is Louis's name in the paper?"

"Read," Annie urged, torn between shame and schadenfreude. She'd been waiting all afternoon for Thelma to come home so she could shove her nose in the paper. Now she'd watch her squirm.

"Is this what you wanted me to see: 'Red Tape Delays Peace Conference'?"

"Not that," Annie said, impatience rising.

"Don't play games, Annie, I'm beat." Thelma shimmied out of her coat. "This: 'London Streets Decked with Flags in Wilson's Honor'?"

Annie sucked her teeth. "Not that, either."

"What then? And where's Julie?"

"With Jesse," Annie said, trying to keep a poker face. "Look lower."

"This: 'Eight Million Killed in the World War; Thirty-One Million Six Hundred Total'?" Thelma plopped on the sofa. Although the girl began weeping at the news, Annie couldn't stomach her tears.

"Take off your boots."

"How can you worry about feet at a time like this? I can't even imagine that many people to begin with—and that many people dead. It's a miracle Louis survived."

"A miracle, right," said Annie. She shifted the baby like a swaddled potato from one shoulder to the other, shook out a burp that launched stringy white spittle over the cloth covering her back. "Read below that article."

"That's local news."

"What does it say?"

"You tell me."

"Look."

"It says, 'Hold 2 as Store Looters.'" Thelma leaned in, placing her forefinger on the newsprint to mark her spot. "With the arrest of Abraham Lorber, alias 'Yiddle' . . ." Thelma looked up, eyes wide. She said in a rush, "Was Abie arrested? Did he telegram? Why didn't you tell me when I walked through the door?"

"He's done it again, your Abie darling, shamed us in front of everybody. Read."

"I can't."

"Since when?"

"Since my heart's breaking. Is he in custody? Have you talked to him?"

"You wanna know the truth about Abie, it's there in black and white for everybody to see." Annie nuzzled Eli's bald head, savoring her sister's distress after her summer of pride.

Thelma returned to the paper, voice quavering:

> . . . 23 years old, of 481 Essex St., and Dorothy Bernstein,
> 19 years old, of 111 Clymer St. . . . .

She gazed at Annie, puzzled. "Who's Dorothy Bernstein?"

"Who knows? But if there's a girl involved, it must be Abie."

"How can you say that?"

"He's a disgusting lecher. Wake up! He's a dirty, rotten *goniff*."

"That's not true."

"Read to the end. He stole from Jews!"

> . . . the police say they have put a damper on store loot-
> ing. The two were arrested by Detective Van Giluwe on
> a charge of receiving stolen goods from the shop of
> Clara Katz, at 17 E. 17th St., Manhattan. They were held
> on $1,000 bail by Magistrate Steers in the Williamsburg
> police court today.

"I don't know where he's going to get a thousand dollars," said Annie. "If we had that kind of money we'd buy a house!"

"Has he asked you for money?"

"He wouldn't dare."

"Is there that kind of dough in a newsstand?"

"Just nickels and dimes," said Annie, downplaying the profits. She did the books, after all. It was a good business.

"What are we going to do?"

"That's his problem," said Annie. "He should rot in jail."

"He's our brother."

"Like that's ever stopped him before. When are you going to wise up? Abie is dangerous to himself and all of us. Ask the parents of Dorothy Bernstein."

"Who?"

"His accomplice. Cut him off, Thelma. He's dead to us. Defend him and you'll end up on the streets, or in the sewers."

"I'll take my chances. It beats your company."

"You've got a lot of nerve, skinny girl. You sound tough now, but don't say I never warned you. Someday you're going to need me. You're going to beg for my help, and then I won't be so nice."

"Since when are you nice? He's Abie. He needs us."

"Keep believing that, sister, but I'm nobody's fool." Annie rubbed her hands together while the baby hung from her shoulder. "I'm washing my hands of this tsuris and putting my children first. Abie? Feh! I'm done."

Chapter 19

1919

Annie claimed to be finished with Abie, but Thelma wasn't. It took more than an arrest to test her affection—and he hadn't even served jail time. Boasting that he was untouchable, he often treated her to pizza at their favorite spot near Nina's house, dropping her off for a visit with the Gigantiellos afterward but never joining her upstairs. Sometimes the siblings would catch a movie or, if Abie had an extra ticket, go to the fights—and sit ringside like big shots. He'd confess his troubles and she'd share hers, and they discussed Louis and the fun they'd have when he returned to New York.

On the first day of August 1919, Abie called Thelma at work and invited her to meet him in East New York, which wasn't a neighborhood she knew well. He said he had a surprise but rang off before she could ask what it was. Having left work early to meet Abie after her boss skipped with the other secretary, she *shvitsed* in a summer shirtwaist that had begun to ripen. Who had time to wash and iron a blouse more than once a week? Who had money for two? Not Thelma, the working girl who took dictation at the women's shoe factory but couldn't afford more than a pair of shoes every other year, especially since Annie pocketed her weekly pay packet for rent and household expenses.

That summer was record-setting miserable, so bad even chatty neighbors clammed up, although they didn't mind their own business. Instead they watched without commenting, saving their strength and collecting gossip for cooler times. In Chicago, race riots exploded. White mobs had killed another colored man, raising the total to twenty-three. In Brooklyn, the heat steamed up from the sidewalk and pressed down like an electric iron. Garbage could be smelled from three blocks distant; a rotting corpse would take days to discover.

The Allies won the Great War and, for once, the Lorbers landed on the winning side. They expected Louis home on leave any day, although he hadn't sent a telegram for them to meet him at the docks yet. Meanwhile, infant Eli was already pulling himself up and threatening to walk (a genius bound to climb Everest!). He'd never met his uncle Abie, who'd avoided Hooper Street since the chilly night of the slap and the *shiksas*, the last time they'd seen Louis before he'd shipped out.

As Abie had explained, he was too busy to drop by, making deals, fixing disputes, and living on Essex Street with a Jewish contortionist who made physical demands he was obliged to keep. Ahem. According to Annie, her brother was an unwelcome *putz*. But it seemed to Thelma that lately there had been some kind of thaw, and she recognized the return of Annie's crafty look in eyes that had softened just a *bissel* during that first year of the infant king's reign.

Hot days or cool, the sun rose and set on that child, whom Abie was in no apparent hurry to meet. On the day he called, he met Thelma on the stoop of an unfamiliar redbrick house at 265 Montauk Avenue between Sutter and Belmont, five miles east of their Williamsburg apartment and Nina's Our Lady of Mount Carmel parish. From what she could tell by the mezuzah nailed to the doorframe, this was a Jewish neighborhood. She worried that the owner would rush out any minute and shoo them off his steps. Still, Thelma didn't question why her brother wanted her to meet him there; she was accustomed to going easy on the questions since his December arrest. She didn't condone stealing, but she wasn't her brother's keeper and, after all, it wasn't a violent crime.

The Montauk row house was about Thelma's age, a two-story brick building identical to its neighbors with five cement steps built to last. A door and two windows fronted the narrow porch, and a second floor with three rectangular windows perched above that. A pretty redbrick facade rose atop that like a paper crown, with a graceful arch and three decorative diamonds. It was nothing fancy unless an immigrant family believed that owning a house on a quiet street with a tree out front was a dream too far, a making-it-in-America fairy tale that folks had heard about but never achieved.

"What I'm saying, Temeleh, is getting arrested and paying bail— *that's* the cost of doing business, the unavoidable expenses that cut into your profit. Ask Annie the money counter; she'll explain."

"I'll skip it," she said, jealous and disturbed that Annie and Abie kept secrets from her.

"Okay, I'll take a stab."

She jokingly raised her hands as if to defend herself. "Don't hurt me!"

"A guy like me pulls a knife once or twice and nobody will ever let him forget it."

She punched his arm, teasing to mask her concern. "Oh, poor baby."

"Not so poor."

"I'd rather have you beside me than shekels in my pocket," she said.

"Why not both?" he asked, raising his eyebrows.

"If you continue breaking the law, Abie, you'll end up in prison stripes—and they're not your style." She needed him more than money, but he just patted her knee and laughed. She knew that's who he was. That's how he got his kicks. Good citizenship was for suckers. He was cocky that way—and she worried that if she scolded too much, he'd disappear.

"You worry too much, little sister," he said. "This arrest thing is a racket, a way to shift cash around to the bail bondsman, the cops, the lawyers, and the judges without wasting a brown paper bag. It's lubrication, like oil, to keep the system moving."

"So getting arrested doesn't discourage you from breaking the law?" she asked, fearing deportation for anything worse than cheating on a math test.

"Why should it?" he asked. "What a *shvits*! I need a drink. I'm guessing you're not carrying?"

Thelma shook her head and laughed. "I'm worthless."

"Beat yourself up on your own time. As for me, I have no more shame than John D. Rockefeller or Cornelius Vanderbilt. I'm never going to be a big *macher* at the synagogue—and if I wanted that, I'd make a hefty donation. That's how things work in America. I am who I am."

"You certainly are. Annie thinks you're the devil."

"Not so much lately, but I'll get to that. Now focus. You're a smart girl, but here's a lesson you don't get from school. The coppers haul me in. They stick me in bracelets to make a big show. Maybe it winds up in the papers to shiver up the good citizens and scare the neighbors who cry for more cops on the beat."

"Annie didn't take it so lightly. She rammed the paper down my gullet, and my throat still hurts. A summer of Louis being a war hero, wiped out by a single burglary."

"Well, it wasn't a single one, more like a looting spree, but I didn't need handcuffs. I didn't hurt anybody. I'm not on the lam—I'm a local businessman with ties to the community—it just doesn't look so good to their bosses if they bring me in nicely and we're all smiling and clapping each other on the back."

"So the police are your friends?" she asked, screwing up her forehead.

"I won't confess to that, Madame Prosecutor. Between you and me, I'll admit we're business associates."

"Monkey business?"

"Oy. Are you going to nudge me to the bitter end here? I go to the precinct house. I pass around some Cuban cigars. We *kibitz*. I tell them some things about people I don't like. They tell me who they have locked up and who looks nice for certain crimes. I clear my throat. I nod. I make a face like something stinks. I point them this way or that. We have a laugh. It's not them or us except in the minds of the sister-hood broads gasping at the *shonda*. The shame is we aren't all born rich with a martini glass in our hands and mink diapers."

"I wouldn't want to change those!"

"It's a metaphor."

"So now you're talking in metaphors, Mr. English teacher? You didn't finish school."

"School of life, Temeleh. It isn't fair, but it adds up. For every arrest, I pull four or five jobs that go unnoticed and I line my pockets. That's why we're here."

"Sitting on a stoop in the wilds of Brooklyn? Why *are* we here?"

He pulled out a set of keys with a pleased look on his face and dangled them. "I bought us a house."

"Are you kidding? You, a homeowner?"

He raised both eyebrows. "Not just me."

"This is ours?" It astonished Thelma, something entirely out of the blue. She'd never thought she'd have that kind of security—or that Abie would be the one to provide it. This was supposed to be something that you got by scratching and saving for generations, putting aside fun for frugality. That wasn't Abie's way. "What's the catch? Is it for you and me and the contortionist?"

"No. She's no housekeeper. The only way she'd be seen in an apron is if she wasn't wearing anything else. And when she gives you a spanking, it's an ouch to remember!"

"Now that's something I'll never be able to forget," Thelma said, placing her right fingers on her solar plexus. "You're giving me heartburn."

"Don't say I never gave you anything."

"I never gave you anything."

"I told you not to say that." He leaned back and examined his fingernails. "Annie was right: you never listen."

"Since when are you talking to Annie again?"

"Since I had a windfall—I need to park some cash."

"Isn't that why God created banks?"

"Did he? Doesn't seem like his style. Banks—I don't trust them. A mutual friend introduced me to the homeowner, Mrs. Reckholder. When her daughter married and moved to Philly, the widow wanted to sell and join her. Now, thanks to Uncle Abie, she can—with her mortgage transferred and a sack of cash. It's a good investment and it doesn't hurt for me to have a permanent address when the cops show: ties to the community."

"If they met Annie, they'd know you're still a flight risk. Something stinks."

"Trust me. This way, when Louis gets his discharge, he has a place to live, raise a family if he wants. It was Annie's idea."

"I just shivered, and it's a heat wave. Nothing good ever comes from Annie."

"Don't worry. I got this. Nobody cons a con. She said it was a peace pipe, but I know better, since I'm fronting the tobacco. What Annie wants more than anything else is a castle for her little king with a backyard and a front porch. And it's me that's giving it to her, not that *meeskait* Jesse."

"So suddenly you care what Annie wants? What about me?"

"I got you covered. What's mine is yours. I brought you here first so you can pick your room before Annie arrives and *geschreis*. Let's see if she can be an ungrateful bitch once I hand her the keys."

"I wouldn't be surprised. Is it in your name?"

"What?"

"Is your name on the deed?"

"What, now you're a lawyer?"

"What's the angle?"

"There's no angle."

"You forget I've known you all my life. Spill."

He raised his hands in mock surrender. "You got me. On Tuesday, we're going to the clerk's office on Joralemon Street and I'm putting it in Mama's name."

"Why would you do anything for them? Why put it in her name?"

"You're still a minor, and if the cops want to put a lien on what I own, they can't, because it's not in my name. But you and I, we know who bought it."

"I hope you didn't outsmart yourself."

With nimble thief's fingers, Abie jiggled and then rotated the key in the lock. He shoved the door and ushered Thelma inside while glancing over his shoulder. As they entered the tiled entryway, heat and stale air smothered them. Thelma hesitated, unsettled. It didn't smell like the home of a widow who'd recently left, but something more vinegary and sadder. She eyed Abie, who bemusedly removed his jacket and looped it on the brass doorknob.

"Welcome to Lorber Hall. It's not bad, huh, Temmy?"

"I hate to look a gift horse in the mouth, but did somebody die here?"

"Not me!" he said, and then, "Look, it's the Ritz: upstairs and downstairs."

"All you need is a top hat and tails."

Abie danced up and down the staircase along the house's shared right wall. He was a regular George M. Cohan, raising his cap and kicking out his legs. When he returned to the bottom, he grabbed Thelma's waist and whirled her around the empty living room. "You're the only girl for me."

She snorted like a mare, which made them both laugh. Dancing madly, he shook out her worries. Still, she wondered who, without a gun to their head, would have chosen the brown floral carpeting. It seemed to be defending the floors from filth by being uglier than dirt. Empty walnut curtain rods hung above the pair of windows with the rings askew, as if someone had hurriedly yanked away the fabric.

Breathing heavily, they strolled through oak pocket doors into the dining room with a built-in buffet. Because it was a row house, the absence of side windows darkened the interior rooms. Below them, the parquet floor had a Greek key design forming a bracelet around the perimeter. Through a swinging door, a window overlooking a fenced-in concrete patch brightened the kitchen. Thelma crossed the room and squashed her nose against the glass, imagining nights under the stars catching a breeze and releasing it.

They had their own private piece of the world. She should be thrilled, but what she felt was anxiety and she couldn't figure out why. Putting on a smile, she turned and grabbed Abie's hand and said, "Thank you."

"Aw, it was nothing," he said. "Let's pick your room."

"So this is what it's like to be rich."

"Minus the diamonds and chauffeurs," he said.

When she thought of wealth, she remembered that kid sitting opposite her in the streetcar when they went to visit her brothers at the orphanage. The two girls hadn't exchanged a glance: she'd stared and the other had ignored her. She'd been invisible, a bundle of rags with a shorn head trapped between two mountains, Mama and Annie. She recalled the bright-red wool coat with the mouton collar and the black Scottie dog that licked his owner's lips. But more than that, she considered the girl's self-possession, her ankles crossed, secure in her perfect coat with black velvet buttons, bearing a dog and her privilege.

At the time, Thelma had wanted to change places, to go where that girl was going, drink her hot milk and honey with vanilla wafers, warm her feet in the stranger's slippers. And when she'd gazed at Mama, she'd felt more hostage than daughter.

Abie poked her and pointed to a door off the kitchen. "How about this room, princess?"

She wrinkled her nose and then realized how strange it felt to reject something on offer, suspicious there wouldn't be another choice. Still, she said, "Better for Mama, right?"

"Never underestimate the advantage of a quick back-door exit."

"I don't see myself shinnying over the fence," she said. "I'm too clumsy."

"We don't want you to break that magic leg."

"Let's try the second floor. Can you believe it—a house with upstairs *and* downstairs? I never thought I'd see the day."

"You gotta dream big," he said, offering his elbow. "Shall we?"

"Let's!"

On the top landing, Thelma cracked a door to a narrow room. She pulled a string dangling from a lone bulb. "Bedroom or closet?"

"Closet," he answered. "That broom is a dead giveaway."

"Smart," she said, shadowing Abie into the big front bedroom as wide as the building. Light flooded through three double-hung windows facing Montauk Avenue and splashed across the window seat. She cracked the doors of a built-in closet and (despite a mothball blast and an undernote of exotic oriental perfume) imagined a yard of gossamer dresses above three pairs of shoes. She was happy but immediately suspected her elation, searching for the catch. She turned to Abie. "Did someone die in here?"

"Still with the dying: Did anyone ever tell you that you're morbid?"

"You taught me everything I know."

They sat beside each other in the window seat. She looked away from him and he took her hand. When she looked back, his eyes were studying her face. "What's wrong?"

"It's wonderful, Abie, a home of our own."

His eyes didn't leave her face. She looked down, playing with his pinkie ring. "Tell me, Temmy. What aches?"

"It's perfect, Abie, I'm just overwhelmed, *verklempt*."

"No, you're not," he said, softening his voice and focusing all his attention on her. "I can see bees buzzing in your head. Tell me what's what."

"It couldn't be better," she said, stroking his cheek. "It's a happy ending."

"You want to sleep with Mama your whole life?"

"You know that's not it." The seventeen-year-old wondered what she truly wanted—and presented with the house, which should have been a dream, she felt in her gut that she needed something, some acceptance, that wasn't four walls and a roof. "Who cares what I want?"

"Try me," he said. She bit her lip. "Let it out."

"Abie, you share everything with me, and nobody treats me better." He raised his eyebrows, creating a cliff on his forehead. "But?"

"But nothing," she said. "It seems that whatever it is I want, whatever that turns out to be, can't be found at the end of this hallway, or that one. I don't know. I feel like I want to break free."

"Ah," he said, nearing her and not letting her eyes wander. "Now we're getting somewhere."

"I don't even know what I want, exactly, or how to string the words. I have to figure out who I really am in the world, not the husband thief, the wicked little sister, the runt." She didn't know how to explain that she wanted to feel the way she'd felt with Giorgio: light on her feet and beloved, sparklers everywhere and singing in the shadows.

She knew what she didn't want to be: judged by a hanging jury. Fame or infamy: not for her. She wasn't obsessed with becoming someone who made the papers, like her brothers. She wasn't good enough to perform onstage, but she wanted to dance through life, to feel that joy she'd felt downstairs, her elation in her brothers' company. She wanted to love and be loved.

He touched her cheek. "What are you afraid of?"

"No one ever asks me that. I'm afraid all the time. Annie scares the hell out of me. I'm afraid that everything she says about me is true. I'm afraid I'll be stuck with her forever. I'm afraid that I'm unlovable."

"I love you," he said. "And I don't throw that around like loose change."

"The feeling is mutual," she said. "From that first time you rescued me from Annie, you've always seemed certain who you are. I don't know who I am."

"I don't, either." He looked down at his shoes, licked his finger, and wiped away a spot. "I know who they made me."

"No one is more his own person than you!"

"That's what you think, kiddo." He laughed. "Who had time to bother with who I was, or what I wanted, before the knives came out? I know what I don't want—and that's somebody else's boot on my neck. Not Annie's, not that stupid jerk Nathan Rothman or his bosses, not the cops nor the army neither. I'm tough, sure, but it's not like I had a choice."

"This house isn't for us, is it, Abie?" she asked. "It's wonderful— don't get me wrong. But it's Annie's dream, not mine. What I really wanted when I came to meet you was to escape Mama and Annie."

"I understand, Temmy, I do. The best cell in prison is still behind bars."

Chapter 20

As they walked from room to room on Montauk Avenue, Thelma asked, "What other bedrooms are there?"

"Not big enough for you, Temmy?"

"This one's for Annie."

"Who cares what Annie wants? She's getting a house from stoop to nuts on my dime. You'll never get what you want if you don't take it."

"I'm not picking a fight from day one."

"Since when is me giving you the best room picking a fight?"

"Don't futz with me, Abie. She'll explode and I'll be yanking shrapnel from my *tuchus* for months while you're out playing the joker. Who needs the *shpilkes*?" Not her. But tsuris seemed inevitable, because she heard her sister's shrill voice inside her own head. Annie made everyone miserable until she got what she wanted. If she wasn't allowed to control the situation, to decide who was coming to Passover, when the meal would start, and when everyone would leave so that her children's precious bedtime wouldn't be disturbed, she'd melt down. Everyone in the household, even Mama, dreaded that outburst. Not Abie: He didn't do fear. He did revenge.

Abie could handle the consequences, not the thin-skinned Thelma. He'd go to any extreme to slice Annie down to size. He played dirtier than she did and then sneered as he danced out of reach. To Thelma, his personality appeared sandblasted and immutable, his confidence as pure as the color blue. Not her. She questioned who she was, dependent, scalded by Annie's tongue. She had a generosity her sister lacked and yet she felt inferior—didn't Mama love Annie but not Thelma?

Unlike Abie, who reminded her that seeking Annie's approval was like trying to squeeze blood from a stone, she still hungered for intimacy with her sister. If only she did this kindness, behaved that way—but it was a fool's errand. And, for now, she was that fool. It shamed her that she still cared what Annie thought. Even though she told Abie almost everything that was on her mind, she guarded this weakness from his ridicule. She still hoped that, if she could restrain herself and not attack, Annie would ultimately accept her. It was ridiculous, because she suspected she'd only please Annie by submitting completely, extinguishing the light that shone so brightly within her, the spark that had attracted Giorgio. She'd have to disappear, even from herself.

Thelma didn't yet accept that unconditional surrender was the price of peace (as it had been for the Huns). She kept trying to connect, to somehow do the right thing to appease Annie, making the older sister recognize and protect the younger, as she did with her own children. It aggravated her that Annie could nurture Julius, Adele, and Eli and, with a swivel of her head, spew dragon fire toward Thelma. She was caught between her desire to get this kindness that flowed from Annie toward her children and her need to expose Annie for the cruelties visited on herself, Abie, and Louis. That was who Annie really was, sadistic and hateful, that was her core—but that's not who Mama saw, or Jesse, or the trio of kids.

Right now, Thelma wanted to discover who she was in the world, but she kept hearing Annie: "Nothing, a schnorrer, going nowhere." Her legs were too long, her kinship with her brother criminal. She wasn't affectionate, she was clingy, and yet, as Abie led her down the murky hallway, she felt the warmth of their connection through their entwined fingers. They passed three identical windowless chambers.

"No," he said. "No. No."

They entered the larger of two sunny corner rooms overlooking the rear. She overplayed the game, trying to recapture a lighter mood despite the sweat soaking her pits. She shuffled across the bare wood floor, toeing aside a dead iridescent fly.

"This is it," she said, spinning around. Dizzy, she flung open a window. A ginger tabby slunk into the jungle of the neighbors' sunflowers. "I want this one."

"It's nice, but why not the biggest?"

"This is more private."

"Pick the fancy closet, because that pig Annie will want that room. And when she blows up because your dresses are already there, you'll be in a position to negotiate. You'll get the room you want—and a leg up."

"She'll be ferocious."

"Enjoy the fireworks."

"It's the cost of doing business, huh, Abie?"

"You're learning."

"Which room is yours?"

"I'm staying with the contortionist. At least there I know where I stand."

"On your head," she said, disappointed. "You're a good man, Abraham Lorber."

"Not common wisdom but much appreciated, sweet little sister. You've got a big heart, but beware—it makes for a big target."

Later that week, when Annie arrived, Thelma had removed her meager wardrobe from the master bedroom closet where Abie had hung it. She'd taken the easy route. Content to hide at the back of the house far from Annie, reading movie magazines, she waited for Louis to return and share a wall, taking the other bedroom at the back. This would be *their* home as much as Annie's, and she'd have an ally. She'd smiled at the thought: how he'd always had her back and held her secrets. A brother like that was worth a thousand Annies. She remembered how he was that day at the orphanage, his pants too big, spotted and torn, his lip split and his eyes holding the floor until she took his hand. He'd looked up and she'd soaked in his sadness and shot back love, devotion. It was like she could think a feeling even then and mail it through her eyes to him. His postcards from the front had been a continuation of that: he could say so much to her in short sentences. He wasn't dumb; he was just cautious with his emotions.

She waited, but Louis didn't come back to Brooklyn. He'd broken up the band without as much as a warning telegram. He didn't have the words for cruelty, and he would have known how devastated they'd be. She and Abie had just assumed he'd train it home as soon as he was demobilized to collect the respect he now deserved. They would be there to share in the glory—he wasn't just a war hero, he was *their* war hero. Their brother was the pride of the Brooklyn Dodgers without ever having thrown a pitch. How could they be no good if he'd fought alongside the greatest in the Great War?

But, no, after being promoted from private to corporal and cited for bravery, Louis reenlisted. Now he was stationed at Camp Pike in Pulaski, Arkansas, near Little Rock. It could have been the moon. Jews just didn't go to Arkansas. In New York, you could be Jewish and, if you didn't leave the neighborhood, you'd hardly know there were Christians, except for the Italians, and they shared a similar system of guilt.

Louis occasionally wrote Thelma, informing her that he had friends where he was, fighting men who understood him, his band of brothers from other mothers. She kept the letters tied with penny ribbon, gray for his eyes, treasured beneath her pillow, where she could finger them at night. He told her that he appreciated army discipline and he didn't mind obeying men who made sense to him. They were working together with a shared goal: he liked that. If he followed the rules, he got along, praised even. Chaos was the battlefield, but there was an order among soldiers and officers. She understood what he left unsaid: that he despised living under the rule of Annie, the randomness and ferocity of her anger. He would rather die from an enemy's assault than the thousand pointless cuts at home. She sensed, and felt jealous, that he'd found a family in the army and, though she would always be close, there was no place for her there. He'd invited her to visit, but she'd never make it out of Brooklyn. She was stuck and tangled here. He'd made it out.

He'd found a local sweetheart. Louis deserved a honey, a thousand honeys. But she knew he was the kind of man who, unlike Abie, only wanted one, not one and change. He claimed he'd worked his Brooklyn charm on a doll named Lucille—a Gentile. It *was* Arkansas, after all. And maybe he was getting serious but he didn't want her anywhere near their older sister. Lucille wouldn't understand, and he liked the girl too much to have her suffer the Annie treatment. Thelma comprehended the way Annie's ridicule held them hostage, chased away happiness. He'd earned respect in the Thirty-Eighth Infantry, and he didn't want anybody he loved to see that disgust in Annie's eyes when she looked at him. That was the problem with having a sister as an enemy: all the fighting was dirty and he couldn't use the proper weapons in his arsenal. He was brave but he wasn't stupid—that's how he'd survived France. A frontal assault would never work with Annie; better to know who she was and withdraw to higher ground.

Abie took Louis's absence hard at first, bellyaching to Thelma—and then never mentioning it again. He adjusted. He always had. The brothers had been a team. They were only two years apart and Abie lacked memories from before his brother was born. Louis had been his conscience and compass. Too reckless to protect himself, Abie guarded his younger brother. But he didn't brood after Louis reenlisted. He smothered whatever feelings remained in booze and girls, throwing himself off cliff after cliff to see if he'd always land on his feet. *Have knife, will travel.* He had his grudges but never against Louis. He explained to Thelma on one of the many nights they shared the stoop on Montauk Avenue—never taking the chairs on the narrow porch—that it wouldn't have been a snap for a decorated war vet on the streets where rules of combat didn't exist. And he didn't want to pull Louis down, since, as he told Thelma, "I'm having a run of bad luck and I have no one to blame but me."

Mistakes were the cost of doing business: a person was high, then low, but rarely in the safe middle. He confessed actions he shouldn't have, like that Rothman stabbing, saying that when he'd poked that stranger because another man asked him to, he'd crossed a line. He hadn't been angry, or vengeful. He didn't cry. He called the kid's bet, that's all. He explained that not many people had this ability, which had been both a good and a bad thing. He did it and then he forgot it.

Remorse was for suckers, Abie explained to Thelma. "I know guys like that. I just wasn't one of them. I didn't want to get caught. If I didn't do it, somebody else would've." He was just the blade, and someone bigger and meaner wielded the handle. He reminded Thelma that a person had to enjoy the here and now because there wasn't any heaven later. His pleasures weren't fancy: not cuff links and champagne but bagels and broads, the taller the better. And she recognized she was more like Abie than Annie. She wanted pleasure in this life, not scraping for a secure future that might never arrive.

He made the papers again in early 1921, terrifying the nineteen-year-old Thelma and inspiring a heaping helping of vitriol from Annie. The police arrested him as a material witness to the murder of gangster Edward "Monk" Eastman, onetime head of the Eastman gang and veteran of both the US Army and Sing Sing. He'd made the war hero and gang boss mix work—but not for very long. The shooting had happened the day after Christmas at 4:00 a.m. outside the Blue Bird Café on Fourteenth Street and Fourth Avenue—three blocks from the family newsstand. Nothing transpired on Fourteenth Street that Abie didn't know about—including the killing, which he explained was a fight about money that got out of hand. The bloodshed, which inspired Thelma to fear for her brother's life, recalled the Rothman stabbing that had climaxed in a bloody pool in the same vicinity.

While the Eastman hit wasn't a victimless crime, it could be viewed as gang warfare that didn't imperil honest civilians. Abie coolly assured his sister that he'd just stumbled past the scene on the way to the newsstand. Despite the papers and the police interest, he'd assured Thelma he'd had nothing to do with the crime. She wanted to believe him, so she did; she refused to see him as the stock villain Annie claimed him to be. Since he didn't snitch, ultimately the coppers stopped bothering him and he appeared justified in his protestations of innocence. As Abie explained, exit Eastman, enter another mobster to pay bribes and settle scores. He'd had a long run—and then he'd run out. In Abie's opinion, there was no reason to pity the Monk, because he knew he wasn't in the longevity business—and if he'd wanted a long life, he'd have been thankful to have survived the Great War and lived quietly on his pension.

Abie was more bothered on the night he slunk home wearing a wedding ring. Thelma had thought the gold band was a prop for some kind of scam, and in a way it was. He'd gotten a Jewish girl from the Bronx pregnant. Her parents, Mr. and Mrs. Chersonsky, insisted he marry Tillie, who was a mere year older than Thelma. He rescued her from embarrassment, but Abie told his sister that was the last time he'd let anybody tell him what to do without a weapon to his head—and a baby was no shiv. He twisted the dull gold band on his finger as if it were a noose that only tightened more as he squirmed. At first, it hurt Thelma that she hadn't been invited to her own brother's wedding, and then he explained: it hadn't been by choice, a mitzvah. He'd had more fun at his arrest—and he had no intention of inviting his sister to his hanging, either. Thelma knew he was kidding, but only just.

Thelma ended up comforting Abie, because he was so uncharacteristically pathetic, lamenting, "I married Tillie like I was supposed to, but she doesn't take to me being who I am. I might as well have married my own mother, or Annie." They both winced at the thought. That settled it: Thelma knew that her brother would never welcome another woman like their sister into his life by choice. "I'll pay. It was my *putz*, after all. I don't begrudge a dime. But I'm not sticking around and praying."

The following September, Abie made the *Standard Union*, which boasted that it had the largest circulation of any Brooklyn newspaper. Only days before Tillie delivered on September 14, Detectives Dowling and Miller arrested "Little Yiddle" at the corner of Broadway and Chambers for assault and robbery. He'd ambushed a jewelry salesman, Isidor Lipsky, in the foyer of his South Second Street apartment in their old neighborhood beneath the Williamsburg Bridge. Abie had snatched $2,127—a fortune—in cash and jewels. And he'd added his signature: the participation of two women who had preceded the theft, approaching the salesman in the hallway to inquire where the Rosenbergs lived. While the ladies distracted Lipsky, Abie pounced. He said it served the dumb schmuck right for carrying that kind of change in an immigrant neighborhood without a bodyguard.

Upon his arrest, the police captain, his lieutenants, the beat cops, the bail bondsman, and the judge all got their share of the take, and Abie was back out on the streets without a day served. It wasn't so easy slipping the baby, who stuck around and grew, as these things do. He'd named the boy Julius, like Annie's firstborn, after their father. Jonas had had the sense to escape Annie and Mama by any means necessary, leading Abie to refer to him as the lucky stiff. Annie made a bigger fuss out of the arrest than the arrival of her first nephew, but Abie didn't think either of them was such a big deal. Julius was Tillie's burden—she'd had, he confessed, wonderful tits. He'd only wanted to cop a feel, not feel as though he married a copper. If only she'd kept her drawers on like the good girl she'd claimed to be. All that moaning and sighing was not for him. He missed the contortionist, but she wouldn't bend over for a married man.

During that time, Abie got Thelma a job as a shopgirl at Gertz's Glove Sales and Repairs. It was on Pitkin Avenue, which was beginning to boom with the IRT elevated train to New Lots Avenue ushering in new residents and increased foot traffic. Mr. Gertz was a husky Orthodox Jew with teddy-bear ears and shifty dark eyes too small for his giant brisket of a head. He was furtive and secretive by nature, no natural salesman, particularly because he appeared to recoil at the sight of women's hands. While Thelma worked for him, he remained in a state of constant fearful agitation, which kept his sweat glands working overtime. Women would enter the shop, setting off the tolling of the bell, take a sniff, and retreat.

The narrow store fronted Pitkin Avenue. Disembodied hands covered in cloth and leather crammed the single display window, elegantly pointing toward a heaven that must exist. It was best not to peer too closely, as hell was a graveyard of flies that, having thrown themselves once too often against the glass, fell dead of exhaustion, their gossamer wings collecting dust, buzzing no more. Stacks of cardboard boxes of dove gray and mustard lined shelves on three sides of the store. They contained every model and size imaginable and some unimaginable things. Mr. Gertz kept tight track of inventory, occasionally looking over one monstrous shoulder and then the other before fingering a box from the middle of a column, clutching it to the ledge above his belly and moving surprisingly lightly to the rear, which held a small windowless office backing onto the alley.

In that airless back room, the real business occurred, which provided the reason for Thelma's ease of employment. The bachelor Gertz had two primary problems: he'd never met a pair of dice he didn't want to throw until his luck ran out, and he had a mother who believed the sun rose and set on his broad back. He was, in his mama's opinion, a giant among men, the repository of all her affection and shmaltz after his father passed and bequeathed the business to his only son. She called him Ketzele, or little kitten, which was what Abie and the boys now called him. Sometimes they would just meow as if they were in heat, a raucous chorus of men who had no love for cats. These shadow businessmen were the sweat that dampened Gertz's armpit hair and raised the physical stink that arose from fear that they would tell his mother he'd been a very bad boy. The lads, Abie included, had no interest in gloves, although they weren't above grabbing a few boxes for their girlfriends; what they liked was that it was largely a cash business with a legitimate delivery operation, which they used to move money around Brooklyn like a personal courier system.

Despite being forced upon Gertz, Thelma enjoyed working for the mama's boy. He was, if not happy for the help, then at least polite. He seemed to sense that she meant him no harm. She was a punctual worker and could sell kid gloves to the biggest pinchpenny while *kibitzing* with anyone who entered, never forgetting the quirks of a finger, the size of a hand, and airing out the salesroom when the owner's stench became toxic. She went so far as to make a deal with Spritzer's Perfumerie de France down the block to exchange gloves for scent, posting a little card on the counter with a 10 percent discount coupon. Spritzer the younger, still a bachelor at forty-eight, flooded her with samples, tiny vials, and doll-size flasks—and once even slipped a tiny bottle of racy Chanel No. 5 into her pocketbook.

As an added bonus, she had a hand model's slender long digits and could now afford the blue-red polish that made her shapely nail beds movie-star glamorous. While at work, she typically covered up with the prim white gloves called shorties that bore pearly wrist buttons so small they were almost impossible to fit into their holes. On slow days, or when men entered purchasing items for their wives or mistresses, she modeled the exotics: black lace gauntlets or, her favorite, buttercup suede opera gloves that rose over her elbows and made her feel so much more elegant than Pitkin Avenue deserved.

Most of the time it was boring the way it was for most clerks, a lot of time on her feet, chewing gum then swallowing it when the doorbell tolled. Because Gertz got flustered at such close quarters, brushing against a woman with beautiful hands, he often disappeared, leaving the shop to her. On the rare afternoons when Abie and his friends took over the back, Thelma did as instructed and ignored them in the spirit of *ask me no questions and I'll tell you no lies.* The gang tended to work the night shift, leaving detailed instructions for Gertz in a locked drawer for the next morning.

This setup granted Thelma hours of unmolested quiet, allowing her to flip through *Photoplay* between customers. Jutting her hips against the counter, she joined the rest of American womanhood mesmerized by Rudolph Valentino's eyes. She'd even gone so far as buying a cheap aluminum frame and clipping a magazine portrait, placing it beside her bed as if he were her sultry sweetheart. In 1922, *Blood and Sand* and *The Young Rajah* premiered. She'd become hooked the previous year with *The Four Horsemen of the Apocalypse* and *The Sheik*, occasionally dragging her Italian girlfriends to the Rialto in Manhattan if she could lure them away from their kids with the promise of Valentino. As much as she loved her schoolmates, she knew how overwhelmed they were and was in no rush for the obligations of pregnancy and marriage. Her time would come, but in the meantime, that left her available for the movie star if he ever made his way to Brooklyn.

In the pages of *Photoplay*, she learned Valentino had been born Rodolfo Alfonso Raffaello Pierre Filibert Guglielmi di Valentina d'Antonguolla a year after Abie. Unable to find work in his native Italy, Valentino sailed to Manhattan via Ellis Island and would have been welcome among the Williamsburg immigrants she knew so well. The movie star was dark, not fair like Giorgio. Tall and slim, he slicked his hair back with Vaseline (leading to the nickname Rhubarb Vaselino, a character Stan Laurel played in the spoof *Mud and Sand*), exposing smoldering eyes that always seemed to be looking deeply into her own and mining her soul.

Sure, there was the first marriage that ended abruptly on his wedding night and was swiftly annulled. The gossip columns exploded with it, along with the bigamy charges when he remarried less than a year later, the legal limit, in May 1922 in Mexicali, Mexico. Earlier, he'd testified in a lady friend's divorce case that her husband had strayed and, not much later, the wife had shot and killed her ex. Life was messy for Valentino, but Thelma was no one to judge. He was complicated. She wasn't seeking a saltine. And although American men tended to question his masculinity, preferring the swashbuckling Douglas Fairbanks, they hadn't a clue about the power of Rudy's smolder on the opposite sex, the broody mystery behind his eyes that led to his appeal. She'd take him up to her room anytime, even if that meant passing the gauntlet of Annie and Mama. Wouldn't that shock the old shrews?

After she'd been working for about a year, a young stranger crossed the threshold as if she'd wished him into being with her dreams of Valentino. The bell tolled. Tall, black haired, and handsome, although pale skinned where her matinee idol was tan, he first entered the shop the week before the high holy days. Harried, she glanced up and caught his eye and smiled, as she would for any customer, her practiced salesgirl welcome that expressed "I'll be with you shortly." His dark eyes slid shyly to the left, as if her gesture were more freighted.

Female customers taking their time making a serious wardrobe choice with the few pennies they had to spend packed the small sales floor. He patiently waited his turn, fedora in hand, as first one *bubbe* and then the next tried to stuff their swollen hands into white gloves the size they'd worn at their weddings. By the time the man's turn arrived, he'd found his smile. He stood at the counter surrounded by a pack of wives and mothers clucking and shifting their paper-wrapped purchases from a day shopping on Pitkin Avenue.

The stranger addressed Thelma leisurely, as if they were the only people in the crowded shop and he had all the time in the world. "Can you show me some gloves?"

"You've come to the right place," she said. "Are they for you?"

"For my mother," he said.

"What size?"

"She has tiny hands. Do you have size five?"

"We do, but are you sure?"

"Positive." She began with the less expensive models, but he examined the material carefully, turning them over in his attractive square hands, rolling them between his thumb and forefinger and then rejecting them with a shake of his head. She noticed his fingertips trembling slightly but didn't comment. After she laid out the items of better and best quality, he chose the most luxurious yet conservative styles, two pairs of white fabric with pearl buttons. He paused, smiling to himself, and, as if having a last-minute inspiration, sent Thelma back to the stock boxes for soft leather longs in jet-black, which made him smile again when she placed their best pair before him. The sale would thrill Gertz, because they rarely sold that quality, particularly in a size five, and they were dear.

Around the gentleman, the other shoppers were growing restless but, having waited his turn, he took his time and Thelma didn't rush him. He paid in new bills, and she noticed his wallet was pebbled brown leather and full, embossed with the gilded initials *P. S.* It screamed that he was too fancy for her. She wrapped his purchases carefully, despite the teeth sucking of the impatient matron in line behind him. And when she handed him his parcel, he tipped his hat to her, replaced it on his head, and didn't smile. Instead, he looked her deeply in the eyes, no longer shy, and she could have sworn he'd stolen that soulful smolder from her Valentino.

Thelma's knees might have buckled but she had to snap immediately to attention when Mrs. Hirscheimer clucked forward, squinting her eyes in disapproval. The kosher butcher's wife demanded to see those same black-leather longs in a size eight, admiring them, tugging them on, pulling them off, setting them aside and picking them up again before buying a more humble fabric pair. She spread out an assortment of change down to the last penny owed and hawkishly watched Thelma count them.

After the high holy days, Thelma often saw the young man who'd bought the store's priciest gloves strolling past Pitkin Avenue. It was a

busy thoroughfare and she assumed he lived nearby. If she was looking up, he'd tip his hat and smile enigmatically. Sometimes he'd stand
outside the window and imitate the plaster display models, raising a
hand and posing his graceful fingers. She began to nurse that kind of
crush one developed for a stranger, feeling the charge when she saw
him through the window, unconsciously seeking him out as she crossed
Pitkin Avenue toward Montauk. One chilly day, she felt a warmth on
her cheek and looked up to see him looking at her, only to have him
tip his hat and walk away. It was a game of catch—he saw her, she saw
him—an impossible flirtation. She wondered what it would be like to
talk to him outside the store, just the two of them, but she didn't know
what to say. How long could they talk about whether his mother liked
her gloves?

As Hanukkah neared, he entered the store again and approached
the counter without hesitation. Noticing Thelma was reading *Photoplay*,
he asked, "Do you want to see my Valentino impression?"

"Sure." She shrugged, caught unawares and unaccustomed to
receiving young men in the smelly little shop. She felt more vulnerable than she had on the busy day when he'd first appeared among the
neighborhood *yentas* before her crush had ripened. Embarrassed, she
covered her hands with the cheap white cotton shorties she'd removed
to avoid ink stains.

He showed her first one side of his face with his chin down while
gazing up through dark eyes. She laughed. "Want to see it again?" he
asked, and without waiting showed her the other.

"Pretty good."

"People call me the Sheik."

"Do they?"

"No. Only my little sister, Pearl. Everyone else calls me Philip—
Philip Schwartz, or Phil to my friends."

"So, Mr. Schwartz, I'm guessing you're not Italian."

"You're a regular Sherlock Holmes."

"Can I help you with something? Gloves, maybe?"

"Yes," he said. "Can you show me some gloves for Pearl? She's eight."

"Do you want weekday white ones?"

"Not exactly," he said. "I have an idea for white gloves with a bow, maybe a pink one, at the wrist."

"You're a good brother," she said, walking self-consciously to the wall, only then realizing she'd slipped off her heels. She blushed as she returned to slip them on her feet and then spun on her heels and efficiently pulled out the relevant boxes. "Does she like polka dots?"

"Who doesn't?" he answered. And he bought two pair, one with a pink bow and the other red-and-white polka dots.

After that day, he began to visit once or twice a week, right before she switched the sign from **Open** to **Closed** for lunch. At first she refused to join him; she'd brought her lunch from home and it wasn't much to share, the daily beef liverwurst sandwiches on rye with a dill pickle. But, later, he brought a bag lunch, too, and they walked to the park nearby, shared a wrought iron bench, chatted, stood up, ambled, fed a few pigeons crusts, and talked some more, brushed elbows. She'd begun to understand what Mama Allegra meant when she said that someday Thelma would fall in love with a particular man and not just with the idea of love. She'd loved Giorgio's company, but this was different—she was falling for the man himself. He began to invade her daydreams. And, at night, when she went to bed, she looked at her framed picture of Valentino, and began to think of Phil.

Chapter 21

1923

The following summer, Thelma and Phil visited Coney Island on their first date away from Pitkin Avenue. It was one of those sunny Sundays that appeared endless, a gateway to a better, happier adulthood. Phil offered to pick her up on Montauk Avenue. He lived a mile away in a fine two-story brick row house with double windows overlooking tree-lined Wyona Street, having by then revealed that he was the middle son of a successful Rumanian immigrant who owned apartment buildings, which accounted for the fancy gloves.

Thelma declined Phil's offer. She didn't trust Annie with strangers, particularly those of whom she was fond and wanted to impress. Her sister the shamer would interrogate him about his intentions for her skinny little sister, mock his hat, or probe into his father's finances. Entering Montauk Avenue represented hostile territory where the women's low opinion held Thelma hostage. As she'd leaped out the front door, her sister had squawked, "Cover those toothpick legs."

Ignoring her, Thelma skipped down the street and rode the new subway to the sea for a nickel. At the final stop, Phil awaited her by the turnstiles. His dismayed face cracked a grin when he saw her, as if he'd been as nervous as she was about being ditched, as if this adventure represented as much to him as it did to her. It meant everything, even if she tried to quash her enthusiasm and expect the inevitable disappointment for which Annie had prepared her.

Phil was on time and well dressed in the middle of the day, pleats in his pants and a handkerchief in his breast pocket. Annie had never dated a man so fine. Thelma let herself gloat that this looker under the Panama hat had been waiting just for her, even if that brief bliss made her fear he would immediately withdraw. *Don't give yourself a* keyn *eynhore,* she thought, the evil eye that spoiled everything one treasured.

Don't want him or he won't be yours. It was such a twisted way of thinking she'd inherited—this mistrust of joy. It had no apparent impact on Abie. If there'd been an evil eye, he'd once bragged, he would have spit in it. He had no time for old-world superstitions in Brooklyn. But she was different. And yet she didn't want to hex this date; she was putting her best self forward, lively enough but not so excited that she'd scare Philip away. When she pushed open the gate, he lit up a matinee-idol smile that sent sparks shining into his dark eyes.

They joined the hordes pouring down the street from the end of the subway line, crushing toward the shore. Most other visitors carried food baskets, beach balls, and umbrellas, herding brats and the elderly, heading to the sand, their swimming costumes puckering their street clothes because they couldn't afford the price of a changing room. Unburdened, Philip grabbed her hand. It felt awkward at first. She was so hyperaware of their connection, her left palm in his right, that she almost didn't feel the press of any other bodies for the touch of his.

As the crowd carried them along, Thelma's purse tucked under her free arm, full of coins nicked from Annie's secret jar, he said, "The beach is for suckers." They agreed: she was no Miss Coney Island sunbathing on the sand, *shvitsing,* being pecked by pigeons and prodded by other people's kids.

In the past, when she'd come to the beach with Annie and Mama, her bare body in a bathing costume had shamed her: the spindly legs, angular hips, tiny breast buds she'd waited impatiently to grow. They hadn't. She'd felt uncomfortable on the hot sand, wanting to hide beneath her towel. Vulnerability had been a dangerous condition around Annie and Mama as they carped on the physiques of the people strolling past, laughing at this one's little pecker visible in swim trunks too small, that one's jiggling fat rolls as she lunged for a rogue rubber ball. *Meeskait*, they'd pronounce, *little ugly one. What a* tuchus, they'd say and point at someone with a seat that could fill a subway car. And yet, the pair hadn't been bathing beauties, either: the walrus and the sea lion. Mama covered in a floral muumuu and Annie squeezed like a sausage into a swimsuit one size too small, revealing back fat that she didn't notice from the front, impressed by her own cleavage.

Oblivious to their own looks, Annie and Mama had judged Thelma—scrawny, knobby kneed, titless. Their voices had permeated her thoughts so that she'd been constantly comparing and contrasting herself to the parade of bodies, filling her alternately with envy and disgust. That self-consciousness had scraped away the joy of sun and sand. And waves, of which she'd been justifiably terrified. Like her kin, she'd never learned to swim. Who would have taught her? It had been hard enough for her mother to learn English; the ocean itself had been a foreign language.

Many summers back, when Thelma had still played with buckets of water at the ocean's edge, the littlest Rosenzweig boy had drowned. One minute he'd been digging with his toes for sand crabs and the next he'd disappeared, last seen by a stranger with his curly head bobbing far into the tide before anyone raised the alarm with the lifeguards. The young cousin who'd been left to watch the smaller child melted into tears, carrying two drippy ice cream bars until all he had was two sticks and an eternity of guilt. The doomed lad had been marked for life: the one who killed his cousin, a child who'd never cried a night in his life, an angel, destined one day to be a banker, a lawyer, a *macher*. Those who'd died young were angels; the devils grew up. Husbands that couldn't be trusted around other women became saints to their widows when they entered an early grave, escaping the nagging of existence.

As long as Thelma avoided the sand, she loved Coney Island. Beside Phil, she smelled fat frying at Nathan's, kosher dogs, knishes. She'd felt less self-conscious about her body because fashion had caught up with her figure: clothes suited her slim frame, especially the drop-waist dotted swiss she'd sewn over the last three nights and worn that day. It revealed her calves and shapely ankles above cutaway T-straps she'd dyed canary yellow when they could no longer pass as white. Phil wore a three-piece khaki summer suit—she didn't know another man who had pants so light, so vulnerable to dirt. She could hear Annie's voice in her own head: *What if he spills something?* Phil breezily angled his Panama hat low over his right eye, not quite cocky but not just another man in the crowd.

They paused to watch a bowler-hatted barker hawk his freak show—the bearded lady, the world's thinnest man, a human corkscrew, whatever that was. But Phil led them on, past the man hammering five-inch nails into his *schnoz* for free on the stage before the canvas tent. She couldn't help peeking at the performer's bald head out of the corner of her eye.

For all the noise and distraction, what she felt most intensely was Phil's large hand in hers, dry and cool despite the late June heat, casual. He had this day covered. He knew where they were going. She only needed to follow—and have faith in him. Even if they weren't meant to last forever, even if he never asked her out again, she surrendered to that single Sunday, to being connected to a beautiful if mysterious man. She wasn't alone. The excitement of all those people, those children, to have a free afternoon under the sun, eating buttery corn straight off the cob burned from the grill and drinking fizzy soda, talking loud and laughing louder, jumping the waves, playing catch. Shabbos had been behind them, and the workweek, the unemployment line, would never arrive. In a world driven by yesterday and tomorrow, the distant *shtetl* across the ocean and the successful future just out of reach, there were these golden hours. The sky didn't disappoint. A sweet westerly breeze blew them a kiss.

Phil slipped through the throng, leading Thelma through the amusement park, past the haunted house's obscene devil's tongue to the no-name bar fronting the new boardwalk. When they procured a metal table out front, she sipped root beer beneath an umbrella's shade, feeling nearly attractive in his reflective glow. He ordered limeade in a thick-bottomed glass and, because it was Prohibition and alcohol sales were forbidden, he topped the drink off with vodka from a silver flask. She looked away to keep from staring: his narrow, clean-shaven face that ended in a square chin, dark eyes deep beneath thick, expressive brows, his shiny black hair slicked back like Valentino's when he removed his hat.

She might have already loved him then, just the surface beauty and the lazy self-possessed way he poked fun at all the people who soldiered past, sandy and dripping out of their ill-fitting swimsuits, naming the animals they resembled, strange beasts like okapis and marmosets. He called himself the albino because he was so pale, and she argued that he shouldn't knock himself because he was so handsome. At least she hadn't said "dreamy," but she still blushed because she'd given herself away. He didn't seem to notice, looking out to the Atlantic beyond that mass of bodies crawling over themselves like drones without a queen.

He drank through the afternoon and only got more charming. Her cheeks hurt from laughing; she must have given him a bruise from how frequently she punched his arm. She hardly noticed his narrow hands shaking as he evaded any questions about his family on Wyona Street. He stuck to current affairs and politics, passionately denouncing the self-interest of bankers, an issue that couldn't have been further from her mind. She knew no one who worked in a bank, although she knew the unemployed men who gathered in front of the Brooklyn Savings & Loan Association arguing socialism versus communism, hoping to be hired as day laborers. She knew newspaper salesmen and jewelers and thieves, not apartment building owners like his father.

Beneath the table, she kept her T-straps near his tan bucks. But she never made the first move. She didn't want to scare him away. As dusk fell, he helped her up and they strolled, arm in arm. She admired the fun land's jewel-toned fairy lights, the enchanted Wonder Wheel, filled with little human ants smooching or spitting on the chumps below. As they walked together, lazily, leaning on each other, they seemed to change from two separate people into a couple without words to barter the arrangement. All she could see was him in the twilight, the gentleman in the well-cut khaki suit. Everything else was lights and whistles, whirling blurs. He changed her entire balance, ripped her from the not-good-enough noise in her head.

They made a handsome couple in a way she'd never experienced alone. She with her bobbed hair and kohl-rimmed green eyes, long lashes, pale skin, red lips; he, tall and lanky, broad shouldered, with that Transylvanian pallor. His lips were red for a man's, in that long face now darkened by bristles. They matched. It was as if they, just the pair, not their parents, grandparents, sisters and brothers, had been family—just Phil and Thelma. That was enough.

Entering Nathan's to buy nickel frankfurters, they joined a line fifteen deep as the mob stopped on their way home, fulfilling the day's final promise. Across Surf Avenue, the carousel produced the saddest jolly music in the world. Thelma felt a hollow in her stomach like a hunger that couldn't be satisfied with frankfurters. Her loneliness returned, the low after the high, a wave of doubts washing over her. Phil had grown quiet. His eyes seemed pensive and distant, his lashes wet. His hand remained on her shoulder to protect her from the crush, but the gesture seemed absentminded, as if he'd been here before with other girls.

Across the street, the merry-go-round slowed between rides. The organ music became lethargic: *the end is near, the end is near.* In line at

Nathan's, a tough guy with a fight-flattened nose pivoted from the front counter. He clumsily sluiced pickle juice on her new dress. She'd raised her right fist and opened her mouth to give the fella hell. The bruiser braced for a fight despite holding a semiwrapped pickle in one hand and three dogs in paper sleeves in the other.

Phil interceded. "It's only a shift, even if it's a very pretty one. No one ever died from a little dill on a dress."

Cowed by Phil's manners, the bruiser apologized by sharing two of his three franks. Philip accepted graciously. He held the treats aloft as the pair slithered out to the stand-and-eat counters that rimmed the stand. Surrounded by the buzzy crowd, they chewed their mustard-drenched dogs in silence.

"Don't say I never gave you anything," Phil teased, wiping mustard from her mouth.

"You never gave me anything," she said. And then her words tumbled, unfiltered—"except the best day ever. Spray me with ketchup and I wouldn't care."

"Tempting as that offer is, I'll pass."

"I don't want to leave yet, Phil."

"We can't: What's Coney Island without riding the carousel?"

"That's kid stuff," she said with a tough-girl growl, shaking her head dismissively. She lied. How could she confess how much it meant? She'd never ridden a carousel. Annie's voice: *A waste of money. It's over in a minute.* She wanted that ride so much she feared making a fool of herself.

"You're never too old," he said. She gathered their trash and tossed it gingerly in a barrel swarmed by yellow jackets, fearing their stingers. They started toward the subway, past the sword swallower and the fire breather. She took his hand, abandoning all pretense, and said, "Can we go for one ride, please?"

"Anything you want, sweet cheeks," he said. They spun around, jaywalked across Surf Avenue, and joined a serpentine line. To their left, the gilt-and-mirror-trimmed carousel circled, casting mad reflections of the riders' gleeful grins. When their turn finally arrived, they surrendered blue paper tickets, but others had claimed all the prized prancing ponies that moved up and down. She panicked and began to run around like the loser in musical chairs. But Phil found her an available perch. He boosted her onto a stationary rooster, which was not quite the steed of her dreams. Then he stood beside her, his hand on the fowl's painted saddle.

When the ride began to lurch forward, she held tightly to the pole. That was when he kissed the ringlet at her nape. She felt his lips' softness, the damp tickle. But the gesture didn't make her woozy with affection. She flinched, thinking: that was it. The sun set, the moon rose, and the moves began. Annie's voice squawked, *He's like every other punter making a play.*

Sure, Phil was slower and slicker, but maybe she wasn't worth the rush. With her bobbed hair and short skirt, her kohl-rimmed eyes, perhaps he'd considered her a dime-store vamp from the very first hello at Gertz's.

After kissing her, he rested his hand where his lips had been, rubbing her neck softly. She twisted to look at him, feeling foolish astride that big chicken. She stared straight into his eyes, where she'd recognized a vulnerability that matched her own. She read a plea for mutual understanding and an escape from loneliness. It didn't seem cynical or carnal.

"I'm not who you think I am," he said softly as the ride slowed, the words nearly drowned by the crush of children rushing to exit. She ignored the warning. He grasped her by the waist and lifted her off the seat. When her T-straps touched the floor, it felt like the ride was still moving. Her knees buckled, but that wasn't why she laughed. Because she wasn't the shopgirl he thought she was, either. She was Little Yiddle's little sister.

That golden day in Coney Island, Thelma began to view herself as the desirable, good-hearted woman reflected in Phil's eyes. "I never want to go home again."

"We can't go home," he said. "It's not a date until we go dancing."

She couldn't hide her absolute delight. That would've been canny. *Retain some mystery. Get to know Phil better. Press your thighs together.* Besides, she had to work the next day. Piles of Sunday ironing for the entire household awaited her on Montauk Avenue, with clock-watcher Annie tapping her toes. But when he suggested dancing, her heart surged. They separated to pass through the turnstile. But on the far side, she threaded her arm around his waist under his jacket, pulling closer.

Never let this end, she thought, closing her eyes to make the wish come true.

They rode to Manhattan while she dozed on his shoulder. Gently, he nudged her awake after Times Square, just managing to slip through the closing doors at Fiftieth Street. Philip led the way, knowing which steps to climb and where to descend. Suddenly, they escaped the piss-and-exhaust stench into the sweet June evening. Broadway lights radiated a dazzling daylight. She felt jazzed, every nerve ending as electric as the Roseland Ballroom marquee up above. A photographer snapped pictures of the swarm with a Speed Graphic camera, flashes blinding.

Philip angled his hat and offered Thelma his elbow, which she grabbed with both hands. He skipped the line, the bouncer ushering them in through red-upholstered doors. She felt exalted and awestruck: so this was living. Men looked at her as she passed on the stairs; Phil nodded to acquaintances. A sharp orchestra grooved from above as they rose to the second floor. On the bandstand, a girl singer lamented lost love in a tinsel dress surrounded by tuxedo-clad musicians. Thelma's soles itched to swing.

He checked his hat, her pocketbook, smiled at her and winked, in no apparent rush. She admired the cozy way the items looked side by side, his and hers. And then he led her to an enormous dance floor. He swayed and caught the music's beat. She followed with an ease she'd never known before, under his arm and out into the floor.

Part of the jiving mass that covered the giant floor, they hoofed it as if they'd practiced all their lives. She knew the familiar steps, turning under his right arm and his left, the dishrag, the pretzel, sliding doors. He taught her new moves. When she confused her feet and hissed under her breath, he reassured her with his touch. He sent her swirling faster and faster, a top in his hands. She laughed out of a giddy fear that she might lose the beat. She didn't.

First he removed his jacket, then his tie. He rolled up his sleeves. Sweat drenched her homemade dress. By the seventh song, other dancers stopped and watched the new couple. The crowd parted. He picked her up and slid her between his legs. And then he pulled her back, popped her over his left shoulder and swiveled her up so that her toes pointed skyward. She'd worried strangers would see her cheap underwear, her mended garters. Then care evaporated. He caught her. He settled her on her feet, clasping her right hand in his left. A physical connection shot through her entire body. He pushed her away for one last turn and then gathered her in for their lips' first meeting: fire in flight.

Chapter 22

According to Annie a knock at the front door past midnight always signified trouble. And this pounding wouldn't quit, waking Annie, who'd fallen asleep while awaiting Thelma's return from Coney Island with Philip.

"Open the door in the name of the law!"

Annie's heart palpitated as Eli began wailing and Adele joined him, while Julius ran into the bedroom to announce he'd had a nightmare. Annie pushed him toward his sleeping father as she sneaked back the curtain and inspected Montauk Avenue. In the lamplight, she noted a black Hudson paddy wagon bearing a gold shield on the passenger door. Since the front porch blocked her view, she couldn't tell who was down below.

"Enough already," Annie yelled out the window, her voice scratchy with sleep and agitation. "You'll wake the whole neighborhood."

As if on cue, lights came on across the street. Annie hurried to head off the neighbors, feeling her hair curlers, an automatic gesture to ensure they remained in place. She unhooked her chenille bathrobe from behind the door. This was too much. She'd gone to bed steaming that Thelma hadn't returned from Coney Island, that tramp, leaving the weekly pressing pile to her. She'd awakened angrier still, feeling the iron burn under petroleum jelly on the inside of her wrist. What would the people across the street think—that she couldn't control her own sister and, now, here was the police, too? They lived here, for God's sake; it wasn't like the family could flee and shed the shame. They owned this house. They would be shunned—because that's how she would have treated neighbors who brought the coppers down on Montauk Avenue past midnight.

Annie checked the clock—it was 4:00 a.m.—and poked Jesse. Deep in her stomach, her *kishkes*, she felt foreboding. Something had happened to Thelma, something bad the girl deserved. She'd never disappeared for the entire night since they'd moved to this house, but that didn't mean she wasn't up to mischief. Her middle name should have been *mishegas*, she was so much trouble. In her mind's eye, Annie beheld a picture of Thelma, a flapper floozy wearing that skimpy dotted dress, barely a slip, with legs akimbo in dirty yellow shoes, stuffed headfirst into a garbage can outside Nathan's. Staying out all night like that was begging for trouble. What did she want from the world that she couldn't get at home? As if she could attract the honorable attentions of a Wyona Street boy, a landlord's son. He hadn't even had the respect to pick her up at the front door and meet her family. That date was probably a hoax and she'd been catting around with the Italians instead. Just what Annie needed: another jailbird and more shame on the family. She didn't deserve the aggravation. If Thelma wasn't dead, she'd toss that girl out on her skinny rump roast.

More banging, to which she yelled, "I'm coming. You think I'm deaf?" She threw the bolt, opened the door, and faced two tense and sweaty Irish policemen who'd clearly been up all night. They flashed their shields.

Annie asked, "What happened to Thelma?"

"Who?" asked the taller of the policemen, a regular giant with hands as big as waffles. His partner stood beside him, hardly out of his youth, with a pockmarked face and a nose that had been flattened sideways uninvited. They both carried hats tucked under their armpits and wore looks of concern and urgency that were unwelcome, whether at 4:00 a.m. or high noon. Even as they stood in place on the porch waiting to be invited in, it was as if the lawmen were still rushing, running on adrenaline, cats pursuing a rat.

"What?" Annie touched her upper lip, which felt sticky. She'd forgotten she'd left on the cream to dye her mustache and was mortified, but there was nothing she could do now. No one else in the house could handle the police, not Jesse, not Moe.

"Do you know Abraham Lorber?"

"Do I know Abie? What's he done now?"

"Are you his mother?"

"Sister," she sniffed. "I'm his sister Annie."

"Well, then, Miss Annie, I think you'd better sit down." He stepped into the stairwell, belatedly introducing himself. "I'm Detective William Asip, and this is Officer Joe Corrigan."

"He's dead, isn't he?" she hissed. Hearing Mama enter the living room from the back, she turned and said, "Abie's dead." Mama began to wail, falling to her knees in a puddle of stained nightgown, while Jesse descended carrying the inconsolable Eli, a weeping Adele attached to his pajama leg.

"Can we cut the circus, here, Mrs. Lorber?"

"Lazarus, Mrs. Lazarus."

"Your brother isn't dead, but he's no picture of health. He's been shot, twice."

"But what about Thelma? Where's Thelma?"

"The lady's in shock, Bill," said Officer Corrigan.

The detective put out his hand. "Smelling salts, Joe." After forced administration of the restorative, Detective Asip dragged a straight chair over. He spun it around and straddled it, which Annie found unnecessarily aggressive even through the sting of the salts and the fog, and all the tears from young and old. She could see the bulge in his pants and she tried to keep her eyes on his watery blues, but she kept looking down and then away.

"Mama, take the kids into the kitchen. Give them the leftover *kichels*."

"It's too late for sugar cookies."

"Then give them Corn Flakes, Mama, just get them out of here."

"What about my Abie?" Mama said, her voice squeezed like liver through a grinder.

"Mama . . ." Annie threatened. She'd been expecting this day since Abie had torched her underwear drawer. It was as if she'd wished the gunfight into being with her own hate and resentment. Nothing he deserved more than two bullet holes in his fancy-schmancy lapel. If she'd been man enough, she'd have done it herself.

Brushing her gaze on the carpet, where a dust clump shocked and annoyed her, Annie tried to dredge up some scrap of sympathy that her brother was in agony, hanging on to the ledge of his life with dirty fingernails. But she felt nothing. Triumph, maybe? Yet that wasn't the face to wear with these policemen. She needed to appear sympathetic in the eyes of the law, to demonstrate enough empathy not to seem responsible for the violence, but not enough to suggest that she would conceal evidence to protect Abie. She could tell these men in blue stories about him, but how would that benefit her?

Her brother's comeuppance should have been more satisfying, and yet, even though she'd long predicted his downfall, the idea that he'd been pierced by lead frightened her. If the gunmen came for him, they could come for her and her children. Thelma would lead the villains straight to the front door. It could just have easily been the assassins as the police who knocked. She heard Jesse ask, as if from a great distance, "Where's Abie?"

"Coney Island Hospital," said Asip.

"Shot in the arm," said Corrigan, pointing, "and another in the chest."

"Who did it?" Jesse asked.

"That's why we're here."

"What happened to my baby brother?" asked Annie. She'd never called him that before, but she was circling her wagons. These officers were goyim, after all. They wouldn't understand a rift between brother and sister in a good Jewish home—and she was determined to show that they were standing in a stable Hebrew household, not a *shtetl* flophouse or a den of thieves. She couldn't leave herself open to their judgment.

"Here's what we know," began Detective Asip, who flipped open his notebook and revealed that the assault had occurred at two that morning. When the victim had briefly regained consciousness, he'd told the officer that he was loitering on the corner of West Twenty-Fourth Street and Mermaid Avenue when a well-dressed blonde had made eye contact. The beautiful stranger had approached him, asking if he knew of a speakeasy nearby. Then she'd started posing personal questions, and when she inquired where he lived, he balked. After that, she inquired if his name was Samuel Lorber and he replied, no, he was Abraham. And then she twisted her scarf so that the knot faced the rear and stepped past him before turning and pointing straight at him.

The detective thumbed the notebook page, found his place and continued: a Packard wheeled around the corner carrying four men and squealed to the curb. The passenger-side doors exploded open, and two unfamiliar gunmen jumped out. They drew pistols and hit Lorber in the arm and chest, and he collapsed, unconscious.

"That's all your brother told us before losing consciousness again at the hospital," said Asip. "He acted confused about why he might have been the target of a hit. He claimed he didn't recognize anybody in the car and he had no outstanding beefs. Everybody loved him, he said. He told me he was a clerk, but we know Little Yiddle when we see him. We have reason to believe the assault stemmed from a fight over an unidentified female."

"Well, that would be Abie all over, wouldn't it just?" said Annie. "If there's a fight over a girl, that's Abie. He just never got shot over it before. You know he's married with a kid, so maybe you should be questioning his missus. I can get you her address. I don't know what you're doing here."

"We thought you'd want to know your brother's condition—and you might have information that leads to the gunmen."

"Fat chance," she said. "His business is his business, and we don't want any part of it."

"Nice house," said the detective.

"Mortgaged," said Annie.

"But not rented."

"Officer . . ."

"Detective."

"You know more than we do, *Detective*, and we want to keep it that way. We're hardworking folks trying to put food on the table—"

"Is he going to survive?" interrupted Moe, who had remained quietly in the background tucked in his mocha-striped bathrobe.

"Is *who* going to survive?" asked Thelma. She'd sneaked in the front door, dress disheveled, cheeks glowing, shoes dangling from her hand, and bare feet blistered. If Annie wasn't mistaken, her sister looked radiant, like a girl floating in love without a care in the world. That wasn't going to last long.

"Who's this?" asked Asip.

"I'm Thelma." Her face fell. She dropped her shoes, which clattered on the tiles.

"Pick those up. I'm your sister, not your maid," Annie said before turning to the detective. "She's Abie's sister."

"I thought *you* were his sister?"

"She's his *unmarried* sister."

"Does she live here, too?"

"When she shows up," Annie said, making no effort to hide her disgust in front of the cops.

"Isn't it late, miss? Where've you been?"

"Coney Island," said Annie.

"You were in Coney Island, too?"

"Who else was there?"

"Abie," said Annie.

"Let me handle this, lady," said Asip. "Were you with your brother in Coney Island?"

"No," Thelma said, the color drained from her cheeks. "I was with a friend."

"What friend?"

"I'd rather not say, Detective. I don't want to get him involved."

"You'd rather not, but you're going to. We're investigating a shooting."

"Who's hurt?" Thelma whipsawed from the policeman to Annie. "Where's Abie?"

"Just answer my questions, young lady: Who were you with?"

"Philip," she said. "Philip Schwartz. But we didn't see Abie."

"Where were you at two in the morning?"

"Yes," said Annie. "Where were you, sneaking around?"

"Mrs. Lazarus, desist. Let her answer."

"We weren't anywhere near Coney Island." Thelma looked at Annie, her eyes a startled mix of panic and pleading. "We were dancing. He took me to the Roseland."

"In Manhattan?" asked the detective.

"Yes," said Thelma. "Have you ever been there?"

"Manhattan? I've heard of it."

Annie shook her head. "You went all the way from Coney Island to Manhattan on a Sunday night while I was doing your ironing? You should see the burn I have," Annie said, lifting her wrist, shiny with Vaseline. "It blistered. Who gave you permission to go to Manhattan?"

"I don't need your permission."

"As long as you live under my roof . . ."

"Your roof—since when is it your roof?"

"Ladies, we have bigger fish to fry. Did anybody see you there?"

"At the Roseland? Scads, but nobody I knew."

"It's seems like a big coincidence that you and your brother were in Coney Island."

"Half of Brooklyn was in Coney Island, Detective."

Moe approached with a straight-backed chair. "Temmy, you need to sit."

"Why?"

"Sit," Moe said. "Something's happened to Abie."

"Why didn't you say so when I came in? Where is he? Will he be okay?"

Asip looked at Corrigan and shook his head. "He's unlikely to recover. He's at Coney Island Hospital with two gunshot wounds, one to the chest."

Thelma's face collapsed. Her jaw worked, but she only squeaked. She lost control of her features, becoming ugly and unglued. It appeared to be quite the performance in Annie's opinion, but she looked sideways at the police, and they were buying tickets. She could see in their faces that they'd registered a lot of reactions to bad news, and Thelma's was authentic. She realized belatedly that this should have been her response: tears and trauma. The suspicion fell back on her, but nobody in the room was checking her reaction anymore. Thelma was a regular Mary Pickford, upstaging Annie again. She stroked her blistered wrist as her anger rose, but she swallowed her rage with spit. It was unsafe with lawmen dragging dirt on the carpet.

"We need to be at the hospital *now*," Thelma said, jumping up. "Let's go! Annie? Jesse?"

"Don't be stupid. He's unconscious," Annie said. "He won't even know we're there."

"He's alive and he needs me," Thelma said, making for the door. With her hand on the knob, she turned back. "I know where I belong, even if you don't."

"You're wearing *that* to the hospital?" Annie asked.

"I'd go naked. I'd even go in your shabby bathrobe with curlers in my hair and bleach on my mustache. We have to save Abie. He can't die. He can't leave me alone."

Annie heard the unspoken: *with you.* "How are you getting there?"

"I'll walk," Thelma said.

"We'll drive you," said Officer Corrigan.

The detective put on his hat. "We're done here—for now."

"You know where you can find us," said Annie.

Moe followed Thelma and the retreating policemen, bent over the tile, hooked something on his fingers, and called after them, "Shoes."

Chapter 23

At Coney Island Hospital, twenty-four hours had passed in the darkened ward. Thelma clutched her hands together, praying for her brother's survival. He remained comatose, tubes entering and exiting his body. He wasn't some random newspaper thug—he was her brother. She willed his eyes to open. Seeing him tiny and inert, a waxwork dummy, shattered her.

Averting her swollen eyes, she scanned the room, counting ten beds, five on each side. Just enough room for a fat *bubbe* to visit, or a doctor and nurse to fiddle with a patient's catheters, separated them. Occasionally she heard the three boys with alcohol poisoning retching out their guts, one starting and his buddies chiming in. There were the groans of the grandfather and his adult son who'd gotten sunstroke at the shore on Sunday, the scrabbly sound of rats' paws racing in the ceiling. Stationed just outside the ward, the policeman whistled a tune, which might have been "Yes! We Have No Bananas," but he wasn't much of a whistler.

After a while, the uniformed guard shifted to "Who's Sorry Now?" *I am,* she thought, shifting on the hard visitor chair. She hadn't eaten since Nathan's on Sunday. Nothing sat on the side table but a copy of the *Brooklyn Daily Eagle* and an untouched water cup with a straw—not flowers, not grapes. The policeman kept associates from visiting; their family was another story, the schnorrers. She shouldn't be alone: Where were Mama, Annie, and Tillie? Her sister wouldn't be lording it over Montauk Avenue without Abie.

A light shone over her brother's head, because he remained under constant observation. An opaque tube drained fluid from his chest. A bag of yellow liquid hung from his bedside attached to his body by a catheter. Brown blood stained a spot over his left chest, and sometimes she'd look up and there was a fresh red pool in the middle, right where he would have pledged allegiance if he did that sort of thing, which he didn't.

Abie didn't shame her—the women of her family did, abandoning him at the Coney Island Hospital, at the New York Hebrew Orphan Asylum. She was the one here beside him, if he ever woke up. His hair gathered in greasy whorls on his head, which was too big for that little body under the pus-stained white sheet. With his eyes closed and his mouth shut, he shed all that was big about him, his flash, his energy, his daring. On any given day, he was a carefree guy looking over a precipice to face down hell—but he'd always gambled he had years before the unavoidable descent.

But, to Thelma, it seemed like the inevitable had caught up with him, and she didn't know where to shelve her heavy heart. As the hours passed, anger scorched her until she could hardly sit. He'd risked everything, and for what? So he lined his pockets; she could live with that crime. But the escalating violence terrified her. What had he done, who had he crossed, to inspire gunfire?

Sorrow replaced Thelma's anger. She deceived herself into believing she didn't have any more tears to cry, lulled by the banality of the hospital, the smell of antiseptic and shit and sour towels, and the way she was disconnected from the outside world with no solace and no way to comfort the wax figure lying before her. He couldn't fix this situation, and neither could she. A lonely wind howled in her belly, and she squeezed her brother's hand, which was small and callus-free, the nails long and pinkish shiny, unchanged, as if he were her sleeping beauty.

But he was oblivious, bloody and broken. On the cusp of thirty, the assault reduced him to this: a little man with a strong chin stripped of his spirit, wearing a hospital gown that exposed his ass when the nurse flipped him over for his sponge bath.

The white-capped sister of mercy had commented how light Abie was for all the police bother. The guy in bed number ten didn't seem that dangerous, the nurse had confessed. Thelma imagined the rage and resentment that ordinarily would have animated her brother given this level of disrespect. Instead, he breathed, his eyes fluttered beneath the lids, occasionally he jerked a limb like someone who stumbles in their dreams. But even that didn't awaken him.

Thelma had sent a telegram to Louis at the base and he'd responded with one word: "coming." Not when or how but he was on his way. Another day passed and she remained alone. She ate the Jell-O from Abie's tray, which tasted like cleaning fluid. At dusk on the second day, Abie still hadn't regained consciousness. Not Annie, Jesse, Mama, nor Moe had appeared during visiting hours. Thelma had expected Tillie to show in a tattoo of heels on the cement floor and a cloud of perfume, dragging their son behind her, but she hadn't come, either. Abie's stubble grew. His hair matted. The nurse came and wiped him down. The doctor took his pulse and peeled back his dressings and sniffed. The boys with alcohol poisoning began to laugh and, within hours, exited the ward. The man with sunstroke left his father behind and went home with his wife and kids. An Italian boy who'd fractured his femur on a construction site entered screaming on the shoulders of his crew and then fell silent after a shot of morphine. And still Abie remained in absentia, the body in bed ten without a soul.

Thelma needed to go home, bathe, and change clothes. She itched between her legs and under her armpits. A whitehead throbbed on her chin. But she couldn't face the crew on Montauk Avenue, inquiring after Abie while refusing to visit, all under Annie's thumb. And, then, late on the third day, while the custodian slopped his mop, singing

"Sometimes I Feel Like a Motherless Child," she heard shoes hustling down the hallway well after visiting hours ended. She untucked her feet from under her and nearly fell when she tried to stand up and there was Louis.

He dropped his duffel bag and hugged her hard until they were both breathless. He rested his hand on the back of her head to notch it into the bend of his neck, his fingers slipping through her new bob. His company was comfort. He'd come home from the war in his uniform, finally, with medals, even. He'd been promoted to sergeant, someone who gave orders as well as took them, a part of something bigger than family, an American. She could feel that solidity in him: he was a grown-up, separate and accomplished. And, despite her sadness, she felt proud. He was still her brother, but he had entered the larger world beyond Brooklyn and survived—thrived, even. He had escaped.

When they detached, he eyed Abie and said, "Jesus."

"Mary and Joseph," Thelma said.

"I only have forty-eight hours—and it took eighteen just to get here."

"Maybe he'll wake up now that you're here."

"I'm not promising miracles, but it's been known to happen." He approached Abie with his hands clasped behind his back and peered down while asking, "Has he said anything?"

"Not to me. He talked to the police that night, but he wouldn't or couldn't tell them who shot him," she said, hovering behind him. "And he's been unconscious ever since."

"Do you know who did it?"

She shook her head. "Does it matter?"

"No," he said. "It's done."

"Will he make it?"

"Sure, Temeleh, sure, he'll make it."

"You're just saying that."

"He's alive and breathing. He still has some kick in him. I saw worse in France, and they popped open their eyes when they smelled whiskey." He extracted a dinged metal flask from his chest pocket, unscrewed the cap, and passed it under Abie's nostrils like smelling salts. They stood in silence, just the rats running relays in the walls, but the liquor had no magic effect. He nodded. "I've seen worse come back, Temmy."

"Can he hear us, Louis?"

"Maybe or maybe not: you never know who's gonna rally, but I'll put cash money on Abie. Just don't reveal any secrets—I remember a guy in a coma whose best buddy confessed he'd bedded the victim's wife and the wounded soldier woke up swinging."

Louis scraped up another chair and they sat beside the bed. He shared the flask with Thelma, who took a small sip, and then a gulp. Her head immediately whooshed because her stomach was empty. She glanced over at Louis in uniform and briefly believed he was a mirage. As welcome as his presence was, it also confirmed how dire Abie's situation was. She focused her attention on Abie. "Hey, schmuck," she said, "Wake up! Louis's here."

"C'mon, you *putz*; I brought you a hot redhead." Nothing.

To an outsider, their exchange might have seemed jocular, blasé— but it was anything but. So much emotion vibrated between them while their words were as clumsy as children's wooden blocks.

"You look good," Thelma said.

"You look better." Louis hung his hat from the corner of the sickbed.

"Liar," she said. "Tell me about the army."

"Now?"

"We've got time. If I had a deck of cards, I'd beat you at rummy."

He sighed, apparently reluctant, and she couldn't determine whether he was being modest or if the memories triggered images he'd rather avoid. He spoke softly now, although his voice echoed in the otherwise quiet ward. He told her about the battle, the big one at the Marne in July of '18 that continued for days, the final German drive that should have sunk the Allies, the moment when the Americans turned them back and seized the offensive. But they didn't know that then. The Thirty-Eighth Infantry was green. They'd hardly had any real battle training, rushed as they were to France to help their beleaguered allies. They'd been honed in action, sometimes fighting under French command. They were just boys in the woods and, on the riverside, fresh meat. He'd taken to it better than most—he'd always relied on his sense of direction—but this was countryside, meadows and steep wooded hills, meandering rivers and slippery swamp, and he didn't know how to plot his location by the stars. He couldn't even find the Big Dipper in the Brooklyn sky.

They couldn't even pronounce the places they were expected to protect, mangling the names: Château-Thierry and Chalon and the Surmelin River valley. He told her how first there was silence and darkness like a person never witnessed in the city. Their ears tuned in to every noise. The waiting had its own sense of dread, and they couldn't even whisper for fear of drawing enemy fire. And then it was like wind, the sound of the German artillery rushing across the Marne, the whiz and bang, the shells exploding, cratering the earth and sending out shrapnel and body parts, the hands of friends. The bombardment continued without pause. They were at the front.

They put on gas masks, which were their own suffocating torture, but nothing like inhaling mustard gas. A soldier couldn't recognize the man beside him, a monstrous bug who could only nod and gesture to communicate. His own wheezing was louder than the sound of the incoming assault, so he had to calm it, breathe slowly, move quickly, even as German soldiers crept over a footbridge and attacked. He had a revolver and his orders: keep the Huns from getting traction on the river's west bank by any means necessary. By then, he'd already killed one mother's son and buried a pal under a wooden cross in Courboin's churchyard.

What was it like? He wasn't any other place, any other time. There was just the now, the inching forward. He was scrambling and fighting and protecting his brothers to his left flank and his right. He wasn't reckless but he didn't flinch, and so his pals figured he was brave. He just did what he'd learned from Abie. If you're going to fight, you can't be of two minds. You're as good as anybody, and you don't need to be any better. Use your weapon. If their artillery is bigger, persist, because what choice do you have? War is hell if a person hasn't grown up in the New York Hebrew Orphan Asylum or been raised by that wolf Annie. At least a soldier knows who the enemy is.

"Are you two girls going to gab all night?" asked a hoarse voice from the bed. "How's an invalid supposed to sleep?"

Thelma leaped from her chair. "Thank God!"

"He had nothing to do with it," squawked Abie, his voice strained from the effort to expel air out his lungs and past the chest pain. "Temmy, can you help me here?"

"What do you need, baby?" She exploded in an exaggerated nursey energy. She'd wash his wounds, wipe his brow. He'd risen from the dead. Thelma would nurse him back to health and give him whatever he needed, as long as he just stayed with her. "Should I raise your head?"

"That's a start," he said. She rearranged the pillows, trying to be gentle while lifting his skull so that he could see them. He grimaced and groaned. "Are those tears?"

"Dust, tough guy," she said. "Should I call for the nurse?"

"Is she good-looking?" He tried to laugh, wincing instead. "No rush. I'm not going anywhere." He squinted, drawing a short breath. "You should see your faces."

"You should see yours," said Louis. "I've seen better-looking corpses on the battlefield—and you were no beauty to begin with."

"It's rude to insult the dead. Better to do it behind their back while they're alive," Abie said. "So, Louis, what a sight for sore eyes: my brother the war hero. I'd salute, but I can't raise my right arm. What, do I have to get shot for you to come home?"

"Some headline: I survived France and you got plugged in Brooklyn."

"Coney Island, what a toilet! Who shoots a guy on Mermaid Avenue? Harpooned, yes, but shot?"

"You made the *Brooklyn Daily Eagle*," said Thelma.

"What was the headline?" Louis asked.

"Lorber Shot Down by Two Men in Auto Directed by Female."

"Did I make any other papers, Temmy?"

"Just the one," said Thelma. "But you got page three above the fold. The subhead was 'Victim of Coney Island Assault Reveals Very Little to Police.'"

"And I'm staying ignorant. It should have read, 'Coney Island Victim Clams Up.'"

"You got good placement, right next to the report that actress Marjorie Rambeau was suing for divorce on account of her husband beating her."

"She's a good-looking dame," Abie said. "I met her once at a speakeasy."

Louis stretched his legs. "Now you have another story you can't tell your kids. Where's your wife? Why isn't Tillie here?"

"That's a funny story."

Louis crossed his right leg over his left, removing his cigarettes from a pocket and then putting them back. "Why do I get the feeling she doesn't agree?"

Abie scratched his ear. "You want the long story or the short story?"

"The truth, maybe," said Louis.

"You know I didn't want to stand under the chuppah with that broad in the first place. I'm not the marrying kind. I did right by her."

"We'll see," said Louis.

"First, she complained that I never came home—but why would I want to live in the Bronx near her mother?" So, Abie explained, one Sunday he sent some of the boys up to her apartment and shlepped her and the kid and the double bed down to a two-bedroom place on Rodney Avenue in Williamsburg. After that, he came home but, wouldn't you know it, she missed her mother up in the Bronx—and she didn't appreciate it when he called Mrs. Chersonsky an old yenta. But, what, she couldn't handle the truth? He was her husband. That's what she wanted, a man around the house and that's what she got: a man, not a patsy. If he paid the rent, he was going to pick the place. They all wanted to stick their fingers in his business, those Chersonskys. Feh on that: take the money and yaps shut.

So maybe that was why she wasn't at his bedside, but she *was* a pill. The more time they spent together, the less they liked each other. She couldn't keep a secret, either. Anything that happened, every hangnail, she told her mother. She began to complain that he was sitting around the apartment in his ratty underwear. So what did he do? He took them off. He thought it was funny. Who knew she lacked a sense of humor.

When Tillie *kvetched* that now he was exposed in front of the kid and it's disgusting, maybe it hurt his feelings a little, maybe he didn't feel like being told what to do in his own house where he paid the rent—and the electric and the grocer. So he made it a habit of never wearing clothes on Rodney Avenue. Like a baby: bare-assed. It got so that he unlocked the bolt and dropped trousers just inside the door. She told him to get out. He said "with pleasure." He got her to agree that it was her idea that he'd never cross that threshold again. That's how he fixed his marital discord. He could write an agony column, he was so proud of himself. She needed him, but not vice versa.

"That's quite a story," said Louis. "Even an angry wife shows up at her husband's deathbed. Now I know why she's not here."

"Nobody's perfect."

Thelma arched her eyebrows. "I'm guessing we won't be having Passover at your house anytime soon."

"The contortionist makes great lasagna."

"She took you back?" Thelma asked.

"She's flexible," Abie said. By then, the early-shift nurses had realized the patient in bed number ten had regained consciousness. And while they checked Abie's pulse, they fussed even more over Louis. Thelma had never seen it before, the way women responded to him in uniform.

"Hey," Abie asked. "Did Annie show up? Mama?"

Louis and Thelma looked at each other. She shrugged.

"Screw them," said Louis.

Thelma sighed. "What else is new?"

"I guess I gotta change my will."

"While you're at it, can you change jobs? This life is going to be the death of you," Thelma said, feeling more emotionally out of control than she cared to express, blinking back tears. "And me, too."

"She's right," said Louis. "If your enemies had better aim, we'd be tossing dirt on your corpse."

"Any chance you could work a desk?" Thelma asked.

"Don't push me, Tem. I know what I'm doing."

"That's clear: knocking on death's door with your ass hanging out."

"Leave it," Louis said, sending a warning glance Thelma's way. "It's too soon, Tem."

"This isn't the kind of business where I can apply for a transfer." He looked at her for a long time, holding her gaze until she glanced away. "So I really scared you this time?"

"Worse than Frankenstein," she said. "I wasn't sure you were going to make it . . ."

". . . but I did. It takes more than a bullet to the chest to kill Little Yiddle."

"Don't take that for granted," said Louis.

"I don't take anything for granted," Abie said. "Look, it's not a total loss—I brought the three of us together."

"I'd rather meet in better times," said Louis.

Abie coughed and grimaced. "Beggars can't be choosers."

"Abie, promise me this won't happen again," Thelma said.

"We'll see, Temeleh. It's not exactly up to me, but I'm in no rush to meet my maker."

"As if he'd recognize you," Louis said.

A matron in white with brisk movements and soft eyes approached. "You have a visitor."

"Me?" asked Abie, digging his free elbow into the bed and trying to lift himself up.

"No," said the matron. "Your sister does—at the main nurses' station."

"That's strange," said Thelma. Without thinking, she hoped it was Philip. But she'd never want him to see her like this, still wearing the same dress three days later at the bedside of her mobster brother. But his was the first name that came to mind.

She rose and stretched before entering the hall and nodding to the disheveled policeman, who'd slept through the awakening. He looked like a man who'd spent the night playing stethoscope with a nurse, and he smelled like it, too—funk and rose water. She rolled her eyes and then proceeded down the quiet corridor. Her footsteps in her dirty yellow T-straps echoed as she passed an open door. Peripherally, she viewed an old man's yellowed feet as twisted as tree roots. She felt the patients' loneliness as the hospital began to stir.

At the nurses' station, Moe stood waiting for her in his coarse brown weekday suit, the skullcap pinned to his scalp, the *tsitsis* stringing down at his hips and visible at the jacket's hem. He held a large brown-paper package wrapped in string. His chin jutted forward and she noticed, as if for the first time, the underbite that suggested a stubbornness she knew lay beneath. She wasn't sure if he was forty-three or forty-four by now. She avoided keeping track.

"What a surprise!" She felt an awkward heaviness. Any more emotion than she was already carrying was unwelcome. When she got within a few feet, her stepfather extended the parcel, saying, "I thought you'd need clean clothes, maybe a change of shoes."

On impulse, she peered at her T-straps that had had so much dance in them and now looked as worn out as she felt. She didn't know what game he was playing. She didn't want to know, yet it impressed her that he, of all people, had done the right thing and made it to the hospital. "Do you want to see Abie?"

"I have to get to work." He shuffled backward in his scuffed shoes. "Don't tell Mama I was here."

"Short leash, huh?"

"Arf," he said with a basset hound's sad, shiny eyes. She began to turn back toward the ward with the bundle beneath her arm. "Wait! I got something else . . . for you."

She turned to see him fumbling in his jacket pocket, his jeweler's fingers failing him. He extracted a small paper sack and rattled its contents. "Lemon drops," he said with a shy smile, "your favorite sweet."

"Thanks." She wasn't a little girl now, but she still loved candy. Nevertheless, she kept as much distance between them as she could when she plucked the bag from his grasp, awkwardly extracting her fingers when he tried to hold her hand. He had something more to say, their encounter pregnant with it, but she cut him off. "I have to get back. Abie woke up."

"Should I tell Mama?"

"Don't bother, Uncle Moe. You don't want them to know you visited the hospital to see your stepson like any good father would."

She turned and gave him a good, long look at her behind, which she was sure he was watching. By now, as an adult, she understood that he hadn't wanted to be married to her mother: Who would? But he'd been Mama's husband when he'd touched her. And she'd been a child; she saw that so clearly now. He'd exploited her and left her to the wolves, unprotected. But few people were just one thing or the other: she still saw the kindness in him, the gentleness and warmth, the thoughtfulness of his creeping to the hospital before work to bring her clean clothes. She didn't know, again, where to put that gratitude, how to sort that push-pull of affection and betrayal, the disgust she felt for this aging stranger, her stepfather.

In the distance, she saw Louis talking to a nurse, who was showing exaggerated interest in his medals. Carrying his duffel bag, her brother turned toward her and began slicing the distance between them. "I have to go back," he said, and her heart sank. "Say my goodbyes to Mama and Annie."

"I'm not taking *that* bullet. They won't be pleased that you came to Brooklyn and didn't pay respects."

"I was right here. If they'd been where they belonged, they would have seen me."

She smiled: her brother, the man of few words but true. "Forget them. It made me so happy to see you, and see you thriving. Just go out there and be happy, Louis—love who you want and come back when you can. We'll be here. Or at least I'll be."

"Abie's in good hands. What a relief he's going to make it. I'm so glad I got leave. I wouldn't be here without that crazy mensch," said Louis. "When I'm done with the service, I'll come home to Montauk Avenue. I'll bring Lucille. You'll like her. And our kids will play together."

"Maybe I should marry first." She wanted to believe what Louis said: that they had a future together, that their children, cousins—even Abie's son—would play catch and hopscotch on Montauk Avenue. Why not? Stranger things had happened. She put her hand up to his cheek where the stubble was gathering. Even bristly, he looked handsome in his uniform. He seemed to finally fit in his skin, to have found his place in the world. When they hugged, she tucked the bag of lemon drops into his front pocket. "Don't be a stranger."

"I'll never be a stranger to you, baby."

Chapter 24

Thelma didn't return to work. Instead, she remained close to home for the next six months, surrendering her bed to the convalescing Abie. He was a nasty patient, a bear ripped from hibernation too soon. He'd seen the afterlife, and it was no picnic, a glaring white light in the distance and angels squawking and his emaciated papa stretching out his hand and coughing at him to come quick, join him. He'd hitched the first ride back to consciousness.

At night, she slept lightly on a heap of featherbeds on the floor, listening for her brother's snoring, awakening if she heard an irregular gurgle. She'd do anything to protect him. She figured it was what he'd do if the situation were reversed. Through Abie's frequent sleepless nights, she entertained him with childhood stories or movie magazine gossip. They preferred Polish-born femme fatale Pola Negri, who, according to *Photoplay* and *Movie Weekly*, demanded rose petals be strewn on her dressing-room floor, drank champagne from a footed ice bucket, and danced the Charleston to burn off excess energy between takes.

By 1923, the star of *Bella Donna* and *The Wildcat* had tossed fiancé Charlie Chaplin while keeping his diamond and was cycling through European noblemen and costars while partying with newspaper magnate William Randolph Hearst and his mistress, movie star Marion Davies, at their San Simeon mansion. Rumored to be Jewish, the five-foot-tall, dark-haired, pale-skinned spitfire wasn't wrapping her love in tinfoil and saving it for some future happy ending on- or offscreen: she relished a be-here-now character that burned brightly before discovering a good man to make her an honest woman.

Thelma had hoped Phil would be her good man. She hadn't spoken to him since he dropped her off after the Roseland. Assuming he'd follow the newspaper reports like everyone else in the neighborhood, she didn't reach out. His father owned buildings; her brother was in a less savory business. If Phil had really been interested, he knew where she lived. He could always knock.

Besides, Thelma had her hands full. Up in her second-floor room, Abie thirsted for fresh air, demanding she throw the windows open, because she apparently required a constant reminder that he was alive and breathing. Annie would hustle in to shut them, complaining that they had to pay for the heat, and he would bark her out of the room, saying, "Take it out of my pension." Pain still plagued him, but being dependent bugged him more. He wanted to move, to get back in the game, to escape the house and the order of women.

Slowly Thelma began to assist him out of bed, watching him flinch as she helped him put on his robe, and trying to be cheerful enough to encourage him but not so chirpy that he snapped, calling her Nursey. Gradually they reached the point where he could creep downstairs, holding her shoulder with one hand and the banister with the other. He spent the next three days on his back, exhausted, but then he pushed himself, refusing to stay in bed like an invalid and appropriating Annie's favorite parlor chair. In the coming weeks, they'd trace the block together, down Montauk, across Sutter Avenue, up Milford, over Belmont, him straining with effort and acknowledging that Mama could beat him in a footrace. Over time, their circuit became larger, taking them two blocks to Pitkin Avenue and returning down Shepherd. He eventually recovered his wind, began to straighten shoulders that had been curled inward to avoid stretching the scars. They'd stop at the luncheonette for a grilled cheese and an egg cream, teasing the paper-hatted soda jerk behind the counter. When Abie could swallow an entire hamburger steak, he began to discuss girls again.

During Abie's convalescence, a weekly courier arrived with daisies and a yellow envelope. When she inquired what the thick packet held and who'd sent it, he'd answered that they were love letters from Tillie. He let that sink in and then added, as an apparent afterthought: *don't open the door if the guy doesn't have the flowers.*

The payoffs' arrival stoked her dread that Abie'd brought the danger of the streets to their doorstep, but she'd never abandon him, considering the transaction the cost of keeping him safe and close while he recuperated. She hoped that when he improved he'd be more cautious. In the meantime, he paid the mortgage, the electric, and the grocer, while she devoted herself to his health, which meant avoiding aggravating questions. He requested meals from Mama and Annie: hold the tsuris. Annie acquiesced, but only if he took out a life insurance policy naming her as the beneficiary. If it would shut her up, he'd do it, even if he called her a vulture as he signed the document she pushed in front of him.

He had no love for his niece and nephews—not for him to treat them as precious cargo after the way Annie had raised her brothers and sister. The kids were more than a little afraid of him. He liked it that way—and it amused Thelma, always his best audience. He growled. He told Julius, Adele, and Eli, now twelve, ten, and five, stories about orphanage life, threatening to send them there if they didn't behave. He offered to show them his wounds and let them put their fingers in the bullet holes, but he had no takers among the timid trio.

Abie's near-death experience changed him. He was sullen for long stretches of time without explaining what inspired the moods. The attack had given his heart a shock and, while it returned to beating, it carried more resentment and less generosity. This was who he was, only darker. And Thelma still stood by him. When he could walk without a cane, they started testing the limits of his range. After a few weeks, they could make the mile west on Sutter Avenue to the Premier Theater, stopping en route at the candy store to get a Hershey bar for him and lemon drops for her. Inside they'd buy a soda with two straws and share.

Smuggling in contraband enhanced the pleasure, but mostly entering the high-ceilinged movie palace offered a sense of almost religious awe and an escape from drudgery (and Annie). Plush red carpets muffled the sound of their footsteps. Crossing the lobby, they'd pass a goldfish pond and a wishing well. They had their rituals, stopping for Abie to hand his sister a shiny penny to toss over her shoulder—bye-bye President Lincoln—Thelma silently wishing Abie good health and a safe job.

Inside, Abie led them to their spot on the left aisle—and beware anyone occupying his favorite seats. He preferred swashbucklers, like Douglas Fairbanks battling through *The Thief of Baghdad* without breaking a sweat, ever charming, lethal—and the slapstick of Laurel and Hardy shorts. Sitting beside Abie, Thelma noticed, as customers shifted their seats, that he had become notorious, recognized as the hood who'd survived the hit. He was about as subtle as a dueling scar—and he didn't seem to care. If he knew why he'd been targeted for death, he'd never explained it to Thelma.

And, as the months passed, it was as if he'd turned the theater into an office. Once the feature started, he'd sometimes excuse himself with a grunt. She'd put her hand on his arm and say, "Stay," or "Don't leave me in the scary part," but she had no apparent influence over him as he slowly navigated up the incline to the balcony steps. She knew he was gravitating back to his old life, his old friends, one reel at a time, but she felt powerless to stop him. If the audience was quiet, she could hear his heavy breath as he climbed, having warned her not to look back or up.

It was on one of these days, late in 1924, when Thelma was watching Negri tilt her chin and flash her eyes as Catherine the Great, notching off lovers, zesting for life and ruling Russia in Ernst Lubitsch's *Forbidden Paradise*, that Thelma first noticed Phil. He sat alone two rows down and to the right. She split her time watching Negri ("Pola's

Catherine is what one might call a good bad woman. But her wicked-ness is done gorgeously and regally," *Photoplay* had raved) and the light flicker off Phil's profile. She remembered him teasing, "Do you want to see my Valentino?" And, then, "Do you want to see it again?"

Yes, she thought, *I do want to see it again.* She tried to stifle her tears during a comic scene without a weeping audience to provide cover, recalling how complete she'd felt that day they'd shared, how meant for each other, how every tune was played for them. And then that dream had been shot right in the heart (technically above and a life-saving bit to the left). She'd read that Negri had abandoned her hunt for the one great love and was now diddling her costar Rod La Rocque. Thelma would have to discard her one-and-only dream man, too, she thought as Abie returned to his seat, handing her his hankie and asking, "What's up?"

She gestured toward Phil with her chin.

"Who's that?" Abie asked in full voice.

"Shh." So mortified, she could have crept under her seat.

"Is he *the* guy?" he asked, lowering his voice to an audible stage whisper.

She groaned as half the theater turned around to see who'd spo-ken, but Phil kept watching the screen. When intermission came, she returned Abie's soggy handkerchief and began to gather gloves and handbag. "I believe you know this gentleman," Abie said as Phil loomed above them in the aisle.

"Phil," she said, in a fruity formal voice that sounded plucked from a cinematic garden party, "how lovely to see you again."

"I do declare," teased Abie.

"I'd like to introduce you to my brother Abraham."

Abie clutched the armrest and began to rise from his seat.

"Don't bother," said Phil.

"No bother," said Abie, reaching out to grab Phil's hand and using it to leverage himself up.

"Check your arm for your watch," Thelma said. The men greeted her joke with awkward silence, so she plunged ahead. "Abie, this is Philip Schwartz."

Abie looked Phil up and down as if assessing horseflesh. "It's nice to meet you at long last."

"Are you two staying for the second feature?"

Thelma looked to Abie for a cue. He said, "Excuse me, but I gotta see a guy about a thing," and then he winked at Thelma before asking, "Could you see Temmy home? My sister's a little shy."

"Suave," she said, pronouncing it with a long *a*.

"Yes, Your Majesty," Abie said.

Phil took Abie's vacated seat beside Thelma. She felt her cheeks flush. She crossed her ankles and then her knees, smoothing her skirt, which wasn't her best. She tried to look sideways and tilt her chin up like Negri as he said, "I love the way this picture leavens drama and tragedy with humor."

She paused, trying to join him on safe ground with a smart comeback about the movie. Instead, she betrayed herself with earnestness. "It's nice to see you, Phil."

There was a long pause. "You, too, Temmy. Can I call you that? Temmy?"

She relaxed a smidgen. "Call me anything—as long as you call me."

"Have you been dancing?"

"Not since . . . ," she began.

"I get the papers, too."

"You know my brother . . ."

"I've read about your brother," he said, "and I know you. You don't have to explain."

"Maybe I want to explain."

"There'll be plenty of time."

"How do you know that?"

"I believe in wishes," he said. "And I've been wishing for you at the well every time I've crossed the Premier lobby."

It was just the kind of dumb, mushy thing the youthful hero might say, bounding off the court and serenading the heroine. "Has anybody ever told you that you look like Valentino?"

"Never," he said. "Well, almost never. Do you want to go up in the balcony?"

"My regiment leaves at dawn."

"Is that a yes or a no?"

Maybe she should have been more suspicious, but she was Pola Negri, spontaneous and dangerous, a good bad girl. She said, "I'm a woman of the world, and that's my air of mystery."

"So that's what I smelled. Follow me."

Chapter 25

After reuniting at *Forbidden Paradise*, Thelma and Phil circled each other for a while without making any overt declarations of affection. She feared getting hurt but was available and easy to find, regularly attending the Premier with Abie while he gradually recovered his strength—if not his sense of humor. Her brother was getting antsy again, an itchy scab. He began to debate the pros and cons of returning to the old neighborhood under the Williamsburg Bridge. When Thelma squeezed his good hand, half jesting as she pleaded, "Don't leave me," like a damsel in distress tied to a railroad track, he promised to fix a retail job for her on Pitkin before scramming. He knew a guy. He always knew a guy. She didn't want to be alone again on Montauk, but she knew he wouldn't remain forever. He'd leave when he couldn't tolerate Annie anymore, and their sister was already way up his nose hairs.

"Can't live with her, can't shoot her" became his motto. Years before, Abie had lost the capacity to trust, and now, following the shooting, his eyes shifted constantly as he tried to see around corners, anticipating the next threat and the one after that. He might have been considered paranoid if it weren't for the matching bullet-hole scars and the nerve damage in his left hand.

It didn't take a genius to sense that she wouldn't have Abie around much longer and that, on some level, she now depended more on him than vice versa. He was giving her a gentle push: She had to start looking ahead, too. She had to make a life for herself separate from his. As winter hit and the slush iced over, the movie audience expanded to include those who begged pennies on the corner to enter the heated auditorium. Frequently Phil would arrive, strolling past their aisle in a business suit, carrying his overcoat, hat, and popcorn. He'd settle two rows down and, at Abie's urging, she'd join him. When she glanced over her shoulder, Abie was gone. After a few weeks, when the Lorbers saw Phil, Abie would gather his gear and shuffle away while the young man took his seat. As cowboys fought Indians and hussies hustled their next mark and toffs downed martinis, the pair ascended to the sparsely filled balcony with rising excitement and a sense of daring. She found the spontaneity intoxicating, even if it was true that their actions mimicked those of young lovers on the screen. He would loosen his tie and she would ease her garters, teasing, "Wanna see my magic leg? Wanna see it again?"

"Yes," he whispered. Beneath the rafters, they rubbed against each other and did those things a man and a woman could do fully clothed in semipublic. Sometimes they had to shoo away neighborhood rascals who crept up to watch, incriminating themselves with giggles and sighs of "Oh, baby, baby." When they broke for a smoke, she'd leave her leg hooked over Phil's knee while he puffed cigarettes and drank from a flask; she popped lemon drops from a paper sack he'd brought, or Jordan almonds. She had an endless sweet tooth.

She convinced herself they were happy for months at a time in the company of Valentino and Negri, Chaplin and Mary Pickford. The future didn't preoccupy them when all they hungered for was each other, the touch and feel, the awkward bumping of noses, battling frustrating armrests, as they adjusted to each other's preferences and pace. Gradually, they began to wonder aloud if they preferred movies with happy or tragic endings. Was there a wedding in their future (or an abyss)? They lived with their families and couldn't afford to marry and set up a third household. Besides, they preferred spending money on movies, dance, and drinks at basement speakeasies. Only suckers saved for a rainy day.

Throughout 1925 and into 1926, every Wednesday they went to the pictures: Negri's *A Woman of the World* and Valentino's *Cobra* and Chaplin's *The Gold Rush*.

They spent weekends together: their golden thirty-six hours viewing the cherry blossoms in the spring at the Brooklyn Botanic Garden and the leaves rusting in the fall, returning again and again to Coney Island without ever getting sand in their shoes, riding the Wonder Wheel and relishing the private time it allowed them to survey Brooklyn as if they alone could lay claim to the world below, passing the flask that Phil inevitably carried. Meanwhile, they ascended in status at the Roseland, becoming one of the privileged couples that danced in the center during breaks, introducing new steps, teaching the tango, the dance that had made Valentino a star. (Only three years before, the actor had traded his screen career for an eighty-eight-city tour dancing onstage with his second wife, Natacha Rambova, née Winifred Kimball Shaughnessy.)

The couple excelled at that most intimate of dances—the tango. They danced chest to chest or upper thigh to hip in close embrace. It required intense focus to perform the elegant, serpentine steps, but the footwork was nothing compared to the emotional immediacy that rose to a torrent of passion—man leading woman, woman leading man—so that each fluid movement forward or back became a sensual act. For Thelma, these moments were exhilarating, Phil's gaze arresting hers with an intensity she'd never seen off the dance floor, his breath filling her lungs. Her worries fled like gamblers from a police whistle. She fell on him, her chest balanced on his as he carried her weight, dragging her first this way then that until she reached up and smoothed his hair, then ran her hand lovingly down his neck, caressing his chest. Then he pulled her close again, twisting her around and bending her back until her bob brushed the floor and she looked up to the stars sparkling in the ceiling. Then he reeled her back into his arms for a final embrace, their lips brushing each other with heat but going no farther.

The tango was a dance of absolute trust. It couldn't be faked. The couple lost track of the audience during these interludes: they were performing something very private in public. Often, during their routine, a female spectator fainted, requiring smelling salts to revive. And, if Phil left her side afterward, a line of men formed to dance with Thelma.

Thelma loved Phil for those thirty-six hours a week, and their affection buoyed her for all the time that separated them when he went back to Wyona Street and she returned to her room at the back of Montauk Avenue, a formal portrait of the pair entwined at the Roseland on her nightstand. Over the summer, they attended the Rialto in Manhattan to see if this new thing, air-conditioning, really worked. It did! And she even had to bring a sweater in mid-August to avoid gooseflesh. It was delicious. It was the future. That fall, they queued for hours to gain entrance to the opening night of the Kinema on Pitkin Avenue and Berriman, a five-minute walk from her house.

Those were relatively carefree times, and they floated along on the liberating spirit of the '20s as the weight of their parents' immigrant struggles began to lift from their shoulders. They were Americans. The war was over. The Germans were defeated and they were on the winning side. Even as months passed and they became confident their love was mutual, they avoided discussing marriage. Like saving money, that was for suckers, too. They'd witnessed plenty of relatives standing under the chuppah. They knew children arrived shortly thereafter and raising kids was work—and that it wasn't for them. Not now, not while they were having so much fun. Maybe someday they'd wed and have "their little schmuck," but they seemed content to be Thelma and Phil: partners in life and dance.

In truth, the logistics had been more complicated. Thelma wasn't entirely lighthearted about the arrangement. She had misgivings about Phil's commitment when he arrived quiet and distant or disappeared for weeks at a time, only to return as happy to see her as ever with no explanation for his absence. These occurrences fed into her doubts about being good enough for him, but she kept them to herself, letting him lead on and off the dance floor. She would have happily escaped Montauk Avenue and Annie with a clenched-fist send-off. However, Philip was more reticent, seeming to appreciate their limited time Wednesdays and weekends to bear the rest: selling ties by day on Pitkin Avenue, moving from one unsatisfying job to the next, nurturing his mother, Mildred, and his younger sister, Pearl.

He didn't talk much about life on Wyona Street, but gradually Thelma culled the essentials: his father, the landlord, stayed in an apartment near his office on 79 Fifth Avenue, spitting distance from the newsstand. This rejection tore the Schwartzes apart: on one hand, mother and children had financial security in a brick house the Rumanian immigrant had owned since 1904; on the other, they'd been discarded by their father the *macher*, who'd seemingly paid his way out of family obligations with his American financial success.

On Friday nights, Solomon Schwartz punctually returned home for roast chicken, delivering the strict household budget with all its conditions and demanding that expenses be recorded in a leather-bound ledger kept in the sideboard beside the good silver. He expected the family, including older brother Herman and younger Samuel, to preserve the fiction that he'd been home all week. He demanded to be treated like the pillar of respectability who deserved obedience he presented to the public. The lie of this situation, and Mrs. Schwartz's howling sense of betrayal, brought Phil's despairing mother to the edge of hysteria that had her fingering the carving knife at the Shabbat table. Her outbursts appeared to justify the father's contention that he couldn't live under the same roof with his crazy wife, and he was being merciful not to have her committed.

Born in Rumania and wed to Solomon before they had Herman and emigrated, Mildred, called Minnie, was a passionate woman—and they didn't have a single set of dishes that wasn't missing a plate she'd smashed in anger on the kitchen floor or tossed at her husband's head. According to Phil, he felt obligated to play peacekeeper once his older brother Herman got married, taking Samuel to live with him and his wife. Phil remained on Wyona Street, becoming the partner his mother so desperately needed. She was a woman who lived for family, and her husband's absence was a sharp rebuke to her skills as wife and mother. Because she often became agitated, one minute weeping about the loss of her spouse and then raging at his villainy, at first tearing her clothes and then cooking elaborate cakes to woo him back that went uneaten, Phil worried that if Thelma joined the family, his divided loyalties might send his mother over the edge.

The one thing Phil's combative parents could agree on was that Thelma, the Galician gangster trash, wasn't good enough for their intellectual son. With his looks and money, any mediocre matchmaker could find him a better bride—but they hadn't convinced Phil. Unlike his father, he was a romantic to his core. Once he'd fallen for Thelma at the glove store, even before the magic legs walked around the counter, that emotion only increased in intensity with the passage of time.

The couple was in no rush to settle down among one familial hornet's nest or the other. Meanwhile, Abie set up shop in a basement flat on Marcy Avenue in the shadow of the Williamsburg Bridge. Not far from Our Lady of Mount Carmel, Abie's scantily lit subterranean apartment doubled as a social club. It featured a cramped bedroom, a kitchen that doubled as an office, a rectangular living room with a bar and three round card tables—and a back door for quick escapes, always necessary in Abie's world. He'd spent his time recuperating wisely, planning a hangout where Brooklyn boys and Manhattan mugs could meet away from glaring eyes, where the Irish cops he'd known for years could be bribed and he could anchor himself at the center of a net of enterprises while still siphoning money from the newsstand and ongoing rackets. He called it the Williamsburg Boys Club.

Abie granted Thelma a key to Marcy Avenue for emergencies, saying he owed her. She hesitated, but occasionally she and Phil sought privacy in the late afternoon when the business that had no official office hours was more or less shut. Despite its dankness, the flat provided them the luxury of sharing the single bed where Abie slept. Even now, as they twisted around each other in the twilight of the darkened room on sheets that had likely not been washed since they were new, they felt as if they were resting on satin, just because they were alone together. She reclined on her back as he stroked the curls from her forehead, discovering that if he softly scratched her scalp, her entire body relaxed into a puddle where there was no future or past, just the security of his touch until she dropped off to sleep.

Thelma awoke to a strangling sound. In the murk, she recognized Phil hunched against the wall, his legs tucked up, his arms crossed over his knees. He was so vulnerable in his underwear without the armor of suit and tie and hat. She realized that the horrible sound had come from Phil. He was weeping and struggling against it, hiding his head in his arms. She'd never seen a man cry before, and her shattered heart cried out to console him as she had so often wanted comfort alone in the dark. She felt a level of tenderness, raw and powerful, that she'd never experienced before.

She knelt across the mattress, reaching a hand to his face. He batted it away. She flinched. She watched his face as it moved uncontrollably, collapsing, shifting like he could no longer rule his jaw, his lips, or his chin, as if there were a stranger strangling the sensitive man she loved and thought she knew. She didn't know what scrape to kiss to make it better.

"Can you hear it rattling?" he asked.

"What are you talking about, Phil? You're scaring me."

"The glass," he said. "I'm sorry. I'm so sorry. I can't go on. My head is cracking. I'm a shell and inside there's broken glass. I can hear it rattling."

Despite her fear, she crawled closer. "I can't hear any rattling."

"Are you saying I'm a liar?" He slithered away. "I'm broken."

"We're all broken," she said. "Look at me."

He tried to collect himself, gulping, his eyes looking wildly at her face, over her shoulder, up at the ceiling. "I'm broken and I can't be fixed. I want to die. Let me go."

"If you go, I go. And I'm not going anywhere." A powerful love expanded inside her and expressed itself as compassion for his broken bits that cut her heart and the beautiful suffering, the black hair falling loose over his broad forehead. This was intimacy like she'd never known before. There was no boundary between them, no tallying of the ways she was unworthy. He was naked to her, a spinning, frightened man not so different from herself. She would find out the why but not today, when he needed comfort, when he needed to be soothed and carried back to the living. She had the strength to hold him together. She had nursed Abie back to life. She had the will to put the pieces of Phil back together. Nothing was broken forever.

She curved her arm around his broad shoulders knotted with tension, feeling the warmth that she refused to let leave that beautiful body. Death wouldn't steal him from her. She would find a way. She must find a way. She pulled him close, settling his head in her lap as she pressed her spine against the wall, rocking him gently, rubbing his neck, stroking the thick eyebrows until he closed his eyelids and the tears flowed without a struggle. The room darkened. She sat with him, realizing the darkness inside her was not singular, something of which she should be ashamed. His sadness was transitory. She wouldn't let it drag them both down. She would scratch her way out of the grave to dance with him again, to walk the boardwalk in their Sunday shoes. She would escort him into the light. Tomorrow would be different.

Phil was breathing heavily as Thelma worried, wiping her own eyes now that he slept. She heard the front door unlock followed by the heavy footsteps of a stranger crossing the living room, dropping his coat, opening a bottle, and whistling the song "Bye Bye Blackbird."

Thelma nudged Phil awake, whispering, "We've got to go."

"Where are we?"

"Marcy Avenue."

"Did I fall asleep?"

"Yes."

"I'm so, so sorry, Temmy."

"I know you are."

"I didn't want it to end like this."

"Shh, sweetheart," she said, fearing the contagion of his panic, "nothing ended."

"I love you."

"Me, too, but we have to scram now."

"You won't leave me?"

"I'll never leave you."

"You should leave me. Run, now, while you still can."

"I'm not going anywhere except out that door before all the gorillas arrive. Someone just let themselves in and I can tell by the heavy footsteps it's not Abie. Now, please, Phil: get dressed."

They rushed in the dark, standing separately, their backs to each other. While he knotted his tie, she made the bed, thinking it was a wasted effort in this dump. She tried not to contemplate who had lain in the bed before them and what might happen there tonight. She heard the man in the other room shove the swinging door into the kitchen and the tap turn on. "Now, Phil, let's go now."

Chapter 26

1926

After leading Phil from Abie's apartment, Thelma became confused. The neighborhood's Italian women were weeping openly on Marcy Avenue, old and young hanging on to each other's sleeves, wailing. Mourning hung in the air like ashes, smudging anyone in the vicinity. Thelma stopped one lady after the other, asking, "What happened?" Had the Great War to end all wars failed and another started? Had the typhoid returned? On the corner, an excited newsboy hawked her answer: "Rudolph Valentino, Movie Sheik, Dies."

She flushed. "That can't be true, Phil, can it?"

He shrugged, still distant. "What's truth?"

Thelma pulled him along like a child with one hand while digging three pennies from the dust and gum wrappers at her pocketbook's bottom. She bought the *Brooklyn Daily Eagle*, reading the subhead aloud:

> Screen star, operated on for appendicitis and gastric ulcers, had made heroic struggle toward recovery until pleurisy assailed him and toxic poisons spread. Last English words to doctor expressed hope to fish with him next week.

She looked up at Phil, who still hadn't registered the news but resembled the saddest living Valentino in Brooklyn. "He was only thirty-one, Phil. How could he die?" And, yet, there it was in black and white, a publicity photo of the Latin lover in profile under the caption "Movie Star Dead." Those three words united her, the neighborhood movie widows, and fans across America all the way to his paramour Pola Negri's Beverly Hills mansion, where she was undoubtedly weeping, too, only in ermine and silk.

Valentino had reached his virile peak, riding the comeback wave with *The Son of the Sheik*. And yet, in the photograph, Thelma recognized the actor's melancholy as he stared into a future that would never unfold. Glancing at Phil's profile, she saw an identical dismay. Underlying her shock lurked her intuition that if Valentino could die so young, so could Phil.

The Latin lover's tragedy resonated among the locals circling the plaster statue of Our Lady of Carmel in her grotto, asking the Madonna, "Why? Why?" Like the kneeling women, Valentino was an Italian immigrant. His mother's pet and his father's disappointment, he'd been the black sheep, sailing to America to discover himself, finding work washing cars and dancing with women for tips long before becoming famous. Valentino had been stardust, providing his fans with an escape from sickness, from mopping, from the shirking husbands and the disrespectful children who snapped back at their mothers in a foreign tongue. If Valentino succumbed with the best doctors money could buy, how could they survive?

To bawl for their individual sorrows was self-pity but, together, the women's grief chorus formed a collective cry of loss. Clutching to Phil, fearing he might drift away, she read,

> Valentino died practically alone . . . Twice divorced,
> his sister Maria in Rome, his brother Alberto in Paris,
> were across the seas. His two wives were out of his life.

> Pola Negri, who declares she was Rudy's fiancée, was
> in California. As tender-hearted Norma Talmadge, led
> weeping from Rudy's room last night said with tears:
> "He's lonely, the poor boy is lonely."

It was hard for Thelma to comprehend how a famous man could feel isolated when surrounded by adoring fans, but when she turned to Phil, she began to understand the gap between a man's suave appearance and his private heartache. They walked for miles from the old neighborhood to the new, Williamsburg to Brownsville and East New York, hearing sobs everywhere they went. Newsies hawked death on every corner: "Valentino Passes with No Kin at Side; Throngs in Street."

∿

Before long, at Manhattan's Frank Campbell funeral home, "film's greatest lover" lay in state under a mountain of flowers, including an ostentatious wreath of scarlet roses with "Pola" inscribed in white blooms at its center. Rioters broke windows, trampling each other trying to gain entry, restrained by mounted police. Negri, having rushed cross-country by train, appeared days later in widow's black. Exhausted from her trip, she collapsed on the coffin. But, rather than being sympathetic to her pain, the sheik's frenzied fans rose up like hordes of jealous women who rejected Negri's claim to be Valentino's fiancée. Skepticism met her extravagant display, which was perceived as a publicity stunt. The intensity and voluptuousness of the Polish woman's grief alienated an American public who had applauded the identical overwrought behavior on-screen.

Not Thelma. Rather than rejecting Negri, she identified with her. If Valentino's death had stirred up a nation who had only known him on-screen, imagine the feelings of a woman who had shared his bed, read his poetry, and been his "Polita." She believed in those feelings, that Negri met the sadness in Valentino with her own sadness, without judging, and that she and Phil were tied to each other in the same way.

Brokenhearted, Thelma had a premonition that life was short for those who burned brightly. The lucky ones, like Valentino, experienced a brief, ecstatic burst of pleasure. Perhaps it seemed desperate, but she had to grab this imperfect love while she had it, suddenly afraid of dying alone, without family, like Valentino. In the following months, Thelma and Phil clung to each other, enjoying more good weeks than bad, catching fireflies of joy. Having confessed his secret, Phil relied even more on Thelma, but they remained in the bubble of each other's company, isolated from their fractured families.

At the Roseland, their popularity soared. They perfected their tango, becoming more fluid, welding technique to their deepening emotional connection, as the circle of spectators widened around them. More often than not, women cried, throwing scented handkerchiefs and exclaiming, "Rudy! Rudy!"

Valentino died, and as Negri's star faded, fickle Hollywood moved on to Mexico-born Ramon Novarro. Thelma and Phil spent 1927 watching movies about life in a glittering Manhattan where women jiggled in revealing evening gowns and men swanned in tuxedos, nourished only by music and martinis. They'd leave the Premier momentarily stunned beneath the marquee's brilliant lights, adjusting to the world outside, the *schmutz* and hustle, the cries of children as their mothers smacked them, imagining they themselves belonged to another life buoyed on vodka and repartee. They dressed the part, with Thelma going full flapper in her drop-waist frocks that revealed her knees when she crossed her legs. Fashion that was adored at the Roseland often met with critical sidelong glances at the local, and while she'd been in the bathroom, she'd overheard a friend of Annie's call her "cheap."

They were living in two worlds, which were about to collide. Since, if the movies were to be believed, marriage was the ultimate happy ending, the pair began to circle the subject. He'd first floated the idea during one intermission that he was ready to take the plunge whenever she was. The following August they exited the wrenching war romance *Wings*, starring Clara Bow, and were strolling Pitkin Avenue to share a banana split when she spun around, spurred on by the movie's tragic love triangle, and asked, her mouth rushing ahead of her common sense, "Will you marry me?"

"I thought you'd never ask." He picked her up, twirled her around, and the borough spun as he bent her back in the move they'd perfected at the Roseland, his eyes locked on hers. A turbaned washerwoman leaned on her broom and clapped, igniting the applause of a series of strangers who paused on the sidewalk to watch with giddy smiles. Afterward, they walked until late, wasting shoe leather, eating grilled cheese at an all-night diner, and making plans. Within two days, they visited the Brooklyn courthouse, got a license, paid for a witness, and became man and wife on August 2—all without inviting their families.

Following the "I dos," they telegraphed Abie with her new address on Wyona Street and got well oiled on martinis at the nearest bar. They enjoyed a liquid wedding feast, flooded with toasts from Wall Street drunks on their way home. The financiers predicted great times ahead for the couple, many children, bushels of happiness, and an era of prosperity like America had never seen before.

Afterward, Phil poured Thelma into a cab to ferry them to Wyona Street. He carried his bride over the threshold (stumbling only once) into the house filled with books and his mother's screams. His thirteen-year-old sister, Pearl, seated on the brocade sofa and flipping through a *Felix the Cat* comic, looked up with infinitely sad, dark eyes and said, "Go while you still can."

They ignored the teenager at their own peril. From that moment, it was like they'd slipped on a banana peel while doing the Charleston. There'd been a reason they'd protected their relationship from their caustic families. Thelma had leaped out of the frying pan of Montauk Avenue into the fire of the Schwartz household, no more wanted by Phil's mother than by hers.

As bitter as horseradish, Minnie was a small, anxious Rumanian immigrant of forty-seven. She pulled her white hair tight into a bun, covered herself wrist to ankle with handmade clothes that had been outdated decades before, when she'd arrived in New York via Ellis Island. Her beauty, though faded and crosshatched with anger lines, was evident: the prominent cheekbones, almond-shaped brown eyes, and arched brows that had remained defiantly black. She must have been as attractive as Pearl, who shared her mother's features but peered at the world suspiciously through identical dark eyes, rarely speaking and remaining in a state of suspension unusual for a girl so young. She watched. She waited. Another shoe would inevitably drop.

The following Friday, Thelma met Phil's father when he arrived for Shabbat dinner to a house scented with fresh-baked challah and chicken broth. Like Phil, Solomon was tall and trim, but that's where the similarity ended. Stern and sober and judgmental, he was a man confident in his ability to make money through hard work and other people's sacrifice. The father's arrogant blue eyes seemed to tally the value of this over that, estimating punishments to fit the crimes surrounding him. According to Phil, success had only solidified his assurance that he was the smartest man in any room he entered.

Mr. Schwartz handed Pearl his hat and coat, admonished her not to drag it on the floor because it cost good money, and assumed his position at the head of the table. He performed the *HaMotzi*, the prayer over the bread, in a commanding voice that could have filled an entire synagogue—although it overwhelmed at a mahogany table with seating for eight. When Minnie poured the wine, her husband cleared his throat as she came to Phil. Her head bowed even farther, if that was possible, and she left her son's glass conspicuously empty, following suit with Thelma's. That was when Solomon stared fully at his new daughter-in-law, who had never known a father and lived in hope. The patriarch shook his head. "She's not much to look at," he said as if she wasn't in the room. "I suppose she has money. What does your father do?"

Verbally slapped, Thelma fumbled to recover from his insult. "Not much," she said. "He's dead."

Her father-in-law pushed back his heavy chair, tossing his cloth napkin in disgust beside his china plate. He sucked his teeth and sighed with the burden of authority. Minnie rushed to collect the napkin and refold it. He approached the sideboard, where the perfect roast chicken gleamed in all its headless glory, inserted the silver meat fork, and began his methodical cutting with the wings. Thelma shivered, crossing her arms over her chest. As he severed the flesh from the breast, he began to speak again, without looking away from his task. "Well, Miss Thelma Lorber, dead man's daughter, how do you expect to live with my son Philip?"

"Papa, stop, please," said Phil. "By law, we're man and wife. What God has done, let no man put asunder."

"What does God have to do with it? You chose a judge over a rabbi."

"It's legal. There's nothing you can do."

"That's where you're wrong, Philip. Be quiet or I'll commit you."

"Daddy," Pearl pleaded.

"Ah, she speaks. Boo, little mouse, boo." He dug the knife into the thigh joint until there was an audible crack. "Thelma, do you think you're going to move in here and sponge off my son and myself like the gold digger of Montauk Avenue you so obviously are?"

"I love your son," she said, looking at her Phil. He tried to wink, she saw it, and she willed him into the response she needed to hear. She wanted to be at the movies. She wanted to be out dancing. She'd rather be in Abie's moldy lair alone with her man than here watching his father flay him as only family could. Maybe losing a father wasn't the end of the world.

"Don't look at him, miss. He's not in charge here. This is my house, my table, my chicken, my son. Not your husband, my son. You look shocked, but why should you be? Are you aware of Philip's fragile health? There's a reason he didn't ask our permission to marry you:

we'd have forbidden it." He changed his tone. "Would you like light meat or dark?"

"White meat, please."

"I bet you would. You'll take anything you can get, anything that's not nailed down." He sliced the oval knob from the tail end, the *tushie*, and handed his wife the shameful delicacy to serve to his daughter-in-law. After that, Solomon served himself a thigh and a drumstick and returned to his seat, leaving the rest to his wife. "He's damaged goods. Ask Mildred. They're all sick in the head. It runs in her family. All you had to do was ask. At least my wife's family had money."

Minnie picked up the carving knife and pivoted, beginning to raise the blade up over her shoulder until Pearl rose from the table to disarm her mother and remain to help serve the meat. There was a knock at the door. And another, followed by a pause and then urgent banging.

"Don't answer," said Mr. Schwartz. "It's Shabbos."

Thelma looked at Phil, who was now far away, his blank face leaving her painfully alone to contend with his father.

"Temmy," a disembodied Abie called from beyond the oak door followed by more banging. The doorknob rattled. "Open up! Now!"

"It's my brother," Thelma said.

Mr. Schwartz glared at her. "Don't answer." Thelma disobeyed, rising and hurrying to the door. "Don't break the Shabbos," he said as if he were Moses wielding the Ten Commandments.

Ignoring her father-in-law, Thelma turned the knob. Abie stood on the doorstep wearing a green tweed suit with knickers that ballooned below his knees, argyle socks, and two-toned spectator shoes. Her first reaction was embarrassment at his garish outfit, as if he were visiting a racetrack, not the home of a businessman who owned buildings. What would come out of his mouth in front of Mr. Schwartz and expose her and Phil to more ridicule?

She immediately sensed his distress. It was like a buzzing energy around him—his hands twitched, his feet shuffled, he rubbed his nose. Entering without invitation, Abie told her, "You've got to sit down."

"I just got up," she said.

"You're not welcome," said Mr. Schwartz from his place at the head of the table. "We're eating."

"Good for you," Abie said. "Where I come from, when family shows, you set another plate."

"We don't come from there," Mr. Schwartz said.

"You come from Rumania. I'm not impressed," said Abie. "I know you."

"That's not possible."

"I never forget a mug. You're that Schwartz of Shyster & Shyster at 79 Fifth Avenue."

"I won't be insulted in my own home, you criminal."

"You come by Lazarus & Sons. I've seen you lay down cabbage on the ponies, the ones with showgirl names. I never forget a bet."

"Abie, drop it," Thelma said.

"You've got me confused," said Mr. Schwartz.

"Don't blame me for your confusion, Mr. Shyster," said Abie, appearing unaccountably angry so that Thelma, who'd been merely embarrassed, now feared violence.

"You need to leave," said the father.

"I need to talk to my sister."

"What is it, Abie? We're eating."

"Nice dishes," he said. "Sit down, Tem."

She sat. He removed his cap, crushing it between his hands as he knelt beside her. "I hate to tell you this," he said, leaning on her knee, locking eyes as he inhaled and lowered his voice. "Louis is dead."

A wail rose up from her navel. "That can't be!"

"It can't, but it is."

"Was he shot in the streets, too?" asked Mr. Schwartz.

"Who asked you?" growled Abie. "My brother was a war hero, you schmuck."

"I don't believe a word you say."

"I don't care what you believe. Rock of the Marne, you heard of that? Turned the Hun around and kicked their backsides. What did you do in the war, old man?"

"I bought war bonds."

"Not quite fighting on the front lines."

"Louis's dead?" Thelma repeated. Shell-shocked, her ears buzzed. Everybody in the room receded but Abie. "What happened?"

"He died in the Philippines."

"Is there a war over there, too?"

"Influenza," said Abie. "He has a kid now. A baby named Shirley."

"Had a kid," said Thelma, looking down at Abie's flashy two-toned spectators. Her voice broke. "He survived France. Where the heck are the Philippines? He's supposed to be safe."

"No, baby, nobody's safe."

"He's never coming home?"

"He's never coming home."

"He'll never see Montauk Avenue? We'll never live together again?" It was strange, but that was what she thought: that they'd bought the house so that someday Louis could come home and they'd be a family, secure together in a home where they belonged, a house he'd love, a stoop of their own, with Philip, too. And that was a lie. She'd been sold a bill of goods. It would never happen. And the last time she'd seen Louis was at the hospital when she slipped lemon drops into his pocket, believing his promise that they had a future together when he left the army. He died in uniform in a foreign country as far from home as he could get.

She crumpled into Abie's arms, soaking the scratchy tweed until she felt Phil's soft touch on her neck. She turned away from her brother toward her husband, who looked at her with sympathetic sorrow, and found that spot between his neck and shoulder where only her head fit. Behind her, the door slammed.

Chapter 27

1927

Louis's death blew Thelma sideways, while the postwar world plunged ahead. On "dish night," locals flocked to the Kinema, where the owners distributed one plate a week; if theatergoers returned, they could acquire a full set. Actual dishes! Free! The first feature-length talking picture, *The Jazz Singer*, opened on October 6. It starred Russian-born Asa Yoelson, aka Al Jolson, as a cantor's son who finds jazz but sacrifices his Orthodox traditions. At the Roseland, dancers packed the ballroom every Saturday night. With Babe Ruth and Lou Gehrig on the team, the Yankees (nicknamed Murderers' Row) swept the World Series. Meanwhile, disconnected, Thelma felt unable to explain that her world had stopped while theirs continued.

After Abie barged in, Solomon abandoned his Friday nights on Wyona Street for months. As the roast chicken congealed, Minnie sobbed her voice raw, plucking hairs from her head that could be found all over the house, silver threads with roots. Phil began sleeping on the floor in his mother's room. Once she recovered enough to bake bread again, Phil retreated to his single bed, the old one in the back room with the basketball trophies, the leather-bound set of Goethe and the works of Sigmund Freud. During that period, Thelma attended her husband, and Pearl cared for her. The sisters-in-law slept in the double bed intended for Thelma to share with her husband in the sunny second-floor bedroom overlooking the street, the room that Minnie had shared with Sol and refused to enter.

Now, if Thelma went to the movies, it was with Pearl, not Phil. She didn't care what movie was playing on dish night—everything made her cry. Romantic comedies became tragedies. War pictures made her crazy. She stood up in the middle of the Kinema, her hands over her ears, screaming, "They're going to die! They're *all* going to die!" In a theater that had pretty much seen every kind of behavior, that was very bad form. She became *that* girl. Get too close and her terror became contagious.

In January, Solomon returned. The cycle of despair reset. From the outside, it was such a pretty redbrick house, so graceful in detail, a place to put down roots shaded by a mature tree.

Later that year, the voters elected Herbert Hoover, and the younger Schwartzes had begun to find each other through the gloom. They didn't go out as much as when they were single, but they always held hands and treated each other tenderly. They found simple kindnesses—a hot-water bottle brought before bedtime, breakfast on a tray with a bright daffodil in winter—to demonstrate that theirs was the true bond they'd always believed it to be. They went to the Kinema, but Phil never felt like leaving the neighborhood to go to the Roseland. Instead, he looted the household money to upgrade the family Gramophone. He began to collect jazz records. They loved George Gershwin, Irving Berlin, and Cole Porter, "Someone to Watch Over Me," and "Blue Skies." Phil would shave in the evening so that Thelma would have a smooth place to rest her cheek, and, having pushed the heavy living room furniture aside, they would swing dance in the middle of the Persian carpet. They moved together effortlessly, two bodies as one, hip to hip, loose limbed, so whether they were in their living room or at the Roseland, they were in heaven. They were less showy and more fluid than in public. Even Minnie would lean in at the door and smile, strangling a kitchen cloth.

The couple was scratching their way back toward happiness, one fox-trot at a time. They even began to discuss maybe, just maybe, having a kid, their little schmuck. They'd name him after her brother Louis, maybe calling him Lawrence or Leonard; Laura if she was a girl. Sometimes Phil would get a burst of energy and Thelma would grab on, pulling him out the door before his mother could piss on their adventures. The older woman warned that they'd catch their death—but they figured it was coming anyway and would find them inside or out.

The couple loved exploring Brooklyn in the winter, seeing icicles dripping off Coney Island's Cyclone, walking among the beautiful town houses of Brooklyn Heights, choosing which one they'd buy if they struck it rich, wishing for sanctuary up the elegant stoops, behind the leaded glass as the grainy snow swirled around them. They merged for warmth, sharing his coat, her scarf. If they heard their favorite tunes, they'd dance right on the street, misbehaving as the somber homes of the establishment stood in stony judgment.

Phil introduced Thelma to Green-Wood Cemetery. For privacy, they entered at the bank on Fort Hamilton Parkway. Arms linked, they climbed the grounds' sloping drive with its six-sided paving stones, the crypts to their right, minimansions of death surrounded by angels with raised, wind-bitten hands. He led her to the graves of the famous: composer Louis Moreau Gottschalk, Boss Tweed, and Horace Greeley. Civil War Union general Henry Wager Halleck rested near Confederate general Nathaniel Harrison Harris, who surrendered at Appomattox. There was even a horse somewhere and a handful of faithful dogs.

It was luxuriously quiet in the enormous cemetery, built to be both park for the living and repository for the dead. In wintry January, the lawns were burned and crunchy. Overhead, crows gathered atop twisted trees, glaring down intruders. It was spooky and foreboding despite the spirits refusing to manifest themselves and howl. They ascended a gentle hill under Mr. Loftus Wood's stern gaze, his statue presiding over the family mausoleum with one stone hand stuffed in his vest. They were beneath him, even in his loneliness.

Leaving the path, Philip wandered over the graves into the Boggs family plot. Thelma followed, trying to avoid squashing someone's skull beneath her toe. They read the stones together: patriarch William, born December 10, 1838, had died September 5, 1913. He'd had two wives named Sarah. The inscription on the gravestone of the first read, "Very pleasant hast thou been unto me. Thy love to me was wonderful." She looked at Phil to smile, but he seemed lost in thought; should she pull him back from wherever he was or let him wander? She waited, daring to recline on Sarah E.'s grave, smelling the damp and wet earth while doves cooed in the shrubs. A dry leaf turned over nearby.

The sky became gray and close, clouds huddling together for warmth. There would be snow later in the day. She felt her heart expand: at this moment they lived more fully in the present than anyone else they knew—except for Abie. They would be a couple from now until long after death. It was something wonderful and, yes, pleasant, especially here in the shared silence away from their families. She glanced down a long, gentle slope, deciding to roll to the bottom, spontaneous, doing something a married woman wasn't supposed to do in a graveyard.

"Hey, Phil," she said, breaking the silence, "catch me." She pushed off, rolling hip over hip on the dead grass, gathering speed.

"Wait for me." She heard Phil drop and roll behind her. Over her shoulder, she saw him stop between revolutions and push off again, until they heaped together at the bottom, tangling arms, legs, removing grass from his crow-black hair, her antic curls. Phil helped Thelma up and they climbed the hill again, Phil tugging her hand as he danced ahead of her. They rolled again, smelling the sweet, damp earth, observed by the critical birds. They tumbled together: Mr. and Mrs. Schwartz. He rolled. She rolled, seeing first sky, then earth, then sky.

As they knitted back together, the times began to change. The '20s had roared right into the Depression. On Black Thursday, October 24, the stock market began to plummet, crashing the following Tuesday. The events unfolded in newspaper headlines like that of the *Brooklyn Daily Eagle*: "Wall Street in Panic as Stocks Slide." Suicides followed, although there was some questioning in the press as to whether the rate was actually increasing. That seemed academic when confronted with the images of the jumpers of '29—rich one day, broke the next—who launched themselves out of skyscrapers and off bridges. Others turned on the gas or loaded their guns or put stones in their pockets and slid into the Hudson River. They couldn't block the images: fallen bankers arms akimbo on the sidewalk, bodies on the crumpled roofs of automobiles. Nervous breakdowns spiked.

As the economy tanked, so did Phil's tenuous optimism. The following year, the Great Depression engulfed the country, a gaseous plague. During those months, Phil had good weeks and bad, joining Thelma in their bed and then retreating to his boyhood bedroom. He visited doctors for treatment and showed signs of improvement. One medical man took Thelma aside and suggested that if the couple had a baby, Phil would rise to the challenge of fatherhood and be cured.

In late March, after walking through the cherry blossoms at the Brooklyn Botanic Garden, the couple conceived. She bloomed, but the pregnancy seemed to have the opposite effect on her husband. After early hopefulness, he began to have headaches and insomnia, which he medicated with vodka and gin, passing out facedown on his single bed and sleeping through the daylight hours. He stopped eating.

Phil promised he loved Thelma but insisted she lacked the power to rescue him. "There's nothing to save," he told her late one night through a cigarette-smoke haze. "Let me go."

"Hold on, for me, for the baby." She couldn't coax him out from behind the mask of sadness that resembled him but lacked his animation. She saw what he'd look like old, with crumpled forehead and hollow eyes, but worried he'd die young. "Please, Phil, hold on."

"How can I explain that your love won't rescue me? It's not enough. That sounds like I'm blaming you, Temmy. I'm not. Nobody's love can make me whole. We had our dance. It was grand. There's no one else. But now it's over, at least for me. Whatever the doctors promised about getting pregnant scaring me sane, those quacks were just trying to think of something to say. You demanded they tell you something, so they did."

After that, Phil stopped speaking for days at a time, then weeks, retreating into his books and cigarettes, never venturing farther than the stoop. Loneliness returned like smog. Nothing had ever hurt so hard. On a sunny September Sunday, she sat in their front bedroom, feeling the baby kick impatiently beneath her swollen fingers. On the bed, Phil lay sleeping in his drab pajamas, curled in a ball, oblivious and lost inside himself. She could hear Minnie crying in the kitchen, alone. It was an unbearable solitude that she tried to counter by sheltering the second heartbeat inside her body.

At 2:00 a.m. on December 9, 1930, Thelma went into labor, the liquid splashing the floorboards between her legs. After mopping the spill, Pearl held Thelma's hand. They dispatched the neighbor's boy to get help and then collapsed into hysterical laughter. Neither knew the first thing about what came next. They shared the window seat while Thelma's contractions increased. Hours passed, and they both turned serious as the city slumbered and Phil remained behind a locked door, refusing to come out despite his sister's entreaties. Other than the midwife, the teenager was the only witness to the swirling hell that was Lawrence's birth, the baby upside down and backward, a cord encircling his neck. The old woman put her arm up to the elbow in Thelma and made a worried click with her tongue, her ear resting like a dried peach on the ballooned belly. Thelma felt intense pain at the top of her womb as the old woman shoved the baby up to the roof of her insides to ease the umbilical.

She wailed, "Save the child, take me instead!"

She cried, "Philip!"

Convinced that she and the baby were both disappearing from the earth, she believed they'd beat the father to the grave. She felt the darkness, the dirt hitting her coffin. But, miraculously, they survived, the ordeal ending for the new mother with an under-the-counter laudanum cocktail as Pearl held the boy who arrived with all his fingers and toes, his little schmuck encased in foreskin.

Grandpa Solomon soon returned regularly on Friday nights to assume his place at the table's head as if nothing had changed. He presided over the child's *bris* and expected his grandson to be quiet during dinner. The birth did not improve his opinion of Thelma but, for a while, he tolerated her. He promised that, no matter what happened, he would always be responsible for the child's Hebrew education. She didn't understand the implied "and nothing else." He hadn't become rich by being generous.

As the months passed, Solomon became increasingly angry and righteous. Phil didn't magically rise to the demands of fatherhood and seek work. Solomon didn't expect much: let him sell ties on Pitkin Avenue. He railed at his son for not pulling himself together. He wished he still had the body of a young man like Phil, and his book learning and command of English; if it were him, he'd take over the world.

Around the high holy days, Solomon launched a virulent attack on Phil, who had made it to the table and contributed his voice—cracking and out of practice—to the prayers, blessing the apple slices dipped in honey. For Thelma, this return gave her hope for a future sweetness. They'd ridden out another attack and he'd improve, slowly, with tenderness and empathy. She'd done it before, letting the nervous attacks run their course, even if they'd lengthened. She found the patience she'd never had, the forbearance of a child bride in the old country unraveling a knotted skein of yarn to prove herself fit for marriage. And she got her small rewards: every once in a while, Phil had put on the Gramophone and played "You Were Meant for Me," even if now they only did an awkward box step.

During Rosh Hashanah, Solomon apparently decided to put his house in order. Perhaps he thought he was fixing a problem as he might have treated a tenant who refused to pay or negotiated a building's sale. He threatened Phil, "Either you pull yourself up by your bootstraps, sonny boy, and get a job, or I call the doctors and commit you. Either you belong in the world or you don't: choose! You're a father now. You need to act like one, or I'll throw you and your wife and baby out on your ears."

"No!" Minnie wailed.

Phil stared at his mother, his face contorted. He'd become emaciated, his eye sockets protruding, his good suit baggy. He removed his napkin from his lap and set it by his plate of hardly eaten food. Thelma witnessed it. He was going under the wave. He'd just needed a final excuse to surrender. Thelma tried to catch his gaze, but he looked down. He said the kaddish, the prayer for the dead, closing his eyes and rocking. He thanked his mother, apologized to Thelma as if she were a stranger whose toes he'd clumsily stomped on the dance floor, and went upstairs. He'd sat down at the table as one survivor struggling forward, and he rose with an unstable manic lightness.

Within an hour, a bang on the front door heralded two oversize men in white coats embossed with "Brooklyn State Hospital" who failed to wipe their steel-toed boots as they entered.

"Take my son," Solomon said, leading the burly strangers upstairs as Minnie began to scream Yiddish obscenities at her husband and Pearl cleaved to her mother. Thelma pursued, reaching the second floor, where her father-in-law bent over the lock on Phil's bedroom door, using the passkey he kept for delinquent tenants. At the front of the house, Lawrence shrilled from his crib like an untended kettle. But she let him scream as she watched the door fall open, revealing Phil. He lay on his bed in his slippers, smoking a cigarette, his hand shaking. He glanced up from his book, surprised, his eyes wide in their protruding sockets. His mouth moved, but words failed him.

Thelma rushed forward. One of the orderlies seized her elbow. Her body bent toward the pain point where he cinched her. It gave her a taste for the medicine awaiting Phil at the institution. The other man unfurled a straitjacket. Resigned, Phil seemed to have regained his composure, rising and extending his hands as if being measured by a tailor. She needed him to fight, to struggle, to lose his composure to regain his freedom. She wondered if Phil believed his father would relent once the elder Schwartz had imposed his will on his son completely. She realized before Phil did that this was no pantomime—she'd learned the lengths family could go when Mama and Annie had shunted her brothers to the orphanage.

Once swaddled in the starched coat—his arms immobilized and cinched behind his back—panic consumed Phil. His wild eyes found Thelma's, pleading, don't let these monsters steal his identity. His autonomy was all he had left. Even if he still breathed and swallowed, he was dead without his will. She feared he'd never be the same if these cruel men took him away; terror twisted her features, not reassurance—and so his eyes filled with dread.

Freed by the hospital worker, Thelma now had Pearl clinging to her waist while Minnie knelt at Solomon's cuffs, begging her husband to relent, saying, "Solomon, he's a good boy. We'll take better care of him. We won't cause you any trouble."

"He's not a boy, Minnie—he's a man. You spoiled him. Now I've taken care of the problem once and for all. He won't cause any trouble to anybody outside the hospital. What's done is done."

"You can't do this to my husband, Solomon," Thelma said.

"Watch me," he said. "If you can't take care of this situation, I will. Either today will scare Philip sane, or the doctors will cure him."

"That's not your decision to make."

"When you pay the rent, you make the rules," Solomon said. He turned his back on Thelma, following the orderlies who manhandled Phil downstairs, lifting him when he struggled and kicked so that his feet didn't touch the wood. Her father-in-law straightened a framed photo that had been knocked askew in the fray.

Thelma heard Phil yelling all the way out into the street and felt helpless, split in two. She entered their bedroom overlooking Wyona Street and watched the orderlies stuffing her man into an automobile like sausage meat, as they joked to each other before driving away. It was the absence that cut more than anything that preceded it. She stood in their bedroom, thinking she'd failed that beautiful man. He'd warned her that she couldn't save him, but she'd known better—until she didn't.

The baby's wailing pulled her reluctantly back to the present. She turned toward the crib and picked him up, feeling the soaked diaper through her sleeve. Spreading a towel on the bed, she laid him out, his face spitting angry, as she wrestled with the unruly pins, removed the sour cotton, crying along with him.

Afterward, Thelma settled Larry in the middle of her bed and climbed in beside him, curling around the baby, comforting him as she wished she could comfort her husband. She assured him everything would be fine—she'd find a way, she'd break his father out, they'd be happy again, the three of them. She fell asleep fully dressed with Larry cuddled in her arms, her nose in the freshness of baby.

At dawn, without knocking, Solomon entered carrying a suitcase. "Minnie wants you out," he said. Thelma's arguments had no more impact on her father-in-law than Phil's had on the orderlies. Begging, pleading, or threatening: he was impervious. She sensed he wanted to escape the house as much as she wanted to remain near the bed she'd shared with Phil. He said, "I'm leaving now. Either you pack or you leave everything behind. It doesn't matter to me."

He drove her to Montauk Avenue, dropped them off, and sped away. As she climbed the stoop, she anticipated the fight to come with Annie. Distraught, mother and son crying, she tried to open the door, only to find the locks changed. Her anger swelled up in her before she even saw Annie's face. She craved tenderness and empathy and, for that, even as she rapped on the wood, she knew she was knocking on the wrong door. This was the last place she wanted to be—and she knew that her sister would exploit her homecoming to the hilt.

Annie opened up a crack, her platinum hair newly shellacked from the beauty salon. "Well, if it isn't the queen of Sheba," she sneered, relishing the moment. "I was wondering when you'd come crawling back with that brat. Did those fancy-schmancy Schwartzes put you out with the trash?"

"Just let us in and shut your trap," Thelma snapped, crossing the threshold and heading toward her bedroom when Annie seized her upper arm.

"You're in the room at the top of the stairs."

"The broom closet?"

"It has four walls, doesn't it? It's a room."

"Who's sleeping in my bed?"

"It's not Goldilocks; it's Eli. He needs light and air for his school-work—he's going to be the first Lazarus to go to City University."

"I'd go to college, too, if it meant escaping you."

"He's a good boy who loves his mother."

"I'm guessing he doesn't know you weren't wearing kid gloves when you raised me and my brothers. There's something seriously wrong with you, lady, and Abie and I can bear witness. You sent our brothers to college, too—the school for violent criminals, that orphanage. Do you have any idea what happened to him and Louis there? I doubt it. What would he have been like if he was spoiled like your precious kids? You threw us under the train and took everything you could grab—the cash from the newsstand, this house, Mama. I'm happy to share those sweet family memories with my nephews and niece now that they're old enough to understand who their mother really is."

"If I'm so rotten, turn around and you never have to see me again."

"This house is as much mine as yours."

"Not anymore, sweetheart. I live here. I take care of Mama while you're off dancing and dropping your knickers. Do you pay the mortgage or the electric? You never even paid the milkman, you schnorrer."

"Me, a schnorrer? That's rich, Annie. If it weren't for Abie, you'd be living on Hooper Street taking in laundry. Abie made Lazarus & Sons, not your lapdog Jesse. You don't buy a house selling newspapers. You did the books. You know the score."

"Abie's a dirty *goniff.* They didn't kill him last time, but he's not going to be so lucky when it happens again. I've been telling you for years: don't depend on him."

Thelma shook her head as the baby tried to wiggle loose. "Lay off, you fat bitch."

"Spoken by the round-heeled floozy that makes Popeye's Olive Oyl look like a great beauty," Annie shrilled. "Is that even Phil's baby? I doubt it, with him sick in the head. He was the only man crazy enough to marry you when he could get the milk for free."

Thelma knew that kick in the chest. It was as familiar as breath. Her sister pushed every button until the little sister lashed out with something uglier, until she became so angry that it was her flaming rage that became the problem, not the evil that prompted it. She wouldn't go back. She wouldn't get sucked in. She considered her beautiful Phil and grasped his love, ending the conversation by saying, "I'm going upstairs to cry. And when I'm done, I'll cry some more. Take Lawrence. He's hungry."

The baby almost slipped through the sisters' fingers as Annie tried to deflect the imposition, but Thelma insisted. "Just don't burn him. I'll be upstairs in my closet. Let me know if you need the dustpan."

∿

During that time, Thelma returned to North Eighth Street to visit the Gigantiellos' apartment in Our Lady of Mount Carmel parish above the Knights of Columbus. She brought the baby, ascending the familiar steps and then turning around, ashamed of her sadness and fearing she might be unwelcome. She descended halfway with Lawrence in her arms, then spun around and ran upstairs, the way a swimmer might leap into a cold ocean so that there was no retreat.

A brown-eyed girl of ten or so answered the door with high seriousness, demanding to know who the stranger was and what she wanted. Thelma paused before the child that resembled Nina in everything except her shyness and said, "I'm Thelma and—"

"*Stuzzicadenti!*" cried a woman's voice from beyond the door that the child guarded with her slight body that was beginning to sprout but had not yet bloomed. "My *stuzzicadenti! Entra!*"

Crossing the threshold, she encountered a swarm of children who crawled and skipped their way around Thelma as Mama Allegra, carrying her wooden spoon, exited the kitchen in her apron to welcome the guest. She plucked Larry from Thelma, burying her lips in his cheeks and then cradling him in her well-worn baby place of comfort. This was a woman who could cook a holiday meal for twenty with a child on her hip. After he stopped fussing, she lifted him up to get a good look. "A beauty . . . like his mama."

Thelma's eyes moistened at a greeting that couldn't have been more different from Annie's reception. "I'm sorry it's been so long," she said, hanging her head.

"You've been a little busy." Mama Allegra shrugged. Her hair had gone silver so that the elaborate braid encircling her head seemed crown-like. "But here you are, bringing me a baby boy. What's to apologize? What's his name?"

"Lawrence, after my brother Louis."

"May he rest in peace having known the hell of war." Mama Allegra bounced the child, shifting him so that his head was over her shoulder, and he burped.

The grandchildren laughed, and the girl who'd opened the door explained, "No burp can escape Nana."

Looking on proudly, Mama Allegra said to the girl, "Teresina, fetch your mama from her nap."

"I don't want to wake her," Thelma said, putting up her hands and rising as if it were already time to depart.

"Sit! I haven't fed you yet, and Nina won't want to miss you!" said Mama Allegra. "Look at this baby! Bright eyes! *Occhi vivaci!*"

Mama Allegra continued to cuddle and coddle the son, requesting a child to bring her a handkerchief before wiping Larry's nose, patting his bottom, and asking, "A change soon, maybe?"

"I forgot to bring . . . ," Thelma began, embarrassed. Her visit had been spontaneous, a walk around the block becoming a train ride out of East New York to the old neighborhood.

"No problem, Temmelina," said Mama Allegra. "You think we don't have diapers?"

"We have plenty of diapers," said Nina, who appeared in the doorway. Wan and tired, she carried an infant low in her belly. Looking at her school friend, she patted her stomach and said, "Octavia or Octavio: the eighth."

"Always with the math," Thelma teased, rising to hug her friend, who fell into her arms.

"I have a head for algebra," said Nina, "and a body for childbirth." She bent her knees and reached back to the sofa with one hand before lowering her tailbone onto the cushions. "My Tonio works day and night to support the family, but he won't stop making babies."

"Nina is the envy of the neighborhood," crowed Mama Allegra.

"Right, Mama, I'm the regular Madonna of North Eighth Street." Nina laughed.

"Shh! If Our Lady of Mount Carmel hears you, she might teach you a lesson for your pride," said Nina's mother, raising her wooden spoon in warning.

"Let her teach," said Nina. "You just missed Giorgio."

"Giorgio," said Mama Allegra, shaking her head sorrowfully, patting the behind of the now sleeping baby.

"He's happy, yes?" Thelma said, trying to navigate the shoals of conversation. She remembered the pair of them pushing against each other in the darkened stairwell, and blushed. It had been so long since she'd thought of him and what she remembered were his broad shoulders and how they felt under her hands. It wasn't a memory she wanted to have while sitting across from his mother.

"He's happy not so much," said Mama Allegra.

"It's the wife that's unhappy," said Nina. "She spent the day kneeling in front of Our Lady, praying for a healthy child."

"Doesn't he have children?" asked Thelma.

"They come," said the grandmother. "They go."

Not knowing how to respond, Thelma said, "I'm sorry."

"We're all sorry," said Mama Allegra, "but this is life. Nina wants a moment of peace to read a book between children, and Giorgio would give his right arm for one healthy boy. And look at this: you arrive out of nowhere today with this beautiful boy, a blessing."

"A mitzvah," said Thelma, shaking her head in agreement without looking either woman in the eyes.

"Tell us about your husband," Mama Allegra asked.

"I love him." Thelma looked away. "And he loves me."

"Then why the sad eyes?" Mama Allegra asked.

"They took him away." Thelma pointed to her head, because she couldn't say the words out loud. "Brooklyn State Hospital."

"Here, Nina, take the baby," said Mama Allegra. She looked at Thelma and said, "Come. I'll braid your hair. Teresina, fetch the brush."

The older woman took the younger mother's head into her lap and brushed the wild curls until they unsnarled and Thelma became relaxed and heavy. She felt a sharp tug and then another. "A gray," Mama Allegra said. "My Giorgio was serious about you and I wouldn't let him be. You were too young, but so was Nina. I thought life was a stew I had to mix. I gave my blessing to a neighborhood girl. He married into a good family—too good. They treat my golden boy like tar. Who knows where the road leads and, still, I pretend to stand at the fork and point as if I know the way."

∿

After that reunion, Thelma often left the baby with the Gigantiellos when she went to visit Phil. Thelma knew in her gut that robbing Phil of agency would be the death of him. Still, she was unprepared for the man she found at the enormous Brooklyn State Hospital at the corner of Albany Avenue and Winthrop Street three miles west of Wyona Street. He showed no light of recognition when she entered the lounge, where he sat slumped over in institutional pajamas and worn slippers. He had drool in his stubble and his jaw was slack, revealing broken teeth on the bottom gums. He blinked as if cigar smoke stung his eyes. She sat with him for an hour, stroking his hand, sending out beams of love from her heart through her fingertips so that he'd know she was there, that she adored him. His left eye twitched. The sides of his head were shaved, and there were skin burns from the electrodes.

When she began to talk about Lawrence, Phil became agitated, standing up and sitting down, standing up and sitting down, so that other inmates of the room began to repeat his motion, rising and falling, rising and falling, until a barrel-chested old man pointed an accusatory finger and said, "Guards, arrest him!" The white coats came and removed Phil like a boy who had sneaked under the tent and into the circus and must form a lesson to all the other sneaky boys.

Thelma returned every day, but, after that first visit, she wasn't welcome. Initially, she believed that it was the doctors who refused to let her pass, until a Dr. Nelson came to the nurses' station and told her flatly that Philip didn't want her there. He softened briefly and said, "Your husband doesn't want you to see him like this."

"Will he get better?" she asked.

"I'm a doctor, not a fortune-teller. Hope for the best; expect the worst."

"You're not much of a greeting card, either, Doctor."

The weather turned bitter as October faded. November spat rain in her face. Every day she sat on an iron bench in front of the hospital, an imposing redbrick structure that reminded her of the Hebrew Orphan Asylum, where they'd dumped Abie and Louis. And every time she thought of that, a lump blocked her throat. The image of Louis and Abie sitting back-to-back on the orphanage floor in short pants, slaying dragons passing themselves off as Jewish children, haunted her. She wanted to spring Phil, but she didn't know how. She could barely take care of Lawrence alone, but the two of them? That would never fly.

One day, when it was pouring rain and she was soaked to the skin, a nurse in a white cap tucked under an oilskin ran toward her through the puddles. "He's inconsolable," the hospital worker said.

"Why?" she asked, but the answer washed away with the storm.

The man in the loose, stained pajamas she encountered in the locked ward who cried "Temmy" over and over wasn't her husband. He was a lost child, emaciated, burn marks on both sides of his head, his teeth cracked and broken. "I'm so tired, sweetheart," he said. Wet as she was, she embraced him, laid his head in her lap, and stroked around the scalp scabs until he settled down, humming "Someone to Watch Over Me."

She would watch over him every day if only he survived—but deep inside she knew that wasn't her sophisticated Phil in the shabby cotton sack of bones. She could have saved him. She knew it. If she'd had more time, if old man Schwartz had left it alone. The shock treatments had sapped her husband's will but not soothed his mind. Once he fell asleep, the nurse led her back out through one locked door and then the next until she couldn't have found her way back to Phil with a loaf of bread crumbs.

That night, he escaped into the courtyard, swallowing buckets of rainwater, like a turkey that looks up at the clouds and drowns. The certificate put the cause of death as acute exhaustion and acute mental disease. She blamed old man Schwartz, sitting in his Manhattan apartment, pulling strings with money attached, and she became enraged. She was angry that her beautiful dancing man had been ripped from her, that her love hadn't been enough. A partner's suicide was the ultimate form of abandonment.

Chapter 28

1932

After Phil passed, their baby seemed to be the absolute denial of Thelma's present situation. Larry adored her with bright eyes, a fat-cheeked child whose curly crown was the envy of bald men everywhere. He was quick to grin, but Thelma struggled to smile back in a way that reached eyes gummy with sleep. She failed at common tasks: mistakenly stabbing his chubby thighs with the unwieldy diaper pin. It wasn't the kid's fault. No natural mother, Thelma was Vesuvius angry and impatient.

When she left Montauk Avenue, she wept on the el and in the corner grocery. She wasn't alone. Given the desperate economy, grown men could be seen sobbing as they loitered outside the bank seeking day work. Arguing politics, socialists and communists battled over dogma and voiced frustration that they'd struggled so hard to raise their heads above water and now they were drowning along with their families. She walked in the neighborhood's collective gloom, the arrogant widow Schwartz, who'd exchanged flapper dresses for shapeless black shifts. When women stopped her to compliment the sunny child smiling back at them, snug in his battered pram, she snickered sarcastically, and the strangers hurried past.

Her father-in-law still blamed her for his son's death, having buried Phil in the family plot at Mount Hebron Cemetery. He'd told his daughter-in-law that there was no space for her beside her husband when the inevitable occurred. She didn't want the old man's dirt pit, but she could have used child support. She was now dependent on the kindness of something worse than strangers: Mama and Annie.

Uncle Abie dropped in occasionally, *kvelling* over his growing nephew without acknowledging how many months it had been since he'd visited last. She couldn't depend on her brother, resenting his freedom to come and go while she remained with Annie and Mama. Abie gave her a camel-hair coat that had fallen off the back of a truck, as stylish as anything on sale at Saks Fifth Avenue. She looked askance at him, asking, "Do I look like Joan Crawford?" When he got huffy, saying he'd return it if he could find the receipt, she clung to it. She needed the fur-trimmed garment, however impractical, too fine for Larry's perpetually sticky fingers.

Sometimes Abie slipped Thelma cash, but she couldn't rely on irregular handouts to move out and pay rent. Although he hadn't been arrested since the shooting, he had his own problems—worry aged his face. When Thelma complained about their sister taking over the house, he shrugged, saying, "I got bigger fish to fry. Handle it."

She tried. She'd hoped now that she had a child she'd never be lonely, but, with her rage and bitterness, her hatred of being under Annie's thumb, she had trouble achieving a sense of maternal connection. As he aged, the kid still irritated her: his constant neediness, his cries when he wanted milk and bread and when the spiky teeth forced themselves through his gums. He was a good sleeper, but he awoke with the energy of three children, and Thelma, increasingly plagued by insomnia, couldn't keep up. Every day he grew, every new change, reminded her of time's passage and Phil's absence. He was another child growing up in a house of mourning. Although she wanted to protect the hazel-eyed boy who began talking even before he pulled himself up around his first birthday and slung his small body like a drunken sailor across the living room, she found that she was as dry as a crone's breast.

Thelma either ignored or spoiled the child. As time passed, they celebrated his second and third birthdays. She hoped that by the time he could form his own memories she would have shed her grief and her guilt for believing that if she had a child, her late husband would magically improve. The boy became his own little man: antic and angry, affectionate and physical, intensely competitive and demanding always to be the center of attention. He never saw another child's toy that he didn't grab for himself. At times the three-year-old got so angry he bit his own arm.

Annie called him "bed wetter" and "nose picker" and felt no responsibility to help raise Thelma's son. Annie's own well-behaved children were a generation older, now fifteen and twenty and twenty-two, and while they tolerated their cousin and occasionally tended him for short periods, their mother's disgust tarnished their affection for their aunt. The house was theirs, and they swaggered in it from top to bottom, ignorant of how it had entered the family's possession, treating Thelma and her bawling brat like poor relations.

After Larry turned three, doctors diagnosed Mama with a congestive heart condition. Her ankles swelled with fluid; she retired her apron. "Don't worry about me," she'd say. "*Oy, gevalt!* I'm going to meet my Jonas." Thelma didn't tell her mother that her husband was probably looking down from heaven with his beloved first wife, in no hurry to welcome the second—and, if there were servants above, she'd probably be charged with scrubbing her predecessor's halo.

To escape their toxic home, Thelma would shlep Larry to the movies. It was bitter cold outside when she took him to see one of her favorites, *It Happened One Night*, at the Kinema around the corner. He almost ruined it, chattering the entire way through, running up and down the aisles, his mouth only quieted by licorice Twizzlers. The sugar powered another energy burst that spun into a tantrum when she tried to drag him out, landing him flat on his stomach beneath the marquee in a fit bigger than Clark Gable's name in lights. The disgusted moviegoers glared at them. She'd come a long way from the glamour of Rudolph Valentino and Pola Negri, but Phil would have liked the movie. She missed him, and if he'd been around, she'd have given him a good piece of her mind. She wasn't single-mother material.

When she was flush with Abie money, she spent it, vaguely aware that folks who can't envision the future don't save. She bought Larry new clothes and dressed him like a little man with a yellow tie and tweed short pants. His hair parted down the middle and slicked with Vaseline, they'd hit the soda fountain, splurging on grilled cheese and egg creams with Fox's U-bet chocolate syrup. They'd sit side by side on red vinyl stools at the counter, with Larry wearing a paper hat that he'd schnorred from the soda jerk. He'd swivel back and forth and she'd let him, smoking a cigarette while they waited for their meal. He looked at her with such love, so grateful when she cut the crusts off his sandwich and wrapped them in a napkin to feed the birds at the park afterward—and she tried to mold a tender smile on lips that resisted. He was the same age she'd been when she'd hidden under the table with Schmulie's lighter. She knew how much emotion—love and hate, curiosity and jealousy—came wrapped in that small package. They'd hold hands and walk to the park to feed the *katchkas*, the ducks, and she'd let him tire himself out chasing tail feathers while she created a small campfire of cigarette ash by her scuffed shoes. He'd run back and jump in her lap and she'd encourage him to lie down on the bench beside her, running her fingers through his hair, rubbing behind his ears, wiping the crust from his nose.

But as he aged, days came when she hungered to revive her old life and rebelled against the constraints of single motherhood. Her magic leg was withering, and it tapped at the edge of the playground, calling out to her to go dancing. A Friday night arrived and she wanted to go to the Arcadia Ballroom, which wasn't nearly as grand as the Roseland, but the dance floor was darker and she would find men to lean on all night long who wouldn't care that she was over thirty. And so she went.

When Larry was nearly five, he constantly asked where his father was. In the Philippines, she'd answer, or on a spy mission, or ice skating in Central Park with Sonja Henie. She'd tell the kid anything but on a lonely hill at Mount Hebron Cemetery in Flushing, surrounded by that snobby family of his. The truth hurt too much.

Despite Phil's assurances to the contrary, the guilt that she hadn't saved him gnawed at her. She beat herself up, brooding if only she'd been different, stronger, less buffeted by Abie's lawlessness, she might still have that beautiful slim man with the black hair and dark eyes, her dance partner and dear friend. Her hopes of creating a happy family in which she could be herself and radiate love, him leading her in a twirl, had evaporated before the music stopped.

One Thursday, when Montauk Avenue seemed as cold and unforgiving as Annie, Thelma was leading Larry to the building on Sutter Avenue where the beggar/baby-minder Rivka squatted in a ground-floor room under the stairs. The five-year-old trailed behind Thelma, throwing pebbles in her direction, occasionally being bold enough to wing her.

"Don't run my stockings," Thelma snapped, distracted and rushed, her hair curlers covered by a scarf. After dropping him off, she planned to return and finish dressing so that she could attend ladies' night at the Arcadia Ballroom. Trudging behind her, Larry raged. She turned impatiently, just wanting to shimmy away the blues. He aimed another pebble, and her left hand struck out and snatched his throwing arm. She sensed she was overreacting, out of control. She unleashed her anger at the little man who didn't deserve it, yet she couldn't reel herself in once launched.

Responding to the bruising grip on his arm as much as her gigantic anger, he cried out. The terrible sound cut through her. "I want my daddy," he screamed.

"Don't we all, kid?" She stood, tapping her toe, confused: Turn around or continue? Pushed too far, she opened her mouth and spewed words she'd wanted to gift wrap with tenderness and empathy. "Wanna know where your father is? Dead and buried, just like mine. I'm all you've got."

"I have Annie," he said, throwing a pebble at her nose with his left hand. It stung, but not as much as his words: "And I've got Eli and Adele and Julius and Uncle Moe. I love them. I don't love you."

No object could have stung her like that phrase. She felt bathed in horror, shaking and furious, looking at that defenseless boy who only wanted affection and protection. He cut her a sour look, flashing hatred in eyes that mirrored hers. Snatching him by his curls, she hissed, "Stop it!"

Larry's body went slack on the sidewalk. Strangers hurried past, hurling sidelong glances. She felt shame mixed with anger, her head pounding. She squatted beside Larry and found herself begging him to get up, to come into her arms, but he shoved her away and she fell on her tailbone. She cursed herself that the love he wanted cost her nothing and yet was in such short supply. Trying to woo him back, she promised he could go to the Kinema and see *Billy the Kid* that Saturday. He brightened. She promised he could go, not that she would take him. She wasn't even sure *Billy the Kid* was playing that Saturday. She recognized the beginning of mistrust in the squint of his eyes. Her heart cracked, but she didn't change her plans. She was going dancing.

Later that night in September 1935, when she returned from the Arcadia, her stockings ripped, a cigar hole in her camel-hair coat, she checked in on Mama before she went upstairs. The old woman lay on her back, her head raised on three pillows, her hands over the chenille as big as pot holders. Thelma sat down beside the bed, snapped open her garters, and unrolled the ruined stockings with a sigh. She stroked Mama's scaly forehead, finally understanding how hard it was to nurture a child when you felt abandoned and couldn't find anything to love about yourself.

Chapter 29

1935

Mama lay in her nightdress, panting, when Thelma entered her bed-room beside the kitchen. She was so short of breath it was as if she'd just hung a load of sheets. But she hadn't left the room in three days. It was Sunday afternoon, September 29, 1935, and for the past two years, since Dr. Pearlstine had begun to visit and diagnosed her with conges-tive heart failure, she'd been telling the family that she wasn't going to live forever. Mama wasn't going to sugarcoat that, but Annie's response was always denial: "Ma, you're going to live forever."

Live forever? As if Mama wanted to spend another day like this. Exhausted, she was a living lake, fluid around her heart, in her lungs, and pooling in ankles and feet bloated beyond recognition. If she remained still, her head propped on three pillows, a luxury of feathers, then it almost felt like the Sabbath, a day of rest without the responsibil-ity of cooking, cleaning, the constant pointless drudgery, her shoulders always bent to the task as if she were carrying the dual-pailed yoke of her girlhood. She was still a little sister in her own eyes, in her dreams, barefoot and full breathed, capable of appreciating sunflowers and shar-ing warm breezes with the fields of wheat. But when she awoke and pinched the skin on the back of her hands, it didn't snap back but remained raised and wrinkled—a crone's skin.

But at least she finally had her own kitchen under her own roof where no one would throw her out on the street or make her lie with a man she didn't know. She thanked Annie for that, although that wasn't who sat in the chair beside the bed. Thelma hummed while she read the *Brooklyn Daily Eagle*. She flapped the newsprint and looked over, saying, "Ah, you're awake. Do you want me to read to you?"

"If you want," Mama said. "I'm not going anywhere."

"Do you want some water?"

"No more water. I'm drowning."

"All right, Mama Mia, here's something: 'Progress Is Pushing Pushcarts to Oblivion.'"

"That's progress?"

"You want me to read it?"

"Go ahead. What else do I have to do?"

Thelma folded the paper and recited,

> Picturesque as they may be, the pushcarts must go. Perhaps not tomorrow or next year, but some day, it is now sure, the little carts will be swept away by the forces of progress into neat new stalls in large airy buildings. The pushcart people know this. They have known it for a long time and they wait with varied emotions for the day that is sure to come.

"That would have made Jonas happy, right, Mama?"

"I could be an ox—not him. He was too good for manual labor."

"Tell me about him."

"What's there to know? He's dead. And I'll be with him soon."

"Are you going to give him a piece of your mind?"

Mama grunted, because it hurt to laugh. Thelma set aside the paper. Mama felt her daughter take her hand, rubbing her thumb on the gold band trapped in swollen flesh. Larry came in, and despite Thelma's vigorously shaking her head no, he climbed onto the bed beside his grandmother, resting his cheek on her breast above her dying heart and casting his free arm around her belly. He squirmed and nuzzled her with his sticky nose, until his breathing became regular and he fell asleep. "Larncy," she said. The last grandchild.

She looked out the window while listening to the boy's breath rather than her own. It was autumn light, bright, filtered through the canoe-shaped yellow leaves of the tree in the backyard. When had she had time just to look out at the sun, the sky? The leaves rustled in the breeze, golden yellow, backlit by the sun, so many colors that she couldn't name in English. A goldfinch fluttered onto a leaf and paused, such brilliant beauty in such a tiny, perfect package. This was the gorgeousness of the world she was leaving, and only now she stopped to hold it in her heart. This was fall without winter, warm and nourishing, framed by the windowpane's rectangle.

Feeling the child heavy on her chest, but comforting, she took the hand her daughter offered and stroked it as she had stroked those of her sisters. There was a lullaby she knew, but the notes failed her. She felt the end as close to her as this child, but not yet there. Appreciating the luminous leaves, she drifted off and felt the hands of her unborn children reaching out for their long-awaited reunions, the hand of her beautiful young Moishe, who had waited so long for his mother. How come she'd taken so long? More than sixty years on this earth. She didn't know what sisters awaited her—"Heaven, I'm in heaven"—or whether her mother was there. And then, it was as if she were in a crowd: unborn sisters and brothers she didn't recognize, the throng of unborn and unnamed, Jonas and his other wife, their pale and sickly boys. There were so many hands grabbing for hers, reaching up her arms, encircling her legs.

Opening her eyes, she couldn't move her feet; liquid pooled everywhere. A pain radiated out of her stomach, and she felt the bile try to choke her despite the lift of her head on the pile of pillows. The room had gotten darker; the boy had disappeared. A candle dripped wax at her bedside and, still, there was the woman who'd been there before, who looked up and said, "You're awake."

This was the girl she could have, should have, loved, but didn't. It was such a hard thing, a heart turned to stone. She'd been weak then, and Annie had been strong. Mama had made a choice. This child was tall and thin like Jonas, but she had a spark they both lacked.

She remembered how Thelma looked that day they visited the boys at the orphanage, the child's hair shorn by Annie so that the girl should have been ashamed and ugly, runt of the litter. And yet Thelma sat on her brother's knee as if it were a throne, radiating love, defiant. But had that been disobedience in the girl's eyes—or need? The child had demonstrated her loyalty to her brothers despite the cost, because they shielded each other. They were a family unto themselves.

And this was the part that now burned in Mama's belly: the realization that what they'd needed protection from was her and Annie, that awful two-headed beast they became together, born out of Jonas's death and her subsequent collapse. Maybe if Mama had just risen from her bed of pain and demonstrated kindness, a shred of love, her children wouldn't have turned so hard against her. If she'd remained the mother and reined in Annie instead of acquiescing to her will, taking the path of least resistance. If she'd had the strength to defy her eldest and taken the boys home that day. She'd seen their cuts and bruises, the anger in Abie's eyes and Louis's fear, and done nothing. If, if, if . . .

Cringing at the choice she'd made thirty years before, she couldn't blame Jonas, her father, the matchmaker, or even her beloved Annie: this was on her. She remembered Thelma's joy on her seventh birthday, learning the box step with Moritz, all attention on the pair—and how Mama couldn't stand that about her, the showiness and the need for attention, already with the long legs and the promise of beauty, the dancing heart. The way the child threw back her head and laughed, breathless.

She was just trying to be happy, and Mama had even begrudged her that small joy. She'd sneered and judged. She'd grabbed the strawberries meant for Thelma because she herself was so hungry and plain, so unloved, so out of place in America, so alone without her sisters and mother to guide her, to support her when her knees buckled. But if she'd reached out, collected the girl on her lap instead of letting her cling to Moritz, maybe that horrible thing wouldn't have happened. If she'd held her close, she wouldn't have sought comfort in that wolf in sheep's clothes. She recalled kneeling outside the bathroom, pleading with Moritz to come out, her back to her crying daughter. The memory cut deep. This wasn't who she was. This was who she had become.

She couldn't summon her anger to justify her past actions, as she had for so many years. The rancor had dissolved and left her empty. She fully saw the daughter seated beside her. She wondered why Thelma and not Annie, but she knew the answer. Until then, she'd only seen this girl through the veil of her blame, but now she recognized that she herself was at fault. She was flooded with an unaccustomed tenderness for this, her daughter-rival, the husband thief. How cruel, that name. It wasn't this child's fault. And yet, she'd never allowed herself to view her in full, to empathize, and in the candlelight, in the last moment, as she felt the dead grabbing at her wrists, her ankles, she saw this widow's goodness and hardship. Mama realized the love Thelma gave her brothers would have easily been shared. She was a bighearted girl. She felt a sense of loss heavier than her abandonment by Jonas: it was too late to change course. She should have been generous enough to rescue an abandoned infant, to nurture the helpless: that, at least, she owed God, if not Jonas.

Mama had fluid everywhere: her lungs, the sac around her heart, her ankles—but she couldn't raise a tear for herself. She hadn't protected the girl, and still she sat here by her side, vigilant.

It was quiet in the room, although she could hear the sound of water boiling in the kitchen and a knife banging a chopping block. She pulled the girl's hand closer, feeling each of her fingers, and said, "You were a beautiful little girl. Were you a dancer! You couldn't stand still until you learned to dance."

Chapter 30

Mama had died and Thelma had witnessed it, shutting her mother's eyelids with her fingertips in a final act of intimacy. This woman who'd overshadowed so much of Thelma's life was now no more animated than the stained featherbed she'd stitched with her sisters in Drohobych that covered her corpse. When it was new, she'd wrapped it in tissue paper and carried it to Jonas's house across the village. Stuffed with local geese feathers, crafted from the finest cotton, produced when such a handmade featherbed was a prized possession and, blessed by the rabbi, intended to blanket a long and fertile marriage. In his prayer, the holy man had omitted happiness.

Thelma straightened the comforter, reversing the roles of mother and daughter. Feeling strangely privileged, Thelma sensed magic in the air, as if she could hear the rush of the spirits that had swirled into the room before shuffling away with Mama. She wondered whether she'd been meant to be beside her and whether, after a lifetime of being at odds, they'd finally united. Had they made peace? Not in any mathematical way, no final reckoning on life's abacus. While still confused, she reveled in an unexpected state of grace that eased the undertow of death.

Her mother's last words had been spoken to her. Thelma had been seen.

She snuffed the candle that had witnessed their goodbye. She felt relieved of resentment's heavy burden. Outside the breeze whipped into a wind that shook down the tree's last leaves.

When she entered the kitchen, the water roiled, spreading the stink of cabbage. She said to her sister, "Mama's dead."

"Why didn't you get me?" Annie flew into a rage, throwing a pot lid at Thelma's head. "I was right here."

"We didn't want you there," Thelma said, unclear whether that was true, but beyond caring. Let Annie grieve the way she wanted to grieve. She wasn't her sister's keeper.

Tearing off her apron, Annie said, "You robbed me of our last moment together. You could have called me and you didn't. You could have knocked on the wall. Do you think Mama loved you? That's a laugh. You disgusted her. And if you think I don't know you're sneaking out at night, you're sorely mistaken."

Thelma said nothing. She closed her eyes and swayed, trying to keep the calm she'd felt before she'd extinguished the candle. This was her grief. She wouldn't have it dictated by Annie. She tried to gather her feelings, to honor them.

Meanwhile, Annie took charge after twenty minutes of crying with Adele and Eli. She sent for Jesse and Julius, the doctor, the undertaker, the rabbi, and the neighbors. In front of Thelma, she fell to her hands and knees, reaching deep into the back of her mother's underwear drawer for the jewelry made by Moe that her mother had stashed in the darkest corners, not wanting to wear the gold but knowing its value. She pocketed the items, claiming that they were promised to her.

The family had sat shivah and then Annie had gone out of her way to make it clear that she was now mistress of Montauk Avenue. Mama had bequeathed it to her surviving children: Abie, Thelma, and Annie. Her heirs. Abie had never once appeared over those seven nights when she and her sister had sat alongside Moe and Jesse with torn dresses and sheet-draped mirrors in honor of the dead, beside a table laden with delicatessen and sweet, yeasty babkas, and kosher pickle spears to stoke the living.

Over the next month, Annie exploited her position as mourner in chief to consolidate her power within the house in Mama's absence. Whenever Thelma got dressed to go out, Annie would say just as she was heading out the door, "I'm not taking care of that bed wetter of yours."

"Who died and made you czar?" Thelma asked. This house was a third hers, but she'd have to fight for every square inch. Occasionally she'd slip babysitting money to her twenty-two-year-old niece, Adele, with promises to cover for her on the nights she stayed out late.

After a month, sick as hell of living under the hammer, she'd fled to dance cheek to cheek at the Arcadia Ballroom under the big crystal chandelier that scattered rainbows on the wooden floor. She'd met up with a friend of Abie's there. He was no great beauty and had two left feet, but he led her down to the alley by way of the stage door, all those metal stairs in her high heels. He said he gave her what she wanted, but it was a long way to go for attention. He didn't even lend her a handkerchief to wipe her hands afterward.

It was after 1:00 a.m. when she left by herself, feeling heartsick, missing Phil and ashamed if he'd seen what she'd become without him. The subway trip that had once been so secure with her man beside her now seemed sinister when she was alone. She got as far as Williamsburg before a trench-coated stranger began circling her, moving from one side of the car to the other, sitting ever closer. When he stood up and unzipped his pants, she fled for the door at the next stop, her coat catching in the gap until she pulled it out with a streak of grease.

All she'd wanted was a little joy, a little sweetness, a swoop in a strong man's arms while the saxophone played. The words *heaven, I'm in heaven* stuck in her head. But, aloud, she whispered, "I'm in hell."

Frequently glancing over her shoulder, she hurried shadowy blocks in high heels, finally arriving outside Marcy Avenue. Heavy curtains covered the windows, but she could see a crack of light between the panels. She knocked. Nobody answered. She rested her ear against the door: muffled movement. She felt a sense of dread and a desperate need to fall into her brother's arms, to be consoled. From her change purse, she fished out Abie's key that she hadn't used since Phil was alive. She hoped it still worked.

It did.

She crossed the empty living room and stepped behind the wooden bar that spanned the left wall. She poured three fingers of vodka in a jelly jar without spilling too much, leaving the martini glasses for the members of the Williamsburg Boys Club. After hanging her coat on a hook beside four others, she looked over at the bedroom and thought of Phil, and then that bruiser she'd followed into the alley behind the Arcadia, and felt repulsed. She'd known love, and she wasn't good enough to keep it alive. Still, what was so wrong with wanting to rub up against a man from time to time? But she had her answer—if it was only rubbing and went no further, it just didn't feel the same. Dancing wasn't a pleasure with the wrong partner. But it was still dancing.

Entering the bathroom to wash her hands, she stared at herself in the mirror—the gray circles beneath frightened green eyes, the fair skin with the mole beside her ordinary nose. She sucked in her cheekbones, replenished her scarlet lipstick, moved her hairpins around so she looked the right side of tousled. She reached for the towel, which was whitish with blue lettering—THE FRANCONIA—and filthy.

She had a bad feeling about a night that was already circling the drain. All the songs in her head were out of tune. She couldn't get a beat. She didn't know how far she could push Annie, or what she'd have to do to earn a living and escape her with a kid in tow. Still, it was her house: Why should she leave? The answer was simple: her skin wasn't thick enough. She didn't think she could ever be happy under Annie's thumb.

When she reentered the living room and replenished her glass, she smelled fear: a salty, sour sweat swirled with sickening aftershave. She heard groans from behind the swinging door—and not the kind of noise overheard beyond a bedroom door that rose to a climax. She had plenty of time to run from Marcy Avenue. But she stayed, sitting down at a card table to play solitaire with her shoes off under the table until Abie entered, rolling down his sleeves.

"What's that, Abie?"

"Believe me, you don't want to know."

"Who's in the kitchen?"

"I'm opening a kosher deli."

"In the middle of the night?" she asked.

"It was the only time the rabbi could come."

"That doesn't sound like a blessing to me," Thelma said with a strained laugh. Unsmiling, he clenched his jaw so tightly it was a miracle teeth didn't come shooting out of his mouth. "What have you gotten yourself into now?"

"Don't ask. You gotta get out of here. Now! Grab your coat. Go!"

"I'm not leaving until I know you're safe."

"What: You plan on moving in? Why not bring Larry, too?" He sat down across from her. Abie was jittery. Not himself. He kept scratching his forearms, rubbing his nose. "I can take care of myself, Temmy. It's you I'm worried about."

"If you're so worried, tell me what I'm supposed to do."

"Go home to your kid."

"Thanks for the advice. I wouldn't be here if I wasn't down in the dumps."

"Your mood won't improve if you stay."

She held on when she should have folded. Afraid of walking back to the train this late on the dark Williamsburg streets, she weighed whether it was more dangerous inside than outside. But here was Abie and there a stranger loitered beneath the onramp to the bridge. Rather than mentioning the man in the hat for fear of adding to the tsuris, she asked the first neutral question that popped into her head. "How am I supposed to find a cab this late?"

Increasingly impatient, Abie said, "Maybe you should have thought of that before you came knocking."

"Since when is your own sister unwelcome? What: Are you Annie?"

"She wouldn't be so dim to come here this late."

"Kick a girl when she's down."

"Get in line. Take a number." Abie fumbled for a cigarette. "You gotta learn to pick yourself up, Temmy. This is my last warning: get out."

Thelma turned her head away from him but lacked the energy to rise and be alone on Marcy Avenue again, so he said, "It's your funeral," grabbed the cards, and riffled the deck on the felt. They came loose from his hands, and he gathered them again.

"You're shuffling like an old lady."

He looked at her now, full in the face, the whites of his eyes wide. She'd never seen him so terrified. But if it was meant to scare her away, it had the opposite impact. She wouldn't leave. They belonged together. She'd be there for him. "What can I—"

"Play cards."

"Deal," she said.

Abie dealt, and she collected her ten cards for gin rummy and sorted them into melds, aces to the left and deuces to the right. They played hand after hand, in the trance that comes from being inside a game with identifiable rules. Concentration was both a means of escape and a connection between players, a shared trance before the other shoe dropped (maybe a pogrom, maybe a shotgun wedding). He'd always been competitive, and she was good at counting cards. Before the shooting, he'd been cockier, but he'd changed, becoming increasingly cautious and secretive. They tended to *kibitz* while they played, but today they were quiet, sharing her glass. The cards slapped the table.

"Gin," he said.

"Already? I can't even knock. You're killing me."

He snorted, shuffled, and dealt a new hand. The swinging door opened. A stout stranger drenched in sweat poked his pockmarked forehead out, looked from brother to sister and said, "Bring me the girl."

"What's he talking about, Abie?"

"I told you to go. Now you're here. I'm not calling the shots."

"But we're in your place."

"Right, like I planned on being a kosher butcher. Mama would be so proud. Now, shut up and do what he tells you. You'll be okay. I got your back."

"It's my front I'm worried about." She squeezed her blistered feet into her shoes, winced as she rose and smoothed her skirt. This was no occasion for a red party dress. She yanked up her neckline, but it wasn't getting any higher.

As she passed Abie, she squeezed his shoulder. It was pure steel. He flinched. "Stop looking at my cards," he said.

"I'll be back and beat you blind."

"Keep dreaming."

She entered a kitchen ravaged by blood and gore. She'd never realized the floor was uneven until she saw the blood pool in front of the icebox. It was a random thought, the kind a person gets when they're in shock and can't register the carnage before them. She gagged. How could she have stayed with only a swinging door between herself—and this slaughterhouse? She could have left, but her need to be near Abie, someone who understood her and still loved her, was too great—and now she'd landed here. Abie had urged her to leave for her own good, and she hadn't listened. What else was new?

"Strip," said a tall stranger with a commanding, even handsome, forehead above thin lips on a sardonic mouth. He was wearing tailored woolen suit pants with an undershirt, and his arms were the kind of muscular that came from constant use. When she hesitated, scanning the kitchen for a bloodless spot to land if she fainted, he growled,

"You're not my sister, sister. But I'm not going to touch you. Why should I have chopped liver out when I've got steak at home?"

"Since you came late to the party," said his partner, the pockmarked thug built like a fireplug, "take this bucket and mop and clean up."

She removed her dress and shoes. Even after the tall man's insult, he eyeballed her every move so that her red-painted fingernails fumbled with her garters as she unsnapped her stockings.

"You got a runner," he said.

"You don't," she said, casting her eyes at the leaky bundle wrapped in chenille, the head covered while two Florsheims splayed at odd angles. The well-made wing tips probably had another ten years to them. Not the owner.

"You want the shoes?"

"Thanks, no, thanks."

"Let's shlep him out the back and into the trunk," the tall man ordered the *shvitser*. They weren't using names. Together, the killers manhandled the corpse out the alley door. Afraid of waiting until they returned, she tucked her slip hem up into her bra like she would if she were cleaning at home and knelt at the shore of the scarlet slime. The more she tried to swab it, the more the goop radiated over the linoleum. It was hopeless. She panicked. She wouldn't be able to clean the mess and they'd slap her around—worse, add her body to the pile. She was no housekeeper, but she didn't stop, pausing only to gag, to stand up and swig vodka from the bottle on the table beside the dead man's glass. The liquor loosened her limbs and she scrubbed with a great yellow sponge she'd found under the sink, putting both shoulders into the work, until the red went pink and the pink cleared. Just when she thought she'd eliminated all traces, she eyed a blood clot beneath the icebox rim. And then she found some skin and viscera on the metal chair legs where the deed had been done. She wiped the vinyl down for good measure. It was brutal work, cleaning up after savage men, that made changing diapers or nursing a child with stomach flu seem like a dream.

Afterward, when she'd sluiced herself with water in the bathroom and vomited in a toilet that hadn't been scoured since the Great War, she perched on the edge of the tub and slowly put on her ruined stockings, hardly able to get them over her sticky feet but not wanting to start all over again. She stepped into her heels and the tight dress she'd once thought was so smart and now seemed Brooklyn chippie cheap. She'd never be able to wear it again without thinking about the dead man wrapped up in chenille. After rinsing her mouth, she stared in the mirror and saw holes where her eyes had been, long corridors to nothing and nowhere. She took a long time putting on her lipstick, because her hand was shaking and she now despised the color red.

When she left the bathroom, Abie waited with her coat open and her purse over his wrist. "C'mon, we gotta go."

"Where?"

"The Navy Yard."

"Gonna enlist?" She followed him out the door and tried to keep up while he hustled down the darkened street. He got behind the wheel of an unfamiliar late-model sedan. She climbed in beside him. "If you had a car, you could have driven me home."

"Sure, Pola Negri," Abie said, agitated, scratching his scalp. "I could've left those gorillas to play chauffeur to my baby sister, saying, 'Pardon me, gents, can I borrow the getaway car?' That wasn't in the plan."

"What was?"

He snorted. They shared a cigarette until she noticed a Buick in the rearview mirror that flashed its headlights twice before slithering past them. Abie pulled out behind the green sedan. He ground the gears trying to put it in first and then lurched out behind the other car onto Marcy Avenue, crossing under the ramp to the Williamsburg Bridge.

"Pretty suave, Abie. Let's not attract attention."

"It's too late for that, Temmy."

"Have you ever driven?"

"Once—I got a lesson."

"Maybe you should have gotten two."

"Can you leave it? Jesus, Thelma, can't you see I'm scared?"

"What kind of man would you be if you weren't?" She looked at him, shifting, *shvitsing*, checking the rearview maniacally. "What just happened? Did you know that guy?"

"Pretty," he said. "Pretty Amberg."

"Isn't he a *macher*?"

"Not anymore."

"RIP," she said. An awkward silence fell, and she felt compelled to fill it. "Is there anything I can do?"

"Haven't you done enough?" He let a lot of room slip between their car and the Buick. He had trouble shifting into second; it growled into third. He bit his left middle knuckle and then exhaled. "Why'd you show up tonight of all nights, Tem?"

"I never had the best timing." After that bloodbath, she wasn't about to *kvetch* about her problems: the groping goon at the dance hall or the meat flasher on the train; how much she still ached for Phil. She had adult needs a widow was supposed to suppress. She'd skipped her period and was going to see Abie with her hand out for a fix just in case.

And now, she'd followed him into an inescapable hell. Just when she thought she couldn't fall any lower, her heroic Abie had guided her down to a desperate place. How long could she fool herself? Even killers had kid sisters—but she wasn't a baby anymore. She had a boy of her own who needed her alive.

Abie ground the gears down to second, turning right on Flushing Avenue. "You never show up like that, Tem. Who knew you still had a key?"

"You can have it back." She didn't want to explain, to ask him for money, so she just said, "With Mama gone, it smelled like death at home and I couldn't sit still. Trust me: I didn't know how crappy death smelled until I cleaned up after Pretty."

"You didn't meet him under the best circumstances, not that he was ever Mr. Popularity. I wish you hadn't come, Temeleh, but now you're here. I'm up shit creek, little sister, not some little tsuris like pissing off that bitch Annie. Tonight I crossed a line. I did something I didn't want to do. I'm more the mind-my-own-business type, but there's a change in the wind and I got squeezed."

"What change?"

"Pretty was in—and then he got in the way. I fingered the guy just like that dame fingered me on Mermaid Avenue. And it feels lousy. The East New York crew said that if I wanted to play ball, if I was the real thing, I'd invite Amberg over to the Williamsburg Boys Club for a dope party—and he'd end up being the dope. They said they'd do the rest. They didn't. They played with him. That was Pep Strauss, the tall gorilla."

"He's a real stinker, that one."

"You don't know the half. I've done bad things before but, Temmy, this guy is one sick *meshugener*. We sliced Amberg like pastrami. It took all night. I don't know what they were waiting for, but we kept him alive well past the begging." The car slipped through the darkened streets behind the Buick. Now he couldn't stop talking. "I knew this schmuck, we'd *shtupped* the same broads, he wasn't exactly a friend, but in this business, who is, right?"

"I wouldn't know."

"I wish we'd kept it that way. I had a choice: be a *shlepper* or a doer—so I did. Am I happy? Could I make it clearer? This is not me, or who I was, but it is who I am tonight. I'm alive, not dead. Those were my choices. Do you want me to draw you a map?"

She shook her head, observing Abie in her periphery. His protective mask had slipped. For a minute, she saw the brute Annie must have seen—and he repulsed her. He'd always been on her side, at her side—but when she looked at him behind the steering wheel following the corpse car, she couldn't keep his different parts in focus. It was as if she viewed him simultaneously as a police photo, Little Yiddle with dead eyes and a sneer, and as her savior, who'd always rescued her from Annie like some screen swashbuckler. It shook her deeply. She felt her love for him begin to tear and, because that love had glued her together, she ripped, too.

She fumbled a Lucky out of his pack on the dashboard, lit it, and puffed. Between shifting gears, he explained what the deal was, and she grunted occasionally in response. He said that his Williamsburg crew had aspired to be like the more established Brownsville Boys, Lepke and his pal Gurrah Shapiro, with their syndicate ties. What made that night different from all others was that, on Lepke's orders, they were proving themselves by killing Amberg, a man they knew. The hit was the B card on the fight for Murder Inc., Jewish and Italian killers for hire. The main bout (the A card) had been Dutch Schultz's shooting over in Newark earlier that night. On contract from the syndicate, Lepke's inner circle meticulously planned and performed that hit on racketeer and bootlegger Schultz. In contrast, the Amberg slaying at the Williamsburg Boys Club was improvisational.

So was the outdoor shindig with the ladies' auxiliary, the gang's girlfriends and wives, that greeted them when Abie pulled up behind the Buick that held the body. In the distance, a bonfire blazed in the weeds beyond North Elliott Place near the Brooklyn Navy Yard. After Abie set the parking brake, he said, "Stay here."

As soon as he hopped away, she ignored his orders and opened the car door. She missed the running board and stumbled on the dirt, leaning over to heave, still stupid enough to worry about whether she'd get vomit on her coat. She stood up to take deep, smoky mouth breaths as Abie hustled toward Strauss, Lepke's enforcer. The broad-shouldered gorilla peered down from beneath his mountainous forehead and bushy eyebrows and grasped Abie's hand in solidarity.

To Pep's left stood a shellacked blonde in a kelly-green cardigan. Who wore cashmere and pearls to a bonfire? Clutching the arm of the party's coldest killer, Pep's date giggled as her man announced the plan in a loud voice. Whichever wife or girlfriend got the short straw would become Miss Murder Inc. and toss the honorary first match on Amberg.

Willing or not, her brother had pulled Thelma into the center of the action like never before. Her nausea gave way to adrenaline as she watched the flames that rose from a nearby metal barrel. Approaching the green car in the middle of the field, she smelled gasoline. Wives and girlfriends surrounded her, laughing and nervous, their elaborate hairdos sprayed stiff. Some wore furs; others flashed cocktail rings. At least she was wearing her good coat, her dancing dress. But underneath, blood caked her slip.

She gazed through the crowd toward her brother and Pep. She could see that Pep's girlfriend won, because she flashed a toothy triumphant smile. She accepted the matchbox from Pep like it came from Tiffany's wrapped in a bow, leaving his side to cheers of "Evelyn! Evelyn!" The dame picked her way toward Thelma, the matchbox in a gloved hand. Thelma recognized from her shopgirl days that they were fancy gloves, a paler shade of green than Evelyn's shamrock-colored sweater, completely impractical.

While Evelyn had left Pep's side with bravado, she slowed down as she approached the Buick that held Amberg. She fumbled with her gloves as she tried to remove them, possibly realizing that this was what the jolly Jewish martini guys were doing while she was home polishing her nails—and she didn't have the guts to get her hands dirty herself. When Evelyn caught Thelma's eyes, seeking mercy, Abie's sister reached out for the matches. As Evelyn withdrew, her rescuer glanced over to where Strauss stood beside her brother. She made eye contact with Pep and saw rage in his eyes. She realized too late that she'd put another wrench in his plan. It dawned on her that the point was to imprint the night on the lovely Evelyn, to make her remove her gloves and recognize the high cost of the pearls around her neck. In a flash, Thelma realized she was an extra who'd crossed into the star's spotlight uninvited. Still, with all eyes on her, Thelma ignored Pep's disapproval, pivoted, advancing toward the Buick. She'd already cleaned up after Pretty once—why not finish the job?

Thelma faced the sedan. If she couldn't create, then she had the power to destroy—to fly high and fall hard. Asserting herself, she seized the night, the fire starter. *Look in. Light the match.* With the gang's attention on that flame between her fingers, she said, "He doesn't look so pretty now, does he?"

The match licked the fuel until Abie ran forward, yelling, "What are you, *meshuge?* Back away, Temeleh."

She heard a whoosh, which almost tore the tags from her life. But where would that leave her kid? What a miserable mother she was, dragging Larry along in her crazy wake. Maybe time remained to salvage the wreckage of her life, to protect her only son by putting him first.

Chapter 31

The next morning, the autumn sun was already high on Marcy Avenue when Thelma awoke with a hammering behind her left eye. Sharp memory shards—blood, flames—stimulated self-loathing. She panicked. She'd hoped to meet Annie's daughter, Adele, and Larry at the el station to take him to Hebrew school—and she was going to be very late. She dressed hurriedly, rubbed tooth powder around her mouth, and leaped out of the empty apartment, but not before dropping the key on a card table.

When she arrived at Saratoga Avenue, she peeked through the streaky window and spotted Larry beyond the station's iron bars, waiting for her. He clung to the metal, a mischievous monkey in short pants, shirt untucked, and a hand-me-down corduroy jacket with sleeves that were too short and exposed bony wrists. He hopped from foot to foot as if he had to pee, all knees and elbows and a nose into which he hadn't grown. His warm, open face beneath a flop of unkempt curls radiated hope, then registered disappointment, then hope again, as he scanned the train, squinting.

She sank low on the seat and let the doors open and close, open and close. How could she save her son when she couldn't save herself? She couldn't meet him nauseous, bees buzzing in her brain, blood on her slip. He needed her, and she had nothing to give. So she flung Larry away, like snot, because she was falling, the floor below her crumbling.

And she didn't want to take him with her. She'd come back later. She'd make it up to him. They'd go to the Kinema.

After the train left the station, she sat back up, clutching her pocketbook. When she got to the end of the line, at Coney Island, she wandered under an overcast sky toward the Wonder Wheel. She nodded at the gnarled Italian who ran the ride. When he belatedly rose to help her, he dropped the newspaper on his red-painted stool. She read, "Dutch Schultz Dying; Two Aides Slain."

Pretty hadn't made the *Brooklyn Daily Eagle*'s headline. Then she noticed the name Amberg just below the boldface type, shuddered with fear, and glanced away to avoid suspicion. The old man raised his tufted eyebrows, more gray than black. "Wanna ride?" he asked. "I'll make you a deal."

"No, *grazie*." She spun around as soon as she recognized her own melancholy mirrored in his eyes, and his pity. Happy people didn't ride the Wonder Wheel by themselves on a chilly Thursday in October.

She was a material witness—more, an accomplice. She knew what that meant: bad on both sides, the cops and the cons. Abie had brought her into this, let it happen. He'd been a material witness once, the killing of Monk Eastman at the Blue Bird Café back in 1920, when he was still getting caught for stuff he did. He'd danced his way out of that somehow, telling the cops one thing, the fellas another. But she wasn't that kind of dancer. Abie knew that. She knew that. No poker face. She couldn't even meet Larry standing at the subway entrance, ready to scoot under the turnstile to greet her. Tokens were for sissies.

Expendable: that's what she was. That's what she'd always been. Even the Wonder Wheel man could read it in her eyes, as plain as the Schultz headline or Mussolini's push into Ethiopia. She had blood on her slip, burns on her hands, and moth holes in her heart. How had it happened, all the cumulative tears, the loss of a father before you had even felt his breath in your face, learned his laughter, caught his large hands meting out justice in caresses and slaps? Good girl, bad girl, no longer a girl at all. She was old enough now, a mother herself, with that itch to scratch between her legs and alone again. And yet she circled back and back: Why? Why couldn't she escape? She knew the answer; she just couldn't bring herself to say it.

To be fatherless, to be rudderless, and to be left with those bitches, Mama and Annie: How had they lacked even a blood drop of compassion for the smallest child, the littlest girl? They tamped down everything that was her, every bit of fire, and still she sparked. She must have been her father's daughter, only who knew? She was born as he departed, raised in an apartment with mirrors covered in sheets and a landlord knocking for the rent. Mama lost in her widow's mourning. Her bereft sister played mother without the milk of human kindness, strong enough only to care for herself and Mama. Annie treated the baby like an unwanted obligation, when Thelma would have lapped up any teardrop of love and been grateful.

How could they love each other so much and leave nothing for her? And then, how could she, carrying their rejection around like a pocketbook of pain, turn around and bring a beautiful son into the world? She should have loved Larry the way he deserved to be loved. What had he done, this child? Nothing. But Philip crumbled, she saw it, as she held the baby, the two of them crying, Larry and Philip, because her husband knew—feared?—that he couldn't rise and so began falling more than he ever had, into the mental hospital and the treatments that erased all that was Philip, all that was joy. Soiled pajamas and slippers: all that remained. Until they told her not to return. They told her to hold on to her boy, to give it the love of a mother and a father, and she awoke to the truth: that in her arms was another fatherless child and she couldn't follow Philip into the hole, the smell of feet and fungus, the syringes, the terrifying electric treatments.

Be a mother: But what did she know of mothering that she hadn't learned from Mama or Annie? Had she become her mother, incapable of loving her own child? Had Annie won, with her three fat children, the doting grandmother dead and buried, the house on Montauk Avenue, the smugness of it all? Thelma fought. She laughed. She danced. She drank. But who could she turn to, now, the day after Pretty Amberg's death? Seeking out Abie in her sadness had started it off, not being aware of her own surroundings, of the danger that the Williamsburg Boys Club was no club at all. They weren't boys—they were fellas, mobsters. She knew that, and still she'd gone. Now to whom could she turn?

With Luna Park and the Cyclone to her left and the Atlantic Ocean to her right, she stumbled along the boardwalk, shoulders jutting forward. It looked colder than it was, but the wind bit. She was never warm enough these days, except when she'd stood too close to the flames. If Abie hadn't called out to her, she would have lost her eyebrows last night, her lashes. Pretty lost more than that. So many cuts on that body, so much blood, so little left to the fleshy face that earned him his nickname. Oddly sad, shredded and slit, the nose in pieces, two lips into six, ears fallen upside down.

The memories came up like bile: Amberg's fancy shoes poking out from under her brother's familiar blanket that she used to play tent beneath, alone and temporarily safe from Annie; the blank stares of the strange men from another neighborhood, their matter-of-factness and her brother's sweat, his odd servility. He was someone else with them than he was with her; she sensed how they treated him as something lesser. Or maybe it was just the nature of the beast, the nerves hidden or exposed by the violence. They were in the murder business now. Had she seen it coming? They didn't joke that Abie was quick with a knife for nothing. But they'd been so slow last night. She had had plenty of time to run from Marcy Avenue. But she'd stayed.

Now, in the aftermath, she was a lone refugee at the ass end of Brooklyn, prepared to throw herself into the sea and be done with it, meet Phil, dance below the surf. But she wasn't made like Phil; she gasped, but she gasped for life. She wouldn't even make it across the sand. It would ruin her shoes, her only semidecent pair.

Wild hairs escaped from their pins, whipping around her cheeks. When she cleared the coarse strands from her lips, she smeared her lipstick. She was a mess. She felt despondent and then angry, a Cyclone of feelings, up, down, ferocious, floundering. She had tried, really, to pull herself up, to be strong for Larry, whatever that was, to be a wife, a widow, a sister—at least to Abie and Louis. She had smarts. She had skills; she could type. She knew how to love, but she kept being pushed out, onto the sidewalk, unprotected: black sheep or stray cat or loose end. All her defenses spent, she felt rubbed raw. This was where Annie wanted her to be: alone and vulnerable and begging to crawl back and submit. Stop rocking the boat—and it was Annie's boat, her own mother sacrificing Thelma, and Abie, and Louis. The boys didn't care— Abie, the orphan, had honed his hatred into a shiv. But her grudges weighed her down.

She felt her own fat, slow tears betray her, like that child, alone under the table, clutching the lighter. It was wretched to know she would always want what she couldn't have, that she couldn't tame the love hunger. She couldn't funnel it into violence against anybody but herself. Crying in public on the Coney Island boardwalk was so pathetic. She didn't want bags to form under her eyes, gray circles. The immigrant scourge: rouged lips, sad eyes. She was already thirty-three. She would never find another man if she didn't look gay, if she didn't hold on to her waist, her ankles, her laughter. Wasn't that really what it came down to? That she felt unworthy of love, not incapable of loving. That she didn't have the strength to put herself aside and be a mother. Or was she selfish, sluttish, dissolute, or depraved? She had to force Annie's and Mama's voices out of her head; they were like bedbugs in the mattress of her brain.

Stepping on chewing gum, she cursed. She stopped, scratching her right sole on the rough planking until it lost its stickiness. "Feh," she said, as if the shoe damage was part of a string of disasters that included her stained slip, ditching Larry, and setting a gangster corpse alight. She felt waves of disgust and fear, her hands shaking as she reached into her pocketbook, detaching the wrinkled handkerchief from the mess inside.

Was it possible to feel worse than she had scrubbing the floor the night before? Or was the shock wearing off and now came the pain— straight, no chaser? She needed more drink.

Walking the relatively solid boardwalk, Thelma felt herself falling. It was as if the boards were shifting back and forth under her feet like a moving funhouse floor. She couldn't regain her balance. Her knees hurt from last night on the linoleum, scrubbing away a man's guts, the goo of it, the stringy membranes.

She eyed the crappy little no-name bar that opened like one end of a shoebox between a corn-on-the-cob vendor and a midway, both shuttered for the season. She saw metal chairs clustered around rusty tables, no longer fought over by the summer throng, barely recognizable from her first date with Phil that summer of 1923.

When Thelma entered the dive, she recoiled at the sour beer stench. She craved hooch to clear her head. Would the police find her? She'd brazenly set the car alight before who knew how many snitching bitches. She'd scoured the kitchen after Pretty Amberg's killing. Was she a fugitive, an accessory after the fact? Or was her crime aiding and abetting? She laughed bitterly. Not even the police would have eyes for her: "Unwanted for Murder: Thelma Schwartz."

Damn Abie and the Williamsburg Boys for getting too big for the neighborhood. Damn Phil for giving her a taste for vodka and then leaving her with a kid and a pincushion heart. Damn Annie and Mama, as long as she was cursing, for offering barbed wire when she needed soft shoulders. Damn her stepfather for showering her with affection and curdling it with that pickle of his, providing her mother and sister more reasons to blame her for souring the milk. Was it wrong that she still felt more for him than her own mother? How screwed up was that? Twisted like licorice.

Inside the bar, her shoes rustled the peanut shells that covered the cement floor. Once she became accustomed to the murk, she spied a row of rummies staring back at her with rheumy eyes. They were the sitting dead, drinking the slow poison. She felt herself floating toward them, the desire to just let go and die. But then she jerked herself back: she'd seen mashed Amberg in the Buick's back seat. She wasn't ready to join him. Larry depended on her, however undependable she was. She'd never thought she'd become so foul a mother. That added another weight to the chain she rattled.

The wiry bartender turned his hostile gaze toward her. "Whatcha want?"

She winced at the potato-shaped boil on his nose. "Vodka."

The Irishman circled his wet rag on the bar, looking her up, then down. "Double?"

"Are you paying?"

"Do I look like a Rockefeller?"

"Make mine a single." She fumbled for change in her pocketbook. "I'm taking it outside."

"Suit yourself." He poured with a heavy hand then slid the glass across the bar. She sipped the drink's surface to preserve every drop and swiveled away from the boozers, keenly aware rungs existed farther down the ladder. She didn't want to tumble any lower, but gravity pulled her down.

Chapter 32

Carting her cocktail, Thelma shuffled onto the boardwalk. A startled seagull flew up, screeching like a human child. She scraped a seat closer to a vacant table, setting the glass down and spreading her hankie on the chair to protect her coat. Once settled, she sipped and then dived into a big, oily gulp.

She gazed across the boardwalk, over the deserted sand to the ocean's sullen waves. Slap, slap, slap. An olive-skinned brunette in a mink strode past, alligator pumps clacking. There'd been a time when Thelma had hoped that would be her future, the marvelous Mrs. Schwartz, secure and loved, maybe even in furs like Pola Negri, no more clawing just to stay in place. What a laugh! She'd been sold a bill of goods. She'd dreamed of places to go and things to do, caring people awaiting her, scolding her affectionately for being late.

Thelma's empty stomach lurched at the alcohol, but she didn't stop. She watched one wave smack the next. Pushing up her coat sleeves, she leaned her elbows on the gummy table, cradling her chin in her palms. Her drink was dry when she heard a familiar voice calling, "Temeleh."

Abie parked opposite Thelma, his back to the ocean. He huffed like an old man, traces of sweat dried on his forehead. He seemed coiled and nervous.

"How'd you find me? I don't even know how *I* got here." Her path had been random; she couldn't retrace her own steps. Still, Abie's arrival meant she wasn't completely alone.

"Larry told me you skipped Hebrew lessons," Abie said, snapping his fingers at the bartender, who had poked his head outside. Ordering for them both, he withdrew a roll and peeled off a bill. "I met him at Midnight Rose's Candy Store. My nephew was running phone calls for Kid Twist at a nickel a pop."

"Not quite the *alef-beys*." She'd left him alone on the street, hoping that Adele was nearby but not checking. She'd been full of cares and careless. While she'd lacked the pennies to front her kid a paper sack of caramels, she could scrape together enough for booze. She'd become the horror her sister had warned her about, Annie with her three ducklings in a row. Thelma wouldn't cry now. Not if she hadn't last night on her knees.

"That's how the fellas rope a boy in. A little pocket change for candy your own mother's too cheap to buy you. It ain't hard to get a kid hooked on sugar." Abie dug a half-smoked cigar out of his breast pocket and lit it. "Larry's quite the character—got a lot of brass for a skinny kid. But he's more mouthy than smart."

"The family curse."

"He'd tell a stranger everything about you for a nickel," Abie said, then shut up when the barman delivered two shots. Abie made a twirling motion with his index finger directed at the table. "Another round."

Once the Irishman disappeared, Abie continued, "I gave him a quarter. He told me he'd waited for you but you'd skipped. He was mad as hell. He called you a few names. Naturally, I agreed. Who knows you better than me? After that, finding you was easy. I knew a guy who knew a guy who saw you in Luna Park."

"Jesus."

"Mary, Mother of God, and Joseph, too, for all the good they'll do," said Abie. "Bottoms up."

"Up your bottom." She gagged and then smacked the glass down on the table. Her brother scratched at his stubble and then rubbed his square chin. He looked like she felt. She saw him young, sitting like a prince of thieves in the orphanage with Louis beside him. And she anticipated what he'd look like old, when those worry lines cratered and his teeth yellowed—if he were allowed to age that long. He wasn't in the longevity business. "We're in deep, right?"

"Up to my neck."

"That was some grisly pudding last night." The siblings leaned back.

"And you missed the main course," Abie said, sucking on his cigar.

"I saw plenty." There'd been so much gore, swirling in circles beneath the sponge, under her fingernails, dyeing the bucket water red. It nearly made cleanup impossible. That was how it had to be. It shouldn't be easy to kill a man. It should be messy and tough, because no one had that right to snuff a life, not even Pretty's.

Abie tossed the cigar. Fishing for cigarettes, he tapped out two and lit them. Brother and sister smoked in silence. Abie was visibly uneasy, not just with the overall situation but with her. She could tell he hadn't sought her out to hold her hand.

"Okay, Abie, spit it out. What's the bitter pill I have to swallow?"

"You saw too much, Temmy. You can't be hanging around the clubhouse."

"That's a fancy name for that basement flytrap." Even though she was numbed by booze, his brush-off gradually sank in, magnifying her paranoia. She turned away to hide her sorrow, ashamed and gutted. Forget hope. Forget comfort. Even Abie, her knight in tarnished armor, was joining Annie and Mama. He was telling her she was unwelcome at the one place she knew she could find him when she needed him.

And she always wanted him. They'd been conspirators in life. She'd been his defender in chief, his ally. Overnight, she'd become a liability. Having seen death up close, she fought the rising terror that her end was near, too. She stood up, furious, spun around and began to walk in circles on the boardwalk, frightening pigeons into flight. When she pivoted to confront Abie, she couldn't read his features, because he'd shut her out. She felt like screaming at him until her vocal cords snapped, but that would only supply more evidence of her weakness. She couldn't control herself, her rage, her grief: Hadn't that been what got them here in the first place?

"Sit down, Thelma, before you bring down the cops."

"I don't want to sit down." Yet she collapsed back in the chair, obediently. In a voice strained by emotion, she said, "So now I can't see my own brother?"

"You gotta stay away from me," Abie said. He swiveled his chair to face the water, giving her his profile. This was how he treated everybody else, but not her. He'd always let her in, and she'd never judged. "I'm begging you. There's going to be trouble."

"What else is new?" Thelma laughed. Abie didn't. She changed her tone, pared the sarcasm. "When did you get into the bump-off racket?"

"When you're running the Williamsburg Boys Club . . ."

"Don't bullshit me, Abie. You're no big shot."

"And I'd like to keep it that way. Things are changing around the neighborhood, Tem." Using her nickname softened her. She felt him coming around. Who else could he trust? He wasn't a kid anymore. He was over forty, older than Papa had been when he'd passed. "Those Brownsville boys have ambitions, *shpilkes*. They can't sit still. They call the tune. Either we Williamsburg guys dance or we lie down. I've seen lying down. I don't want to be on the floor when the music stops."

"Why did Pretty have to die? Couldn't they have just given him a beating and a ticket out of town?"

"He stomped into Midnight Rose's making big-man threats, beating his chest. He was going to kill everybody. It was an engraved invitation."

"You didn't have to accept, did you?"

"We were either in or we were out." Abie appeared to drop his tough-guy mask. He'd always talked to her eventually. Everyone had to have at least one confidant, someone with whom the voice in their head matched their conversation. Abie was surrounded by animals, but even a man with a crooked past needed to unburden himself. "I knew Amberg, all right. He wasn't afraid of me. I invited him over to Marcy Avenue for a shot, maybe a little powder. But the party wasn't friendly. The boys tied him up in the kitchen. They gave me the first cut. I didn't like Pretty, but still, I didn't have any heat in me. He was my guest, an immigrant son of a bitch like me. But we had orders. And we had orders to do it slow."

Hunching deeper into his coat, he lowered his voice to a rasp. "They were over shooting Dutch in Jersey. It was going to be a long night. We were just supposed to get the party started. So I sliced his arm with a knife so sharp it took him a minute to squawk. Then we took turns. The bastard talked the whole time, as if we wanted information. He would have given us his kid's bar mitzvah funds, his wife's panties. But he didn't have anything to tell us we wanted to know. He just had to be wiped out of the picture. Things are changing, Temmy. It's the American way. Even killers are incorporating. The big guys have the syndicate. We *shleppers* are subcontractors. We're disposal experts filling orders, only it's not for bootleg hooch but body bags. We steal cars, we snatch guys, and they disappear. If you're not in, you're out. The Brownsville boys say it's the cost of doing business."

"Maybe you should unionize." She cracked wise to defuse the tension, but it didn't work, so she asked, "Why are you telling me all this now?"

"Because, Temmy, I'm poison for you now. You gotta keep your distance. I can't protect you." He coughed in a way that seemed to bounce around his lungs. "I'm a fixer. You know me. Someone wants something, I get it. Two guys don't get along, then I sit down and try to reshuffle the deck. Now I'm fixing this and that, holding my finger in the dike—they should call *me* the Dutchman—but I don't want a big name like Dutch Schultz. That's for suckers, small guys in big hats. I want to be Little Yiddle with a fiddle. I want to stay in the shadows in the neighborhood and collect my rent."

When he said "rent," she realized what worried her brother in the first place: money. Poverty was at the root of all his fears. He took a cut of the club and all the schemes that flowed in and out, including this new enterprise. In the process, he paid a lot of people off. She wasn't his accountant, but she knew that much—and that he was trying to negotiate a takeover and end up profiting. He was the victim of his own success, but he wouldn't see it that way. She prompted him to continue by asking, as if she were a doctor, "So where does it hurt?"

"All over," he said. "Slicing a guy, some guy I know? Pretty? Of course he's mad. They killed his brother. He's crazy with it. It's hard to raise a blade like that, against a guy you've beat at cards, who pulls out his *schlong* when he gets drunk. It's not my style. You know me, Temmy, I don't have trouble with knives, like that kid on Fourteenth Street who gave me grief and begged for it. But this is different. This is icy Italian reptilian shit." He shrugged and sucked his teeth. "And they know where your family lives, so it's not like you have much choice. What am I going to do? Move to Jersey?"

"Over my dead body," she said, feeling a chill unrelated to the wind, like someone had walked across her grave before she'd paid all the installments. She feared for herself and Larry.

"Things have to change, Temmy. I'm not running the show," Abie said, watching the breakers. "I love you, but we can't keep playing this hand. You gotta fold."

"What do you mean?" Thelma asked, agitated, her voice rising.

Abie scanned the boardwalk. "Don't play dumb. You got blood on your hands. I should've kicked you out, but you were such a mess I couldn't turn you away. Not my own sister. But you're not their sister. You're a loose end."

"Forget them. Am I a loose end for *you*, Abraham?" She glared at him as if he were a specimen she'd never seen before—a random thug in a police lineup. The realization that with their two skins on the line, he'd save his own, shattered her.

"What: So they sent you to kill *me*?" Rising, she felt both terrified and outraged. She slammed her empty glass on the ground just to hear something break. It was so thick it only thudded and rolled. She'd felt alone before, but now she felt hunted by the man who knew her best. She'd knelt and scrubbed up Amberg for him. She would have gone to the end of the earth for him—and, now, they were at the end of the earth and only one of them would be returning. "You're *kvetching* to me about some work crap so I can forgive you for making my kid an orphan?"

"I'm not going to kill you, Temmy. Don't go *meshuge*."

"You threaten me and say, 'Don't go nuts'? What is it, Mr. Big Shot with a knife?"

"Things change for me, they change for you."

"I get it: you're the fixer and they said to come and fix me or else." Despite the booze, her mind began to clear. "Was that why you bumped into Larry at the candy store? You were sniffing around the Brownsville Boys for your reward now that you'd crisped Pretty?"

"Keep your voice down."

"You keep *your* voice down, you backstabber." She balled up her hands in anger. He'd seen her since she was a baby; he knew every bit of generosity in her heart and the scars of every cut. All the times she'd been kicked to the curb, Abie had been there for her. Was it all so that he could shove her aside?

Annie would get the last laugh, seeing them in the gutter together. Their sister had always predicted this dire end. "Spit it out, Abie. What's the fix? How do we get out of this mess without digging me an early grave? You don't want me to go out dancing anymore? I'll cut off my right leg. You don't want me to pick up men? I'll become a nun. You want me to make up with Annie and crawl back on my knees? I'd rather clean blood for you than kiss her fat ass. What, Mr. Respectable, are you going back to Rodney Avenue with Tillie?"

"Never gonna happen," Abie said. "Get me my straitjacket and commit me to Brooklyn State Hospital."

She jerked her head away from her brother. The comment was a wisecrack too far. *Just shoot me now,* she thought. *Let's walk across the sand and you can hold my head under the waves.*

The Brooklyn State Hospital was where old man Schwartz had committed Philip. Her husband's biggest fear had been to be caged, stripped of his individuality, and detached from his daily newspapers and books. His father had locked him away to shuffle in pajamas and slippers during the day, hydrotherapy in the afternoon, with lights out at nine and insomnia's black pit. He'd begged her not to let them take him away, but Papa Schwartz had called her a tramp and a gold digger and, in the end, sent her packing to Montauk Avenue.

Philip had been harmless the way he was. Maybe he wasn't earning a living, but he had an active mind. Sure, he had dark days, retreating to his room to brood and puff. But that wasn't every day. He just needed more love, and patience to let the moods pass. The treatments hadn't fixed her husband; they'd just crushed his spirit and cleaved him from the real world. In the end, the place had killed him. He was as dead as Amberg.

Breaking the silence, her brother snapped his fingers at the bartender. He ordered another round. The Irishman plucked the fallen glass from the boardwalk and searched it for cracks. Abie rolled off a bigger bill. "There are worse places than Montauk Avenue."

"You're shitting me." She clenched her fists, feeling her resentment rise with the mere mention of that house. "Is that your brilliant fix?"

"My dough bought that house. You have just as much right to be there."

"Keep telling yourself fairy stories, Abie. You bought it and they changed the locks."

"Locks don't stop me."

"You talk big. You know Annie won't let you near those precious monsters. The future of the family—I should live so long! You can run with professional killers but you can't handle Annie?"

"Different weapons." He shrugged. "What, you want me to stab her?"

"I've considered doing it myself, but I lack your talent," she spat.

"It's no talent. I just take my anger and turn it out, not in."

"Thanks for the lesson. Put it on my tab."

"I won't charge you," he said. "I bought that house. I bought that respectability. I got them work when there wasn't any. No good deed . . ."

". . . goes unpunished." She felt her anger rising as her options narrowed. She sensed a finality in their conversation that she couldn't quite express. It was as if they were already remembering this moment together, not living it forward.

Maybe she was still in shock. "So I'll go back, play the Cinderella sister act again, is that what you want, Abie? Will that save my skin? No sex for the rest of my life, Larry and I sharing the little bedroom at the top of the stairs until he enlists?"

"That's not a bedroom. That's a broom cupboard."

"Tell me something I don't know. That roof isn't big enough for Annie and me. It can be done, but I don't want to do it any more than you want to sleep with Tillie."

"If only she'd let me rest."

"What's wrong with these women, Abie? Annie wants me to roll up my life like a rug and sleep on it, lumps and all. No more nights dancing. I can see it: smoking on the stoop in my housecoat, drinking on the sly, a grown woman playing the spinster, sitting around with the insomniacs, plotting our escape in whispers. Can you imagine Uncle Moe still mooning over me with apologetic eyes but still begging for a touch? You want that for me?"

"It's not a life, Temmy, I know that. But now you got a kid."

Chapter 33

Thelma stared at the boardwalk, empty now except for the raggedy birds. This was Coney Island, shabby in its autumn coat. She realized she couldn't pry love from her mother and sister. But what ached was how hard it was to find that generosity in her to give Larry.

"Would it have been so hard for them to love us just a little, Abie?"

"Stop kicking a dead horse. The love isn't there, only blood. You and me, Temeleh, that's something else," he said with a softness that caressed the Yiddish nickname. For the first time that afternoon, he looked into her eyes and she saw them, tears. But he would never perform the tell of wiping away the drops.

She half smiled, wryly, the light they shared in the darkness. She was still furious, but she couldn't hate him. She'd followed her brother down this path that landed them at this very table. "I made this bed with the dirty sheets. I get it. It's my turn to lie in it."

"We had a rough start, little sister." Abie pulled her hand close to him and kissed the burn-scarred thumb. She'd never forget the horror of Annie saying, "You'll crisp like chicken skin."

Like Amberg.

The lesson to avoid fire had escaped her. Instead, that day on East 106th Street ignited a never-ending feud. Her first memory was of Annie's treachery and Abie's defense. But what did Annie know from child rearing? She was a teenager fascinated by her own breasts. Her older sister didn't want to be taking care of any kids, much less a mother hardly able to fold socks.

"We had a rough start, Abie, and the finish hasn't been much of a picnic, either." She considered Philip. "Every day I wake up, there's the empty pillow where Phil's head used to be."

"You loved him."

"For all the good it did him."

"Or you."

"*Me?* Who cares?" She shrugged. "I had Phil's kid, and it put that beautiful man right over the edge."

"He already had a front-row seat on that ledge, Temmy. That whole family is thick with crazy."

"His doctor told me: Get pregnant, have a kid. It's just the tonic to mend him. I sensed it was a lie, but I wanted to believe. I hoped to get my old Phil back, the one who danced, the one who loved this, me." She raised her hands and gestured at her scrawny body. She'd stopped eating. She walked miles at night alone. It was enough that she no longer cried on the street, on buses among strangers, in comedies with happy endings.

She felt responsible for Phil's mental breakdown. She'd killed the man she loved because she was broken and he'd cut himself on her jagged edge. She'd been true to Phil from the day they'd kissed at the Roseland. But she'd been born on the back foot, overpowered by the relentless Annie, a charity case for Abie. She drew out the humanity in her brother. She sparked the light in Phil. She wasn't all bad. They'd walked taller together for a time. And when he was gone, when they'd all put stones on his grave in Mount Hebron Cemetery, she was left with a boy and a broken heart. They blamed her. Well, take a number, because she blamed herself first.

Last night, she'd come to Abie for comfort, because he was the only one left who saw her worth and she needed to see that reflected back. That's why she'd gone to Marcy Avenue. She missed Phil, and nobody wanted to hear it anymore. Find a new fella—that's the cure. There'd never be a new fella.

"I miss him, Abie. And now I'm slipping, too. I understand how he felt. I get how much he wanted to be there for me and how much it hurt all the time, the cuts on his arms, the fist holes in the wall."

"At least you loved each other. I've never found that woman for me."

"You're like a kid in a candy store. You can't choose just one. Ask Tillie."

"I got Tillie knocked up, but I could hardly watch a double feature with that cow."

"I'll never know what you saw in her."

"Her tits," he said.

"She does have a pair."

"I just wanted to see if I could get her bra off. I wasn't even thinking. Save me from nice Jewish girls! This ain't going to come out right, but I envy you. You're sad, you're bloody tragic—a regular Pola Negri—but at least you had that love with Phil, the one in the pictures. It's like that song from *The Broadway Melody*: 'You Were Meant For Me.' I never had that. I never will. I ain't meant for nobody, and nobody's meant for me. I just don't feel that way, that fuzzy, warm shit they sell with sex and love in soap ads. I did things in that place where Ma dumped me, the Hebrew Orphan Asylum for the Criminally Unwanted, and bigger kids did stuff to me. I came out backward and raging and unfit for flowers and chocolates, first date and meet the parents. I'm just good for whoring around, which ain't so bad to be when you're in my business."

He'd never confessed this before. She knew not to question, to contradict him and bullshit, say that he'd find that one sweetheart who was meant for him. It was hard enough for him to crack open this far. She felt the hush of intimacy between them, and she let it hover for as long as it lasted. She reached over, took his hand, and squeezed. This wasn't the image she'd had of him, the cocky king of the orphanage, protector of little Louis. He'd always seemed so tough, but he hadn't had a choice. He'd been a child thrown into the lion's den. They sat for a while, watching the clouds drop lower. Drinkers slunk past, entering the bar to avoid the coming rain.

"I have another idea, Tem, but it's got drawbacks."

"Mr. Fixer."

"I can get a place for you in Manhattan."

"Why didn't you say so to start?"

"No kids allowed."

"I can't do it."

"You *gotta* do it. I don't have any other cards up my sleeve. It's Montauk Avenue with Larry or Manhattan without him. Take your pick. The apartment's a single room with the bathroom down the hall, on Twentieth Street between Eighth and Ninth: a decent neighborhood, a crummy walk-up. I'll arrange a union job. You can even go dancing at the Roseland. I just can't protect you any longer."

Abie reached for Temmy's hand and squeezed it. They studied the greasy Atlantic. "Tem, if I'm going to survive, I can't be tied down. I love you, you know that, but I'm not ending up like Pretty. Not me. Sometimes you're on top, sometimes the bottom. But if you push too hard, pretend to be higher than you are, someone will reach over and shove you just for grins."

"But if I'm in Manhattan in a single-room occupancy, what'll I do with Larry? Annie won't take the kid. They'd ruin me for him and him for me. She'd make sure he knew he wasn't his cousin Eli, the Prince of Montauk Avenue."

"All hail the prince," Abie said. "What about your girlfriends? The Nina, the Pinta, and the Santa Maria? They have four or five kids each already—what's another one?"

"What kind of life is that? He'd be like a puppy on a pig. Sure there's a teat, but who will he be? Will he still be my kid, or Phil's?"

"Can you leave him with Phil's sister?"

"They don't want him on Wyona Street."

"You're giving me no choice. What, you wanna put him in an orphanage?"

"You know I wouldn't do that to a kid of mine." Abie blinked and got quiet in a scary way, as if he had something in his eye that could only come out with tears—and he'd do rage before tears. She asked, "Why does Annie have to be such a *farbissiner*, such a sour lemon? Larry has as much a right to that house as Eli."

"Possession is nine-tenths of the law, sweetheart. You'd have to sleep there."

"So we're back where we started."

"What about old man Schwartz with the buildings?"

"He'll pay for Larry's bar mitzvah—screw a roof over the kid's head. He still blames me for Phil. He'd blame me for the Depression if he could."

"So: Will it be the Nina, the Pinta, or the Santa Maria?"

"Maybe Nina's mama until I find something permanent." She sighed. "Larry wets the bed sometimes. Nina's husband, Tonio, has to get up early and doesn't have much patience for Larry's tears."

"Ain't that the way with husbands?"

"Not Phil." He'd loved her. He'd viewed her and, dammit, he'd seen that woman worth loving, that sparky, affectionate, dancing girl. The way they'd comforted each other, spooning through the night when Phil finally stopped talking and fell asleep with his nose buried in her wild hair, his arm's comforting weight across her ribs. But it was difficult to sustain that self-confidence with him gone. When she studied herself in the mirror, she didn't see the woman reflected in his eyes. She'd died with Phil; the bastards just hadn't drizzled her with dirt, mumbled a prayer, and turned their backs.

Thelma was lonely as a vacant lot, but she wasn't alone. She had Larry, who shouldn't have had to suffer for her choices. He was only as needy as she'd been. She knew he was only tugging at her as she'd reached out to her own mother: seeking warmth, understanding, and protection from strangers. As a little girl, Thelma had cringed at Mama's every sour look and swat, taken every no as a rejection not just of the moment but of every moment returning to her birth. She'd been the needy, unnecessary infant that outlived her father—and she'd been trying to shed that stigma ever since. Only after Larry's birth could Thelma relate to her mother's distress. She lacked the maternal instinct while Annie, born in a different house at a different time, had a mama bear's ferocity.

Guilt and resentment colored Thelma's feelings, but she finally understood that by the time she'd arrived, Mama was done. Mama was only a little sister herself who, at a time of crisis, regressed and reached out to Annie as if she were her mother. They traded roles in that bedroom on 106th Street the day Annie suggested the orphanage for Abie and Louis. Mama consented, giving her teenager power over her younger siblings because Mama herself was too weak to make the daily decisions that had fallen on her widowed shoulders. Annie had rescued Mama and thereafter they were stitched together, with the eldest daughter never afraid of reminding her mother of their exchange and never reverting to her daughter's role.

And so Thelma recognized what her son wanted when he snatched at the fingernails she had just painted Broadway Red, begged for her to take him to the movies instead of going dancing, cried in the night when she joined him in their cot. Even if she tried to reject how similar they were, all legs and arms and boundless affection, she knew the truth: he was more her than Phil. His light-brown hair, hazel eyes, his antsiness: all hers. All those wants, simple and complex, that he had and that she couldn't supply. Her failure made her shrink from him. She recoiled and he moved closer. He desired what she had wanted from her mother and sister. He craved comfort and security. He wished to be bathed with care and rubbed warm with a towel. *Kiss my scratches. Forgive my mistakes. View me through eyes of love and welcome.* He deserved to belong, like his cousins Eli, Adele, and Julius.

The straggly, fatherless boy craved his mother's company, however awful her cooking or short her temper, however much she cried like a child when he did, when she turned away from his attempts to cling to her in the night. She'd known that loneliness. Her son just wanted to be close, to be first in her eyes and protected in her arms. But without Phil, she lacked the strength to bury her mourning and make that sacrifice. She'd promised herself on 106th Street that if she ever had a child, she would treat the baby with every bit of her love. That broken commitment haunted her.

A mensch, that's what she aspired to be, to accept and treat herself gently and radiate out from a good heart. She struggled to swim back to her son, to crawl onto shore, to accept motherhood's boredom. She loved his funny stories about the neighbors, when he repeated their arguments back to her in his singsong child's voice as if reciting the ABCs. But she'd been too broken to glue them both together, to hustle the money, to cash out her girlfriends' kindnesses, to set aside her jealous rage that Annie had a roof over her head and Abie had paid for that roof. She craved that stability her son would have had if Phil had survived. She kept trying to keep it together, and then the night would sing out to her and she had to run away toward the music, the men. She despised herself for her weakness. Larry saw that anger and turned it against himself. She didn't hate him, but how was he to know, sensitive little man that he was, before his skin thickened like Abie's?

As she watched, her brother thumbed a few big bills from his bankroll and handed the rest to her. That's where it had started: money. Beside the pervert on the train, she'd hustled to Marcy Avenue on her way home because she had a personal problem. Her period had been two months late. In a panic, she'd entered the hangout uninvited. Abie was always dropping in at Montauk Avenue unannounced. What was the big deal? And she was in such a bad way. Abie wouldn't judge. He wouldn't preach abstinence. Chastity was for suckers. The cash would solve one problem but couldn't ease her fear of botched backroom abortions: coat hangers, curling irons, spoons. Sterilization. Infection. Bleeding out. At her girlfriends' insistence, she'd already perched over a steaming pot of boiling water. That scalding home remedy didn't, as the ads said, remove the "obstruction," return her to "regularity."

Abortion was as old as Adam's right rib, but it was a *shonda*. In her family, you had kids until your innards turned inside out—but only if you were married. That night, she hadn't had the chance to broach her lady problems. When she'd heard Amberg groaning in the kitchen and Abie had entered rolling down his sleeves, her situation suddenly diminished in importance.

Even now, Thelma still hadn't mentioned her condition. She'd taken Abie's bankroll. "Walk me to the subway?"

"You first," he said, raising his glass. "I got some beefs to settle."

She rested her hand on his. "You okay, Abie?"

"Do I look okay?" He withdrew his fingers and rubbed his bristly chin.

"Pass," she said, rising unsteadily. She looped the purse strap over her forearm and tried to make eye contact. He stared away at the Atlantic. Whether he felt the same desolation, she couldn't tell. He wouldn't open up to her again. He'd chosen sides. He'd sacrificed the sister he loved.

Feeling gut punched, she wheeled away. She'd done the unthinkable: gotten down on her hands and knees and cleaned up his violent mess. This was her reward. Abie knew more than anyone else her fear of abandonment—and abandoning Larry in turn. And here he was: shoving her out of the lifeboat. *Sayonara, sucker.* Sure, he had a fix, but there was no repair for cutting the cord between them.

She stumbled back toward the Wonder Wheel. Praying Abie would change his mind, she dangled a free hand for him to hold. But it remained empty when she turned right and crossed the deserted amusement park. She fought tears, but they battled back, slowly slipping down her cheeks. If she could have looked away from herself with revulsion, she would have.

Her swollen eyes throbbed. At some point the spinning had to stop, but not today. With Abie's cash, she could buy an evening dress and hit Roseland. She wanted to shimmy away the blues. Strangers lacked Phil's grace, but beggars couldn't be choosers. In a dancer's arms, she was never lost or lonely. She preferred fellas with broad shoulders but didn't care if they were tall or short, wore a wedding band or had the kind of scars on their faces and throats that only came from knives.

She could still inject shyness in her smile if that's what the guy wanted, pretending she was a new dress on the rack. Moving to the rhythm, she became the clarinet's wild scream, the piano's pulse. She felt alive flying out and being caught in a man's strong arms. Lately, she drank more, laughed louder, and afterward, leaned against alley walls with men whose aftershaves were more familiar than they were.

Phil had hooked her on that Roseland high. She'd been one half of a great dance team. People still remembered that, as they knew he'd died too young. Since he passed, moving to the music was her only escape until the tunes stopped, the lights went up, and reality choked her again, like now when she sniffled beside the Cyclone roller coaster. She dredged her bag for a subway token, tucking the bankroll into the lining.

All Abie's dough flowed from the Williamsburg Boys Club. She didn't need a diagram to tie this cash back to that beast Strauss. She glanced over her shoulder. Would that cutthroat pursue her despite her brother's promise?

Wherever it had all begun, this was where it had to end. She exited the amusement park on Surf Avenue, across the street from the shuttered carousel. Nearby, a newsie at the foot of the subway ramp waved a paper at her, shouting, "Murder in Brooklyn" and "Amberg Ambushed."

She slunk to where he stood, dropping three cents into the boy's grubby palm. Folding the broadsheet, headline discreetly in, she ascended the concrete slope where she'd often strolled with Phil, full up with hot dogs and ready to dance. Today she dragged, as if she were walking the plank on shackled feet. She paused to catch her breath, inhaling a lungful of sewer and damp.

As she passed through the entrance and crossed the dark hall to the turnstiles, she felt a stitch in her side. She recognized that cramp, followed by a dull uterine ache. Small mercies: her girlfriend was back. She dropped a token in the slot and paused in the minimal privacy of the gate, wiggling her privates to check if the bleeding had started, but no, not yet. She'd be needing rags soon. She smiled in relief, looking up toward the waiting train at the end of the line—and spotted Pep Strauss in her periphery.

The killer stood on the platform in an expensive double-breasted gray tweed overcoat. Staring out from under a black beaver-felt hat, he caught her eye with a skewerlike gaze.

Lepke's enforcer didn't move as passengers scurried around him. She feared death: a push, brakes squealing, and a ripping pain away. Pep tugged the cuffs of his black gloves. His lids drooped with menace, which some women confused with bedroom eyes. Not Thelma. Pep's threat pulsed between them. Her nape hairs tingled. She couldn't hold his stare. Glancing away, she eyed a beat cop and flushed with relief. She opened her mouth to scream but realized the futility. Wouldn't the police gloat if she fingered Strauss and then had to explain where they'd met?

She imagined his breath on her neck as she hurtled past him to the train, hopping the gap from the platform. Inside, as she careened from car to car, doors clacked behind her. She found a crowded spot, wiggled room for her rear end between two burly strangers, and when the subway jerked forward, she jumped anxiously.

As the elevated train headed toward Brighton Beach, she hid her face in the *Brooklyn Daily Eagle* with its below-the-fold headline screaming, "Who Killed Pretty Amberg? Brooklyn."

No, she thought, *it's my brother and those monsters calling the shots, the Murder Inc.* machers. She tried to accept that Abie was doing her a favor forcing her out of Brooklyn, but he'd killed any illusions she'd had that he was her hero, somehow different from Pep and Pretty.

Louis had nailed it when he'd told Abie, "I survived France and you got plugged in Brooklyn." Funny, Louis didn't anticipate dying of influenza on the other side of the world—but none of them was a sideshow fortune-teller. When the el lurched left, rejecting the shore and curving across Brooklyn toward the skyscrapers of Manhattan, she watched dusk spread over the flatlands, the clouds peeling back, revealing a plum-colored sky. As lights switched on in bay-windowed brownstones and shabby shingled apartment buildings, she imagined a young couple dancing in the living room—her hand draped around his neck, his lips brushing her cheekbones—as if nothing and no one existed beyond the curtains.

"You were meant for me." The song lyrics washed over her. She loved Brooklyn, the brick and concrete, the characters, the Giglio, the fragrant and fragile cherry blossoms trapped in that walled garden at the Brooklyn Botanic Garden, the koi spooning each other in their nearby pond. That's where she'd been with Phil the day they'd conceived Larry, when she still clung to the dream of a child to chase away the shadows. She had to forgive herself: she'd adored Phil, the curve of his back, the way he sent her out spinning onto the dance floor and somehow her feet balanced on the beat and she became weightless until she returned to his arms. "I was meant for you."

She couldn't afford to be soft, a single mother stewed in heartache, Little Yiddle's little sister. She wasn't going to toss herself off the el. She'd mope. No question. But once that ran its course, ultimately she was a woman who picked up her own pieces when forced. She'd put Abie back together again, hadn't she, for all the good it did.

The fear of being alone had overwhelmed her, but now that she had Larry, she realized how complicated loneliness could be. Thelma struggled to find that generosity inside her to give him, to rally her maternal instinct. She wanted to be a mother, to feel that pull, the urgency and need, that connection, hand in sticky hand. Mama couldn't find love in her heart for Thelma, and she, in turn, struggled to love her son. But Thelma refused to wait until her last breath to right the wrong. She had to learn to love Larry the way she'd wanted to be loved. She had to unleash that devotion she'd had for Phil, for Abie, for Louis—and bundle it up for Larry.

And maybe, just maybe, the kid's love for her would be enough. She'd work hard at the union job, typing her way into a steady pay-check, a pension, and a burial plot. It wasn't dancing and daffodils, but she'd save for an apartment big enough for two and put Larry to sleep every night with a wet kiss on each cheek, the way he deserved to be loved, because that was what a mother should do, no matter how broken.

ACKNOWLEDGMENTS

This was a journey back in time and deep into my heart, and I couldn't have achieved it without the amazing, magical circle of women who made my lifelong dream a reality. Thank you to my lady of the lake, Lake Union Publishing, for her unwavering support and insight: editorial director Danielle Marshall and her entire team, including the passionate developmental editor Tiffany Yates Martin, Gabriella T. Dumpit, Shasti O'Leary Soudant, Dennelle Catlett, and Nicole Pomeroy. I'm grateful to Victoria Sanders & Associates, led by the mighty, wonderful Victoria Sanders, with Bernadette Baker-Baughman and Jessica Spivey. Oh, Benee Knauer, my editorial coach, what an adventure we've had: traveling to the old neighborhoods of Brooklyn, the borough that yielded my father, who could find a Brooklynite on the hillside of Greece's Delphi and would yell across hallowed ground to greet them, eternally embarrassing the rest of us, including my mother, Rosalie.

And then there are the menschen who make my writing a life: Dennis Dermody, Galen Kirkland and Natalie Chapman, Hilton Caston and Robin Ruhf, Paula Bomer, Amy J. Moore, Nicole Quinn, Julie Fontaine, Jane Rosenthal, Berry Welsh, Jill Goldstein, Caroline Leavitt, Susan Shapiro, Nina Shengold, Melissa Leo, Rajendra Roy, Patricia Clarkson, Anne Hubbell, Amy Hobby, B. Ruby Rich, Drew Grant, Emily Assiran, Nick Hitchcock, those heroes of WAMC, Joe

Donahue and Sarah LaDuke, and Lina Frank and Clare Anne Darragh, the powerhouses of Frank PR.

Of course, undying love to my husband, Ranald, and children, Elizabeth and Ranald IV, for their support and perspective that having a mother who's a writer isn't exactly the same as one who bakes cakes and slays dust bunnies, but it has its perks.

ABOUT THE AUTHOR

Photo © 2018 Emily Assiran

Thelma Adams is the author of the bestselling historical novel *The Last Woman Standing* and the *O, The Oprah Magazine* pick *Playdate*. She coproduced the Emmy-winning *Feud: Bette and Joan*. Additionally, Adams is a prominent American film critic and an outspoken voice in the Hollywood community. She has been the in-house film critic for *Us Weekly* and the *New York Post* and has written essays, celebrity profiles, and reviews for *Yahoo! Movies*, the *New York Times*, *O, The Oprah Magazine*, *Variety*, the *Hollywood Reporter*, *Parade*, *Marie Claire*, and the *Huffington Post*. Adams studied history at the University of California, Berkeley, where she was valedictorian, and received her MFA from Columbia University. She lives in Upstate New York with her family.